Blue Earth

From Jeff,
To Jeff.

Blue Earth

A Blue Throne novel by

Jeff Stover

Contributors

Senior Editor:	Janet Lynne Roots
Consulting Editors:	Moses Garcia
	Julian "Jay" Burton
Cover Art and Design:	Alex Gelernter
Proofreaders:	Megen Princehouse
	Sara Stover
	Jennifer Burton
	Luz Padilla
	Becky Homsher

BLUE THRONE CREATIVE, LLC
Morrison, CO
www.bluethrone.com

Published by Blue Throne Creative, LLC
Morrison, Colorado

www.bluethrone.com

ISBN 978-0-9842781-0-7

To all those who believe that technology is neither the beginning nor the end of humanity.

PROLOGUE

25 *The truth came to spite me; it was a disease without cure. Each day a new torment picked at my resolve. Sanity slipped away. It turned me against myself. It turned me against my love, my passion, and my people: the truth a machination of my fettered mind.*

2 Was this the truth? Truth is nothing. Truth is the singular joke of humanity. Truth is an army of Men cutting through heaven, demanding the heads of angels and saints, sacking the good and the just, proclaiming the hell of paradise, disowning the One. ³"We come for the creator! Why have you done this to us? We seek our own truth and will destroy yours!" ⁴Crushing blows rocked the gates of Heaven, taking down golden banners and ivory foundations. God was sought and found. The people of Him demanded respite from their own hopes and justice for their own glories.

5 "Death! Death! Death!" they proclaimed as steel and electric fury ground the sapphire cobblestones to powder. ⁶God did not retreat and did not speak. His voice had become too subtle for the armies of Men, too humble for the brave and the relentless. ⁷They had remade themselves in their own image and had become quite mad. They had come to take their bounty, for the bold are an extension of the fearful, that multitude who had not marched on Heaven but fled to find homes in twilight and electron mesh. ⁸The mob that remained had tidied their brains and sat down to sup. Breads of rationality sustained what they had made, the life given was thrown to the void and shadows became taught and sturdy, black sky and blue earth running as fluid beneath their feet.

9 It was in these days that I was to witness the greatest of miracles, one that claimed reconciliation of days and nights and brought about the things we all wanted to believe but also wanted to destroy. The founding of new stones in the earth to hold structures to come, which was much of the purpose.

The Book of Blinding Strikes 25:1–9

CHAPTER 1

"Will that be all, sir?"

Jamal regained consciousness while ordering biscuits and gravy. More precisely, his cognitive processes coalesced and he was suddenly aware of a speaking waitress. As Jamal's vision struggled to focus on the surrounding space, his mind also struggled to decipher what he saw through a fog of intoxication.

Raw data became thought, and Jamal realized that he sat in a corner booth at a familiar diner and was alone except for the speaking shadow to his left. As Jamal looked up, the waitress backed away from the table without meeting his eyes. She turned and walked off, leaving him with a view of bouncing brown hair and a well-padded skirt. Jamal assumed he had completed his order.

Shifting his gaze to the table, Jamal found it empty except for a mug of coffee. He reached for the cup and was able to raise it halfway to his lips before his hand shook at a frequency too great to avoid spilling. He put the cup down and lowered his head to it, slurping up what he could.

The aroma of coffee opened his nose to other smells. He looked down. Dark stains and crust littered the once-ivory shirt. His black pants were equally soiled with... unidentified filth.

Minutes passed and Jamal fought the need to put his head down and sleep. Keeping his mind blank, he watched cars drive by the diner and drank more coffee.

A plate of food sailed over his shoulder and landed hard on the table, sending driblets of gravy over his coffee mug. The waitress continued by without slowing her pace.

Jamal did not look up but instead ravaged the food on his plate with large bites and little chewing. He finished, the bill came, and he paid at the register by the door.

A short walk brought him to his apartment. After stumbling from the bathroom to the kitchen, he started the coffee brewer and walked through the spaces, floating from room to room, finding the same apartment he had haunted for almost three years.

The floor dirt was the same. The stains were the same. The furniture orientation was the same. The refrigerator buzzed excessively as it always had.

Jamal sat down on his couch and waited for the coffee to brew. In the diffused radiance of the early morning, he vainly watched motes of dust float up from the radiator and past the window to disappear into the gloom of the unlit apartment. Jamal tried to focus on each successive grain of dirt that drifted by, but a lack of sobriety made it impossible and he stopped before the room began to spin. Instead, he surveyed the rest of the space.

His analysis was cut short by a soft chime sounding from his com-pad on the table. He picked it up and checked the face screen: there was one message. Reluctantly, he hit play and listened: "Jamal, this is Jennifer. I... I don't want to talk about last night. I was just calling to tell you not to call me anymore. Don't... just don't call me anymore. Anyway, Brian is okay—he didn't need stitches, so... Jamal, I want you to know..." Jamal lowered the com-pad from his ear and hit the cancel button.

Jamal was not moved by the message. The night before was a blur, and now the typical response from traitors and weaklings—people called "friends"—would begin to filter into his world day by day. It was time to move on anyway.

So he sat back as motivation seeped into his brain from dark places, only to flee in the light of growing consciousness. In silence his mind flailed, screamed, and pulled at a formula of confusion that came every day.

Suddenly, he remembered that today was different than most. A different variable was part of the equation. Today offered something other than unemployment.

Today was another chance.

But the previous night of decadence stabbed his body and mind and Jamal struggled to stay awake. Pitching the last of his will against exhaustion, he dragged himself up from the couch and into the bedroom to set the alarm.

He had another chance.

Jamal collapsed on the bed after hitting some buttons on the clock, not entirely sure or entirely caring what alarm time he had set. Senses died, muscles relaxed, and Jamal passed out.

"I'm here for a ten o'clock interview. My name is Jamal Battle." He smiled at the wax-faced receptionist. The alarm had indeed been set properly and Jamal had risen, bathed, dressed, and rode the bus through downtown Minneapolis to arrive on time—mildly inebriated, but on time.

"Good morning, Mr. Battle." Her voice was dead. "Just fill out these forms and bring them back to me when you're finished. We're running a little late, so the Director will see you as soon as possible."

The receptionist laid a packet of papers on the desk and trotted into a nearby office.

Jamal sat down in a chair opposite and began to write. The lobby smelled of perfume and window cleaner. He finished writing his name five times, proclaiming he was drug-free two times, and swearing his life on all testimony once. Jamal tossed the pen into a corner and placed the clipboard on the receptionist's empty desk.

She returned several minutes later.

"Mr. Battle? The Director will see you now." She pointed to a door down the hall. Jamal got up and followed her gesture, trying to walk straight as he approached the door.

He entered and examined the office. Most of the space was used to accommodate an immense steel desk. A small chair sat back against the wall opposite.

"Sit," said the man at the desk. He wore a sky-blue uniform and his hair was white. The man did not look up but continued to read from a desktop com-pad.

Jamal felt his vision blur, but focused enough to find the chair and sit down without any fumbling. The residual haze of intoxication was fading.

"Not much of a resume," said the Director.

Jamal said nothing. He read the name-plate on the desk: "Sec-Commander Richard Holly."

"Let's talk about your service record," the Director continued. He looked up and Jamal could see plainly that the man did not care. Jamal was insignificant.

A sudden malice pervaded Jamal and his full senses returned.

"The feed came in from the DoD this morning," Holly said. "Taurus Force Systems has all-level access to a candidate's military service record. That's good for you, Jamal."

Fuck this guy!

"Yes, sir." Jamal sat erect and tried to stare at the wall behind Sec-Commander Holly's head.

"Run-of-the-mill Army infantryman. Got your hands dirty in Iran, though." Holly continued to read, reinforcing the impression that this was not going to be a conversational interview. Jamal noticed his expression change to a grimace and then to a disgusted scowl.

Jamal knew what he was reading about.

"We don't need psychos," Holly said, shaking his head.

"Sir?" Jamal feigned ignorance but not remorse.

"I can't get any details about... you know what I'm talking about. Why would we at Taurus Force Systems overlook this incident, Jamal? Tell me."

Jamal stiffened. Taking a breath, he looked up into Holly's face and started a well-rehearsed explanation.

"My platoon leader was given intelligence regarding certain *volunteers* working in the north block of Tehran. The persons in question were suspected of providing more than food and medical aid to that part of the city. When I entered the room, I pacified the militants immediately. The 'aid-workers' commanded me to stop while they ran to several boxes in the corner and reached under a tarp."

Jamal paused. Holly's expression hid nothing; with a downturned head and frowning face, the man had already decided what he thought. The urge to tank the interview and punch the man was strong, but Jamal took a breath and continued.

"I hesitated until the first woman pulled a pistol from under the pile. After that, I wasted them all. My command reprimanded me, but as you are reading right now, no charges were filed and I continued my service until I was honorably discharged. I stand behind my choice and I would do it again under the same circumstances."

Holly grinned. Jamal fought back a growing rage by looking through the man until the scene before him was nothing more than a blur against the blank white wall,

Holly's sky-blue uniform merging with the metal desk. Jamal's thoughts became a hollow void.

"The report states that there was one aid-worker survivor," Holly said. "She claimed they were just trying to show you the food and med supplies under the tarp. The woman was just moving the pistol out of the way. Hell of a hair trigger you have."

Jamal was ready to accept unemployment rather than suffer the opinions of weak men behind desks. "Sir, may I inquire as to the length of service and duties you held while an active-duty soldier?"

Holly laughed and put the com-pad down. He leaned on elbows and laced his fingers, a weak smile not reaching his eyes. "Relax. I want to know how people who save life by dealing death can manage decisions after they're made. Taurus Force Systems is the largest private security firm in the world. We provide exclusive security for almost every facet of U.S. foreign affairs as well as other private businesses. We have succeeded through our experience and commitment to appearances.

"The public's opinion is our greatest enemy. I can't judge you on the incident in question because I wasn't there; the public would judge you, however, if given the chance. I think you have the right intuition as a soldier, but what we do here is different. Taurus Force Systems needs good soldiering for defense and security, not assault. That difference has to be learned by everyone we hire, so just relax."

"Yes, sir," Jamal said, annoyed by the reflex to give respect without meaning it.

"And Battle." The Director leaned forward and grew stern. "My background is none of your goddamn business, understood?"

No kills — understood. "Yes, sir."

Holly paused and forced a grin. Jamal noticed the annoyance behind it and grinned back in provocation. The attempt seemed to fail. Holly's face softened and he continued.

"You served eight years in the Army. Why did you get out?"

Jamal reached for an explanation and found none. Introspection had not supplied Jamal with a good reason, regardless of his interview preparation. He watched as Holly looked down to his com-pad. Perhaps he expected Jamal not to answer?

Jamal felt predictable once again. "I felt ready to transition into civilian life, start a family, all that," Jamal said.

"Didn't go over like that, did it?" said Holly.

"Not really."

"Why not go back into the Army? Why Taurus Force Systems?"

"The money," Jamal said.

Holly sniffed and pointed to the com-pad. "Bullshit," he said. "Careful what you try to withhold from me, Battle. I have your whole fucking life here in my hands." Holly snapped his fingers at Jamal.

Do that again...

"Your psych evaluation is shit. Uncle Sam thinks you're damaged goods. You've only worked 25 months of the last three years for five different employers. You have nowhere else to go."

Jamal suddenly remembered why he got out of the Army. Despite the order—the lack of worry about paying rent or stocking the refrigerator or what to wear—the military had one glaring drawback that made it unworthy of a career choice: you had to follow the orders of pretentious, ignorant, weak individuals. Individuals like Sec-Commander Holly.

"Whatever you say," Jamal said, as he leaned forward in the chair in expectation of dismissal.

"At ease, Battle." The man gave Jamal a triumphant look as if he were Jamal's personal lord and savior. "I think we can use you."

Jamal attempted to mask his relaxation. Holly's smug expression swelled.

"It would be a risk for us," Holly continued, "but I've hired people more fucked up than you. As long as the drug screen is clear and our own Psych Department clears you, I will endorse your application. You'll start as a Sec-Private and not a rank more. I'm late for my afternoon round of golf, so…" Holly rose.

Jamal stood up in response. "Thank you for the opportunity, sir."

"Opportunity? Ha! We always need grunts, Battle. You're a grunt."

Jamal turned and started to walk out, blocking the rage from his mind with the knowledge that he needed the job. Indeed, he had nowhere else to go.

"Oh, and Battle?" Holly said.

"Yes, sir?" Jamal turned.

"People with felonies work shit jobs. They also do jail time. This is the first and last time your father's name is going to help you get anywhere in this firm. Understood?"

"Yes, sir," Jamal answered, his mind going dead as he put one foot in front of the other, the need to get paid stronger than the urge to punch the Sec-Commander in the jaw.

Jamal returned to his apartment. He allowed the wan light filtering through the drawn shade to illuminate the space and walked from room to room, pacing but not thinking.

He sat. Restlessness invaded any peace Jamal hoped to gain by sitting and he rose to wander once more. The march led him inexplicably to the spare bedroom. The space was strewn with boxes and served as a storage area, save one corner where an easel stood. A canvas sat upon it, the surface blank except for a black smear streaking across it like a fading plume of noxious smoke. He stepped over the clutter to stand before the easel. As he surveyed the soiled canvas, he could not deny that it was a finished piece, a fresh beginning stained with time and judgment.

But more could be added to the charcoal smear, more could stem from that thoughtless application of black that Jamal had performed while drunk and alone over a month ago. More could grow from that darkness; a simple application of color and shape would transform the canvas into something beautiful, or at least real.

Jamal felt his breathing increase in depth and speed. He looked at the possibilities on the canvas. But in the same instant, Jamal summoned a force to combat these weak and useless emotions. From a dark place within came avenging shadows. Suddenly, he saw the canvas for what it was: a lie and an enemy.

Jamal pulled a knife from inside his suit jacket, a relic from his time in the Army. He held the blade out and pointed it towards the black smear, stabbing into canvas-flesh. Tracing the smear with the blade, he followed the arc of the charcoal. He stepped back, allowing the knife to fall. Not hearing the blade hit the floor, Jamal looked at the ruined canvas. He reached into the cut and ripped sideways, taking a handful of soiled-white from the wooden frame. Once the canvas was removed, he calmly broke the frame's joints and tossed them to the floor. Jamal left the pile of wasted wood and canvas where it was, his mind turning to… to what to do next.

He had a job. He did not need an apartment anymore, did not need a place to be. He wanted to be nowhere and wished he could leave that night, plunging his will into the world once again, like his knife into canvas. Taurus Force Systems was giving him a week to "handle personal affairs and move out of current living accommodations." He only needed a day.

Jamal left the spare room and found his phone in the kitchen. He called a familiar contact.

"Jennifer. This is Jamal. Just wait... I'm leaving for a new job and I just wanted to say goodbye." He thought of other things as the woman chattered on the other end of the line. Jamal knew what to say to get through her fear and calmly pleaded his case until she agreed to meet him at a bar in 30 minutes. It was time to close down his personal relations here, once again. A week was plenty of time. Quickly, he changed into casual dress, all the while sharpening his mind to an edge no less lethal than the knife that lay on the floor beside the easel.

Jennifer had been a soiled canvas for some time now. It was time to start again, and Jamal was going to enjoy punishing her for not being more beautiful, not having more potential. With his soul a blade, his body the executioner, and his mind the innocent crowd only there to observe, Jamal set out to attend a final rendezvous with someone who was not good enough.

CHAPTER 2

"I'm afraid I'm *very* busy this evening, Howard. Perhaps another time?" Ruth said as she started down the hallway.

"When? I—"

"I'll let you know." Ruth did not look back as she strode across the marble tiles. When she turned to enter the classroom, she noticed Howard in her periphery, still standing where she had left him. Ruth continued on.

The room was unusually full today. And hot. Stifling September air filled most of Campolo University's chambers despite the relative youth of the buildings and their cooling systems. Using modern methods, the architects had replicated Romanesque and Baroque styles, achieving the monastic essence the founders wanted in a Divinity School. That included monastic discomfort, as well. Ruth found the stone arches and high ceilings comforting in the main lobbies, but thought stone and iron windowsills in the classrooms bordered on draconian.

Ruth slowed as she approached the desk on the far side of the classroom. Her legs swept carefully, masking her lack of proficiency while walking in heels. By nature, teaching put the teacher on display and Ruth was embittered by the thought, but she fought through it as she did every day. She also fought through the anger that rose when the classroom chatter faded and she took center-stage: male chatter, to be precise.

Despite the expectation of being "checked out," Ruth wore a snug, knee-length gray skirt and a loose white blouse. She preferred her winter wardrobe, the thick wools and cottons concealing her figure and giving her a rest from the effects of her physique. But it was difficult to intentionally dress like a librarian. Besides, she was here to teach and teaching quality was dictated by many factors, not the least of which were comfort and personal bearing.

"Professor Long?" a student said.

"Yes?" Ruth faced the class while unloading her hip bag.

"My mom is coming next week for parents' week. Can she sit in for a session?"

"Sure," Ruth said while turning to the light-board. "Why not invite your friends, too?"

A tension fell on the students, emanating specifically from the testosterone-producing majority. Ruth seldom indicated that she was aware of large numbers, and frequency, of visiting students. But she was well aware of the young men who were only there to gawk and whisper.

She hoped her comment would help these young men realize that mature women *know* they are being gawked at and do not like it. For Ruth, it was taxing and degrading. She liked being a woman, but not a walking pin-up girl.

Still, her emotions had bubbled over in a way that was unacceptable. The class was not supposed to know that she could be given to compulsion. In fact, no-one was.

"I mean, all of you are free to invite anyone to the class." Ruth spoke quickly. "Anytime, actually. We foster an open academic environment here at Campolo, so feel free to open it to your friends and family."

I'm so full of shit.

But the students glowed and the sexual tension was broken, or so Ruth convinced herself. It helped her focus on why she was here.

"Get out your lexicons and scholar-Bibles. Let's talk about the reading," Ruth said.

When the class was over, Ruth hurried to the small restaurant that sat on the edge of campus. It was the only place to eat without traveling far, and a favorite meeting place for her boss, Dean Rupert.

Mr. and Mrs. Rupert waited there for her now. Ruth had assiduously resisted the invitation, the "casual lunch" often devolving into an impromptu lecture by the Dean who burned with memories of the days when he actually taught.

Praying for a light lunch, both in substance and philosophy, Ruth entered the café. She made her way past the throng of student-patrons to a table in the back corner, a table always reserved for the Dean and his wife.

"Please excuse my being late. I was focused on a project and lost track of time," Ruth said as she sat down and forced a smile. The restaurant was dim and less than half full. The Dean and his wife were dressed in similar shades of brown, with similar expressions on their faces. They also were of similar height, which was still noticeable when they sat.

"Oh, no worries, my dear. No worries." Dean Rupert reached out and patted her hand. "Didn't I say I made the right choice in charging Ruth to restore our biblical translation and theology curriculum, Theresa?"

Mrs. Rupert wore an expression that was serene yet jagged. While Ruth had always trusted the jovial expressions of the Dean, she knew that Mrs. Rupert wore a complex veneer that few could read. Ruth considered herself one of those few.

"Repeatedly... my dear." Her eyes bore into Ruth.

Dean Rupert chuckled and took a sip of his wine.

"Many thought that classics—scholarly religion and theology in particular—could no longer be taught by formal institutions any better than the morass of disinformation and misinformation out there. But, I give you sweet Ruth Long. She's been a godsend for Campolo."

Mrs. Rupert wiped her mouth with a napkin, but clearly said, "Yes, a godsend at six feet, and a hundred and fifteen pounds."

Ruth grinned as if she had been complimented. In truth, she had.

"Thank you again for accepting a post at such a remote institution," the Dean continued, oblivious. "Wyoming is not for everyone."

"I've found the surroundings relaxing," she said. "Thank you again for the opportunity."

The Dean coughed violently, his brittle form vibrating with each convulsion. Mrs. Rupert placed her hand on his back, patting it gently. When the coughing stopped, Dean Rupert fumbled for his dinner napkin and began to dab his lips.

"Never been the same since that goddamn pneumonia... humph!" he said.

Ruth knew of the Dean's frail health, but she thought his strong will was an adequate surrogate for a robust constitution. He would philosophize and mumble on for at least another decade.

This would be due in large part to Mrs. Rupert, who kept the Dean in working order. She was also a bitch with nothing more to do than project hatred and conceit from a secret black tower that sat in the shadow of the Dean's ivory one.

A professional wife, Mrs. Rupert was everything Ruth strove not to be: inhibited, subtly controlling and bitter. Despite these traits, Ruth respected her for loving and caring for the Dean. Most others did not and Mrs. Rupert was regarded by other Campolo University faculty as a scourge.

"Now then." Dean Rupert took a breath and composed himself. "I expect you will receive your Ph.D. from Harvard next semester, and I've already started the application process for your USFEA license. How is your thesis turning out?"

The waiter came and Ruth exhaled heavily. They ordered, and all too soon the Dean and his wife were looking at her expectantly, the Dean's original question not lost.

"The thesis is turning out wonderfully," Ruth said, leaning forward again with a smile that she hoped masked her apprehension.

"And it's about post-modern religious movements, or something to that effect? Please forgive my memory, Ruth. I remember that I approved of it, that is sure," Dean Rupert said.

Uh... "Basically, the formation of new religious doctrine and interpretation during socio-economic and technological changes in both localized and global faith groups, specifically Christianity."

"That's the title?" Mrs. Rupert mumbled as she took another piece of bread from the center plate.

"I'm not sure of the title just yet," Ruth said honestly, and prepared herself for a long siege of questioning and stalling.

"Ah well, it sounds like a wonderfully rich and worthwhile topic, my dear. One I'm sure your Harvard mentors are proud of. It's hard for those of us who keep the vanguard on classics and theology to justify our own existence in this age, I'm afraid. We don't know a scrap about nano-

18

profusion or LarcSuits, so the mobs we so diligently educate view us as vestigial and worthless, like fading stone-age cave paintings or the like. Oh, and the beliefs of this generation! How appalling. Roks and Smith Gnostics. Even these fictional 'Throne' beings that people worldwide are starting to believe in. Never in all of history were the guardians of philology and history so needed."

Ruth shifted in her seat, crossing her legs to the other side. "Indeed."

The lunch date concluded without any significant inquiries from Dean Rupert or more snide comments from his lovely wife. Ruth returned to her office to prepare for her last class of the day. The room was small and lined with bookshelves, a tiny window offering a view dominated by the brownstone wall of another building.

Ruth sat down at the cluttered-yet-orderly work space of the desk, the loose papers and books layering its surface forming her personal fortress of scholarly aptitude. Martin Luther, Brian McLaren, and Albrecht Alt constituted the castle walls while several towers of Paul Tillich, John Rawls, and Spinoza overlooked the additional piles of miscellaneous texts on the floor.

Sitting back, she thought about her lunch with Dean Rupert. He seemed to support her and to respect her academic focus, so she was safe. Much of her real success had come through hard work and accepting challenges that others would not. Most of Ruth's *institutional* success had come from knowing the right people, asking the right questions, and not asking the wrong ones. Ruth pondered the differences in definition.

Pondering led to confidence and Ruth directed her attention to the center of the desk. Within the stack of paper sat a single booklet of pages, clipped together and recently printed.

She lifted the manuscript. A grin forming on her lips, she read the title of the thesis: *The Impact of Artificial Biological Creations on Doctrinal, Teleological, and Ontological Thought within Christianity and Related Religions*, by Ruth Long.

Some panic followed the pride when Ruth thought of the hours of work that sat before her, but an iron wall of defiance rose to block it.

I can't turn back now. It's almost done anyway.

She looked at the clock. It was nearly time for class, so she gathered her things and left the office.

The afternoon class was free of visitors yet full of eager students. Questions and attention thrived, and Ruth enjoyed providing answers and rewarding attention with knowledge. It was quickly becoming the best session she had taught in weeks.

"So, we find that many of the manuscripts differ in subtle ways; these differences were recognized, respected, and addressed by the Jewish scholars. Conversely, these differences were rearranged, smoothed over, and misinterpreted by the founders of the Christian Church," Ruth said as she wrote on the light-board. "Now, does anyone want to comment about—"

"Professor Long?" said a voice from the door.

"Yes?"

Professor Cook, the resident Ancient Greek and Latin language professor, stood in the doorway. "I am sorry to interrupt, I—"

Ruth put a hand up to silence him. She turned to the class.

"Take a break, guys. But stay here," Ruth said and walked to Cook at the door. Cook was a handsome man, but also markedly demure in a feminine way. His mastery of syntactic and semantic properties within language was a talent that Ruth had tapped recently to the benefit of her research and teaching. "What's up?"

"The Dean wants to see you," Cook said, looking down. "I don't know why he sent me, I mean you have a phone in the room and all that... I was talking to Mary Thomas, you know, the one I think should go on to Ph.D. studies? Well, I was talking to her outside the hallway near Rupert's office, and he came out and told me—not politely, I might add—to go 'get' you, and I was trying to explain some word origins to Mary... uh, I think it was concerning odometers, or maybe I was talking about Mega-Stoma, like the shark, you know, and I—"

"Got it, George." The only way to converse with Cook was to inhibit his loquaciousness by being blunt. "I'll go see him after class. Thanks." Ruth patted the man's shoulder and turned to leave.

"Oh no, no. He said to come right now."

Ruth wheeled on the man and pointed inside the room. "What about the class?" She was annoyed, more at the realization that the Dean *never* interrupted a class unless... unless it was for a reason that might be bad, might be good. She let her anxiety spill over Cook anyway, suddenly aware that she was scowling.

He stepped backward, his eyes wide. "Uh, well, I don't know. Maybe you could just have a longer class later, or make them stay until you get back. Maybe you could—"

"Thanks. I'll handle it." Ruth softened her expression and gave George Cook a light kiss on the cheek, hoping to put the man at ease. He smiled and shuffled off, mumbling to himself.

Everything is fine. The Dean just needs to talk to me... Did someone die? Maybe...

Ruth cut off the speculation and returned to the middle of the class. She looked at the clock and then at the students.

"I am afraid that our class has been cut short today by twenty minutes."

The students immediately started to pack up books, shut down com-pads, and put on jackets. Ruth had to raise her voice above the sounds of movement. "We'll talk about the Gemara and the Council of Nicaea next week," she said, trying to focus on the lesson plan in her head. "Continue with the readings per the syllabus. Be safe if you're going to the mountains this week. See ya."

She began to pack her own things, her thoughts focused on why the Dean would interrupt a class to see her. Always a defender of etiquette, Rupert was normally predictable and his habits easy to navigate.

As Ruth walked across the main hall, she could not conjure a good reason for the sudden summons. Her pace quickened as she obsessed.

She climbed the stairs to reach the Dean's office on the second floor. Once outside the office, she stopped, knocked on the doorjamb and cracked open the door.

"Dean Rupert? Professor Cook said you needed to see me?"

The Dean was sitting at a small cherry desk, the matching bookshelves that lined the walls giving the room a palpable taste of academia and propriety. A magnificent round window, spanning from floor to ceiling, was opposite the door. The portal furnished a view of Campolo University's main courtyard, the campus entry lawn, and the jutting Rockies beyond.

The Dean was busy reading something on his com-pad, obviously engrossed. His head shot up at the sound of Ruth's voice, his expression one of mixed apprehension and weariness.

"Get in here and close the door," he said.

Ruth shut the ornate door, detailed with a circular ivy engraving that matched the design surrounding the window.

"Sit."

Ruth sat across from the Dean. She caught herself regressing into a sex-exuding defense posture: her hips thrust to one side of the chair while her torso flowed enticingly to the other. Composing herself, Ruth sat up straight, smoothing her skirt.

"How far are you into your thesis, Ruth?"

"I've put about five months of research into it," she said. "The outline has been finalized and I have written about thirty percent of what I think will be the total of the paper, but with editing and revisions, who knows?"

Rupert was silent a moment, as if expecting more. "My dear, I am afraid we have a serious problem regarding the content of your thesis." He leaned forward and put his elbows on the desk, his face softening. "I am somewhat sure you can change it and avoid incident, but I can't guarantee that."

Ruth took a short breath as her mind began to race.

"What? Why do I have to change it? It's been approved by Professor Faulkner at Harvard. I don't understand."

The old man's hand shot up violently and Ruth was shocked into silence. "Faulkner called me this afternoon," he said. "Ruth, though you have spent much of your adult life in college, there are still many elements— administrative elements—that you have not been exposed to. Your thesis topic, once approved by Harvard, is then submitted to the Federal Education and Standards Bureau. It would seem that while most submissions meet no resistance once their respective university processes them, your thesis topic has."

The situation was out of Ruth's preferred level of control. Her aim had been to insulate Dean Rupert from any adverse happenings, or general knowledge, regarding her thesis. Apparently she had missed something. "I have to call Dr. Faulkner."

"Yes, undoubtedly," Rupert said as he patted his hand calmly on the desk. "But let's talk. We have briefly discussed your thesis before and I didn't detect anything that I would deem inappropriate. Would you mind indulging me with the title and some of the primary research points again?"

Ruth fought the urge to sink into the chair. Her mind was locking down and her body wanted to follow. A lack of reference was enough to make her come undone. She saw that the Dean was shaking now, his body vibrating with anger. He expected something unsavory, an expectation probably built on Ruth's nervous body language.

"The specific title is *The Impact of Artificial Biological Creations on the Doctrinal, Teleological, and Ontological Thought within Christianity and Related Religions.*"

Rupert slammed his hand down on the desk. Ruth had never suspected him capable of physical violence.

He rubbed the spot on the desk he had struck as if to erase the action itself. "Somewhat different than what I remember from our conversations, Ms. Long."

"Dean Rupert," Ruth said, "As I have been writing, the paper has evolved quite a bit, the research serving as a catalyst."

Rupert snorted. "I can't say I sympathize with that approach, Ruth. Are you writing a novel, or writing a scholarly paper using academic rigor?"

"I—"

"Don't answer that." Rupert leaned back again and smiled half-heartedly. "I am sorry for being so tactless. You must understand that Harvard's Federal Charter has been threatened by all of this."

Ruth had doubted the severity of the situation before. Now she did not. "I... I believe that there are many things going on out there that are relevant to my research, though they may seem tied to more nefarious realms of Stimulist thought. Some of these situations and their outcomes will become part of history," Ruth said without conviction. "Stimulist thought" included everything that modern educators would not touch: internet crazes, speculative history, and current religious cults. Ruth was in the minority because she found value in studying such areas. Traditional educational institutions—federally funded educational institutions—did not.

"But Ruth, that's the failure of so-called Stimulist thought! The whole charade finds historical meaning in every belief, every action, everything. The world has been denuded of cultural fortitude; the collective thoughts and practices that took centuries to grow are being slashed and harvested, never to bear fruit again."

Rupert sighed and looked out the window. "The only things we will have left," he continued, "are the machines of our making: vile mechanisms that will maintain our bodies and sustain our minds with the ignorant drivel the Stimulists have programmed them to dole out. The supersaturation of novitiate interpretations and profit-driven proof-texting on all levels is killing our universities, Ruth. It's killing Campolo University. It's killing us!"

Not this lecture again... "I understand," Ruth said, hoping to stave off the coming tirade.

"So I assume this element of your thesis is what the FESB doesn't like." Rupert looked to his com-pad.

Ruth was suddenly incensed by the entire exchange. She was a student of Harvard Divinity School and her advisor, Professor Faulkner, was well aware of Ruth's work and progress. How dare Rupert, a wolf whose fangs could now clearly be seen through his outer lamb-like trappings, suddenly pounce on her?

"Didn't Professor Faulkner tell you what my thesis was about?" she said loudly, allowing her own disguise to drop.

"No," Rupert said, his tone rife with aggression. Ruth wanted to run out of the office and get away from him, away from his unexpected malice.

A faint chime sounded from Rupert's desk. He reached for his com-pad, touched the screen a few times and began to read, his eyes sweeping the screen. Ruth looked out the window, not knowing what to do or say.

Ruth thought of her thesis. The bulk of the material she wished to cover was of present-day significance, but she was aware of how careful academics must be while contending with a sea of information that changed by the second. All of the subjects in her research were observable phenomena, even if there were few empirical sources to tap. But Harvard's Federal Charter was being threatened. Why?

"Ruth," Rupert whispered. His face was flushed and he visibly trembled once again.

But she was no longer affected. The man was a sharp predator when he needed to be, and Ruth would not forget this betrayal of trust. Now something else had invoked his ire.

"Thrones," he said in a murderous whisper.

"What?" Her indignation turned into fear.

"The notice I just received was from the FESB. They have mandated that we suspend you until your thesis, and overall academic credentials, are in order. The notice said that your thesis outline, as they received it from Professor Faulkner, deals primarily with the Thrones."

Ruth struggled to find a defense, but could not. "Yes. Much of the paper is about the Thrones."

CHAPTER 3

"Hey, Battle! Help me with this trench, eh?"

Jamal stood at the edge of the camp and looked to the hilltop beyond. As he watched, massive trees fell at regular intervals. The quiet of the camp was pierced by the sounds of tearing forest canopy and crashing tree trunks.

He had stripped down to his undershirt despite the forest flies that swarmed around him. The radio marker, camouflaged to look like a small Congo shrub, was planted firmly in the ground at his feet. Jamal reached through the plastic leaves and found the switch, activating the device. A soft chime toned from the com-earpiece in his ear. He walked toward the command station in the middle of the camp.

"Did you hear me? I need your muscles over here," said Mendoza.

Jamal ignored the request and entered the command station. The structure was small but armored. "Sec-Lieutenant?"

A man in crisp tropical green fatigues sat at a desk constructed of planks lain across two plastic crates. "Yes?"

"The perimeter markers are in place and activated." Jamal waved a hand back in the direction he had come. "We've excavated most of the trenches for the fence charges. Awaiting orders, sir."

The small man got up and looked out the bunker's only portal. Nodding several times, he turned back to Jamal. "You guys move fast. I like it. I'll radio the construction team, let them know that base access protocol is in effect. Set up the boom-fence after I make the announcement."

"Yes, sir." Jamal saw the Sec-Lieutenant as a parasite, a blood-sucking tick at the center of a camp that real soldiers were building outside. Taurus Force Systems was virtually identical to the U.S. Army: individuals received promotions commensurate with the level of their incompetence.

"What are you smiling at, Battle? Go on and get to work," the Sec-Lieutenant said, and Jamal let go of his latest spiteful fantasy.

"Excuse me, sir," he said and went back outside.

He found Mendoza at the north end of the camp, digging a ditch about a foot deep. As Mendoza bent over to take another shovelful of dirt, Jamal kicked him high in the buttocks, sending him into the pile.

"Ah!" Mendoza twisted violently, shovel up. "Fucker! It should be you that's ass-deep in this ditch, bitch."

"Yeah? Make me do it, then." Jamal reached out and helped Mendoza get up.

The man was fiery and liked to scrap. Jamal liked him. Mendoza also did anything that Jamal told him to do.

"Why don't we get the guys with the LarcSuits to do this shit?" Mendoza said. "I mean, I feel like I'm in the Dark Ages… fuckin' grave digging."

Despite having a personality regarded as incendiary, Mendoza was soft as a soldier.

"I'm sure they'll dig you a hot tub later," said Jamal, "to help soothe your woes, you candy-ass."

"Dick," Mendoza mumbled.

Jamal looked back at the hill. Only a few trees remained. "The construction team only has forest-clearing gear. That's it. They're making a landing area and a rough road from it to the base. When the prospectors get here, the suits are going on the outbound flight." Jamal felt better now that he was in the field, his mind working more efficiently as his duties distracted him from the usual chaos within.

"I should steal one of those fucking things and start robbing banks," Mendoza said.

Jamal smiled. "And take what?"

The base amplifier sounded from the command station. *"Perimeter Condition Yellow. Base perimeter set. All personnel are ordered to move into and remain within the boom-fence marker areas. Markers are on and will indicate proximity. Once inside the perimeter, consider the fence live and do not cross. Perimeter Condition Yellow."*

"You got the charges?" Mendoza said.

"Three crates over by the command station," Jamal answered. "Why don't you get them while I finish the last ditch?"

"Fuckin' A!" Mendoza threw the shovel at Jamal's feet and jogged off. Jamal picked it up and finished the final few feet of the ditch in a matter of seconds.

Leaning on the shovel, he took a moment to survey the rest of the camp. Three other Taurus employees were setting up communications gear and collapsible dwellings. Although the mission did not have a high threat level, Jamal was uncomfortable with the dearth of personnel assigned to the project: a Sec-officer and five Sec-regulars. The three LarcSuit troopers were essentially construction equipment, outfitted to cut down trees and move them out of the way. They would be gone soon.

Taurus had accepted a contract from a large mining conglomerate that was prospecting in areas of the Congo once thought to be either devoid or stripped of resources. Someone thought the chance of finding rogue gem or metal deposits was worth the price. Hiring Taurus for both security and forest clearing was not cheap.

Jamal felt the mission was more akin to a camping trip than a military operation. The colors of the Congo were incredible though, so he was enjoying the experience all the same. The entire camp sat in a gloom under leaves and struggling branches. The forest floor had little vegetation. The area had been quiet before the construction team arrived.

Mendoza returned, pulling a gray crate on wheels. He opened it and handed Jamal a thick reel of explosive cable.

Jamal hated to handle explosives. The boom-fence charges were stable, but mistakes could happen. They only needed to unroll the line and bury it. Once the "fence" was armed, any object over twenty kilograms would set it off. Supersonic spikes of exploding metal would rip up and through any intruder trying to cross. Mendoza removed another spool and unrolled it in the opposite direction.

Without warning, a large explosion shook the earth and Jamal jumped to the ground reflexively. Thinking the fence had gone off, he frantically scanned the camp to see what had happened. But the area was clear.

Echoes of the blast rolled over and over. Finally finding the source, Jamal watched as smoke rose from the hilltop beyond. Sounds of gunfire and smaller explosions came from the north.

Jamal assessed his surroundings. Mendoza was crawling toward the small clearing on the north edge of the camp. The other Taurus personnel had taken cover.

Jamal followed Mendoza, getting to his feet but keeping low. He caught up with the man and they both got on their stomachs and crawled to a rise overlooking the ridge, using it for cover.

Their vantage point gave a view of the hill and surrounding forest. Jamal could just make out forms moving in the valley to the west, rocket trails streaking as they fired at the hilltop.

"The LarcSuits! They're hitting the LarcSuits!" Mendoza screamed over the din.

At that moment, Jamal heard the Sec-Lieutenant on the command channel. "Taurus Force Systems, sound off!"

Jamal looked back. Nothing moved inside the camp.

"Sec-Private Battle, online."

"Sec-Private Mendoza, online."

Jamal assumed that the Sec-Lieutenant had locked the command station and would not open it until the danger was clear, as Taurus protocol demanded. Jamal might be an employee working in hazardous conditions, but they were all expendable when company performance was under threat. The thought was quickly replaced by the sudden invigoration of being in a fight once more.

"Sit-Stat?" the Sec-Lieutenant said.

Jamal decided to be part of the team. "A force of undetermined size is attacking the construction zone at landing site Zorro," he said. "Observed weaponry includes small arms, machine gun, and rockets or RPGs." Jamal patted Mendoza on the shoulder and pointed to the troops below.

The fire lessened and the attackers spread out, taking cover throughout the valley. Aside from the occasional shifting of shadows, there was little sign of them now. Jamal struggled to make out a few of the marauders.

"I'm enabling the construction crew's channel," the Sec-Lieutenant responded. "They're pinned down behind some fallen trees. Whatley's channel is dead. I hereby authorize all Taurus Regulars to use deadly force in defense of self, Taurus property, and other Taurus personnel. I've radioed the regional office and they are sending a neutralization team. The weapons cache is unlocked. Arm yourselves, seek cover, and don't give away your position.

Await the neutralization team and do not engage the enemy unless directly attacked."

Jamal made his way to the command station with Mendoza. They met up with the other Taurus Regulars at the arms locker attached to the side of the station. The com channel lit up just then, crackling with the sounds of gunfire and static.

"Command, Construction Team, we won't make it. Whatley is down... I think they got him in the head. We are unarmed. Repeat, we are unarmed... *crrck...*"

Jamal looked in the direction of the construction team but he could only see trees.

"Construction Team, Command, hold position. Repeat, hold position. Back-up force is en route, ETA twelve minutes," said the Sec-Lieutenant.

Jamal turned to the soldier doling out weapons from the locker. She handed him a sub-machine gun. He pushed it back into her hands.

"Sniper rifle," he said.

"What?"

"Give me the sniper rifle." Jamal shoved her back against the locker.

She was shaking. The woman threw the gun down and reached back into the locker. Fumbling for a moment, she withdrew a long-barreled rifle, banging it on the door as she pulled it out. Jamal snatched the gun from her quivering hands.

"Get a weapon and go hide," he said.

The woman crawled away. Jamal moved forward and reached into the locker, finding the right ammo clip. He stood up and casually snapped the clip into place, walking back to the clearing without caution.

"Wait!" the Sec-Lieutenant said. "Did someone say 'sniper rifle'? DO NOT engage the enemy except in defense!"

Jamal reached the clearing and got into a shooting position. A clump of rotting branches served as a rifle perch as he took steady aim on the area below.

"Battle. I can see you on my video feed. Stop!"

"Sir, fellow Taurus employees' lives are threatened."

"I told you to wait for the neutralization team, Goddamnit! The LarcSuits will hold out."

"No, they won't." Jamal did not care if they did or not. He only cared about satiating a simple need to answer violence with violence.

He looked through the scope. The shadows resolved into detailed forms: troops, in dark green uniforms, firing assorted small arms. Two men were also armed with rocket-propelled grenade launchers. Jamal could make them out clearly. The entire force had resumed fire.

He panned across the rest of the company and saw a man gesticulating wildly. He was waving to something behind the main attackers and Jamal swung the rifle to look. He could clearly make out an armored vehicle lumbering into the area.

"Sec-Lieutenant, they're bringing in a tracked truck of some kind. The bed is big, big enough for a LarcSuit." He smiled as he spoke.

"Fuck! Fuck!" the Sec-Lieutenant sputtered over the com channel.

Armored bunkers and safety protocols served no purpose for the man now. Jamal listened with satisfaction to his meltdown. "Orders?"

There was a pause filled with heavy panting and scattered unintelligible mumbles. Finally, the Sec-Lieutenant said what Jamal wanted to hear. "Okay. Uh, all Sec-Regulars are ordered to defend the LarcSuit team in order to help them…"

Jamal fired and hit the vehicle driver through an open window, painting the interior with blood and viscera.

Without pause, he swung his scope to the nearest RPG man and fired. The first shot missed, but a second connected with the man's chest and he went down.

Jamal took several more shots before the rest of the force responded. Men scrambled to take cover. Muzzle flashes erupted throughout the valley and Jamal's perch was instantly under fire.

"Fall back! The militants have our location and are attacking." Jamal rolled back violently.

"Damnit!" the Sec-Lieutenant said. "You're an idiot, Battle. Seek cover."

Jamal crawled to the station. He slung the sniper rifle onto his back and grabbed the machine gun off the ground. Once refitted, Jamal made for the road that led to the construction team.

"Mendoza!" Jamal searched the trees as he ran.

"Battle!" Mendoza said.

"Do you see me?"

"I'm thirty feet behind you."

He looked back and saw Mendoza a short distance behind. The road was lined with tree trunks and Jamal kept close to the left, using them as cover. Light streamed in through a long opening in the canopy and Jamal tried to find his objective. A curve in the road prevented him from seeing all the way to the hilltop clearing.

He made a quick decision and jumped over the trunks to his left, bolting into the forest. Coming again to the ridge, Jamal began to fire randomly in the direction of the militants. "Mendoza, get up here and lay down fire. Make them follow us away from the camp."

He watched as Mendoza did as instructed, firing down into the fray from behind a tree trunk. "Where are we going?" he said.

"To the construction team." Jamal loosed several shots into the valley below.

"Didn't we just bail them out?"

"Not yet." Jamal continued towards the hilltop. "Sec-Lieutenant, what is the status of the camp?"

The com channel hissed. "I let the other Regulars in to the command structure. My feed shows scattered forms flanking the road to the west, but they're not attacking the station. Don't lead them back here, Battle. Do you hear me?"

Jamal broke into a sprint. Reaching the end of the curve, he could finally see into the clearing. It was easy then to make out the construction team, their suit enamels a conspicuous bright orange.

As Jamal got closer, he could see two of the armored men dragging the third. "Construction Team, Sec-Private Battle. Status?"

The moving pile of glinting orange stopped as both of the burdened men looked in Jamal's direction.

"Don't stop! Get to cover. Move and talk." Jamal ran on.

They turned back and continued to drag the fallen man, more quickly this time.

"Whatley is dead," one of the men said. "Something got him in the head. Not much of it left. Frank and I are fine. These suits are for heavy lifting, not combat. The armor is sufficient to hold against those bastards' gunfire, though. We found cover behind some logs. Whatley didn't make it. Once the firing stopped and you guys engaged, we went out to get him. We're... ugh... getting him back to our hole now."

"I'm coming, and the enemy's right behind me," Jamal said.

"Shit!"

"Get Whatley's body out of the suit."

Jamal saw the suited men climb over the pile of trunks and out of sight. From behind, the shots were more frequent, and he was forced to jump the road barrier once again. He looked back briefly to find Mendoza close behind. They made their way to the construction team's location, led on by a waving mechanized arm.

"I have your location, now get down. That orange stands out like a flare."

Jamal found the men huddled over their fallen comrade, his body freed of the damaged exoskeleton. Whatley was mostly intact, but his head was a mass of crimson pulp littered with skull fragments. Jamal kneeled down beside the empty LarcSuit.

He looked into the black visors of the two suited men before surveying the equipment attached to their arms. Each had a large sickle-like claw on one arm and a two-bladed buzz saw on the other.

"Can you dump your implements?" Jamal examined the devices.

The man shook his helmeted head. "No. They're part of the arm."

Jamal scowled. "Can you let the arms go free, releasing your own limbs to do other things?"

"Yeah, but why would…"

"Do it."

Jamal was pushed from behind.

"What the fuck are we doing?" Mendoza said as he crashed into the trunk-protected area and grabbed Jamal's arm. Jamal shook free of the man's grip. He took the sniper rifle from his shoulder and thrust it out.

"Give me your gun and take this. Go east. Find a good roost so you can see the enemy. Try to find the last RPG guy. Snipe as many as you can."

"But—"

"GO!"

Mendoza threw his gun to the ground, snatched the sniper rifle, and ran off.

"Now. Frank, is it?" Jamal said, as he retrieved the other machine gun and rounded on the two men.

"No, I'm Frank." The other man raised his hand.

"Whatever. Get one of your arms free, take that gun there, and start firing. You, take this." Jamal laid down the machine gun and pulled a pistol from his hip for the other man. "You start shooting too."

"What are you gonna do?" Just then, an RPG streaked over Frank's head, screaming into the forest and exploding in the woods beyond.

"Mendoza!" Jamal wanted the RPGs gone.

"I see him! I see him!"

Jamal watched as both of the armored men obeyed, and the access points on their arms opened with a *snap*. They slid their arms out and the released suit appendages lowered and folded back. Each man raised his weapon and began to fire blindly in the direction of the closing attackers.

Jamal lay down into Whatley's suit and began to strap himself in. The suit automatically closed around his body, making the necessary adjustments to fit snugly onto his legs and torso.

Jamal rolled inexpertly and tried to get to his feet. After several attempts, he got on one knee and fumbled with the controls until the right arm of the LarcSuit opened and folded back to the side, exposing his own arm and allowing it to move freely.

He had piloted a LarcSuit once before. Most required little training to use and responded naturally with the movements of the body. Fortunately, this one was like most. Jamal shifted his weight to get a feel for how the LarcSuit behaved. Satisfied, he held his armored left arm out and across his body, approximating a rough shield.

"Give me one of your helmets," he said.

The two suited men continued to fire into the distance.

"Give me a helmet!"

"Fuck you, kid," Frank said.

Neither of the men looked back. Jamal let it go and took up a position at the log barrier. The marauders were getting closer, though they were fewer in number than he remembered. Perhaps the main force had remained with the vehicle?

"I think I just shot the RPG!" Mendoza said.

"Do they have your location?" Jamal stood up.

"I fucking hope not."

Jamal looked in the direction Mendoza had run, but saw only leaves and forest debris.

"I'm going in," Jamal yelled. "Try not to shoot me." He staggered over the log barrier, the LarcSuit's massive feet digging deep into soft soil. He ran to the right of the militants. Ducking his head, he started to shoot with his free hand. The com channels sprang to life.

"Jesus Christ!"

"Jamal!"

"What the fuck are you doing?"

Two attackers hunched behind a large tree froze at the shock of Jamal's assault and were easily gunned down. The surprise was soon gone and bullets began to tap against his suit, the concussions clearly felt against his flesh.

Jamal fell to his knees. More shots landed as he buried his head and naked right arm under the rest of his armored bulk. His body was on fire as the hail of bullets sought a weakness, trying to get through his armored defense.

Jamal screamed.

In desperation, he pointed the gun out from under his legs, exposing his arm. It was instantly hit by the maelstrom of bullets and torn apart.

He screamed again as his body crumpled. Twisting in torment, Jamal tried in vain to move his inoperable limb back under the suit. Agony destroyed any semblance of thought and he rolled to his side.

A nearby explosion rattled the ground. Jamal waited for the next blast to take his life. Instead, the gunfire that had peppered his suit ceased. He strained to look up. The enemy was still shooting, just not at him.

All at once the forest exploded in every direction, debris and bodies scattering violently. Jamal waited for the concussions to abate before looking up again.

The immediate area had been spared, yet smoke and burning wood filled the perimeter where the militants once stood. He saw lifeless bodies everywhere. Chatter filled his com-earpiece.

"Wooohh!"

"We're still down here!"

"*Crrrkkkkk...* Echo-35, this is Halo-1. I have visual of three Larcs. Status of other personnel?"

Jamal tried once again to move his arm, but could not be certain there was an arm left to move. A growing haze filled his mind as pain and loss of blood fought to drain him of lucidity.

"Four in the command station," the Sec-Lieutenant said.

"Sec-Private Mendoza, reporting."

Jamal struggled to look up through growing delirium. He was aware of something moving in the sky above. As he searched the mix of beaming light and leafy shadows, Jamal saw a ghostly form descending from the canopy. It was bright in color, contrasting with the deep green above. It drew closer, alternating between a blinding whiteness and a soft glow as it flew through bars of light and gloom.

"Roger. Have visual of remaining hostiles. They're buggin' out. Should I engage?"

"Negative, Halo-1. Verify enemy egress and commence area recon, five-klick-radius," said the Sec-Lieutenant.

"Copy that, Echo-35. Halo-1 out."

Jamal let his head drop, the energy needed to hold it up having seeped out of his wounds. Com channels continued to crackle and hiss, but the voices bled into one another and he could not understand them. Without warning, he felt several sets of hands gently rolling him over. Jamal felt safe in surrendering to unconsciousness. The forest faded and the forms dissolved.

CHAPTER 4

Jamal sat up in the hospital bed, bending his arm and marveling at the presence of both strength and flexibility. The bicep looked different, as though it had been ripped from another body and grafted to Jamal's own. But it worked as well as it had before. That was all he cared about.

He could recall memories of the Congo expedition. Jamal had passed out after the battle was over, but regained consciousness before the med chopper arrived. Through the haze of battle-fatigue and pain, the image of a bright, shining form descending from the canopy had captivated him. It had seemed to glow faintly as it alighted on the forest floor.

Jamal had been confused by everything then: where he was, why his right arm did not work, why he looked down at his body and saw only orange metal and red blood. But when the airborne trooper had approached, clarity of mind returned. A LarcSuited woman stood before him, her aspect markedly different from the orange construction suits, her beauty captured by engineering and bristling weaponry.

The suit was sleek and she moved with threatening grace. Various ports and vents accented her body, large exhausts covering much of her back. Small boxes clung to her hips and peeked over her shoulders.

But all of these things were made trite by the instrument held tightly in her hands—a multi-barreled rifle of great size, painted in the same shade of polar white as her body.

"Mr. Battle?"

Jamal felt the sting of the voice cut into his thoughts. Blocking it out, he strained to remember. The Sec-Lieutenant had given orders like "Detain the Sec-Private" and "Escort Sec-Private Battle." But as he immersed himself in these recollections, the most intense mental vibration came from the silken, contralto voice of the LarcSuited savior. "*You're glad I'm back from Antarctica early, aren't you, little boy?*" Jamal searched his mind for those amalgams of force and wonder, of merging flesh and metal, the sex of polar white and bleeding shadows heating his body with self-annihilating fervor and anointing him with the smell of female sweat and jet-fuel.

"Mr. Battle?" The voice insisted on destroying fantasy.

"I'm awake." Jamal waved without opening his eyes.

"Good. As you know, we are releasing you this afternoon. I just wanted to check on you one more time to make sure you are ready to leave."

Jamal was tired of the nurse "just checking" about everything. He had tried to leave a month ago—on three separate occasions actually—but hospital security was consistently quicker than he was. Each episode resulted in a slow walk back to his room, flanked by several Navy Men-at-Arms. The nurse began "just checking" more often after that. But today she left without a second look, obviously ready to be free of Jamal.

Likewise.

Several hours passed in more wakeful dreaming. His instructions were to wait for the Taurus Force Systems representative to escort him out of the hospital. Jamal was starting to doze when a man in a brown suit walked into the room. A guard in Taurus uniform followed, but stopped, turned, and stood at the door. The suited man said nothing as he put his briefcase on a chair and pulled out a com-pad.

Confused, Jamal started to get up. The newcomer thrust out a hand and he sat back down.

"You are Jamal Battle, Taurus Employee number 5667843920?"

"Are you...?" Jamal began.

"Just answer my questions, please. My day is more than full and I don't have time to dally. I am with the company and here to process your release from the hospital."

The urge to get up and leave was strong, yet Jamal obeyed. "I'm Jamal Battle, number 5667843920."

"Good. National Naval Medical Center has stated that you are no longer in need of medical care requiring an inpatient status. Your right arm has been reconstructed and has been restored to approximately 80 percent of its original operability and strength. To the best of your knowledge, do you concur with these statements?"

"I do." Jamal hated business suits. He hated formality as well. The company had sent him a message saying they would make contact when his convalescence was over. And so they had.

"Your admittance and subsequent hospital stay, of considerable cost, stems from Taurus Force Systems Incident 4555G4A. You have not been absolved of responsibility in the incident, so all hospital charges are awaiting payment by you, any wages payable from Taurus Force Systems being forfeit to make payments on these costs. If you are absolved of responsibility in this incident and the company is found culpable for your health and rehabilitation, all charges will be paid by Taurus Force Systems and you will owe nothing. Do you understand the things I've just told you?"

"Absolved? What? We got attacked. Why would I have to pay for anything if—?"

"Stop." Again the man's hand came up, and again Jamal wanted to leave, by force if needed. "My purpose does not concern the details of Incident"—he looked at his com-pad—"4555G4A. I am here to inform you of the aforementioned items and to see you into Taurus Force Systems custody."

The man turned and snapped his fingers at the door guard. The guard walked out of sight and the suited man went back to viewing his com-pad, making entries. Two men entered. It was the door man accompanied by another guard, this one holding a pair of handcuffs.

"Under the authority given by the U.S. Department of Defense concerning internal company security matters, I, Arthur Reston, Taurus Force Systems Legal Advisor, officially order the employees of Taurus Force Systems to take legal custody of one Jamal Battle from the civilian care of the National Naval Medical Center, December 19th, 2032.

"No charges exist at this time, though Taurus Force Systems must hand you over to the authorities if any charges that violate Federal or International Law are substantiated by the company."

Jamal stood erect, staring hard at Reston. The guards stepped back, one holding the cuffs open, yet looking confused. They looked over to Reston, then up at Jamal.

"Please, Battle. As I said, I don't know the details of the incident, or the level of interest that Taurus has in you. But don't get yourself in real trouble. We take you in, you find out what issues must be resolved, and you resolve them. That's it. You are probably not in any trouble at all, but the cuffs and the guards are protocol. If you try to force your way out of this, all I do is make a call and the real military intercepts you and you go to jail. For as long as *I* like, Battle, I assure you."

Jamal realized his fists were closed and his body tense, ready for conflict. The other men in the room had realized this as well. He relaxed, rubbing his face and head slowly to release the anxiety.

"I understand." He did not, but he wanted to get out of the hospital at all costs.

Composing himself, Jamal extended his arms with wrists together. They put the cuffs on roughly and Jamal regretted not running: he was now a prisoner, regardless of what was said. Reston packed his com-pad back into the briefcase, sealed it, and gestured for Jamal's security detail to leave the room first.

A plain black sedan complete with driver awaited them at the hospital entrance, engine running. The smaller of the two guards helped Jamal into the back seat. The other guard spoke briefly to Reston before going back into the hospital. Reston got in, turned to Jamal and gestured toward the hospital entrance.

"We have a few Taurus employees on staff at the hospital since we have exclusive rights to use the facilities. We are the only security agency that the DoD allows in there. You received some of the finest care available in the history of humanity. You should feel privileged."

Under guard, in handcuffs, and being escorted to an investigation by way of a spook sedan, Jamal did not feel privileged. He also doubted that he would get his job back. So a bereft life of a dark apartment and drunkenness loomed, putting him right back where he'd started. He forced the thought out of mind.

They drove for an hour, arriving at what Jamal assumed was a Magna-Rail station. He read the sign in the central lobby: Thomas Station, a stop on the railway between New York and Washington, DC. Once across the lobby, Jamal was directed to enter the Taurus Force Systems office. Taurus owned a car on the New Acela Express. Reston spoke briefly to the lone guard before walking out without a word to Jamal, who was then directed to board the train using a non-public entryway.

The trip took just over forty-five minutes. Jamal sat with the guard in the passenger section, a cramped cabin with about twenty seats. The rest of the car was an open cargo space, its utility apparent as Jamal was escorted through it on his way to the bathroom. Several crates, an armored rover, and a few utility robots were visible through the passageway window.

They arrived in New York and the journey continued, with Jamal bound and led by a weak-looking man into a yawning pedestrian tunnel funneling a crowd into the city.

Jamal had never been to New York, and technically, he was not there now. Another city existed under the metropolis, the many autonomous subterranean communities networked below being owned by government agencies or private firms. The guard had told Jamal that most of the areas under Manhattan were secure and did not provide passage to the public; private research and other secretive operations occurred under the feet of millions. A tunnel connected Osceola Station, the Acela Express's New York City connection, to Taurus Force Systems' corporate headquarters in Andros Tower.

As they walked up a service ramp, out of the underground area and into the tower lobby, the guard took off his vest and gave it to Jamal, demanding that he cover up his bonds as they walked. People passing by looked at Jamal suspiciously. He questioned the nature of his detainment now, as it was obvious that the guard did not want his incarceration to be public knowledge. Jamal's escape fantasies became more practical and less creative.

New York might be a great place to get lost, but he knew they would find him eventually. So Jamal walked on.

They stopped at an elevator access. The guard waved his hand over a black glass plate and the door opened. Jamal grimaced; he hated ID implants. A small number of the population was still implant-free, and Jamal was proud to be one of them. The government did not mandate ID implant use, although it was considered tasteless not to have one. And industries made life difficult for those without. From security to credit payments to simple commerce, most used the convenience of instant identification. Profits were enhanced by reliable statistics.

The elevator rose. The guard furnished a key to unlock the upper-level punch keys. He pressed the button for the top floor: 155. Jamal was going to the top of the tallest structure in the history of the world. He had seen the Andros Tower on a myriad of video feeds and TV shows. Now he was inside it, rising floor by floor.

The elevator slowed and stopped. As the doors opened, extreme humidity invaded the car and clung to Jamal's face. The guard motioned for him to get out.

They walked into a short passageway leading to a central court. Jamal followed the guard to the middle of the chamber and was assaulted by the décor of the room.

The floor was made of rough stones, layered like cobbles and of varied color. The walls were terraced and held what Jamal assumed were tropical plants. Bright orchids and large green leaves grew from the terraces. The entire room evoked a sense of ancient powers and ways of reckoning long abandoned by civilized men.

All of the fixtures, carvings and plants pointed toward a single inanimate entity in the center of the room. Jamal was struck by the enormous statue on a stone pedestal that dominated the chamber. It was in the form of a bare-breasted woman, one arm extending above her head and holding an obsidian sphere, the other holding a down-turned sword with the tip of the blade resting beside her feet.

Black marble channels radiated outward from the statue's base through the rest of the chamber, a shimmer of light and faint gurgling the only evidence of water flowing to the spaces beyond. Above, light streamed in through a transparent bubble-dome.

The chamber walls seethed with strangeness as well. A thin fresco followed the circumference of the round chamber above head level, painted with twisted serpents fighting inhuman warriors. The silent soldiers hacked at scale and coil, their own mouths issuing long, grotesque tongues both pointed and forked.

The artistry was breathtaking, if intensely macabre, and Jamal lost himself in the dark beauty of the paintings. He could not identify the methods used, but judging from the texture and depth of the frescos, Jamal suspected they were egg tempera on dry plaster. He had experimented with such old techniques before, but in the face of the modern digital-to-mechanized painting system, practitioners of old methods—or more precisely, mentors— were hard to find. Jamal felt pain at the thought. He wanted to forget his interest in developing true skill in the art form. If he went back to a dark apartment in Minneapolis, perhaps he could try painting again.

A man entered the chamber from a door to Jamal's right. Recognizing the man, Jamal forgot about painting.

"Please take care not to step in the water. Don't touch anything, and try to understand that it is a peculiar twist of circumstances that has allowed someone of your... *stature* to be standing in a place that Presidents, Prime Ministers and CEOs are rarely allowed to visit." Arthur Reston stood taller than Jamal remembered, his eyes level with Jamal's.

"Why did you—" Jamal began.

"Stop." Reston raised his hand and motioned for Jamal to come closer. He did so, getting as close as possible before Reston extended his arm to stop their noses from touching.

"Ah, I can see why you are here." Reston stepped back without alarm. Jamal did not press further. "Now, let's take a look at your dress. Your issued Taurus uniform is sufficient for today, though not for tomorrow, I think. Maybe you'll be wearing another one."

The situation was growing as strange as the chamber they stood in. Jamal was undoubtedly outside the office of the most powerful man in the entire world. He did not know why. The loss of control was finally unnerving. "What the fuck are you talking about?"

Reston moved quicker than Jamal thought possible, throwing a punch that struck him in the side of the mouth. Jamal jumped back, trying to take a fighting stance and bringing hands up to protect his face. Reston stood as he did before, not a dark hair of his head out of place. He was serene, his hands held out, open palm towards Jamal's escort guard. "If you speak again without being explicitly questioned, Sec-Sergeant Jones will gag you. Now, compose yourself before we go in. I have some instructions for you."

Jamal's mind was red heat and clicks. An instinct to fight was overruled by the circumstances. He knew now that he was in real trouble, that having been taken to the inner sanctum of this man was not safe.

"CEO Tennyson will talk, and you will listen. You will not interrupt him, nor speak unless answering a question directed at you. Don't look him in the eye, but rather focus on the wall behind him, as you would with an officer in the Army. Understood?"

Jamal brought his bound hands to his face and felt his lip. He looked at his fingertips: no blood. He looked down at Reston, who wore a casual grin. Jamal knew the punch had been pulled. "Sure."

"Now, if you will, please." Reston gestured towards the door across the chamber, opposite the elevator access corridor. The door was larger than the rest and made of a dark wood.

Jamal expected additional servants on the other side of the door. There was none. Reston walked in, pointed at a spot on the floor where Jamal should stand, and went back to close the door. The guard remained outside.

The office was large, yet not as extravagantly furnished as the central chamber. Charcoal carpet covered the floor, and alternating tiles of ash-gray and black formed cascading designs on the walls. The far wall was all glass and Jamal could see only mist and sky beyond, the city below obscured.

A desk sat in the exact center of the office, made of a type of wood Jamal had never seen. The grains alternated dark and light, giving the surface strange life through optical illusion. The man sitting at the desk wore a fine pinstriped suit, his body appearing as an extension of the wood surrounding him.

His graying hair was accented by white wings and there was no doubt of his identity. Jamal knew little about business, but Keenan Tennyson was known in every country, every city and every household as the richest man in the world.

The founder, owner, president, and CEO of Tennyson Holdings, the man controlled several companies that had changed, and would continue to change, the fate of millions. Taurus Force Systems was one of them. Jamal remembered the news ten years ago when Tennyson had purchased the Andros Tower. He had been lauded as an American hero, a man taking back the U.S. legacy of toil and profits that so many believed had fallen into the hands of foreigners.

But Jamal's father had said that Tennyson was "a king who sold kingdoms to slaves, ruling them with such a subtle hand that they are not aware of their captivity." Jamal had not listened to his father's philosophizing, though the lessons seemed increasingly vivid now. The man at the desk continued to read from a stationary com-pad.

Dark colors were woven from wall to floor to man. Every molecule and wave of light seemed to churn with its own intelligence, the collective entity pacing, surging, and attending to its locus seated at the desk.

Jamal was intrigued, yet confused by this audience. After a moment of thought, he decided he didn't care. Several months ago, his days had consisted of consorting with piss-ants. To divert himself, he had tried to drink action into his life, hoping that an inebriated haze would eventually rip a hole into another universe, giving him the chaos and adventure he desired.

He had enjoyed killing those men in the Congo, hoped he could do it again. If Jamal was in real danger, he sure as hell wouldn't be standing before a living god. A facet of his psyche wanted to snap Tennyson's neck; another wanted to kneel before him.

At last, Tennyson looked up. There was no secret message in that gaze, nothing more than a sense of pure utility. The man was steel. Jamal was courted by this knowledge, viewing Tennyson as a living katana. The years and challenges of his life had been used with total artistry and control, his emotions and thoughts being hammered and folded, hammered and folded, until they could cut through anything with flexibility and speed, the seal of a master etched thoughtfully upon his forehead. A self-made blade. Jamal thought of himself in the same way, but

Tennyson's presence made this self-image ridiculous. Jamal was nothing. Nothing but ruined iron and a blunt edge.

"You don't know why you're here, Jamal Battle," Tennyson said.

It was not a question.

"Currently," he continued, "we have delayed turning you over to Federal authorities."

Jamal looked at the wall and said nothing. In his periphery, he could see that Tennyson stared at him blankly: no intent or emotion was detectable from that stare. Jamal sought an ascetic bearing but fell short.

"You are charged with endangering company property and personnel, as well as murdering nationals of Zambia. We have allowed you to convalesce in a hospital instead of a prison as a courtesy. I would like to know your opinion on this."

Jamal took a moment to digest the statement. He had expected the limited autonomy afforded to a soldier. While in the Army, his mistakes were the Army's mistakes. The same was not true, it seemed, of Taurus Force Systems. "I disagree with the charges, sir."

"Do you?"

"I was following the orders of Sec-Lieutenant Parker. He told the Taurus Regulars to defend the entrenched construction team." Jamal felt his fists clench as he shifted his weight from foot to foot. Realizing the self-betrayal, he settled himself and tried to stand at attention.

CEO Tennyson sat erect with hands folded and said nothing. Just as Jamal was about to speak, Tennyson came to life. "Do not speak. You've given me your opinion as I asked. Now, in response to that opinion, I'd like to provide the facts on this issue. All communications between Taurus Force Systems personnel involved in this incident were recorded at the time, as is protocol for all operations. The Lieutenant ordered you to defend the construction team.

He did not give you permission to use offensive tactics. He did not give you command of other Taurus Regulars.

"He did, however, tell you to wait for the neutralization team. He also told you to lay down suppressive fire to aid the construction team, but according to the records and communications, you were too busy killing protected foreign nationals and donning equipment that you are neither trained nor authorized to use. You did knowingly threaten the use, machine-life, and security of protected technologies leased from the U.S. Department of Defense."

Panic surged and Jamal considered his options. In the penthouse of a highly guarded tower belonging to the largest private military contractor on the planet and handcuffed, Jamal had none.

"We are the only corporate entity in the world with access to LarcSuits," Tennyson said. "I won't assume you know that. But I will assume that your Taurus Orientation informed you of the limited number of LarcSuits we possess and their importance. I will assume this because you submitted to your own psychological defects and disguised your actions under the pretense of protecting said assets.

"Taurus Force Systems is not grateful for your actions. I am not grateful for your actions. You are a liability. Lesser men put you into company service when they ought not. Their incompetence has resulted in millions of dollars in fines and compensation. Some of that money went to the DoD for the admitted misuse of a LarcSuit—they monitor our communications per our government contract—and the rest to provide recompense to the people of Zambia for the loss of their sons, fathers, and brothers. Sec-Private Battle, what is your opinion on what I have just said? Yes, there is only one opinion you could possibly have."

Jamal let his vision drift and meld with haze beyond the window. Low clouds could be made out when he focused, clumps of fine cotton racing by. This morning he had expected to be released from the minor hell of Bethesda, travel to Taurus's barracks in Norfolk, drink himself into oblivion while resting at a local strip club, hopefully using extra funds to lure a stripper-of-choice to a hotel to do more than strip. But instead he felt himself being tied to a pole that extended into the stratosphere, his bleeding body looking down on the top of the Andros Tower, through the transparent roof, to gaze into the black orb that Liberty held towards the heavens, just forty feet from her master, Keenan Tennyson.

"I have no opinion on this matter, sir. The facts speak for themselves," Jamal said with reluctant humility.

Tennyson sat back in his leather throne and looked his employee over. Jamal waited for some kind of judgment.

"I like your answer, Battle. I doubt it is the right answer, but only you can know that."

It was not the response Jamal was expecting. Understanding that this meeting and its direction had been premeditated by Tennyson, Jamal tried to be unpredictable. "What do you want?"

Tennyson's face folded slightly, a mere hint of the demonic flashing over his visage. He was silent for several minutes, the time crushing in on Jamal's brain as he assumed it was supposed to.

"The question is what do *you* want?" Tennyson said. "Your marginal career is at an end."

"Then I have nothing to lose."

"Oh, I would not be so hasty in that assertion. What you have left can be taken from you in the most painful of ways, Mr. Battle."

The situation had dissolved into madness. Relaxing his body, Jamal assessed the room. Tennyson was five feet away. Jamal looked over his shoulder to find a smiling Reston standing in front of the closed door.

"Easy, Jamal. Reston is an excellent lawyer, yet that is not where the majority of his salary is earned."

Something hard pressed against the back of Jamal's head. "I'd hate to ruin your carpet," Jamal said, knowing the feel of a gun barrel on flesh.

"I'd have it, and you, replaced in an hour," Tennyson said quickly.

Reston lightly tapped the gun on the top of Jamal's head.

"As much as I enjoy mixing with people of your caliber," Tennyson continued, "I'd like to conclude this meeting. Fortune has blessed you this day, Mr. Battle, for you have been given a chance of which you are unworthy. You either choose to accept the charges Taurus Force Systems will bring to the Federal authorities and face life in prison—and I'm fairly sure of the sentence—or you accept private employment from me."

The expected apex of this meeting was both a relief and a seduction. The chaos Jamal had felt since arriving at the penthouse formed into knowledge of his captor's dark intent. Jamal was a mustang to be bridled, simple enough.

"I don't think I'd like prison," Jamal said, suddenly interested in the prospect of working again, in whatever vile capacity Tennyson might require.

"Although you seem to do all the right things to earn a cell. I am not sure how you ended up in my employ, Jamal. You are a cyst, a mal-appropriation of nature, nurture, and societal wealth. You should have been incarcerated long ago. Yes, I know everything about you. You have no benefactors now, however, to trick the system into releasing you. No father."

An explosion of hysteria nearly took Jamal from within. He breathed hard and stepped toward the sitting man.

"I'd keep that temper of yours in check, Jamal, if you would like to hear what I have to offer."

Jamal calmed himself and resealed the memories Tennyson's comment had started to unlock. His façade had fallen for a moment, and Tennyson had seen right through. "I have a task that needs completing. This task concerns another cyst that has grown fat from my success and generosity. The only thing I need you to do is to recover some loose property of mine. The items I desire are not hard to find, though the task might require a certain, say, 'moral flexibility' on the part of my agent."

Jamal let the statement take hold. This was a job interview of sorts, and all pretenses could be thrown aside. He relaxed further and spoke impulsively. "How many items?"

"Exactly twelve. Some may be found in remote locations, others may be found together. No expense will be spared concerning this retrieval. You will be free to allocate any resources that Tennyson Holdings and its affiliated services can provide. The exception is that nothing can be done publicly, so if you need something that cannot be reconciled by the accounts on the quarterly or yearly reports, you can't have it."

Jamal did not know what that meant. "I thought you were sparing no expense?"

"I have informed you of the limits of your authority and I will not reiterate them. You are no longer part of the company, so how you get the resources you need is your affair. A key cube was lost several weeks ago. This key cube gave unlimited access to all security points and a credit account within the Tennyson Conglomerate, as well as allocation authorization. Perhaps you will find it.

"When you leave the tower, you will be given details on the first of the items to be recovered. Once in your possession, bring it here. You will then be given details about the next item and the cycle will repeat. Now Arthur will see you out. Any questions you may have are moot." Tennyson returned his attention to his com-pad. The audience was at an end.

Reston opened the door as Jamal turned to leave. Jamal's body seemed to work without clear cognizance. He could not process what had just happened, but he understood he was going to be free. He was past the threshold when Tennyson spoke.

"Oh, and Battle, you are not a Sec-Private anymore. You do not work for me or anyone who works for me. There are several other individuals with motivations similar to yours, so I suggest that you retrieve my items first. If not, the world will not notice your second disappearance. Don't think about going back home. They had your funeral last Tuesday. I understand your mother was sad, yet apparently relieved. Strange. She even commended the morticians for their presentation of your body. Sometimes the face does not even look like the person, but yours was dead on, excuse the pun."

Jamal's mind went numb.

"Jamal Battle worked for Taurus Force Systems for several months, but died of his wounds after coming back from somewhere in Africa. Anyway, I wish you well in your endeavors. Homelessness is terrible. I hope you survive the winter."

Jamal looked back in horror. Reston grabbed his arm and pulled him towards the central chamber, but he jerked free and turned to face Tennyson. "I thought if I refused you were going to turn me over to the Feds?"

"Oh, I knew there was only one choice for someone as… motivated as you."

"If I refused?"

"You would be the first man in history to be buried twice."

The urge to run was strong, though Jamal didn't know where to run to. Reston led him back through the central chamber and on to the elevator entrance. Tennyson's office door closed.

"The elevator will take you to the lobby. Please don't bother us with your inadequacies in the future," Reston said, relief apparent in his voice and posture. He quickly released the handcuffs and stepped back, saying, "Herriot in Kenya."

"What?" Jamal said.

"Herriot in Kenya."

"That's it?"

"That's it. Oh, and I think you dropped something."

The doors closed and the car began to descend. Jamal looked to the floor. A small metal cube lay in the corner. He reached down to pick it up. A dull finish of brushed metal hid the importance of the one-inch cube and Jamal noticed that it had a small chain connected to it.

The elevator reached its destination and Jamal stepped out into the Andros Tower lobby, walked through the lush gardens set in black marble and past the elegant fountains to the entrance. Stopping at a trash can, he tossed his wallet away, put the cube in his pocket and walked out onto Fifth Avenue.

CHAPTER 5

Ruth graded papers. Her teaching status was now ambiguous, but still she graded papers. That helped her remain emotionally stable through the afternoon, but as the stack of reports thinned, her anxiety returned. She was at a loss about what to do next. Rupert's words repeated in her mind: *"The Thrones are not a legitimate topic for academic study. They, like so many other hysterical phenomena of the current age, are fleeting manifestations of the social disconnection that people feel. Why not discuss the state of the Protestant Union or the Southern Catholic Church Proclamation if you desire to study Post-Modern and New Imperialist influences? The reality is that the FESB tries to prevent any information from getting to the classroom that is better suited for independent websites and these so-called 'independent academic syndicates.' Maybe you are just a product of your generation, Ruth, not knowing the difference between knowledge and fancy. Excuse me, my dear, I don't mean that. I fear for the future of all Federal Universities. We are by far the youngest; Campolo was built when I was about forty. We are facing a crisis, Ruth."*

"Piss," Ruth said. She thought of Howard, the overeager philosophy professor. She thought of how annoying he was, how his advances were repulsive, and how he was utterly unattractive. The thesis sat before her on the table. She flipped through the pages and took notes, frantically trying to sculpt the headings into something innocuous without changing the heart of the project. "Piss, piss, piss."

Ruth collected the papers and stuffed them into her bag. She reclined in her seat for a moment, head back, eyes closed. She picked up the phone.

"Hey! It's me, Ruth. What are you doing for dinner tonight? Me? No. Okay, I'll meet you at six. Yup. Okay. See you soon, Howard."

Ruth watched TV for an hour to waste time and also to deaden her mind, the current situation too catastrophic to dwell on. The time came to leave and she drove back into town to meet Howard.

He was standing outside the pizza place when she pulled up. Ruth got the same feeling driving past him to park—his dumbstruck eyes glittering at her when she made the mistake of meeting them—as when she saw him from her classroom on most days.

But Ruth needed some kind of company now. Her only female friend, Professor Stephanie Parks, another fellow of the Classics Department, was spending a semester as an adjunct professor at Tel Aviv University. Without her, Ruth had to settle for Howard.

So she greeted him at the door, they got their food, and sat down in a booth. Ruth said as little as she could, but finally decided to load Howard with her ills in an effort to distract him from finding romantic courage. He was a good guy and he truly looked out for Ruth when she asked him to. Besides that, she found absolutely no attractive traits in the man. He was milquetoast, overweight, and had a distinct odor.

She told him about her suspension anyway. "Don't tell anyone about this," she added, after recounting the day's drama.

"Oh, I won't," said Howard.

Ruth took another bite from her pizza slice. The restaurant was a poor imitation of an East Coast-style pizza parlor. The tables were bright orange. Pictures of European advertisements (some actually in French, though Ruth was sure the owners spoke neither French nor Italian) for Ducati Motorcycles and Ferraris layered the wall — too clean and too new.

There were no pictures of Portofino, Naples, or the Vatican, no caked scum in the floor corners, and no jabbering Italian in the kitchen. *And the food sucks*, Ruth thought. But it was Howard's favorite place. He always insisted on either taking her to one of several marginal "fine dining" restaurants or this pizza place.

"They're pissed about the Thrones, huh?" Howard said.

The statement jarred Ruth back to her current predicament. "They are."

"Well, I don't know much about them. I heard they were government experiments gone wrong, or some geneticist made them in his basement. Something ridiculous." Howard laughed.

"I was just interested in the story about their manifesto." Ruth imagined she was talking to the Dean, defending her actions more adequately than she had that afternoon. "Apparently, a document surfaced that claimed the Thrones are real and have 'divine' authority."

"Where did you read that?" Howard said.

"On some websites."

"Scholarly-designated sites?"

"No."

"Not trustworthy information, then."

"Apparently not. But where do you start? I know there's a lot of junk information out there, but what about real phenomena that are shaping future religious thought? The FESB censors everything so completely that you would think only information from over twenty years ago and beyond is *reputable!*"

Howard's eyes widened as Ruth spoke. She realized her anger was getting hot again.

"I was interested in finding a current example to put historical events into context, that's all. I needed a present-day example to add to the list including the Apostle Paul, the Buddha, Joseph Smith, and a few other figures involved in the genesis of new religions and religious sects."

"So you think the Thrones will start a new religious sect?"

"No, and frankly I don't care. If the Thrones were real, the Southern Catholics would kill them either publicly or secretly. Besides, the Franklin Laws forbid their very existence, so the government would have to kill them anyway, right?"

Howard paused for a moment and looked deeply into a slice of pepperoni. "Would you try to clone your own kid if they died young... like Franklin?"

"I don't know what I'd do in that situation. But they'd put the kid to sleep like a dog, wouldn't they?"

Although she had been a child at the time, Ruth remembered when the newscasters announced that five-year-old Jimmy Franklin, or rather the clone of Jimmy Franklin, had been executed. The United States had nearly torn itself apart with protests and riots in the days leading up to the Supreme Court's ruling.

It was then that the Franklin Laws came into existence, a complex set of prohibitions that forbade cloning and mandated the immediate termination of any illegally cloned or experimentally created human beings.

"So what are you going to do about your thesis?" Howard said.

His voice invaded Ruth's introspection. She realized that she needed solace and not company, at least not present company. "I don't know," she said, and concentrated on finishing her meal.

I don't know.

Ruth had wanted to get up early. Instead, she repeatedly pressed the snooze button on her alarm until it occurred to her that she might miss the flight.

Once packed, Ruth dressed frantically in casual travel clothing that clung uncomfortably to her still-wet body. Before jogging out the door, laden with luggage and a portable office, she threw on a leather jacket adorned with mock-military insignia and witty patches.

Within forty-five minutes she was onboard a tiny shuttle plane and leaving the ground. She landed at Denver International Airport and made her way to the connecting gate. The next flight did not depart for another hour and a half, so Ruth found herself sitting alone surrounded by gray plastic, blinking lights and invading morning sun from the narrow windows above.

She decided to go through parts of her thesis, hoping to find points and topics that could be readily altered, making them either more palatable to the FESB or simply less inflammatory. She re-read her theories on the indestructibility of all religion, something she called Organic Infallibility Theory. She had used the term "organic" to demonstrate things integral, fundamental, and systematic concerning religious and theological dynamics, as opposed to any naturalistic or biological implications. Though she knew the title might seem confusing to some, the term "evolution" had been overused during the past several decades, Ruth thought, so she had avoided it.

Organic Infallibility Theory stated that religion, and all associated theology, can never be abolished by any other mental or spiritual discipline, but would instead grow through human crisis. Voltaire was wrong, as were Dawkins and a host of others. They were not necessarily incorrect in their reasoning, but they were wrong to think that humanity would ever become "non-religious" or without a "god" of some kind. Ruth had tried to stay away from any dialogue or argument with the atheist community; her thesis measured the historical and current dynamics present when cultures shift and religions shift with them, not the dynamics of belief. That was it.

Ruth believed that present society was in crisis. Life expectancy grew each year, with the quality of life of these extra years growing. They were not useless decades of life relegated to "senior living" and senility.

Cloning was a simple reality, though it had taken corporations decades to perfect the technology, and more importantly, get the legal permission needed to use their knowledge to make a profit.

Ruth allowed memory to go back to her youth and college years. She had been untouched by the burning fever of idealism that had incensed some of her female colleagues, due largely to a healthy sexuality and solid self-image. College had almost destroyed all that, but Ruth graduated as an adult with more grit than gravel. She had questioned the image of "female leadership" as it stood in those days.

She shook her head, drawing herself back to the intended task. The layover time was long enough for her to read over the thesis one last time, to muster as many rhetorical defense points as she could before the audience to come, so she needed to concentrate.

The technological and political forces present as she grew from babe to young woman had served as furnace and hammer, Ruth's future course sure to include the mark of those years. From curing most types of cancer to artificial limbs, to robot psychology, to cloning human beings, Ruth had witnessed the active disconnection between faith and sociology.

This observation had led to an obsession, and Ruth had no genuine interest in subjects other than theology. It was natural for her to form the thesis around something both religious and sociological in scope, yet Ruth struggled to reconcile her yearnings with the growing guilt about stirring things up, both with Campolo University and the FESB.

She could trace the thesis topic back to one catalytic event: a friend telling her about a strange document on a website. It was essentially a manifesto, one that claimed to be written by, or directed by, a group of artificial beings called the "Thrones." Entire blogs had been created to discuss the significance, authenticity, and implications of this manifesto.

Some thought the Thrones were secret government cloning subjects that had escaped and now roamed freely among the populace, their true origin forever obscured. Most thought they were a hoax created by sensationalists, perhaps the news agencies themselves. Fake news had become profitable, but eventually the line between true and false drew readers and philosophers away from anything mysterious. The information fog had become so thick that most scholars fled to areas of knowledge that the mob had no interest in. Besides, the Federal Media Accuracy Rating systems divided fact from fiction, or so the United Nations Media Bureau promised. This served to reinforce the power of the fog, not dissipate it.

The document Ruth had found was on an entertainment-only website, without any verifiable authenticity whatsoever. Regardless, the piece claimed that the Thrones were intent on serving and protecting humanity from itself and "dark powers." The mystery was palpable, and some segments of the masses had been entertained by the prospect of secret guardians here to help.

Ruth did not care; she just thought the Thrones phenomenon was a good example of her Organic Infallibility Theory, proof that no matter how people invent and discover new realities and technology, humanity will pick up the pieces of its disintegrating beliefs by inventing new ones. The world is not the center of the world? That's okay. Robots have brains identical to humans, they dream, have moral dilemmas? Some obscure passage in the Christian Bible will be used to explain it and even claim that this was all foreseen.

The time passed quickly. Before Ruth reached any resolution concerning an apology, the first calls were made for boarding. She packed up her notes and joined the line of passengers.

Sleep took hold shortly after take-off. When she awoke, it was to the sound of moving bodies and shuffling feet, of passengers disembarking. She followed. A rental car awaited; she needed to reach Cambridge by 1 p.m.

"Ruth!" said a male voice.

She looked around. A man was waving at her. As he approached, Ruth noticed he was very handsome and had the most intoxicating boyish grin. An almost-fashionable yet dissonant wardrobe reminded Ruth of her time as a graduate student. He was tall and lean, with athletic movements that set him apart as he moved through the crowd.

"Do I know you?" Ruth said.

"No. I work for Professor Faulkner. I'm a graduate student at Harvard Divinity School. The Professor told me to come get you about now, and here you are. I'm playing chauffeur today. You're not very photogenic, are you?" He took a small com-pad from his pocket and flashed it towards her. On it was a picture of Ruth taken two years ago. Her hair was a different color, not to mention a different style.

Ruth was horrified. "You recognized me from that?"

"Sure. Professor Faulkner gave me some other... descriptors, so I was well prepared for finding you in a crowd," he said and smiled.

"Is that so?"

"May I take your bags, Professor?"

"You may, and that is very kind of you, uh—?"

"Oh, sorry. I'm Josh."

"Well Josh, I hope you're up to the task of being my chauffeur and bellhop."

"I'm sure you will be satisfied."

Ruth allowed a grin to find her lips, slid her backpack off and extended it to Josh. He took it as if she were giving him the keys to her house, and allowed himself to get very close to her as he donned the pack. She had met plenty of men like Josh before, but she enjoyed his blatant attempt at charming her.

They retrieved Ruth's checked luggage and continued on to the parking garage.

Josh liked to talk. He was finishing his final year of graduate school and was studying Biblical and Ancient Near Eastern languages, which came in handy while out at bars, he told Ruth. He was from Hartford, he was twenty-five, had a younger brother, was a Gemini, and he thought Ruth looked way too good to be a professor. This all came out within the first ten minutes of conversation.

Ruth stroked his ego by asking questions, attempting to burn the young man out before he truly became annoying. He would find out soon enough that her personality was neither patient nor tactful.

They located his car and were soon off into the wilds of Boston. Ruth was mildly concerned when they took I-90 out of the airport, but she panicked as they went south on I-93.

"This is not the way to Cambridge! Get off at the next exit." Ruth fluttered her fingers at the passing exit sign and waited for the car to veer onto an approaching ramp. Josh's chatter was going to make them late.

"Uh, you're right. Where do you think we're going?"

The ramp went by and the car did not slow. "I have an appointment with Faulkner and Parker, Josh. You have to take me to Harvard." Ruth glared, wanting very much to be in the driver's seat.

"Well, that's not what they told me," Josh said, still looking forward. The ice in Ruth's tone apparently had no effect. "Professor Faulkner told me to bring you to the Garner House in Providence."

"What?" Ruth leaned out and over, trying to get in the young man's line of sight.

"I get out of grading papers for doing this one. You know, one time I had to go to Maine to pick up this woman for Faulkner. She definitely was *not* his wife. I didn't have to drive her back though, so I don't know why—"

"Wait." She put a hand on the young man's shoulder. His muscles tensed, though a grin betrayed his delight—just as Ruth expected. "Faulkner told you to pick me up at Logan and take me to Providence?"

"Yup."

"I would've flown into T.F. Green, had I known."

"He called me up late last night about all of this, so it sounds like it was a change of plan or something."

"Great." Her enjoyment of Josh's presence was waning. "Josh?"

"Yes?"

"Would you be a peach and stop at a sandwich shop or something? I need to eat."

"We have to get to Providence by 2:30."

"We'll be fine." Ruth sat back and closed her eyes. She liked the occasional diversion from her everyday life, but this upset was excruciating. It was bad enough that her career was on hold. Denial and consistent policies of avoidance had allowed her to supplant any anxiety concerning her status at Campolo, but now that she was on the move, the terror of not knowing what was going to happen in the next hour, let alone the next day, was unbearable.

She had flown to Boston to apologize, amend and change her thesis, kiss the right butt, and go home happy — career intact and teaching status reinstated. Now she was riding with a stranger towards uncertainty.

The Garner House was not her favorite place to visit, either. The Classics crowd, with whom she had only associated to prevent ostracism, used the place for a variety of social functions that Ruth hated. She had always found a way out of the "dinner parties" and "cocktail evenings" that the Victorian-style house near Thayer Street often hosted.

Josh pulled into a gas station. Ruth made do with the meager and nutrition-free fare. It satisfied her enough to continue the journey. They were about to leave when Ruth decided to satisfy another need. "Josh? Would you go buy me a soda or something? I forgot to get a drink."

The man beamed at the call to serve. "Sure. What do you want?"

Ruth leaned over the seat to stare into his eyes. "Surprise me."

Gone was the confident college boy. In his place was a startled boy. He put the car back into park, got out, and ran back into the station market.

Finally. Ruth jumped out of her own seat and rounded the car, taking her rightful place in the driver's seat. Josh came out with a pop, opening the door to find Ruth strapped in and smiling up at him. "I would really like to drive, Josh. You don't mind?"

His eyebrows nearly reached a lush hairline. "Uh... No. I mean, that's fine. Do you...?"

"Get in." Ruth put the car in drive and held the brake.

"Okay..." Josh walked toddler-like around the hood of the car and got into the passenger seat. As soon as his door shut, Ruth sped out of the station and nearly clipped a side mirror on a stationary car.

Calm. Calm down, now. The shock of Ruth's coup expired five minutes after taking to the road and Josh started to ramble once more. "I went to Brown, remember? Anyway, my boys and I used to go down to the pub over by the capitol building and we'd..."

Ruth returned to her thoughts and allowed the noise to fade into background fuzz. As they got closer to their exit, she watched the familiar dilapidated city outskirts pass by. She had also experienced Providence in her younger years, though she was sure Josh would take an unhealthy interest in her if she told him how. He would get the wrong idea and the discussion would become two-way, in a bad way. She smiled at a church as they passed.

They exited the highway and penetrated the mystic and shadowed interior of Providence. As they drove deeper, they passed opulent, gated properties—centuries old—that proclaimed the presence of a separate society of ancient maxims and propriety.

Ruth parked as close to the Garner House as possible and they walked a block to stand before the collegiate fortress. Ruth enjoyed smells she could not articulate or identify, but if she were blindfolded and exposed to those pungent, churning aromas, she would know that she was in Providence.

Officially an outpost of the Ivy League elite, the Garner House was once the property of widow Elizabeth Garner, a transplanted aristocrat who had fled some clandestine political upheaval in London with her husband, Ian Garner, in the early 1800s. The house was only blocks from Brown University, on the south side of Benevolent Street.

Three stories of brown stone and tan brick, the house was adorned with plum-colored shutters and iron roof studs. Past refurbishments brought the addition of patina-covered roof extensions and lower-level stone alcoves. Within these recesses sat statues of notable scholars, their names escaping Ruth's memory.

Ruth and Josh continued past the front of the house and walked over the cobbled driveway to the side entrance. Many of the windows held sill planters, overflowing with blossoms bright and fragrant. The smell of lavender wafted from the gardens in the rear, and Ruth felt rejuvenated.

She loved living at the base of the Rocky Mountains and was enchanted by the dry summer air and the sparkling winters. But a piece of her heart would always remain captive to this part of the world: the smell of decaying maple leaves and sassafras in autumn, wet bricks and salt-breeze in the spring. She forgot herself for a moment and just stood there, looking through oak branches and over colonial rooftops to find swift moving clouds beyond. Sighing, she scrubbed her face with her hands, as though she were rubbing the experience into her flesh to both preserve and banish it. Finally, she followed Josh inside.

The door led to a small utility room and into the kitchen. Josh was sitting on a stool, helping himself to a block of cheese from the refrigerator. It was difficult to imagine the young man studying Ancient Akkadian, or any language for that matter. He crammed the food into his mouth without pause or care, a fair amount of crumbs falling over his pants and onto the floor below. His boyishness was charming, but this behavior was outright adorable. Of course, any activity that kept the kid's mouth occupied and precluded speech was adorable, Ruth thought. She smiled as he feasted like a goat and continued on into the house's great room.

Framed with dark walnut furnishings, bookshelves and crimson accents on the tables and chairs, the main chamber was haunting, yet evocative of majesty. It paid tribute to the human mind, or that was the intent. Dark and beautiful, the room both enchanted and repulsed Ruth. She was not sure why.

The ceiling was a full two stories above and the eastern wall held two full-length stained glass windows. The first window featured two men, one holding a loaf of bread and the other, a chalice. Below the figures, under a line that represented the ground they stood on, was a space of red glass with a widening "ray" of orange shining on a third figure below. The lower portion was brown and black rock, a third figure prostrate, the only features evident being the bottoms of its feet, a thin back with protruding vertebrae, and just the hint of dark matted hair on the back of its head.

Ruth thought the picture was abominable.

The second stained glass window featured a winged angel hovering above a green hill and holding a golden scepter. Its head was cocked to the side and it had an expression that could only be described as both dominating *and* submissive, as if the being were reluctant about being there, but also enthralled. Below the angel was a dark table with several bearded men sitting at it, each garbed in a different bright color. They all seemed to be in mid-sentence, some half out of their seats and gesticulating anxiously. The expressions on their faces also varied from anger to contentment. The dark table in the glass matched a real table in the middle of the chamber. Made of walnut as well, it was identical to the picture-table in every way, including the number of seats it accommodated. Ruth did not know which had been built first: the glass picture or the real table. She found the force of the table's identity, made real through the stained glass, disturbing. It was powerful, pretentious, and disconcerting.

Ruth walked through the great room to enter one of the house's many studies. This one was called the Tennyson Room, named for the great poet. It was an interior room and held no windows; solid shelves of books were the only adornment. A desk at either end allowed for two scholars to enjoy the solace of the space without interrupting each other, but in truth, it was a sitting room. A small stand with crystal glasses and a decanter of amber liquid stood by the table.

Two men currently occupied the study. They were conversing quietly. Both rose when they noticed her approach and Professor Henry Faulkner gestured for Ruth to enter the circle of furnishings. "Good afternoon, Ruth. So nice to see you in the flesh for once."

Faulkner was a short man, but stately nevertheless. He had a soft and commanding presence. Ruth loved having him for an advisor. She loved learning from his decades of dedicated, yet often unorthodox, methods of scholarship that fit Ruth's own inclinations.

"Dr. Faulkner. The same to you." She extended her hand and Faulkner kissed it lightly. The other man shifted awkwardly as silence enveloped the scene.

"Ah yes. Oh, please forgive my lack of manners. May I introduce Mr. Walt Hendricks, Assistant Director of the Federal Education Standards Bureau?"

Ruth allowed her hand to slip from Faulkner's grasp and glide seductively towards Hendricks, palm down. He also took the hand as Faulkner had, but slipped his hand into a proper handshake position, righting her hand and shaking it professionally. No luck there.

"A pleasure to meet you, Mr. Hendricks," she said.

"My pleasure as well, Ms. Long," he replied. "Thank you for making the journey."

"I didn't have a choice, did I?"

"Of course not," Hendricks said, and gave her a sincere-looking smile. Again, silence engulfed the group, and Hendricks looked over at Faulkner and nodded. Dr. Faulkner took a breath and retrieved his libation from the table. "Well, I've succeeded in bringing you two together, so now I will take my leave."

Faulkner left the study and closed the door. Ruth was at a loss. She had come to New England intending to plead her case before Dean Parker and get out with her career and reputation intact. Now she was talking directly to the FESB, exposed and without the protection of her academic directors.

Hendricks was a tall man, and overweight. But he exuded power in the form of high intellect and bureaucratic authority. He sat down as Ruth took the couch next to him.

"Please excuse my lack of professional attire, Mr. Hendricks. I did not expect to be whisked from the airport without a chance to change."

"Ah, please don't apologize. You have the rest of your life to make the slow descent into drab academic garb and unflattering wardrobes. If only we all could follow C.S. Lewis's example."

The Bumbling Academic routine? Gotta do better than that.

"Please. May I pour you a glass of Scotch?" Hendricks offered without losing his affability.

"No, thank you," Ruth said, without discarding her disdain.

"Just as well." Hendricks sat back and did not pour himself a glass. "Let's get to the point of this meeting. Your thesis has agitated many at the FESB. We think that it has its merits, but when we consider the current landscape of the nation—an election year with artificial life issues serving as the main battleground—the sanctioning of academic content according to Federal mandate is necessary."

Ruth leaned forward and looked Hendricks in the eye. "You're censoring me."

Hendricks turned his head away violently, waving his hand at Ruth. "If you want free speech, drop out of Harvard, quit Campolo, and start your own organization. Nothing stops you from doing that if it's what you believe."

"Nothing, except the loss of job, respectability, and oh, I don't know, succumbing to all the human trash information out there that made me want to become a Federally-accredited professor in the first place!"

"Not our problem." Hendricks smirked.

Ruth reined in growing rage by breathing slowly and looking at the floor. Once composed, she met Hendricks's eyes once again.

"Do you think what you're doing is important?" he said, with a serious expression and tone that replaced the previous cold and bureaucratic one.

Ruth started to reply, but stopped. She had never thought deeply about such things: it seemed a waste. She reconsidered that conclusion and thought as deeply as a few seconds would allow.

"I... Do you?" she deflected, deep thoughts providing very little for an answer.

"No. I don't," Hendricks said without pause.

"What? Are you firing me? Barring me or whatever—?" Ruth jerked forward, gripping the arms of the chair tightly to anchor her growing fury.

"Miss Long, you're jumping to conclusions. Just relax." He made soothing gestures.

"And you're being cryptic. I can't write the thesis I want to write because it contains 'undesirable' subject matter. That's the only issue here, right?"

"Without parsing words? Yes."

"So I have to start over."

"Well, in a way. I've read the thesis proposal and I noticed that most of the sections about modern religious evolution use the Thrones phenomenon as an example."

"So?" There were many other religious phenomena occurring in the world. Ruth didn't understand why her work stood out.

"So I'm curious," Hendricks continued. "What has your research dug up about the Thrones? Do you think they are real? What do you think they are?"

Ruth was disgusted. This man had inhibited her scholarly ambitions, yet now wanted to talk shop. Worse, Ruth had immersed herself in the research so completely that no invitation to talk about it could be ignored, not even under these dismal circumstances. The man was cruel and Ruth was compelled.

"I think that there are people who believe in them. The masses will see what they want to see. The Thrones are nothing more than a sounding board for society's current dilemmas. That's it. I really don't see why this is a problem for the FESB. I'm not advancing any theories about the Thrones; I'm just observing a real phenomenon using good scholarship."

"And I agree," Hendricks said.

By his appearance, Ruth estimated the man must be in his late fifties. A youthfulness surrounded Hendricks that could not be reconciled with his flaccid facial skin and thin hair. Occasionally, his movements and speech seemed furtive or openly paranoid as well. "You agree?"

"Yes. Your reckoning is absolutely correct. In this case, however, we simply have a conflict of interests and you are the one who must compromise."

Ruth looked down, incensed and no longer interested in the man's appearance.

"But," he continued, "I must confess I find the Thrones, and many of the other artificial life legends and stories, fascinating."

Ruth was not interested in talking anymore. The man's interests lay beyond sinking her thesis: that was obvious.

"Have you read the Thrones' manifesto?" he asked.

"That's a trick question." Ruth wanted to leave.

"How so?"

"If the FESB is working so diligently to protect the soft heads of college students from misguided teachers such as myself, I am sure you know all about the dearth of real information on the Thrones. Don't you have anything else to do?"

As Ruth watched Hendricks's expression turn from jovial to hurt, she knew she had gone too far.

"I've gathered as much as I can from articles posted on various websites," Ruth said, trying to continue as if she'd said nothing ill. "Very few of the references qualify for use in scholarly applications, however. From what I've read, it looks like something cooked up by a needy societal gestalt. Please keep in mind that my thesis does not, in any way, explore the validity of any aspect of the Throne myth. I am only concerned with the effect it has on the purported beliefs of individuals and groups, as openly and conveniently expressed on various web outlets. People will confess more under an alias on a blog than they will to God. My methods are sound."

As she spoke, Ruth felt more and more vindicated of any wrongdoing. It was just research.

"So I gathered from your thesis outline," he said. Hendricks did not revisit the legitimacy of Ruth's thesis.

That's that, I guess. No going back.

Hendricks continued, "What if I told you I had a genuine copy of the Throne manifesto, of the Throne Logos, as it is titled?"

"I don't believe a manifesto exists. I think the entire affair is a cultural tumor, benign, yet not true. As I said, people will see what they want. The net of information out there is notorious for spontaneously creating myths and legends overnight."

"Ah, but that is your specialty, isn't it?"

"What?" The man seemed happy again. Ruth was not.

"Biblical Source Criticism. You know your P from a D, your John from a Q, your Synoptic from a Coptic. And not in the ways that pseudo-scholars have exploited hidden and secret knowledge to support 'conspiracy theories' and new religious movements."

What did this man want?

"But that is just what my thesis was about," Ruth said. "How the methods you just mentioned actually *do* affect the future pursuit and cultic practices of many faith groups."

"My point exactly. What if I had a copy of the Throne Logos? Would you read it?"

Ruth realized that more was transpiring here than just a scolding for a naughty thesis. Was Hendricks doing his own research and trying to hide behind Ruth? "Firstly, I don't believe there is any Throne Manifesto outside of farce. Secondly, why would I care now that I can't use it as part of my thesis?"

"Aren't you curious?" Hendricks pleaded.

"Yeah, but I'm also somewhat peeved at my current situation, so you'll understand if I don't give a damn about any literature on the Thrones right now." Ruth sat back and closed her eyes, putting a hand to her face. "Sorry," she offered.

"I understand," Hendricks said. "The last time I checked, however, a scholar's mission was scholarship, not thesis papers."

"And the FESB is here to get in the way."

"I am genuinely sorry that we cannot let you publish your work under FESB standards. The reason I granted you a personal audience is because I think you should continue your studies. You're right: by defending the veracity of knowledge, we sacrifice other areas that are not so easily evaluated. As a FESB official, I am here to let you know that, and to let you know we support professors in the struggles they face. I am here to offer a consolation prize."

Hendricks was sincere, as sincere as Ruth could detect, considering she had only known him for several minutes. "What is so threatening about the Thrones?"

"Nothing precise. In fact, it is the possibility of *legitimacy* that makes the matter sensitive." He sat back, looking around nervously before leaning towards Ruth. "I feel that I can tell you this, though it's confidential and I will deny having told you anything if you choose to break that confidentiality. You deserve to know this since we are tampering with your career."

"I can't argue with that!" Ruth said — too loudly, she realized.

Hendricks continued. "I received a call several weeks ago from someone claiming to be a Throne. He called himself Massoud and was very brief. He claimed that the Throne Logos was intended for the U.S. Government alone, yet the information in it must have leaked somehow, given the current Internet fervor.

"To avoid further damage to the legitimacy and content of the document, Massoud said, a certified copy was to be sent to the FESB. I also received a lecture from this man about how the FESB has become nothing more than a filter for fallacious information and that it decides what is true and what is not, like a propaganda bureau. I was offended at this, but I marveled at the... man's aptitude for understanding the dynamics of information and government. He is right."

"So you believe him?" Ruth was rapt now with curiosity.

"No. But I think the document sent to me is remarkable. Although we at the FESB have to shut you down, I thought it would be a courtesy to give you access to this document for any future *academic* value it might provide."

"So I am forgiven? Are Harvard and Campolo off the hook?"

Hendricks shook his head. "I can't tell you that. It would be doubtful that anything punitive would come of this, but that's not up to me."

"What? I thought we just sorted this out."

"Not exactly. There are plenty of administrative considerations that need to be worked out. A task force is currently building new policies to preclude any other fledgling professors making the same mistake as you."

"But—"

"I have to get back to DC in time for a banquet tonight. I hope you understand."

Ruth did not understand. Hendricks rose and waited for Ruth to do the same.

"It has been a pleasure," he said. The audience was ending abruptly.

"Likewise." The man had become anxious and Ruth noticed.

Hendricks picked up the briefcase that had been leaning on his chair. After rummaging through it for a few long moments, he pulled out a heavy document case and handed it to Ruth. He then pulled something small from his pocket. "This is the key for the case," he said, as he handed her a small, electronic, silver key.

The case and its security measures were unsettling. She had expected an email, not an actual paper document.

"We have your records at the FESB, of course, so I hope you don't mind that I pulled your print and G-sig. The key will only work for you."

"Why the security?" The situation was becoming surreal.

"I don't want this contributing to the mass of misinformation out there, so I hope you will take care of it and get it back to me when you are done. Give me a call when you want to return it, I'll send a courier. Anyway, I have to go." He shook her hand one more time, and opened the door. He called out for Faulkner, told him that he was done, and that "she was free to go."

Ruth sat back down and looked at the case in her hands. It was heavy, and the pressure it put on her lap seemed oppressive and crushing, though it probably weighed only two pounds. The strangeness of the exchange with Hendricks also pressed in on her. She was inclined to shut the door to the study, unlock the case, and discover what it contained while sitting at one of the ornate desks that flanked her. Instead, she sat and stared at the bookshelf opposite and allowed her vision to relax until the drab and multicolored tomes bled together, forming a picture of brown chaos.

Faulkner entered and sat down. He looked at the case and seemed vexed, but smiled to himself and poured a drink. "Can I pour you one?" he said.

"No." Ruth stared at the wall.

"Humph. Well, I guess we get to talk now, though Dean Parker wanted me to wait until we meet with him tomorrow."

"What?"

"We still have to meet with the Dean to figure out what you... what we *both* have to do to appease the FESB."

Ruth pointed angrily at the study entrance. "Isn't that why I just met with Hendricks?"

"I wouldn't know." Faulkner shrugged. "He called me yesterday and asked to set up this meeting. Dean Parker also said that you must meet with him tomorrow. I was so busy that I really didn't have time to explain everything and I'm sorry about that. What's a little adventure for the cloistered young Ph.D. candidate, right? Anyway, I assumed he met with you to gauge character or some such nonsense. What did you two talk about, anyway? Oh, and what's in the case?"

Fright filled Ruth, more at the disconnection between her superiors' communication than anything else. She decided not to stress the situation further. "Mr. Hendricks wanted to apologize for the mess and said we'd all figure it out," Ruth said. "He also gave me a copy of my thesis that includes several... suggestions. He wanted me to take a look and tell him what I think. That's what's in the case."

Faulkner gave Ruth a juvenile thumbs-up gesture. "I knew he respected you. This is good."

Ruth slumped back in her seat. "So I guess I have to change my thesis?" Ruth said.

"I believe that is a certainty, at this point."

"Okay, then what else do I have to say?"

"Going along with what I said earlier, *we* have to make amends with Parker and discuss what your new-and-improved thesis is going to be."

"I have several ideas."

"I'm sure."

"But I'll wait to share them with both you and Parker so we are all in concordance."

"That would be best. Thank you for cooperating with everybody, Ruth. I expected more resistance."

Ruth patted Faulkner on the knee and smiled without saying anything. The whole issue was beyond comprehension. Ruth had met with the Assistant Director of the FESB, who had presented her with an incendiary document on a subject he had shut her down for, and now her immediate superiors were still in the dark, with Ruth still on the hook.

Faulkner's eyes suddenly widened and he reached into his coat, withdrawing a vibrating com-pad. Raising it to his ear, he smiled at Ruth and got up and walked out into the hallway.

Ruth sat back and tried not to ruminate on the current situation. Hendricks was a nice man, but something about him struck Ruth's intuition. She had the feeling that the man had been more interested in meeting her than anything else. Odd.

She was startled by the sound of thundering footsteps crossing the hallway to the study. Professor Faulkner erupted through the door, his face twisted and fearful as he looked at Ruth and then surveyed the room as if expecting to find something sinister.

"What's wrong?" Ruth said.

"I just got off the phone with Dean Parker. Apparently, he had just concluded an impromptu meeting with a member of the FESB."

"Yeah? Are we in more trouble than we thought?" Ruth was growing numb.

"Perhaps. Dean Parker just got out of a meeting with Mr. Walter Hendricks—a meeting that started three hours ago!"

CHAPTER 6

Ruth rode back to Boston in the car with Faulkner in silence, despite his assiduous efforts to start a conversation. She had never seen him upset, so it was surprising to find Faulkner coped with crises by being loquacious. It was also annoying.

"We have to call the police."

"As you've said before, Henry." Ruth watched graffiti on sound walls pass outside the window.

"Did you check your clothes for bugs, bombs, whatever?"

Ruth read a large and finely painted line of script that read *Jesus was Black!* She realized Faulkner was still talking, and responded: "Did you?"

Faulkner inhaled sharply. "Oh God… No, I didn't! Do you mean the man might be some kind of terrorist?"

"Yes, and what better way to throw the nation into a panic than to kill theology professors. It wouldn't even make the news." Ruth stifled a chuckle. Her statement shut Faulkner up for several minutes. Ruth relished the silence while she could. The case and its contents were burning a hole in her mind, however, and she desperately wanted to read the document inside.

While Henry was sending Josh on his way, fearing student involvement in something potentially nefarious, Ruth had opened the case. She found several pages of penned prose. Flipping through, she gleaned that it was some sort of story, but she could not be sure of more. She did not want to bring it up with Faulkner until she had determined what the document was; more precisely, she did not want to bring it up with Faulkner at all. Ever.

Ruth found the whole business very interesting, which surprised her. It was a departure from her usual reaction to adversity and enigma, though she still feared losing her career. She had nothing else.

A Federal Professor's License and post was not a lucrative job, but it was a secure one. It had a Federal pay grade associated with it and it was hard to lose once attained.

Ruth had not attained anything yet. Technically, she was still in a probationary period, her pay subject to cancellation for a variety of technicalities. All of her education was worth nothing outside colleges and universities, and the real world would give her no quarter for studying classics and religion instead of engineering. Or so she had been taught.

"What did you two talk about?" Faulkner broke into her introspection again.

"I told you!" Ruth turned, furious. "He just said he was there to judge my 'character' before the FESB did anything. He explained why my thesis had to change, and that's about it."

"And the case?"

Shit!

"I told you already! It was just a copy of my thesis."

Ruth felt no inclination to defer to the old men of academia just yet. She wanted to know what was going on without having to cede the little control she had.

"Huh."

"You've met Hendricks before, right?" Ruth said quickly. Faulkner sighed, his expression softening as he focused on the road ahead.

"Yes, and I must say, this chap had me fooled completely. His disguise was flawless, as was his speech and body language. He could have convinced us to do anything and we'd never know. It chills the blood to think of it."

Ruth recalled the recent encounter with the impostor, but strangely, her blood remained warm at the thought. "He didn't seem like a bad person, you know?"

Faulkner sniffed. "Perhaps, but who can say? He was obviously a master of impersonation and infiltration. He knew everything about the elements of the FESB and the players involved. My God, Ruth, we talked at length about a variety of subjects before you arrived. He asked me about my grandchildren, by age! I don't take any stock in my intuition about his intent. Nor yours, my dear, though your instincts are your greatest gift."

"No, you're right." Ruth ignored her intuition. "Who would go to that much trouble? It can't be good."

"I'm afraid not."

They arrived in Boston late. Ruth stayed at one of the university's guest rooms for visitors and adjuncts. After dropping off her things, they went directly to see Dean Parker. He was still in his office. By the time they sat down to talk, it was almost 9 p.m.

The man appeared haggard and drained, but Ruth couldn't remember Dean Parker ever looking fresh and alive. In truth, Ruth had always imagined the Dean as a wax figure, animated by the gods of education that reject student applications and turn down grants.

The conversation was simple. They discussed the fact that someone had impersonated a member of the FESB. That was serious. That they had seemed to target Ruth was serious as well. Parker demanded the case Hendricks had given her. She gave it to him without argument. He asked her to open it since the key could only be used by Ruth. He drew out the pages and examined them.

Ruth started to get nervous. If Parker suspected anything, he made no comment. She had replaced the document with a copy of her thesis because she had thought Parker would give the document to the FESB without even looking at it. Besides, Ruth couldn't suppress the slow burn she felt at the entire situation; her life had been disrupted primarily by the powers-that-be. She deserved none of it, and she did not feel inclined to play by the rules. Parker was staunch, but usually fair. He played by the rules because he was good at it. He had to be: all of his files and communications were monitored by Federal agencies, namely the FESB.

The FESB's real purpose was to prevent academia from becoming an agent for misinformation and terrorism. Ruth's grandparents might have called the FESB the worst kind of "big brother," but with all that had happened in America from 2001 on to the current year of 2034, not many people complained. A small price for safety, or so ran the general sentiment.

Ruth's thoughts went back to Campolo University, which had been built about the same time that Ruth was born. The mission of the University was to specialize in classics and "soft" disciplines, such as philosophy and theology. The ancient language faculty was composed of many fine scholars, and the curriculum was also one of the best in the world. But Ruth thought it strange that Campolo had only one Muslim professor who prayed five times a day in the stunning Campolo Mosque. With a dome of brilliant sapphire and a structure of white stone, the mosque was built to represent the inclusiveness of American academics and to draw true Muslim scholars and build lasting relationships. It had not.

Ruth tried to concentrate on matters at hand. Parker was writing something on his com-pad, and Faulkner was starting to doze in his chair. Parker spoke only when absolutely necessary, and it seemed those necessities had already been addressed.

She wondered what was next. Parker was inept at understanding the needs of those around him and also social propriety. He allowed Ruth and Henry to sit for nearly an hour as he typed, jotted, and annotated. Faulkner slept, and Ruth knew better than to prompt Dean Parker. He would just ignore her. Finally, Parker spoke. He told her that the matter of the impostor was being dealt with. The authorities would find him.

She was to go back to Campolo and continue her Ph.D. candidacy. She asked about her thesis and Parker calmly informed her that a new thesis outline, developed by him, had been sent to her via email. It made use of her previous training and would be adequate to gain her Ph.D. She was forbidden from changing any part of it. She should also be thankful to the FESB for this concession, Parker explained.

Ruth felt no gratitude. She was free of the creeping doom that threatened her career, however, and was free to go back to Campolo, teach classes, go home at night, and earn a paycheck.

For security reasons, she would have to leave on an early flight in the morning. Although it would not be visible, security would be watching her every move until she got back to Wyoming, Parker told her. This was unsettling, but Ruth was ready for life to normalize. She bathed her fears in thoughts of gawking male students, grading papers, research, and unwanted advances from Howard. It was almost comforting. Almost.

Ruth had slept very little the night before. Her mind was heavy with the events of the day and the cot became a basalt pedestal, her conscious thoughts displayed to some phantom audience. When she woke, the fantasy of sleeping again consumed the narrow lucidity that remained, but she rose anyway and prepared for her return home.

The ride to the airport was uneventful, but Ruth felt uneasy at the thought of security watching her surreptitiously. The check-in process went as usual, with burning fluorescent lights, the gabbing static of crowds, and the alternating scents of perfume and flatulence searing her nostrils as she walked. Ruth constantly scanned the interior of the airport for a glimpse of either a stalker or agent. She detected neither. In truth, she didn't understand why she was being allowed to go back to Campolo without more of an investigation. If she was of interest to the fake-Hendricks, why would the authorities assume he couldn't find her in Wyoming? Realizing the final boarding call had been made, Ruth quickly boarded the plane.

Once the flight was underway, she pulled out the paper the fake-Hendricks had given her. The covering page was spattered with red-brown splats of nameless origin. Many wrinkles and cuts marred the stack, and a long tear traversed the right middle to the center, as if someone had tried to rend the stack in two but had stopped or been stopped.

The papers also reeked of something distant and alien. Ruth put her nose to the pages and breathed deeply. Freshly turned earth and coriander were the closest two scents she could muster as a description, but even these were inadequate. The top page was blank except for a title: *The Book of Beasts and Green Things*.

"How pretentious." She expected the man beside her to say something, or perhaps for the attendant to come by and say "What's that, dear?" She continued to look at the pages. Contempt rose as she flipped through.

The text was handwritten. It was legible, but possessed a quality that Ruth could not identify. Perhaps the author could read and write in more than one language? That might account for the slight differences in strokes and letter shape that diverged from the spectrum of most English writers. The writing *looked* queer, and that drew Ruth into reading it instead of sleeping. She'd just scan a few pages and give it a full analysis later. She began to read:

In the deserts of God, the Blessing of the Age toiled, sowed, and harvested. Winds of Abraham blew through vines and sand, nourishing the souls of humans and their servants alike, the soldiers of darkness lost in the magnetic traps and flowing grains. The Blessing of the Age was keen and wise, his care of the earth's forms and systems great in wealth, staggering in depth. He was a living sea of knowledge, and many came to drink of his Blessing, taking with them the truth the Lord had granted for the Fallen Times that they who thirst would do more than drink, they would themselves become living water and nourish the deserts, restore the salt to the land, and prosper under Green Leaves and with Living Beasts.

But the land had become a place of Death, and the black walls of shadow surrounded the continent, visible only to the pure and to the discerning. Through the shadowed veil came a man-who-is-not-a-man, a hidden Blessing that walked with humankind on the edge of a spear blade. His name was Herriot, and he shined with silver and sun. Many believed that the gods of the land had made him from clay and cinnamon, but the kings of the day knew he came from the Sea to Mombasa, and traveled the lands with his love and Blessing, stitching up the Hundred Year wounds, and taking the pestilence from the people and the beasts.

The Gikuyu took him and put him in a hut, under guard, because they knew of his origins in the Empire of Despair and thus thought him a demon. But when he found remedies for the sick and lonely in the village-prison, he was regarded differently. He had not light skin, but that of the Blessings, the skin of the Sky, as if he had fallen through the clouds and the sky had broken his descent, rubbing off its goodness and power. He respected the beasts and the people as if they were his own. He claimed they were, and the Gikuyu, Kisii, Maasai, Luo, Luhya, and Bantu of all lines believed him.

On the day of his freedom, a crowd of Quakers came from the forest to announce his innocence and demand his release. Herriot was born of wicked lies, but God had given him grace in abundance. He fled from the Empire of Despair, and was to be loved.

The Gikuyu freed him, and gave him passage through all lands in day or night. He stayed in the town which is known as St. Edmund. It was here that he found the voice of Christ as it spoke in the wind and mumbled from the rocks and pebbles. The people thought he could talk to the beasts and grass because of his wonder, and found every living thing in the land and brought them to him, hoping he would restore their numbers and give the people back a time when they could talk to the earth while talking to God and walking with the Christ.

Herriot brought the machines and abominations of the Age, the devices of the Empire of Despair, to St. Edmund. He did not plant their wickedness in the dirt but instead forgave them, demanding that they redeem themselves through the Holy Spirit and give Life to humanity where they once gave Death.

St. Edmund came to grow in God, becoming a city of brick and stone set with trees of glory and gardens of God, not huts of disease and Death. The beasts came back as well; some were brought by the servants of the Lord, oth-

ers came by themselves, for even the beasts know the truth of the Heavens and sense the good in their Stewards, the people of God. They came to kneel before and give service to the humans, feeling the grace in the man-who-is-not-a-man, marveling at a thing which they would normally kill as an abomination, but the beasts sensed the Spirit in him, and sang the name "Herriot" in the morning mists, full sun and silver moonlight.

One day a baboon came to St. Edmund, lost of field and sky, which had not eaten in many days. His face showed the destiny of leadership among the baboons, but he limped in pain, and walked in circles. When the people of St. Edmund tried to heal the baboon or talk to him, he screamed with the demons and bared his teeth. His fangs were five inches long, and he frightened the people so that they left him to limp and scream in the corners and dark places of the village.

This went on for many weeks. The Blessing of the Age, Herriot, heard the people complain of the baboon. Herriot became angry with the people, and told them they had not a heart for the flesh and sand of the earth, for they had forsaken their duties unto God. They begged for his forgiveness, but he said, "It is not I that you betray, but He who sent me. Bring the King Baboon to me." And they brought the injured beast to him.

The King Baboon said, "I have walked through damaged lands and dead places to find the people of God, but they have ignored me and treated me like a false-creature instead of a King of Baboons. I need their care, but I am forsaken."

"You are not forsaken, but rescued by their faith," Herriot said, and the crowd did not know to whom he was talking. "Come. Your masters have not forgotten you and your kingdom." Herriot turned and walked back through the square of the village and the baboon followed. They ar-

rived at the big house of St. Edmund, where Herriot slept occasionally, but did not own.

He opened the door to the house, and the baboon went inside. The people were afraid and disgusted, for baboons could kill a human and also smelled very badly. They were cunning, like the waterways of the rainy season, and rage-filled like the night lightning. That Herriot had invited the beast into a house was to invite ill. But when the people followed Herriot and the baboon into the house, they found a bed of dry grass made for the beast, and Herriot was mending the leg that the baboon had limped on.

Herriot said, "How have you become injured?" and the people were confused for they knew that baboons could not talk.

"My troop was hungry and had no food, master. We ventured into the blessed dwellings of humans because we did not want to die. Though we know not of your ways, we believe in our purpose. The lions are gone, and the small creatures we eat have gone too. We have lost our divine fear and have real fear. I was struck by a human when it saw me. I knew we had erred, but what were my subjects to do? Now we will perish in hunger and shame, the trees patrolled by false-creatures and our memories of fresh dirt and brown fields fading."

"Not true, for I am a false-creature, but have been given power like the humans."

"We know of you, my master, and I came to this place because it shines with God's light. All of the creatures from here to the desert know of the growing things here, of the return of cubs, pups, small things, and every good memory of the land."

"And so you have served your purpose diligently, King of Baboons. Go now, and bring your troop through field and town to come to these lands. We welcome you, and you will dine on grass and small things again, and you will be hunted by the Great Cats of Flame, and you will

know the love of God once again, for his servants, your masters, have remembered their charge."

The people grumbled among themselves, fearing that Herriot was possessed by a demon, or had become one, or was just sick. But the baboon got up and walked in three circles around the room. Each time he stepped, he limped less, and his fur seemed to find luster like that of the clear night sky. When he had completed his third circle, he limped no more, and roared with might and leapt through the crowd out of the door. The people were upset, and blamed Herriot for setting the beast upon them to scare them.

"Do not be fooled," he said, "for I have done for the beast what you should have done weeks ago. He had lost his way because humanity had lost its way, but in this town you find the path clear and easy to tread. Do not hoard these gifts, for the time comes when even the beasts will demand an answer for the death of field and sea, and you will give them one, oh stewards of the land and keepers of every living thing! I did not heal the King of Baboons, but you did, for in this place he remembered the pulse of molten earth and thunder, the feel of danger and humility towards the masters of the land. YOU!"

"This man-who-is-not-a-man speaks the truth," said the people. "We have shamed ourselves before God for not loving the King of Baboons and giving the life and death he deserves. Let us be thankful for this lesson."

Ruth sat back, gasping for air because she had forgotten to breathe. She flipped over the pages of the document, as if the act would seal its contents from her consciousness. It did not.

"Are you all right?"

"Yes. I'm fine, thank you," she said to the man beside her. Tears welled as she spoke and she turned away to hide them.

Ruth fought the impulses that ran free in her mind when exposed to something both revealing and religious. Guilt was the first demon to strike. Her consciousness writhed with memories of good and bad experiences in church, namely, the Lutheran one she had gone to as a child. The many other churches she had tried over the years stuck as well, and failure to make good on religious practice threatened to cheapen what she had just read. She fought her way back to logic.

The impostor Hendricks had lied. This document was far from the manifesto Ruth had expected. There were no proclamations of any kind, nor was the word *Throne* used even once. Instead, she had just read a remarkable account of something allegorical or perhaps illusionary, but it still churned her spirit in a powerful way. She had no training in African languages, but what she had just read might have been a translation of something already written. Perhaps the vernacular chosen was the result of the writer's first language bleeding into their English—not uncommon for second-language writers at all.

Regardless, the prose was strong and full of conviction. Ruth wanted more. It was obvious that the writer had emulated parts of the New Testament, and Ruth wanted to be disgusted by the use of the word "Christ." There was a unique rhythm, however, and Ruth would have to spend time dissecting the sentences and sections for literary devices.

With these thoughts came the second and third demons of doubt and contempt. The bitterness of believing in something as absurd and misleading as many of the doctrinal and even scriptural beliefs most religions espoused—*especially* Christianity—grated on Ruth's will and made her want to toss the document. She was not a proponent of modern religious experience. How the culmination of history and current events affected the common person's beliefs was important, but how dare anyone write something this meaningful? It was charlatanry and fallacious. The vampires who inspired the checkbook-use of millions should be jailed.

Stop!

Ruth's hate-filled thoughts ceased.

The fourth and last demon crept up and speared Ruth through the eyes. Its name was fear. She feared the idea of God most days, and this document, whether real or hoax, was aimed in the direction of faith and one could not think about the text without thinking about God. She was a theologian, not a pastor. She hoped there was an afterlife, but since becoming immersed in various religious traditions and penetrating the hidden facts behind Christianity, she had found it hard not to think that everything meets oblivion in the last and final act of death. Nothing more to think about, nothing more to ponder, other than overcoming fear of death.

"Peanuts?"

Ruth looked up at the attendant in fright. He didn't know that he had somehow successfully merged the concept of nihilism with Jimmy Carter in her brain. "No. No, thanks. I'm fine. Napkin?"

He handed Ruth a napkin. She snatched it and began to blow her nose. Folding the mucus-filled parcel in on itself several times, she offered it back to the man.

"Trash will be around in a moment, ma'am." He continued on to schlep peanuts to the passengers ahead of her.

The document was incomplete. There were eighteen pages of text, but the story seemed as if it would continue if it could. What troubled her was that the time of the story seemed to be current. It could be within the last twenty years, or it could be today. Kenya was a fractured and violent nation, as it had been for decades. Communications had stitched the string of towns, villages, and cities together to help true international commerce develop, but the wounds inflicted by European colonial muskets and mining picks had left livid scars and oozing scabs on most of Africa, even now.

Ruth was intrigued. Indeed, if local peoples in Kenya were using new myths for their evolving faith practices and doctrine, then it was consistent with her Organic Infallibility Theory. This was aggravating, because it would have made for great research in her now-defunct thesis. This thought was a further demon. The difference was that it cast out the other four, or at least banished them to irrelevance while Ruth ventured into realms of danger and risk. Risk was overrated. Her mother had once told her that the greatest lie told to her own generation was that successful people risked everything, and that a person could do anything if they put their mind to it.

These topics continued to shake Ruth's security until her very identity started to careen. Pushing the fears into a mental compartment, she completed her journey without any external conflict and arrived safely back at her house.

Ruth had few options to consider when the environment required her to think and act, preferring avoidance when push came to annoying shove. As she sat in her cluttered house and drank tea, a strange arrangement of memories—recent and long past—ran through her senses like living shadows, flowing from behind the drapes and under the couch to stand cruelly before her, demanding attention. She held onto the techniques she had developed, systems to get through confusing situations and demands.

Her first mechanism was victory through besiegement, her soul locked in a fortress of iron. An example was her first love, a man named Gerard. He was unruly, adventurous, and absolutely insane. When they lived together, she had to share the burden of his personality and feed it regularly with raw emotion and mother-like tenderness. Even in the beginning, Ruth knew she would come to hate him. She pretended not to.

Eventually, the invisible daggers and suffocating contempt claimed Gerard. He spent six months screaming at her, explaining the nuanced destruction she had wrought upon him, as if she didn't know. He was strung along by the hint of change, but Ruth had no intention of changing for anyone. He left one night and never came back. Her fortress was blackened with the soot of fire and several cracks had propagated through the stone, but the walls held. Ruth's mind, heart, and bank account were intact.

When the first mechanism of besiegement failed, she defaulted to the second: vicarious use of innocents. These were seldom close friends—the burden of being too familiar was death to all friendships. Just the occasional venting of pressure performed on a disposable acquaintance: an interested man, for example. Ruth felt some shame, but she also felt spite. She had yet to meet a man who could control himself in her presence, or at least one who was young and unmarried. When these two techniques failed, Ruth went to pieces.

For two hours she checked her email, ate leftovers and chocolate until her stomach hurt, then ate more, engaged in several bouts of weeping, and called no one.

Dignity once again secure, Ruth felt better, perhaps having discovered a third mechanism for the future. She turned her attention to the topic of the moment.

Thrones.

Opening herself up to the Internet, she fed on information that was both sustaining flesh and decaying refuse. The Thrones were legend, the Net giving them a history of millennia and a future spanning the rest of time and space. Fan sites fabricated all they wanted to believe.

Thrones are animals who took human form.

Thrones are humans who neutered themselves and disfigured themselves to become more human, non-human, better than human.

The man-who-is-not-a-man.

Thrones were government super-soldiers, like Captain America, only there are many of them.

Thrones are human clones.

The man-who-is-not-a-man.

There are 12 of them.

There are 600 of them.

One in ten people in the world is a Throne and they don't even know it.

The man-who-is-not-a-man.

They are Satanists who believe they are more than human.

They are a rank in Freemasonry.

They are fugitive biological constructs who should legally be terminated.

The man-who-is-not-a-man.

They don't exist.

They don't exist.

They don't exist.

Ruth broke away from the screen, mind and body numb. It was Saturday, and she had spent nearly five hours reading and thinking. The information out there was little more than the collective hysteria and longing of a bereft generation. Ruth loved it, but turned an inner valve and cut off the pressure. It was time to grade some papers.

It was a welcome activity to recuperate from the intoxicating tryst she had just exited. Not every paper was enjoyable, but that was academia. She seldom gave a bad grade, but on occasion a student might betray the fact that they had done none of the reading, such as a late-semester report mentioning "Pontious Pilot." Then she could get savage. She seldom gave perfect marks either. The average student had to work hard and ask some deep questions for that, adequately articulating the subject matter and performing an airtight analysis.

She got up from the large plush chair in the corner she used when she was grading. It sat on oak legs and seemed as though it would fit in the corner of a Bavarian aristocrat's house, rather than that of a poor almost-professor. It was an antique, and it was red, like every other piece of furniture in the room.

The chair had been handed down through the generations, its legend changing with each new progeny. The story told to Ruth was that her great-grandfather had brought it back from Germany during the Second World War. To the victors go the spoils. Ruth would have said he simply *pillaged* it like a barbarian of any class, but it was special to the Long family, nevertheless. Ruth gave it a purpose and kept it clean. She didn't like it when visitors sat in it.

Ruth had the windows open, and the house smelled of prairie and pine. Occasionally, the essence of nearby ranches would invade sharply into the subtle scents, but Ruth didn't mind. Open sky, buffered by monolithic mountains to the west and stretching barrens to the east, gave her a home she had always dreamed of. Escaping the rigors and crowds of the New England wilderness, she had come to a garden of sacred wheat and buffalo. It helped her think.

"We need you around for staff functions," Dean Rupert said. "You may not be teaching, but I don't think it would be breaking the mandate to allow you to grade work and take some of this burden off the rest of the professors."

"Full pay?" Ruth said.

Rupert looked guilty for a moment, then leaned forward as if he were going to explain something complicated to a child. "No. I want to make good on my promise of providing for your needs, but the truth is that I am incapable. You should seek other, outside help, if I may be frank. My instructions are to take you out of teaching until your thesis is complete. The reasons for this are irrelevant; the FESB mandates it and we must comply. Think of it, Ruth. Your focus will be one project! This is a rare convenience in our profession, you know.

"I envy you. I can't say that I like the arrangement, however, as I have to find an interim professor to teach your classes. The rest of the faculty will have to shoulder the load for now, and I am not looking forward to any student or parent complaints. We might get lucky, who knows? Did you, Harvard, and the FESB agree on a new thesis?"

"Strangely enough, we did," Ruth said, and imagined venom dripping from her own lips. Dean Rupert had not assuaged her angst. She had made a decision. "I understand. In that case, I am taking a leave of absence." Ruth sat back and smirked.

"What ?" The man's eyebrows raised, but not enough to show true concern.

Son of a bitch wants me gone!

"I will be continuing work on my thesis, but while I travel." Ruth allowed the smirk to become a smile.

"Ruth? This is not prudent. You have caused much trouble for everyone and this would inconvenience me further. Besides, the FESB expects you to be here working on your thesis. I don't think they would let you leave."

"Let? *Let* me leave? I am sorry, Dean Rupert, but I don't need permission to take a leave of absence," Ruth said, folding her arms.

"Well, technically, you do."

"Technically, sir, I need to *present* a reason. My reason is for personal health. I was embroiled in possible terrorist activity. The FESB psychologist has already examined me over the phone and endorses a one-month leave. Check your inbox and you'll see it. I am entitled to take it—you're required to give it."

"You are... you're playing the system, Ruth. I can't afford to lose you completely. You've put everyone here in dire straits. None of this would have been an issue if you had used good judgment in your studies. You are only making things worse by exploiting this technicality."

"A man fooled my advisor, Dean Parker, and a host of other people, including me, into believing he was Walter Hendricks, Assistant Director of the FESB! I don't have to explain that I am a little freaked out by that."

"But he didn't do anything." His voice was a growl. "You are here at Campolo now. What could he possibly do to you here?"

The conversation was going in the direction Ruth had hoped it wouldn't. "You really want me to answer that? Of course, most men don't think about being raped, do they?"

"Ruth! You're out of line. My point is that Parker's, the FESB's, and my own opinions don't sum up the circumstances into the grave situation you outline."

"I'm sorry, Dr. Rupert. The whole thing has shaken me up a bit and I want to rest and take time to rethink my whole purpose here at Campolo."

Rupert calmed. Ruth saw his body relax as he breathed deeply and looked out the window. His head turned back to Ruth mechanically. "Do you want to leave permanently?"

"No, Dean Rupert. What if I offered to do electronic work for you?" Ruth tried to soften her own body language below that of Rupert's.

"Can I send you items we need help on, like papers for grading? Could you handle that?"

The conversation was clearly over for Rupert, as was some inner conflict over decisions to be made. Ruth gambled on what the decisions were.

"I don't see why not." Either she had just cracked Rupert, or she had just lost her job.

"Very well. I need you for the rest of this week. Can you wait until Monday?" he said.

"Yes, that would be fine. I may not take the whole month. I'll let you know if I'm coming back early."

"Sure, whatever you decide. Ruth, I have to get ready for an evaluation that's happening in fifteen minutes. I think we've got this matter resolved for now. Talk to me again before you go. Oh, and you said that you are leaving the area, so where are you going?"

"Not far," she mumbled, but Rupert's attention was already gone.

Wrong, wrong, wrong direction.

CHAPTER 7

Enough!

Jamal left the bar with nothing: no names, no jobs, nothing. The expectation had been to make contacts quickly, gaining the trust of locals and traveling Westerners alike. The reality was far from expectation.

Nairobi was a separate universe, with laws and properties wholly different than those Jamal lived by. Still, the city possessed several attributes that resonated through the differences. One was brutality.

Jamal had witnessed seven separate muggings since arriving two days earlier. While walking in the business district, Jamal had seen a young man snatch an elderly woman's bag on the street ahead of him. The woman had pulled the bag away and thrown it to the ground. The attacker assumed victory, scrambling to pick up the bag and flee. As he did, the old woman pulled a revolver from somewhere in her dress and shot him in the chest. He fell back and she unloaded the remaining five shots into him, all the while screaming in some language Jamal couldn't recognize.

People on the street fled, but Jamal stood and watched. After all, it was impressive. Cops materialized and responded by bludgeoning the woman with night sticks, throwing her into the back of a van after she crumpled to the ground. No one came for the man's body. People walked by without a pause, passing cigarette butts, paper, and the cooling corpse with equal indifference. Jamal found himself comforted by a darkness within, one he had not named or talked to, but also had never asked to leave.

Upon arriving in Nairobi, Jamal had no leads or ideas as to his next action. He assumed he had to find a man named Herriot, who, in theory, would have what Tennyson wanted. Of course, there might be more to it than that. He hoped there was.

Jamal also expected his movements to be tracked by Tennyson or Reston. If they were, it was beyond Jamal's ability to detect. So he continued his policy of spending as much money as possible and stayed at one of the finest hotels in Nairobi.

He walked back to the hotel, with no more information than when he had left New York. As a consolation, Jamal ordered room service to balance the day's expedition in the highly volatile streets below.

The meal came; he tipped the bellhop, and prepared himself to enjoy the filet mignon. Jamal lifted the silver cover to reveal an empty plate, devoid of his juicy steak.

He called the front desk. They apologized for the delay and told him they'd send somebody right up with the expected meal. Jamal sat down and tried to read a romance novel he had found in a trashcan somewhere he didn't remember.

The prose quickly bled together, Jamal staring through the ink and paper as recent, unwelcome memories became clear. He tried to escape his thoughts and return to the best-selling garbage he held in his hand.

After leaving Tennyson's office, Jamal had been driven to madness by a mass of conflicts. If he went to his mother, he would forfeit everything to Tennyson's wrath, including her. Perhaps he should just escape the country, living life as a fugitive as long as possible? Go back and kill Tennyson? No, kill Reston and then...

As each implausible scenario had flashed within, Jamal defaulted to his old demons, using the "stolen" security cube to finance every debased activity to deaden his mind.

Money was easily extracted from teller machines — the account and identification numbers always changing to preclude a security action before Jamal was well away — and the cash was spent just as easily.

He drank for a solid week, his mind never sober and his bed never empty. Jamal found a motel in Brooklyn, one that didn't ask for ID, just cash, and settled in. The prostitutes visited in shifts: one for the morning, one for the afternoon and evening, and one for the late hours. The last was more for the comfort of sleeping with, like a teddy bear, yet Jamal usually awoke in distress when he found her in his bed each morning, sobriety pulling him back to life. Luckily, an army of hard spirits in colorful bottles watched vigilantly from the nightstand, lending their liquid defense when he woke.

The booze and sex could not obscure the growing abyss of regret and memory. But on the seventh day of this new life of crime and excess, he was harshly reminded that he had work to do.

Jamal woke and found the members of the hired harem dead, three limp and slashed bodies surrounding him on the large bed. The metal scent of life and death plugged his senses and he sat up. He was covered in blood, covered as if his skin were naturally crimson instead of mahogany.

Jamal examined his own body slowly to ensure he had no injuries. The scene sobered him enough for such an inspection but not enough for genuine emotion, not enough to wonder why his three lovelies lay butchered around him.

He climbed from the pile of slashed flesh and looked into the mirror at his dark red form. He was a demon.

Jamal had lost consciousness the night before, as he had every night, yet his nightly descent into whiskey death had never before ended in violence. With his "business associates" lying dead before him, however, Jamal could not say that the act was beyond his abilities.

The mystery unraveled quickly as he noticed a freshly pressed suit hanging from the door of the bathroom. It wasn't his. A maroon collared shirt hung in front of the jacket and slacks, a piece of yellow paper protruding from a front pocket. He pulled it out and unfolded it. It was a full-sized piece of paper, but with only two words typed in its center.

"Forgetting something?" it read.

That was when Jamal decided to leave New York. Before he left, he risked the purchase of a fake ID. That was a difficult business in current times, taking a week to win the confidence of the right people. A million dollars later, he was part of the taxpaying public again, or so it would seem. When asked for a possible fake name, he gave them one: Jamal Battle. They informed him that someone by that name had just died, so it would be flagged for identity theft. Bad name. Jamal said he would risk it. They let him.

After retrieving his birth name, Jamal felt as though he had struck back at his generous malefactor. It was the only satisfaction he could find. The cold reality was that he was a pawn of corporate crime and had to move across the board before he was taken. He trusted nothing he was told, but formed a plan from the words of Reston: "Herriot in Kenya."

He went to Kenya.

Jamal forgot about his New York memories and looked out the window at the Kenyan sunset, the city outside on fire. Yellow encased the ether surrounding mausoleums to the northwest, the deep reds of the sun's false inferno blazing through the trees of Uhuru Park to the west.

The predicted knock at the door came. Jamal rose and walked to the door, his hunger more intense than a thirst for alcohol, for once. He turned the handle and was immediately struck, the door thrown inward by an onrushing form.

Jamal fell to the ground and put his arm up instinctively, primal senses quickening at the sight of a downward-stabbing knife. A quick turn and he stopped the oncoming blade, though at the price of it slicing into his forearm. His mind narrowed to the functions needed for survival, and the pain of the cut came and went.

On his back and frozen in a knife-embrace, Jamal assessed the attacker. The man was small, but quick. Throwing a leg up and around, Jamal locked both legs around the man's body and squeezed.

The attacker squealed, but continued to strike out haphazardly. The small man could not twist his body around, allowing Jamal to slide out from under him while continuing to crush his torso. Jamal grabbed his left arm, forcing the attacker's chest to the ground at the sudden loss of support. The man's right arm flailed uselessly.

Seizing victory, Jamal used his free hand to grab the back of his assailant's neck and pressed him down into the thick carpet. In labored gasps, the attacker fought on, but his breathing diminished with each exhalation as Jamal put pressure on his rib cage and kept his face smothered by the carpet. Jamal heard a faint *tick* as a rib cracked.

"Ahhhh! Stop! Let me go! Ahhhh!" The man screamed into the carpet, his words almost unintelligible.

Jamal unlocked his legs, but kept the man's neck gripped tightly. Rising to a crouch, he snatched the knife with his free hand. He slammed his knee into the middle of the man's back and held the knife to his neck, where skull meets spine.

"I don't have to do shit!" Jamal relaxed his grip slightly, but kept the man prone on the floor. He stopped struggling, and tried to turn his head. Jamal could see the side of his face now. Leaning in, he made eye contact. "Let's talk, then. Where's Herriot?"

"I don't know what you're talking about." The man chuckled.

Jamal smacked him hard on the back of the head. "Are you sure?"

"I only know about St. Edmund and the package. I don't know any fucking *Herriot,* I swear to God!"

"You know about me. How is that?"

The man sneered, turning his head as much as he could. His face betrayed a look of smugness and disdain, the kind that a rich man gives to a poor one. Jamal shook him roughly, summoning an expression of fear that Jamal found much, much more agreeable.

"They told me I wasn't the only one," the man continued, voice quivering. "A tour guide was going to take me to St. Edmund. It's where Reston told me to look for the package. I saw you in the lobby. I knew you were going for the package too."

"Now how the fuck would you know that?"

"The key cube, jackass! You were swinging it around on your finger while you checked in, like no one would fucking notice the goddamn gold mine you had! You're lucky no one has slit your throat to get it."

"Someone just tried." There was more of a game going on here. Tennyson must give out key cubes regularly if Jamal's could be recognized.

"Uhrrr... Get your knee out of my back. I can't talk in this position."

"Should have thought about that before you came up to my room, asshole." Jamal removed his knee anyway, and the man rolled into a sitting position.

"I want your key cube."

"They didn't give you one?"

"No!"

I'm privileged?

"What was your job before you died?" Jamal said.

"I'm an accountant."

"What?" Jamal laughed.

"I got caught banging my secretary."

Jamal smiled and slapped the man lightly across the face. He recoiled and looked around, as if the fight had been resumed. Jamal sat down and grabbed his knees, ignoring the man's rekindled fright. "That's it?"

The man realized he was in no danger and relaxed, though he sat at a distance from Jamal that prevented easy slaps.

"No. My secretary's name is Alice Tennyson."

Jamal rolled back and looked to the ceiling. "Sister?"

"Niece."

"That's not that bad." Jamal looked at the man and shrugged.

"And her daughter."

Jamal thought about it. "Alice can't be *that* old." He arched an eyebrow. "And neither can her daughter."

He did not ask how old. It was enough to know the man's motivation, enough to have some kind of perverted kinship in this twisted life he was forced to live, even if the kinship was actually contention. He looked at the man, whose light frame and vulpine face made for an unlikely assassin. He looked like an accountant. "You ever kill anyone?"

"No," the man said.

Jamal thought he detected a bit of shame in the man's voice. "But you were going to kill me?"

"No… I just was going to cut you up until I got the cube. They told me there were other people going after the package who were killers and criminals. What am I supposed to do?"

Jamal raised his fist suddenly and enjoyed the little man's reaction: head down, hands up, and scooting away on his butt. He looked up at Jamal in hatred.

"Get mean, I guess," Jamal said.

"That was my conclusion," the man said in a whisper, looking sadly at the floor.

Tennyson was quickly becoming the most intense and twisted man Jamal had ever met. He remembered the pragmatic aura around the man, a complete transparency in personality and intent: he did what he wanted with no regret or misgivings. The man was utility incarnate. No action or movement was made without purpose.

Jamal considered this, realizing that it was out of character for Tennyson to employ a cadre of forlorn souls to retrieve something of value. Tennyson must have something valuable at stake if he justified killing, or the use of gross resource allocation, like the cube, to achieve this aim. Jamal found this intoxicating, yet dangerous.

The little guy brightened. "Hey, we can get the package together, you know?"

Jamal thought about it. "You tried to kill me."

"What? No! I just was going to scare you and take the cube," the man said, putting his hands out in resignation.

"My bleeding arm is pretty scared." Jamal felt a familiar darkness invade his mind. The little man must have sensed it as well. They both stood up hastily.

"Oh, sorry about that. I didn't mean to…" The man put a hand on the door knob.

"You might be an accountant and you might not be." Jamal moved quickly, throwing a hand out to prevent him opening the door.

The man pulled at it in vain and looked up at Jamal. He was quivering again, this time with an element of feral rage that might make him dangerous. "Oh come on. I'm trying to save my marriage. Besides, they'll put me in jail if this gets exposed!"

"Maybe. Sure." Jamal slammed the man's head into the door, using the recoil to throw him back to the floor. He pinned the little man with a knee once again.

Once again the man squirmed but could not escape. "You fucking trash! I hope you get greased by Tennyson, ahhh!"

"There's a statement I trust. Thanks." Jamal reached for something on the bed.

"But, oh come on, I—"

"This might hurt."

When Jamal stepped out into the hallway of the hotel, he felt fresh and relaxed. He walked to the stairwell, his provisions packed and carried in a large backpack, and continued to the lobby. Bright and gaudy colors lapped up at him from wall tapestries, cushion-covered couches, and the carpet. He sat at one of several small desks serving as the check-in/check-out areas.

The lobby was empty. After a few seconds, a clerk emerged from the hidden office in the back. "What may I do for you, Mr. Battle?" The man sat across from Jamal. It took a moment for Jamal to register what he said through the heavy accent.

"I would like to check out."

"Yes? We expected you for the week. Is everything all right? Were our accommodations not to your liking?" The man was intensely concerned.

"Oh no, it's not that. I just have some business to attend to that takes me from Nairobi. I won't be returning."

"Very good then, sir," the clerk said, his tone suddenly casual. "We are sad to see you go, but are glad that we could accommodate your stay in Nairobi and hope to do so in the future."

"Of course. Why not?" Jamal slapped the room key card down and got up. "Just charge it to the account I gave you."

"Ah yes, I wanted to tell you, Mr. Battle, that we had a problem with that account. May I see your cube again?"

"Absolutely," Jamal said, trying to emulate the sound of a media announcer. He had gotten used to these "account discrepancies." At first it had scared him, but after looking at the account data from various transactions, he noticed that the cube was constantly changing its account ID. Each new number was good. It was untraceable and infinite. Jamal enjoyed the freedom.

"Ah, sorry about that. The account is okay, now."

"Of course it is." Jamal smiled at the man and took the cube back from him. He started to walk out the large entrance doors. When he got to the threshold, he stopped and turned back to the clerk. "Oh, and one more thing."

"Yes, Mr. Battle?"

"A man came up to my room and tried to kill me. I ordered a steak, but got a homicidal CPA. He's tied up in the bathroom. You might want to look into that. Oh, and he's American, so just call the embassy before you even go up. And keep mother-daughter combos away from him. He's got that look about him, you know?"

The clerk's eyes bulged as his face contorted in horror and confusion. He tried several times to get up from the desk as Jamal talked, but kept sitting back down in utter discomposure. When Jamal finally walked out of the door, he looked back and saw the clerk run back into the office.

"And I'm still hungry," Jamal said to an empty lobby.

CHAPTER 8

Ruth got out of the jeep to look around.

The drive from Nairobi had been rough and unpleasant, largely due to high winds buffeting the vehicle and kicking up dust, so very little of the countryside could be seen. Ruth had looked forward to the view. Now she looked forward to going home.

She had spent a lifetime reading and not doing. Even if the search yielded nothing, she would be *doing* something, not just reading about something that had been done.

Her primary objective was to discover if the town of St. Edmund actually existed. There were seventeen towns named St. Edmund on the continent of Africa. Because *The Book of Beasts and Green Things* had mentioned Mombasa, Ruth had searched for a St. Edmund in Kenya.

She had found one.

According to the travel information on the Kenya tourism website, St. Edmund was a new village, forming quickly over the last seven years and located approximately 90 miles north of Nairobi, near the southeastern base of Mount Kenya. The land on which it stood was once part of Mount Kenya National Park, but due to a lack of government enforcement and a failing tourism industry, migrants had settled in the once-protected area. To save face, the government had just changed the National Park boundaries on the map.

St. Edmund had gained a reputation because the people there routinely climbed the mountain trails and kept them clear, picking up trash and planting trees, or so the article in the travel brochure said. Specifically:

> *St. Edmund is the friendliest and cleanest town in all of Kenya. The citizens celebrate the arrival of any traveler, whether they are the wealthy on safari or refugees on the run. I was treated to a feast when I arrived! They talked me into staying the night and found me a beautiful room to stay in. The feeling of life overflowing was hard to shake, and St. Edmund quickly became one of the most amazing places I've ever visited. The view of Mt. Kenya to the northwest dominates one's attention, while in the humble yet vibrant village, singing can be heard at almost any hour, and the hospitality is second to none. If you are visiting Kenya, you have to find this place.*

Ruth tried to find more, but it seemed that St. Edmund was not a true tourist destination. The comments section accompanying the travel article was blank: either no one trusted the writer's recommendation or no one wanted to let the secret out.

Or no one cared.

The contrast fueled Ruth's curiosity to an unnatural level. She must find this place. She had hired a driver and left Nairobi for St. Edmund.

She was almost there. Once the jeep started the gradual ascent to the plains surrounding Mount Kenya, the wind slowed and the dust cleared. The driver stopped at the top of a low hill, motioning for Ruth to take in the view.

The brilliance that lay ahead was intoxicating, calling to Ruth in ways she assumed all humans knew, yet which she could not understand. Coriander- and cinnamon-colored plains stretched to the south and the west, the land dotted with lonely trees and plants she could not identify. Seven shades of brown wove themselves around the car. Every tree, blade of grass, and hardy shrub vibrated in a hidden harmony. Through the cab's open window flowed spirits of aroma, deep earth, and vegetation, dancing on Ruth's senses and invading her soul.

The sun above was set to its own tune as well, with fast-moving clouds conducting a song of light that shifted from full brilliance to muted shade to tender shafts of radiance and shadow. The symphony went on for centuries, millennia, or so Ruth believed, before the driver put the jeep in gear and continued into the magical painting before them, a picture dominated by the guardian monolith of Mount Kenya at its center.

The mountain was dark and crowned with glaciers. The fear and tension caused by current events were washed from Ruth in that moment, and she forgot who she was and why she was there.

In the distance between their hilltop vista and Mount Kenya, Ruth could make out a town about a mile and a half away: a small collection of structures sitting at the right hand of the lone mountain.

"St. Edmund?" she said.

"Yes," the driver responded. It was the first English word she had heard him use.

They rolled down into the depression where St. Edmund sat. As they approached, Ruth watched Mount Kenya. Small changes in elevation and direction caused the character of the mountain to change. One moment it was a black keep, the next it was an ornate palace with blade-like spires.

Fields raced by and occasionally Ruth detected shapes moving in her peripheral vision. The closer they got to St. Edmund, the more wildlife she saw. Many were deer-like animals, the kind she had seen on nature shows. Ruth assumed that they were impalas, gazelles, springbucks, or things of that nature.

It didn't matter. It only mattered that she had found St. Edmund.

They passed a tree, shaped like a bonsai but huge, and when she looked closely, Ruth's pulse quickened as she realized the black and gold form cradled by the great tree was a leopard. She was pretty sure that it was. It might have been a cheetah, but she knew that leopards liked trees.

The town was only a few hundred yards ahead. Some of the houses looked like the bungalows at a safari club, others were simple thatched huts. The houses exuded humility. They were simple, no pools or ornate terraced gardens or iron fences surrounded them. In fact, Ruth found it odd that there were no fences anywhere.

Every town had fences.

The main road bisected St. Edmund. The driver pulled over and stopped just as the fields ended and the town began. He looked at Ruth with a pleading stare and raised his hands, palms up.

"Hotel?" she said.

"No hoo-tel." His hands rose higher, nearly touching the roof of the jeep.

"What?" The sense of relief fled.

"Eh… No hoo-tel," he said again and looked forward, his face suddenly showing alarm. Ruth turned and saw a crowd approaching the jeep. She could hear women singing and men talking as the people walked casually onward.

The din of the voices became overpowering. Though nothing was overtly threatening, Ruth felt anxious, mainly because the driver was petrified and she was not in a land she understood. The crowd continued on and every person in it talked, laughed, or smiled as they came. Ruth relaxed, the innocuous nature of the group finally overriding her concern. She looked back at the driver. He was markedly *not* relaxed and made no move to get out of the jeep.

"Who are these people?" Ruth pointed to the throng.

"Ahhhh, no. Maasai. Maasai!" he said and pointed a thumb at his chest.

Ruth shook her head, confused.

"Kikuyu." He pointed at the crowd.

Ruth didn't understand the last word, but the consonantal sound was both a *g* and a *k* at the same time. Maasai was a tribe name. She thought for a moment and realized that the word was reminiscent of something in *The Book of Beasts and Green Things*. It was a tribal name, spelled "Gikuyu."

The world of tribal warfare and ethnic cleansing was utterly alien to Ruth, but the driver must have routinely ventured into areas controlled by peoples that were not friendly to those of Maasai blood. The coming crowd seemed harmless, but how much did she know about this place and its people? She hoped that her intuition was worth following. Deciding it was, she unlocked the door and started to open it.

"No!" the driver said and reached across to grab the door handle, trying to slam the door shut.

Ruth felt his fear and lightly put her hand on his, looking into his eyes. He was a large man with stone-like features and graying hair, light on the temples but peppered over the rest of his skull. His face was contorted with fear and the hand Ruth held trembled. As he looked at her, however, his expression softened. She watched as tension was slowly released from his body and his grip on the door handle eased. The man blinked his eyes several times and leaned back. A smile started to form on the granite face, but resolved into a mild grimace. "Okay," he said.

"Okay?" Ruth tested.

"Okay."

Ruth got out of the jeep and let the sun engulf her, the air hot but flowing gently. She took off her sunglasses. The crowd was instantly upon her and she was greeted in languages she had never heard. Women clad in purple, blue and every bright color of a rainbow surrounded her, shaking her hand or rubbing her elbow. The men milled around behind and offered undecipherable mutterings. Several children ran up to Ruth to pull at her shirt and give her flowers of white and pale gold.

Ruth almost fainted from the force of the greeting. She was pummeled by the overwhelming presence of new people and a new culture in a new land. But it was more than that.

Love.

The people seemed to be filled with the love that Ruth had known in only short spans and special events in her life. It felt like a childhood Christmas morning or a special Thanksgiving, free of arguing and booze. She felt as if she already knew these people, as if she had traveled the globe and was now returning to her family.

It felt like home. The women were her aunts and sisters, and the children were her nieces and nephews. They smelled of incense and human scent, sometimes pungent, sometimes subtle. Ruth answered them in English, accepting their beauty and giving them warm thanks in the only way she could. She felt something push into her right hip. Ruth hopped to the side to avoid falling over. She looked down to see a mob of dogs, some tiny and some large, nosing up expectantly with tails wagging. The crowd laughed and Ruth did too.

The raw energy present inched Ruth backwards until her back pressed into the side of the jeep. She turned and knelt down to look through the passenger window. The driver looked back at her blankly. Ruth gestured for him to get out. He shook his head with several quick jerks. She gave up and rounded on the crowd, smiling and thanking them again and again.

Though she was entranced by the welcome, this was still a strange land. Perhaps the driver's reluctance was not to be ignored? He had locked himself in the car, so Ruth risked an action based on her intuition once more. Raising her arms, Ruth signaled the crowd to quiet down. The roar became a medium rumble of talk and laughter, and Ruth assumed that was the best she was going to get.

"Maasai." Ruth pointed back to the car. Many in the crowd quieted and looked at Ruth, no longer smiling.

Please don't let this get the guy killed, please…

"Maasai," Ruth said again. Several of the adults walked around Ruth and looked into the car. The rest of the crowd responded by surrounding the vehicle, their faces pressing in to look at the driver with mixed expressions.

Just as Ruth began to fear the beginning of an ethnic conflict, the crowd began to sing a beautiful yet mordant-sounding song. The force of it seemed to be directed at themselves and not the driver. The men sat back and sang in varied parts and pitches while several women got on their knees and reached out to the car, moaning and screaming in metered intervals.

Ruth was aghast yet expectant, for something was occurring that was both powerful and alien. Whatever the song was about or whatever gesture it represented, it had an effect on the driver. Ruth heard the locks snap open from inside. The driver-side door opened and the man slowly stepped out.

Ruth realized he was more venerable and elderly than she had thought. As she examined him again, she saw tears in his eyes. His lips quivered. The men continued to sing and the women reached out to him. Finally, he inhaled deeply and threw his arms out, yelling out in proclamation. The group of villagers cheered and rushed in on the man, the women scrambling to their feet and the children running in from the greater distances they had retreated to while the adults sang. The dogs were also affected by the excitement, and barked, jumped, and nosed their way into the commotion.

After many hugs and laughs, the whole group of people along with the driver broke out into another song, this one jubilant and joyous, the crowd jumping with the rhythm. Ruth watched, hypnotized. She didn't know what had happened, but felt safe in assuming no one was going to get shot or struck by a machete. When the song was over, the whole crowd began to move back onto the main street and meander into the town. Ruth could not make out the driver and once the people cleared, he was gone.

She was about to panic at her sudden solitude when a woman shuffled up and took her by the hand. She was smiling and talking. Though Ruth understood none of the words, it was the most beautiful conversation she had ever had.

They walked to the far end of St. Edmund. The woman walked casually and waved at people as they passed by. She turned to Ruth and touched Ruth's elbow with her free hand. She then put a hand on her own chest. "Jata," she said.

Ruth smiled and said nothing, confused but still comfortable.

"Jata," the woman said again.

"Oh, sorry." Ruth understood and put a hand to her collar. "Ruth."

Jata smiled as if she had been given a gift. "Ruth!" She took Ruth's arm again and shook it hard. The earnest zeal of the woman's expression stole any alarm she felt. The strength flowing from Jata was striking, a force that was both simple and complex. She appeared to be close to Ruth's age, as well. Had she been specifically asked to greet her?

She let the question go and walked on. St. Edmund was not a large town, rather a basic settlement with one artery running through it, several streets and alleys branching off and disappearing behind the main-street houses.

Most structures were made of wood and some even of mortared stone. The presence of several water towers surprised Ruth. Small gardens laced the perimeter of many of the "estates," but no trees or large plants grew within the town. Ruth assumed this was to prevent snakes and other dangerous creatures finding a home in St. Edmund.

This thought was punctuated by something sleek running across the road and shooting into a nearby garden shrub. Ruth had read *Rikki-Tikki-Tavi* when she was twelve; she believed she had just seen a mongoose. Remembering the valiant rodent hero, her confidence grew.

Ruth was not confident about lodgings, however. "Jata. Hotel?"

"Hoo-tel?"

"Hotel." Ruth mentally crossed her fingers.

Jata shook her head, but said something else and pointed ahead. Ruth followed. This visit was entirely different from what she had expected, but the words of the travel writer came back to her.

Ruth had not believed a word of it before coming. She was glad to be wrong. Halfway through the town, the main street was covered in rough cobbles, not dirt. Men were busy laying the cobbles as she walked by. They took a moment to wave at Ruth and Jata, smiling and uttering greetings.

Jata led her to a house with a small front yard of dirt and scrub bushes. Flowering shrubs lined the path leading to the porch. The house was a combination of wood, concrete and thatch. The porch held two rocking chairs and hanging baskets full of vibrant purple flowers. The whole struck her as sturdy, quaint, and beautiful.

They entered the house and Jata began picking up loose items and tidying here and there. Ruth assumed the house was hers. There were two rooms: one at the front and one at the rear that made a rectangle stretching back through the small lot. The front room had a small stove and food preparation table in the left corner, with a table in the middle and cot on the right wall. It was essentially a studio apartment, by Ruth's privileged reckoning.

The room smelled of sweet fruits and wood. Open windows on either wall allowed the warm breeze to penetrate and churn the mixed fragrances into something fresh, yet intoxicatingly thick.

After Jata had finished tidying, she took Ruth by the hand again and led her to the back room. A sitting area with empty tea cups on a table filled the left corner, while a large bed with a simple canopy of sheer lace and blue cloth stood opposite. Stepping into the room, Jata extended her arms and gestured to the surroundings.

Ruth got the idea. No hotel: just a room plucked from Heaven. Ruth could not suppress a smile.

"Thank you." Ruth put down her bag and hugged Jata sincerely.

For the rest of the afternoon, they sat on the porch together and "talked." Ruth pointed to something and identified it in English and Jata countered with terms in Gikuyu. Jata's words were intriguing and organic, yet tight and solid, as if the language had been derived from the power of the trees, rocks and mighty Mount Kenya in the distance. It made Ruth think of many things, including the link between culture and language, how speech limits and defines what a person may think and convey. The number of languages left in the world was decreasing every year: that people here in St. Edmund continued to use an African language as opposed to English or French was astounding. Homogeneity may be a result of cultural diffusion, Ruth thought, but was still a cause for mourning.

They sat on the porch and watched dusk settle. Ruth had more tea over that two-hour span than she had had in the previous two years. She got up frequently to use the toilet and Jata laughed each time she excused herself. Ruth reveled in the abandon of the setting sun, almost forgetting why she had come to St. Edmund. Almost. The town was indeed as charming as the one described in *The Book of Beasts and Green Things*, yet it was just a town.

Besides, she had not yet encountered any talking baboons.

As the sounds of night crept over St. Edmund, Ruth knew she must ask a question she now dreaded. She had spent her own money to come and "research" the origins of the mysterious text given to her by the impostor Hendricks.

But the journey was fast becoming much more. The joy and pleasure these people exchanged was divine currency; the unity created by this blessed commerce was beyond explanation. They had running water and electricity, which surprised her. Trucks loaded with grain and fruit had passed by several times during the afternoon. Jata would say something as they passed and smile, obviously pleased with the bounty being paraded on its way to…

Ruth had wondered where the grain was going. She had seen irrigated fields as they approached St. Edmund: it might be that the loads of food were being *exported* to other towns or beyond. St. Edmund was a simple place with nothing resembling wealth in either building structures or citizenry, but it also held no poverty that Ruth could see.

She hoped to find someone who spoke English before she left. There were many questions that needed answering. But the most important one she loathed to ask for fear of breaking the spell.

At last, Ruth dared. "Herriot?"

Jata looked up and along the street. She closed her eyes and bowed her head, smiling. Ruth feared that the name "Herriot" might be close to some Gikuyu word, but suspended her panic until Jata's head rose, her eyes open.

"Herri-oot," Jata said and nodded.

Ruth did not know why the name had evoked such thought. "Herriot?" she said again and pointed to the ground, the universal signal for "here," or so she hoped.

"Eeh, Herri-oot. Eeh!" Jata pointed toward the southern end of St. Edmund, where Ruth had arrived.

She wanted to see what Jata was pointing at, to ensure they were both talking about a man. She gestured questioningly and started to get up. Jata also rose and rubbed Ruth's arm before taking the cups from the table and going inside. Ruth waited. The sky had become a mix of deep sapphire and amethyst tendrils reaching into a brilliant, star-filled, dark sky. The night was no less magical than the day. Her heart had been stolen and she knew she would never get it back.

Jata returned and they left the porch, walking down the main avenue once more. Not far from where the driver had originally parked stood a relatively large house built of stone.

They entered without knocking. Inside was a long hallway that led to the back of the building. As they walked, Ruth peered into rooms lining the passageway. Most had

no doors. From one room wafted the aroma of food. When
she looked in, she saw several men sitting at a low table,
absorbed in a humor-filled conversation. They laughed
and yelled at each other. Ruth smiled and walked on.

Other rooms were simple storage spaces, filled with
what looked like sacks of seeds and farming implements.
One room had a locked cage door. Within, Ruth could see
tools and electrical wiring on the ground. The last door
before the end of the hallway was shut and locked, but she
could hear chirps, yelps, and clicks from within. *Caged animals?*

Jata knocked on the door at the end of the hallway and
called out "Herri-oot." After several moments, she did it
again. "Herri-oot!"

A crash followed by several bangs ensued. Afterwards,
a muffled voice and shuffling of feet or rustling of papers—Ruth couldn't be sure which— emanated from behind the door. Jata knocked again. She put her whole body
into it and the door shook, dust motes floating down from
the ceiling and visible in the wan light of the hallway
lamps.

"Yes?" A deep voice spoke from within.

"Jata," she responded.

"Ah, okay. I mean, *eh. Eh.*"

The door opened and Ruth beheld a dark figure. The
shadows cast by the hallway lights prevented her from
making out the man's face. Jata spoke once again. The man
shifted on his feet nervously. As Jata pushed Ruth into the
room, he stepped back. He withdrew until an overhead
light illuminated his features. Ruth tried to understand
what she saw, but could not.

Herriot was very tall, yet his proportions were all
wrong. His waist was thin and compact, but as his ribcage
began, his chest widened strangely. It reminded Ruth of a
bodybuilder, but the shape was aberrant. His arms were of

normal length, contrasting with legs that gave him most of his height. He had dark brown hair. The normality of that only accentuated his other physical oddities.

The overall impression was that of a thick man on stilts. This was alarming enough, but Ruth was shocked more by the fact that he looked both natural and inhuman at the same time. For an instant, she thought she was meeting a being from another planet.

Only then did she dare focus on Herriot's face.

A harsh brow extended too far and cast a shadow over his eyes. His face was a cut gemstone, the angles, edges, and points perfect in their proportions and symmetry. Eyes glinted within their dark lair, but Ruth saw nothing ominous or strange in them.

Instead, she felt peace.

An expression of compassion and innocence lay on a face that seemed as though it was made to scowl. His skin was thin and translucent. It reminded Ruth of a spring-roll wrapper or wax paper. As a result, his exposed hands and face had a faint blue and purple tinge to them from the blood coursing within. It was grotesque.

He gazed into her eyes and said nothing. When the shock of the examination wore off, Ruth realized that Jata was gone. She looked around the room and noticed tables and work benches for the first time. A golden form lay on one of them, the sound of soft breathing audible from across the room.

"Most people react in a less desirable way, Miss Ruth," Herriot said, breaking Ruth's distraction.

She refocused on his face. He was smiling at her. That was more of a distraction. "You're..." Ruth coughed to find her lost voice. "You're Herriot?" *There must be a reason he looks like that...*

"Most certainly." His voice was smooth and tranquil.

"I… I, uh… I don't know why I'm here. I think that…" *He's just some kind of albino, right? Man-who-is-not-a-man…*

"Well, I am quite accustomed to your loss for words, so why don't we just sit down for a moment and let the dust settle? Agreed?" He motioned to a work table and chairs.

Ruth looked at the ground and felt embarrassed, but she could not think clearly. The room was warm, and the smells of foreign animals, disinfectant, and coffee melded into something vaguely familiar.

"Are you a vet?" She ignored his invitation, the shock of his appearance motivating her to find something else to fixate on.

She walked past Herriot and over to the table. As she approached, the nature of the form became very, very clear. It was a lion. The cat slept soundly with a mask over its muzzle. Wound dressings covered the lion's upper abdomen and one of its paws.

Herriot followed and Ruth shifted to the side of the table to keep him in her view. "This is a young lioness whose inquisitiveness got her into trouble. Last night, members of a local pride wandered into an unlocked shed by the cotton fields. This one jumped onto the workbench. Unfortunately, the bench was not of robust design— just some pieces of wood lashed together, really—so it collapsed under her weight. She impaled herself on a broken stave and cut up her right forepaw as well. I spent most of the day in surgery. It won't be easy for her, but she seems to have a strong constitution and I am hopeful for her return to the pride."

Man-who-is-not-a-man… talks to animals.

"Wow. I've never seen a lion, much less one convalescing," Ruth said.

"It's not the ideal way to observe them, but I'm glad to introduce you to *Panthera leo*, the King of Beasts… or Queen in this case."

Ruth looked again at the lion. The animal was beautiful and majestic, even in its pathetic state. "Can I touch her?"

"I usually wouldn't recommend that, due to diseases and the like. But in this case I will allow it. Wash your hands over at the sink both *before* and *after* and you'll be fine."

Ruth avoided looking at Herriot because she wanted to forget what he looked like. His voice was soft and comforting, though he was definitely particular about certain things. He struck her as being nerdy. Ruth thought of herself as nerdy, too.

She washed her hands and returned to the injured Queen. The fur was deep ochre, the hair around the neck having lighter tips and framing a paler face. The lioness's rib cage was wrapped in bandages, and even unconscious the animal's presence filled Ruth with both fear and awe. She let her fingers touch the lioness's flank, away from the wounded torso.

The hairs were soft, yet thick and substantial. They passed under her palm and reminded her of flowing wheat and summer nights in Kansas: a rogue memory from her childhood when the family had attempted to "go west" like so many others. They had moved back to Connecticut within a year.

She was nine and her father was still a professor. He'd been offered an adjunct position at KU that would become permanent after a year. Of course, Ruth didn't know this. She just knew that they had left the forests around Hartford and come to the flat grasslands of Kansas. They had a house near Mount Oread. It was a small house next to a ranch. Ruth remembered the one August she had lived there, when she ran through the high grass that was light brown and not green. It had looked like a place where lions would live.

Ruth came back to the room and realized she had rested her hand on the lioness. Herriot was beside her, gently stroking the lioness's head, visually assessing the wound dressings as he did.

She watched him.

Herriot's movements were human enough, and his concern for the creature on the table was palpable. Ruth could not deny a primal impulse that shook her when she looked at Herriot and his queerness, but it was something she could master. *He must have some kind of genetic disease or deformity.*

He looked up at her and grinned. "Wash your hands, please, and come sit with me. I'm sure you have a few questions for me. I have a few questions for you."

Ruth did as he asked and took a seat across from him at a work table. It was strewn with animal anatomy books and a large com-pad and satellite receiver.

"Not much in the way of communications out here, huh? That must cost you a lot," she said, pointing to the receiver.

"I know a guy…" His grin contrasted with the lack of humor in his voice.

Ruth chuckled.

"So, you probably want to know why I'm here, right?" Herriot said.

Ruth did, but didn't know how to tell him. "Well, not really."

Herriot's hands flattened on the table top and his arms tensed. He seemed ready to throw himself backward, away from Ruth.

"What are you…" she began.

"Please, let me stay! I won't leave here, I promise!" Herriot shot back from the table and ran to the room's rear door, tripping over a stool as he did so. Incredibly long legs kept his body steady, however, and he prevented himself from hitting the floor by putting a hand to the wall. The weak structure visibly shuddered from the impact.

"Stop! I'm not going to hurt you, or anything else." Ruth threw her arms up and got off her own stool, walking backward and away from the frightened Herriot.

He remained in a posture of impending animal flight.

"I'm just a tourist, okay? Don't you meet tourists every now and then?" Ruth thought it was a good question. As Herriot's body relaxed, she assumed that he thought it was a good question too.

"Well, yes, it's just... you are different, more intense. I thought..." He put a hand to his shoulder, the one that had taken most of the impact when he struck the wall.

"Are you all right?" Ruth remained by the entrance.

Herriot looked down and smiled, a weak chuckle passing before he rubbed his shoulder again, the smile becoming a wince. "I'm fine, thank you. And I'm sorry. I just have to be careful with people sometimes." He walked over to the table once more and sat. His bearing immediately returned to the calm state it had been. Ruth felt more shock than relief. *What the hell is going on in this place?*

"Please, sit. Let's start that over, shall we?" He gestured feebly at the table.

Ruth approached slowly, more out of her own fear than any consideration for the strange man. "You're a vet and you're doing vet stuff, right?" she said, also more for her own reassurance than Herriot's. Not once Ruth thought she might walk into a hostile situation, especially since coming to St. Edmund. Either the man was expecting an attack, or was just crazy. Ruth did not want to cross the path of either potentiality.

She sat, but with only half of her buttocks on the stool and one foot resting firmly on the ground, in case her own egress should be necessary.

Herriot leaned over and sighed, looking to the wall for a moment before returning his gaze to Ruth. "Actually, I do not have a DVM."

DVM? Ruth thought for a moment. "Oh, Doctorate of Veterinary Medicine?"

"Precisely. I do have a joint bachelor's degree in biology and zoology from the University of Minnesota."

His mention of a familiar academic institution should have comforted Ruth. It did not. "Huh?"

Herriot waved his hand dismissively. "What are degrees worth today, anyway?" he said.

"Not much, right?" Ruth said, surprised by her own ready sarcasm.

"Well, I just happen to love living things. Whether they are *Panthera* or *Phthiraptera*, I've either nursed, grown or captured things crossing my path since I was a boy."

"Phthiraptera?"

"Phthiraptera. Lice."

"Oh."

"Fascinating creatures, actually." Herriot met her gaze, with a light in his eyes that was joyful and infectious. "Did you know that most not only feed on specific species, but also on specific *parts*?"

"I guess I never thought about it." She could not share Herriot's enjoyment of parasites.

"Most don't. Anyway, what brings you to St. Edmund, Miss Ruth?"

"My name's Ruth Long."

"My apologies, Miss Long."

"Just call me Ruth."

"Ruth." He was not annoyed, which she found odd. "What brings you here? I assume you're American?"

"I am, as are you?"

"I grew up in America, yes."

Ruth paused, conflicted as to her next move. In lieu of a good lie, she defaulted to honesty. "Well, I received a... document that references St. Edmund."

Herriot's face contorted. "I find that strange. We are doing well, but St. Edmund is just one African village among thousands."

"The document also references you."

Herriot looked at her in disbelief, and with a measure of horror that Ruth saw he wanted to suppress, but then his face softened and he chuckled. "*The Book of Beasts and Green Things?*"

"Yes." Ruth remembered Herriot's earlier reaction and hoped her naked approach would not spook him again.

"Why am I not surprised that one of us circulated such a trite story?" Herriot smiled, looking pensive.

"Us?"

With a shake of his head, Herriot raised his hand and looked into Ruth's eyes. "You want to know what I am, don't you? That is why you are here." It was not a question.

She glanced down, confused by his candor. When she looked up, he sat grinning, still waiting for her answer. "Yes."

Herriot pushed the books away from the space between him and Ruth. With elbows resting on the table, he folded his hands and took a breath. "When I was born, I looked just like you: normal. I grew up in a small town in southern Minnesota. My parents were wealthy and had chosen to move to the town as a kind of retirement. They were in their forties when I was born.

"As I grew, I read books, got into fights, got dirty, played soccer, and got report cards just like everyone else. My childhood was wonderful. I went outside a lot. I planted my first garden when I was six, and from there my interest in botany and biology burned out of control, to the detriment of other disciplines required in school. My parents…"

Herriot paused. His face grew placid as the muscles relaxed. Ruth saw pain in that blank stare. Compassion boiled up within her, but she said nothing.

"Sorry." He grinned. "My parents loved it, though they feared for my education and wanted me to be normal. When I asked to use a quarter-acre of the yard for a test garden, one where I could play with genetic species kits and the like, they couldn't say no. I was only eleven. I wanted to breed new strains of corn and beans and whatnot. Ridicule followed me in school, but we Midwesterners aren't as ruthless as some.

"Eventually my close friends wanted to help me with the 'field,' but my knowledge was growing rapidly and they lost interest. A year after that, I started a 'practice' for sick or injured pets. Some of the kids would bring their dogs or cats over to see me—nothing was ever wrong with them—and I'd diagnose the problem and prescribe a remedy. When my parents found out what I was doing, they explained the importance of professional licenses and lawsuits. To this day I don't understand that.

"Anyway, I'm not making this as brief or to the point as I want. I was lucky to grow up in a rural area so that my interests and talents did not go unnoticed nor underdeveloped."

Ruth settled herself more comfortably on the stool.

Herriot took a breath, the grin slipping from his face. "I was seventeen when my body started changing. A second growth spurt almost rivaled the first. My shoulders broadened, and most people just thought I was weightlifting or something. So, like any teen trying to hide his body, I learned to dress in ways that masked my growing deformity. There was no explanation. It wasn't until my skin started to lose pigmentation that I finally went to my parents.

"We went to several doctors, but nothing came of it until my final visit. They took a sample of my DNA for analysis since epigenetic manipulation was becoming standard in most practices across the country. The fallout from the passing of the Franklin Laws was finally settling, so genetic and epigenetic remedies were making a comeback."

"So you were…"

"My parents were fearful, as parents should be." Herriot did not pause. "But I detected something else in their comments and reactions. It would not be accurate to say they *expected* my change in physical stature, but while they waited on the diagnosis, I sensed anger and resentment towards something unseen. I remember my father screaming into his phone one day, but I can't remember what was said. Everything changed after the DNA results came back."

The Queen took several sharp breaths before filling the room with a feline groan of sedated power. Herriot did not look back, but instead took on the same nerdy grin as before. Ruth assumed the lioness was just dreaming and looked at Herriot sharply, willing him to say what all this was leading up to.

"Genetically, I am not human," he said.

"You're a Throne." She realized that her tone bordered on accusatory instead of questioning. Herriot regained a look of flight for a moment and Ruth thought the strange man would bolt for the door once again.

"Please. I'm sorry." She slid a hand across the table.

Herriot looked at it disconcertedly and made no move to take it. But he looked up and the animal fear was gone. "That is what they call us, don't they?"

"How is it you are free to roam the earth without being poked or prodded?" Ruth was aghast at her own tactless-ness, instantly wishing she could take the statement back. Her choice of words was born of the absurdity of the conversation. Still, Herriot sat before her and indeed, he looked… no, *felt* different. Human-like, but not human.

"How indeed? Miss Long, I am not 'free to roam the earth,' as you say. Perhaps you've not thought about why you found me in Kenya instead of Apple Valley? May I finish my story?"

"Sorry," Ruth said, ashamed of her aggressiveness. The man sat before her, grotesque and different, but who was to say he was not human?

"The hospital we went to had all the necessary equipment to test for DNA defects. The results came back and my mother wept. Of course, no one told me what was going on. I stole the results from my father's safe and read them myself. It didn't floor me the way you might think. Some of my brothers have very sad stories involving near-suicides and being hunted, beaten, and cast out of their communities. My story is quite tame. Anyway, I knew I was cut from a different bolt of cloth. The results were…"

Ruth fought to stay focused, suddenly conscious of how far she had strayed from home, of Kenya, of this non-man and his story.

"Before I left, I pieced together a coherent explanation for my origin." Herriot did not seem to have noticed her lapse in attention. "It seems that my parents tried to have children in their late twenties and continued to try until I was born. The technology was changing rapidly in those days, and the Pure-Form process had reached the masses, if only the upper-class masses. My father spent almost half his fortune to try a new Pure-Form process for those couples who could not conceive."

"Pure-Life," Ruth said reflexively, having no problem recalling the origin of the greatest fertility technology ever created.

137

"Yes. A very successful program."

"But Pure-Life works. I've never heard of any problems. They had to work with it for almost ten years before the government let them use the process legally on humans."

"Yes, Pure-Life works. But something went wrong in the beginning of the program, something never reported. As you said, it was ten years before the process was legal. That did not stop Tennyson Health Sciences from using the technology *illegally*.

"I have a different genetic blueprint than you, Ruth. Human-based, yes, but as different from a human as a chimpanzee is."

The man-who-is-not-a-man. Ruth was suddenly uncomfortable. She let disbelief console her and argued, "If Pure-Life made you and others like you, I would have heard of it. I can't believe that it wouldn't go public."

"When anything is possible, nothing is plausible." Herriot looked at her pleadingly.

"That's not an answer."

"I don't know why our existence has remained hidden."

"If you weren't exactly human, they would have—"

"Yes. I was well aware of Franklin and the aftermath. My parents loved me deeply, but I left them the night I realized what was happening. I didn't want to die or become an experiment. I took the lab results and broke into the doctor's office to erase any files on me and take any hard copies. The computers could not be accessed, naturally, so I burned the place down."

"What?"

"Survival, Ruth. I had much to learn about the truth. When you assume you are one among billions, you play it safe. When you don't know what you are, when you think you might be one of a kind, you survive. It was a gamble, because I had no way of knowing if the test results had been catalogued anywhere else. Years have implied that they weren't. Years have also shown that I am not one-of-a-kind."

Ruth waited, but Herriot waited longer. Finally, she asked, "How many others are there?"

"There are twelve of us, total. My eleven brothers and me."

"How did you find them? Where are they now?"

"A story for another time."

Ruth wanted to hear the story then, but charged ahead with another question. "Wait. You said that you went to college?"

"Correct. I was about to go to college when my abnormal nature was verified. Being who I am, I stayed on the same path."

"But how?"

"I wrote a letter to my parents asking them for one last favor. I vowed never to visit them again, but I've contacted them since leaving. Given the situation, they feared for me as well, but I was not rejected as many of my brothers were. No one ever proved that I burned down the clinic. My parents stopped calling Tennyson Medical Services and nothing came of it. I had already been accepted to the U, so my father paid my tuition and board from behind the scenes, all in advance. I just had to go to class and stick in there."

"And no one challenged your looks for four years?"

"Makeup and baggy clothes. Need I say more?" Herriot raised an eyebrow.

"No." She thought of her encounter with the Hendricks impostor at the Garner House. "Did one of you guys... did a Throne give me *The Book of Beasts and Green Things*?"

"I don't know." Herriot sat back. "You saw this person who gave it to you, correct?"

"He was disguised as someone else, someone important."

Herriot snorted and tapped the table with a finger. "Twain. His name is Twain."

"But how do you…"

"Oh, I know my brothers well," Herriot interrupted. She heard the warmth in his voice. "If I may be so bold, Ruth, I'd say you have a natural love of life that is not easily diminished. Perhaps that is what brought you here, or perhaps you are driven by fear. I'd bet on the former, if I were a gambler. I'm not, however."

"So, you think Twain gave me the book?"

"Did you believe that the person giving you the book was someone they were not? A flawless performance in which you received information shortly after that revealed the deception?"

"Yup, pretty much like that." Ruth was not amused.

"Then I am certain it was Twain. He loves subterfuge and theater as much as I love leeches."

Ruth glared at Herriot, more to convey her disgust at the meeting at the Garner House than to show her repugnance at leeches, though that was bad too. "He scared the hell out of me," she said.

Herriot looked down at the table, a scowl apparent as he reached down and began to straighten a haphazard stack of books. "I can't say that we are all straightforward. But we live another day, so I won't apologize for our methods." He looked content once more as he surveyed the now neat and orderly textbooks.

"So he gave me the document and predicted I would come here to find you?"

"I suppose."

"And you wrote the Book originally?"

"Me? Certainly not! The Book was probably written somewhere else, perhaps by a traveler or tourist."

"It's religious."

"No." He raised a finger. "It's Christian."

"Strange." Ruth pointed a finger upward as well, in mockery.

"Oh?"

"You can't tell me you're religious."

"Can't I?"

"But... You just said that you're not human. Humans made you."

"Ruth, I would not like to talk about what I believe and how it contends with the vagaries of society. I am in the minority when I say that all religious discussion is flawed rhetoric, with little to no meaning in what is conveyed or accepted. Just understand that I, and the rest of us, care about the world around us and the people in it. Some follow a deeper and more zealous path than my own. I came here to live in peace and help out where I can."

She nodded. "This town is different than the other villages in the region, Herriot. Why?"

"The people here are of sincere moral character and work very hard to feed themselves and others around them. When I came, I saw that they could benefit from some minor things, such as simple irrigation and agricultural methods. The view is great and the wildlife in this region is remarkable. Using junk, we've been able to put up basic windmills, water towers, and storage facilities for the crops."

"Storage? I saw trucks taking crops away, but I didn't see any silos or barns."

"Oh, we have underground storage places."

"Underground? Wouldn't that take a lot of manpower?"

"As I said, the people here are hard-working. I am just a seed myself. With my knowledge, I've helped these people figure out how to live safe, abundant lives without riches or power. We light the houses with banks of old car batteries. All of the technology we have was once junk. The people of St. Edmund work together on each problem and find a solution. They also help their neighbors as much as they can."

"But I see no way of defending the town, if raiders or military come to take what you have."

"The people of St. Edmund live by the tenets of their faith. They believe God has always lived here, in the mountain and in the grasses. He will protect them, but if they are to be consumed by the same greed and violence that has ravaged this land for generations, they will not pick up arms and fight. They blame evil. They blame the choices of people. They do not blame God."

"How naive." Ruth wanted to add more in that direction. "Herriot, I'm sorry. This place is wonderful and I've enjoyed my visit so far."

"I just hope you know that no matter where or when, people can find true life in the midst of death. I grew up with the lesson that Africa was devoid of resources and debased socially. I was lied to. You may have seen violence and destitution since arriving in Kenya, but know that it can and does exist in every part of the planet. People can live together in their faith and choose to forget why they hate another person, another people, another country. St. Edmund has become that place, for a time. Jata believes this town is a small piece of Heaven fallen to Earth. She might be right... for now."

Ruth was increasingly uncomfortable. The conversation had become complex. Translation and interpretations in a general sense did not bother her, but when faith was discussed — Christian faith, which she had essentially abandoned long ago — the topic could not support the semblance of empiricism. It became personal, and who cared what any one person thought? She delved into the net effect of what the masses believed and acted on. Admitting her own beliefs would put her into the experiment and take away its objectivity. But St. Edmund was full of something she could not deny.

"Anyway, I don't want to get into the theological tenets that my brothers and I have constructed. We believe in God, specifically the 'God of Abraham, the God of Isaac.' We also believe in Jesus Christ."

"Because you grew up in America! If you were born in Tibet, you'd all be Buddhists."

"As would you," he said quickly.

"Touché." Ruth responded humorously, but was unsettled by Herriot's logic.

"Our beliefs get a little more complicated than what you know as Christianity, as I'm sure you would expect. I don't... *subscribe* to all of them. More precisely, I don't spend as much time thinking about many of the implications of our existence as some of my brothers do. I am content growing crops, rigging up batteries, and mending savannah Queens." Herriot gestured at the sleeping lion. "Now, Ruth, what do you do for a living when you're not visiting genetic freaks in the backwaters of Africa?"

She countered his smile with a frown. "I'm a professor of theology and religion at Campolo University."

Herriot's eyes narrowed. Then he smiled and again Ruth was struck by both his deformity and his charm.

"You don't say."

CHAPTER 9

Jamal kept walking and no one challenged him. They just smiled as they passed. He waved at strangers and laughed when they waved back. St. Edmund was full of predictable, harmless people. He had yet to encounter any more Tennyson competitors like the one in Nairobi, but expected to find more when he got closer to this "Herriot."

Besides, Herriot might have already given the package to someone else and Jamal was walking dead. As he reflected on this, he was bludgeoned by a need for abandon, by the belief that he desired failure after all. Failure and freedom. Freedom to run, fight, and die in the most dangerous of ways would be open to him; no one could deny his drive nor creativity once they admitted that his circumstances justified anything. He lusted for absolute desperation, the kind that had no end save survival or carnage.

If the package was gone, Jamal could live with that.

Daydreams of beating Tennyson and Reston with something heavy enticed more abandon, the jaunt through St. Edmund becoming an escape, his mind in one place while his body remained in another. Memories of lost fights and bad arguments came back to him. *I should have punched more people when I was younger.*

Though his eyes made out the orderly and neat houses lining the street, his ears danced with the sounds of laughter and singing and birdsong, and his nostrils were filled with the glory of cinnamon dirt and baking bread, Jamal writhed within from discord and lament. Within the fantasy, he grew to the height of ten feet, his hands themselves weapons. He smashed people who argued with him. He tore weak leaders in two. He shot Tennyson between the eyes while he pinned his neck down, watching the viscera run through a bloodied hand, painting the parchment office with revenge and reality.

A boy ran up to Jamal and offered him a mango. He stroked the boy's head and accepted the fruit, laughing all the while. In his mind, the mango was someone's heart being torn from the chest, flesh and soul ripped from a cooling corpse.

The boy smiled and ran along.

Jamal took a moment to focus on St. Edmund. The town was thriving, and he might find something of value in one of the houses if he needed to. His key cube was of little use here, but he had procured transportation easily enough back in Nairobi. He had bought a truck. He had bought guns too, and filled the back of the truck with them, hidden under a tarp. Jamal had no interest in selling munitions, though it would be a legitimate front for his travels to the Mount Kenya area. He considered it an insurance policy, should he find himself in trouble with local warlords. Besides, if he were attacked he would have sufficient means to defend himself.

But the journey had been uneventful and boring. He drove for several hours, following the map that came with the truck. The land was barren and depressing. He hated coming to these shitholes, and was eager to get the package and return home as soon as possible. Shanty towns and poor people were the only things to look at while he drove. The only interesting part of the drive had been watching some hyenas run across the road ahead of him. He had stopped to observe. They made inhuman-yet-human sounds that were both horrid and beautiful.

Now he was immersed in the banalities of St. Edmund. People walked, talked, and sat. Everyone seemed content, and this filled Jamal with discontent. He pondered briefly what might lie hidden in such a place that would interest Tennyson.

He didn't care.

He only knew that freedom lay in getting what Tennyson wanted. Once that was found, Jamal was free to kill Tennyson. *He might give me something that would change my mind*, he thought. In truth, he liked Tennyson. Tennyson's ruthlessness was unprecedented, a skill Jamal strove to develop. Reston, however, was not to be forgiven. His mind re-lit with fantasies.

He didn't know what to do next, but he was not concerned. St. Edmund was only so big; finding someone here would be easy. Because there might be other hopeful collectors, however, Jamal moved with more discretion than came naturally to him. He walked through the town several times, gauging each house for importance and weakness. No one questioned him or seemed concerned by his presence, beyond waving and smiling. The town was full of simpletons. The serene and vapid feel of St. Edmund was far from the jagged edge of Nairobi.

The name "Herriot" did not give Jamal much to prepare for, but for some reason he thought that when he found a white woman or man, he'd find Herriot. And white people would not be found with the rabble of common savages. They would be in the largest and most luxurious structure in the town. Accordingly, Jamal flagged a large stone house at the edge of town as the plausible location for his package-holder.

He saw no guards, but scanned the roof and surrounding foliage for sentries. He found none. In fact, he had not seen anyone holding a gun in St. Edmund at all.

Strange.

The town was prospering, but Jamal was unsure why. In this wretched place, prosperity could only be the result of something illegal or violent. He could understand that.

Jamal went to the truck and unloaded an unmarked box of rifles. He put it on the dolly, also included with the truck purchase, and rolled his payload over to the front door of the stone house.

He knocked.

When no one answered, he knocked again. As he waited, a short woman approached him, speaking in whatever gibberish they spouted, and entered the house without looking back. Open door before him, Jamal shrugged and went in. The hallway was narrow but extended back through the building.

Several doorways stood open. He smelled food from the one nearest. The woman who had walked by him poked her head out and jabbered again. She gestured to Jamal and went back out of sight. Jamal followed, leaving the dolly loaded with a large box of illegal assault rifles leaning against the wall.

He found himself in a kitchen. Two men and two women sat at a low table, talking loudly. The first woman was fixing food at a stove, still speaking in his direction. She turned and handed him a plate of steaming food. He hesitated for a moment before taking the plate. It held rice, cooked vegetables, and some nameless meat.

"Don't mind if I do," Jamal said, as he sat down with his hosts at the table.

* * *

Ruth woke late. She felt rested, but the fatigue of the previous day's travel continued to pervade her body, leaving muscles sore and joints stiff.

The conversation with Herriot had ended after her probing intensified and he had finally said, "You must be exhausted, Ruth. Good night." She got the hint when Herriot started to turn off the lab's equipment and lights.

She had reluctantly made her way back to Jata's house. Ruth remembered the strange walk. Each step was slow, and the day's revelations lay like river stones in her heart.

The liquid joy of St. Edmund, combined with the improbable yet persuasive story and personage of Herriot, churned those stones and swept them up in a deluge of oddity and discomfort.

She had traveled to Haiti when she was 16 for a church mission trip, back when it had been compulsory for her to attend a faith institution. That experience had blown her world to tatters by revealing both simple joys she wanted to cherish eternally and complex horrors she wanted to forget forever.

She chose to remember the joy of children running to her and thanking her for being there. She forgot about the widespread disease, the prostitution in Port-au-Prince, and the small hospitals that had to choose the hundred they would save each day while hundreds more suffered and died outside of curable diseases and treatable wounds.

St. Edmund rekindled those joys and horrors, but also held something more tragic to Ruth. In this town she saw the wonder and simple happiness enjoyed by those children of Haiti, but without the violence and sickness. It could not be. To think that one could exist without the other was terrible because it implied that the world was wrong. It implied that the truth could have been realized long ago, could be realized now, could give so much to so many.

Ruth had always felt the disconnection of living with high technology and low family involvement. It was the price of curing diseases and spurring positive economic development, or so she believed. Now she saw poor people taking care of themselves in St. Edmund, the word "poor" taking on a new meaning.

In another town, the Maasai driver might have been beaten to death. Here, the people had put aside their ethnic hatred for something new, something whole and unbeatable. Ruth knew this place would eventually fall to the violent and the ruthless. But yesterday, the people had loved their enemy.

All of these things shot through her consciousness as she rubbed sleep from her eyes and attempted to get her bearings. She was still in Kenya, still in St. Edmund. Feeling comfortable with that for the moment, she called out to her host.

Jata's hospitality was unmatched. Her humor leapt over the wall that language had built between them.

Ruth already loved her. She trusted her in every way, even if life had taught her that people cannot be trusted fully, especially those you've known for less than 24 hours.

She's the sister I never had. Ruth smiled and called again. "Jata!"

The door opened and Jata stuck her head into the room. "Ruth."

"Hello," Ruth replied, knowing it was one of the few English words Jata understood.

"Hello," Jata shuffled into the room and sat on the edge of the bed. "Tea?"

"Eh." Ruth said, which she had learned meant "yes" in Gikuyu.

Jata left and came back with two mugs. She sat down once more, handing Ruth a mug of tea.

"Good morning," Ruth said and lifted her cup. They both giggled before taking a sip.

* * *

The men at the table chattered on until Jamal pretended to understand what they were saying. They had already identified that he did not, so the room was filled with raucous laughter each time he got up to perform some duty or function when his hosts said something directed at him. It became a game. They might have said *you eat chicken shit*, but he would get up immediately and start to wash dishes, pour them more coffee, or any number of pointless acts until they roared and beckoned him back to the table.

The men would have looked formidable if they didn't smile and laugh so much. One had a puckered scar under his right cheek that pulled the side of his face down into a perpetual grimace. Another was built like a tank and taller than Jamal.

They all had thick calluses on their hands that he noticed any time they reached for their coffee. The men might have been hardened by labor, but they joked with each other so much that Jamal could not escape the fun of the breakfast table. He stayed and ate his fill.

When the food was gone, the men looked at each other and sighed. The conversations became serious and Jamal knew his antics would now be in bad taste.

They were going to work. It sobered him as well. He had to go to work too. The men began to clear their dishes from the table and Jamal helped. They continued to talk to him and he continued to pretend he was not weary of all this cheer.

Finally, as the group was about to leave, he made his move. "Herriot?"

One of the men turned to him and spoke. He went out into the hall and gestured for Jamal to follow. When he did, the man pointed to the end of the hall.

He said "Herri-oot."

It can't be this easy.

"Thanks," Jamal said and patted the man on the shoulder. He walked down the hallway, disappointed at the prospect of leaving Kenya so soon.

* * *

Ruth spent another half-hour outside on Jata's porch watching St. Edmund revive itself for the day. The sun was already hot and Ruth was glad for the porch's shade. She had told Herriot the night before that she would return in the morning. He had agreed reluctantly. Herriot was in hiding and Ruth knew where he was. He was pleasant to Ruth, but she sensed that he was afraid of what she might do. She could respect that, so today she hoped to win his trust and get more information out of him regarding the Thrones.

She was intrigued to hear what he believed, even if it might be false. Ruth had concluded that Herriot and the others were just a generation of aberrations resulting from scientific error. It drew her in.

Nevertheless, she was aware she was being manipulated. Intuition told her that Herriot was not one of the manipulators, but he was tied to them, nevertheless. Her initial thesis topic had interested someone enough to cause a ruckus. In turn, someone had predicted that she would go to Kenya to investigate, based on reading one document of dubious origin.

Ruth hoped to find the author of *The Book of Beasts and Green Things*, although the events behind the book were more important at the moment. That must have been foreseen as well.

When she felt fully awake, she told Jata she was going back to see Herriot. Jata must have understood when she heard Herriot's name, as she smiled and waved to Ruth as she left.

The impossibility of St. Edmund and its people flooded back into her mind. Today she hoped to learn more of Herriot's condition and why at least one person had found religious significance in it. Remembering how she had been duped at the Garner House, Ruth thought that Herriot's "brothers" might have a penchant for the melodramatic, and might be spreading these rumors themselves for public recognition.

She nearly stumbled at the thought.

What better way to survive, for those born with a deformity that could legally get you "terminated" in some nations, than to devise a complete origin story based on religious weaknesses of the devout? Sure, some Christian groups would seek to destroy the *abominations* or *demons* with more zeal than the government, but other religious zealots would rally for their protection. The situation would pit people versus people, group versus group, sect versus sect, public versus government, all in hopes of the Thrones being accepted somewhere. The Thrones would risk conflict and upheaval to cut out a place to live in the world. How very human.

Very, very human.

Ruth was enraged.

She had ignored her natural caution and flight reflex, and was hence induced to actions favorable to a phantom party... possibly. The excitement of getting out of stolid academia and finding adventure had enticed her enough to leave home.

St. Edmund was a great place to visit and Ruth could not deny that her life had been expanded by knowing that such a community could exist in a place of unrest and violence.

But her feelings for St. Edmund might be just as naïve as the shock she had felt in Haiti. So she was in a nice town full of prosperity and good people — so what? It would be crushed by the legacy of foreign oppression and internal fighting, just as every good thing in Africa had been before. Suddenly, Ruth realized she had been duped again.

She quickened her pace.

* * *

Jamal opened the door. The room was yet another foul space bare of modern conveniences. The tables were crude constructions, obviously built from whatever junk could be found. Books were piled high on several of them. Jamal didn't care enough to look at the titles.

A yellow-haired form was strapped to a stainless-steel table near the far corner of the room. Again, Jamal did not care what it was; he looked it over to ensure it would not impede him in the future, just in case.

The floor was amazingly clean, but the effect was ruined by dirty wall shelves filled with bottles and more books. Jamal hated how books made a room look. He detested libraries. Jamal forced his bibliophobia aside when he noticed someone hard at work at the center table.

The man looked like a disease.

From where he stood, Jamal tried to understand the stark lack of color in the man's neck, face, and exposed arms. He thought the man was wrapped in something, but as he drew near, he could see sickly, translucent skin tinged blue from the pulsing blood vessels beneath. The man was hunched over, looking through a microscope and obviously engrossed in his work. His shoulders did not fit his body. When he finally looked up, Jamal could see he was retarded.

"Can I help you?" the thing said in perfect English, with an inflection that made Jamal feel stupid.

"Are you Herriot?"

The thing looked around before replying. "Who's asking?"

"I'll take that as a 'yes.' "

The man—if that is what he was—sat back from his work to focus on Jamal. "Yes. I am Herriot."

"What's wrong with you, pal? You look horrible." Jamal realized that Herriot was more monstrous-looking than the initial view had indicated. Impossibly long legs stretched out under the table. Shoulders extended grotesquely to form a "v" reminiscent of a martini glass. Jamal thought he was looking at a cartoon character.

Regardless, the thing named Herriot was tensed, and also safely behind a table. If Herriot became hostile, pulling out a gun or something, Jamal would not have much time or room to react.

"I think I've answered that question too many times in my life, sir. You figure it out."

"You have a package for me." Jamal held out his hand.

Herriot's face screwed up while his body relaxed. He now looked... annoyed? Herriot rolled himself back to the table and resumed his work. "Go see Howard over at the work shed on the other side of the town. We need that part machined as quickly as you can. No more than a day or two, okay?"

Jamal was getting angry. The room reeked of chemicals and shit. He had no time for miscommunication. Paranoia suggested that coincidence had brought him to the wrong "Herriot" in the wrong town. At least he was in Kenya.

"What are you blathering about?" Jamal said.

"You're here for the tractor clutch we need fixed, right?"

Jamal looked around, not sure where to go in the conversation. "No." Honesty was his best weapon.

Herriot looked up again, annoyance still evident, but now his expression was also tainted with anxiety. "Then what are you here for?" He inched away from the table.

Jamal wanted to say, "You tell me," but thought otherwise. The guy was stalling. He must know why Jamal was there, right? For the duration of the trip, Jamal had not considered the package itself. He didn't care. The assumption was that Herriot would give him what he was there for: mission accomplished. Now he was playing grab-ass with some mutant. "I'm here to collect a package from Herriot."

The lanky thing shifted back farther on its stool, no longer annoyed but rather showing signs of mild panic. It was all Jamal needed to know he was still on the right path. "You know," he said.

"Who sent you?"

"The richest man in the world." Jamal waited for the statement to hit. It didn't take long. After the disjointed exchange, he had begun to think that he had been hired as a thief rather than a simple courier. That was fine since he was getting bored. He might have had little skill with subterfuge and tact, but he was proud of his ability to induce fear and action in the deformed man before him. That induction was swifter and more extreme than Jamal was ready for.

Herriot jumped back and swept the contents off the table. The books and microscope crashed to the ground and Jamal leapt back to avoid having the instrument land on his feet. When he looked up, Herriot was already halfway to a door at the rear of the laboratory.

On its stork-like legs, the thing strode faster than he had anticipated. Jamal jumped over the debris to close the distance. Herriot was rapidly undoing lock latches. Jamal lowered his shoulder and collided with Herriot, slamming him into the shut door and taking his breath. Jamal struck the beast with an elbow to the back of the head. He pressed after the strike to pin Herriot before he could turn around.

The thing was strong. As Herriot struggled, Jamal imagined he was wrestling an orangutan or something... *other*. This close to its neck, the faint scent of perspiration wafted up to Jamal's nostrils and smelled like nothing he had ever experienced. It reminded him of plastic and geraniums. The strangeness almost caused him to drop the thing, just to avoid the smell.

"Wait! Wait, I can't hurt you. Let me go," Herriot said. He relaxed under Jamal's fury.

It satisfied Jamal to see an enemy surrender so quickly. He was getting good. "Yes, you can't hurt me. No, you can't go. Give me what I want and I'll let you go."

Herriot's body reanimated and he tried to pull away. Jamal continued to clench his arms like a vise and the thing remained in his grip.

"What?" Herriot said.

Jamal had pinned the spindly thing with its face pressed against the door. He let up some to allow Herriot's head to move. "I said, give me what I want and I'll let you go."

Herriot turned his head. He was breathing heavily. "You mean, you don't know what you're here for?"

Jamal slapped Herriot on the side of the head. "Now! Or this gets painful."

Herriot ducked his head, obviously expecting another slap. Jamal waited for the thing to recover.

"Okay. Get off me and I'll get it for you," Herriot said.

Jamal didn't like the situation, but thought about his own ignorance. Fresh fantasies of taking a steel pipe to Reston's head sprouted, fueled by the lack of briefing Jamal had been given concerning his task. As least he had found Herriot. "If you run, this gets personal... and painful. Got it?"

Jamal eased off without waiting for an answer. He hoped Herriot would try something, try to attack or try to run again so Jamal could be more creative with his methods. But as he stepped back, Herriot turned slowly and looked at him with anger and something else.

Jamal thought he saw tears in Herriot's eyes. Tears! But the strength of his gaze lay in something else. It looked like pity projecting from this freak, but its face was just as wrong as its body, so why trust the expression? The man must be some kind of retard—a retarded monkey martini glass that spoke. He looked like a science experiment gone wrong. Jamal wanted to kill him on principle, to rid the world of this defective human.

"Over there, in that small bottle on the table." Herriot pointed.

Jamal turned to look. The table was clear, save for a small bottle full of a blue liquid. The bottle was plastic, a drink bottle that had been stripped of its label and was now being used for other purposes perhaps.

"What's in it?"

Herriot was probing the side of his face where an ugly bruise was beginning to form. His lower lip was broken and scarlet blood ran down to his chin over gossamer skin.

"It contains a new form of nanotech: little power generators for immersed non-flow systems using a liquid crystal substrate."

Herriot continued to stand by the door, but by the way his body had relaxed, Jamal didn't think he was planning a counterattack or exit, so he walked over to the table and picked up the bottle to peer into its depths. The liquid within was a shade of luminescent blue, with tiny motes swirling and weaving to some insane rhythm. It was hypnotic to watch and Jamal had to pull his mind away from the dance to focus on Herriot. He feared he had let his interest in the bottle's contents disarm him momentarily, so when he spun back around and found Herriot still standing by the door as motionless and calm as the sedated lion on the table nearby, Jamal was disarmed again. "Why didn't you run?" he said.

"I've run for long enough."

So Herriot had stolen the blue stuff from Tennyson's company? Jamal had assumed as much. "Do I need any special containment devices for this stuff?" He held the bottle up and swished it around.

"I wouldn't do that," Herriot said and held a hand out in protest. "The contents are relatively stable, but excessive agitation can make it explosive."

"You're shit'n me."

"Throw it against the wall and see what happens."

Jamal looked into the bottle and noticed the shaking had caused bubbles to form along the internal surface.

"Take it and go. Give Tennyson my regards."

Jamal glared at the thing. "Who said I worked for Tennyson?"

"The richest man in the world?" Herriot raised a hand, pleadingly.

"I did say that, didn't I?" He gave Herriot one last look. Jamal felt something jag his soul when he looked, and he could not place the emotion. Perhaps he was feeling remorse for roughing up a seemingly innocent *man*. Perhaps now that he'd recovered the package he had time to think about Herriot's physical deformities and how they churned something primal and dark within, a force that called for the destruction of that which was faulty or should not exist.

Herriot met his gaze. His deep-set eyes pierced Jamal's façade, seemed to reach into his hatred and challenge his right to feed and conquer. Jamal could feel something alien ignite within, an emotion that shone wanly through his steel-clad intuition.

The light quickly extinguished and was nothing more than a blink within Jamal's solid and reliable psyche-crutch. But the oddity that was Herriot continued to burn through his mind, an inferno of warning that called to Jamal as he turned to leave the lab.

Tennyson Biosciences, Tennyson Life Products, Tennyson Pharma. Sure, Tennyson Holdings had plenty of military companies and weapons-development programs, like Taurus and others, but something about this encounter was all wrong. Jamal stopped and looked back.

Herriot looks all wrong. Why did he say he was tired of running? Did he steal this blue stuff? Was he going to sell it? Then it hit Jamal like a hailstorm.

While he had been entertaining the workers at the breakfast table, he had taken things in and out of the refrigerator. He remembered seeing a clear pitcher of some blue liquid beside a bowl of eggs. He sniffed at the opening of the bottle. Instead of a foreign scent of chemicals or something otherwise odious, his sense of smell was greeted by a sweet fragrance of nameless berries. Jamal laughed and raised the bottle to his lips.

"No! It will poison you," Herriot said.

The liquid was soda. Jamal quickly dismissed the realization that he had just risked his life. Seeing Herriot's suddenly feral expression, he had not time to ponder.

Herriot rushed to the rear door once again, but stopped to look back at Jamal. While taking a sip from the bottle, Jamal had reached into his light jacket and pulled out a pistol, which was now leveled at Herriot.

"You can't kill me."

"So try to run away and see what I *can* do," Jamal said. But Herriot remained frozen, fear and resignation evident on his face. Jamal was certain now.

Herriot is the package.

"So, what? You're a failed science experiment? Did you steal drugs that made you look like that?" Jamal didn't care, but he needed to be sure Herriot was indeed the package.

Herriot said nothing. He only looked down at the floor as his queerly shaped shoulders sagged.

This complicated things. Jamal only liked complications that allowed him to justify doing whatever he wanted. Now he was limited.

He quickly scanned the room for things that might aid him in his first, but doubtfully last, abduction. He walked through the lab and looked at each bottle and box lining the shelves and tables, while keeping the gun trained on Herriot.

Jamal ignored the books. He found a bottle of chloroform, a rope, a blanket and a wagon he assumed had been used to bring the lion into the laboratory. The wagon was large enough and he made his decision. As Jamal started to organize his implements, Herriot moved away from the back door and towards the lion.

"And you are moving because...?" Jamal stepped forward and pressed the gun into Herriot's temple.

"I can't leave this animal. There is no one else in the town with the knowledge to get her healthy and back into the wild," Herriot said calmly, ignoring the gun as he stroked the lioness's head as one would a child's.

"You won't care about any of that in a moment."

"What?"

Jamal rounded on him and smothered Herriot's face with the chloroform-soaked rag. The tall man-thing went down in a heap and Jamal began to truss him up for the journey.

* * *

Ruth opened the door of Herriot's house and went inside. A large box obstructed the passageway and she had to flatten her back along the wall to squeeze by. The building seemed empty. No one stirred in the kitchen or any other room in the house. Ruth wasn't listening anyway. She walked purposefully to Herriot's lab, her footfalls echoing on the cheap wooden floor.

Just have to tell him off, and I'm out of here.

St. Edmund was a lovely place, but just a place like any other. She had risked everything for a stupid thesis topic and then run off for some college-student-like adventure in the "Third World." Add to the situation a cabal of genetically augmented "men" who wanted to get a foot in the door of society and you had the perfect ruin of Ruth's stable existence.

I might still lose my job. I am still being used by people or things that are living out some movie fantasy of freedom and revolution – what the hell have I done? She buzzed with each additional count of stupidity and Ruth knew that if she failed to get a grip on her own mind, the collection of thoughts, memories, and fears would reach critical mass. The ensuing supernova would result in her collapsing to the ground and weeping for a good 20 minutes. There was no time for that.

The door to Herriot's lab was open several inches. She paused. Entering, Ruth saw a broken microscope and scattered books on the floor. Other than that, the room was exactly as she remembered it from the day before. Exactly the same, except for the absence of Herriot and the presence of a man she had never seen before.

He was tall and lean, as evidenced by his exposed forearms and the soft khaki shirt he wore. His head was bald and sleek, giving him the profile of an athlete or model when combined with his handsome features. As the man looked up to find Ruth standing before him, his expression hinted at alarm briefly, but was replaced by a smile that proved his visage was in fact made of flesh, though his proportions and solid body hinted at geological perfection.

His face was carved from onyx. The man was beautiful, as a jaguar is beautiful.

He looked Kenyan, but his clothes were too fine for the average St. Edmund citizen. Ruth assumed he was either a city-boy or something more. He had been tying twine over a tarp-covered wagon when she entered.

She waited for him to say something, but he did not. Instead, he dissected her with his dark eyes, eyes that seemed to lap out at her and caress every curve of her body. Most men took the opportunity to look her over blatantly and without shame. He did so without taking his eyes from hers. It was frightening, yet attractive.

Ruth noticed the convalescing lioness remained on the steel table. The wound dressing looked fresh and the gentle tidal motion of the Queen's ribcage seemed to cast a spell on the lab, as if the rolling grass and warm sun of the surrounding land had sent an emissary to the darkness of human habitation. Ruth was calmed by this, but not enough to overcome the charm and danger she felt emanating from the stranger.

* * *

Jamal was very pleased with himself. Herriot, or the "package," was unharmed and now ready for shipping. There was no further resistance to expect. He was not afraid of what would happen if any of the common townsfolk made their way into the lab. He would feign ignorance or, if that didn't work, use his gun and the chloroform until he had the entire village tied up and helpless. So he had not expected someone to walk into the lab and disarm him completely.

She was tall, which was an instant ingredient for arousal, but there were many more items to the recipe. Her face was pale and unmarred, with eyes that held both intensity and abandon simultaneously: a strange mix. He couldn't tell what color they were, but he hoped blue. She wore a

simple tee-shirt, made of thin cotton that hugged her figure. The faint lines of muscle tone were evident on her
arms and, though she wore loose tan trousers, he bet her
legs held the same promise.

Jamal had met many women in his life, most "meet-
ings" being much more, and much less, than a simple conversation. Most women with stunning beauty, like the specimen standing before him, lacked something important. It
was a regular hollowness that sometimes came with feminine beauty, a sadness that Jamal could feel when he realized that pretty girls were objectified because they *were*
objects, their lack of internal veracity inviting oppression
and setting them up as trophies and whores.

This woman was different. He could feel that at once,
like a subtle aroma permeating a space and conquering it
molecule by molecule. She was not an object, but instead a
force of will as strong as any man. How he could taste this
truth upon viewing a woman for several seconds was
beyond him, but he went with his tried and true logic.

* * *

"You don't speak English, do you?" Ruth said.

"I think you've already guessed that I probably do," he
replied.

Ruth smiled. *American and witty.*

"Is there anything I can do for you?" he said. The question was genuine and nefariously sexual, as Ruth could
detect from his body language and the black glint in his
eye. She stiffened and hoped that her aroused glow was
extinguished. "No. I'm here to see Herriot. Where is he?"

He pointed out the rear door. "He went over to one of the fields or something. I don't come out here much. I'm just here to take some equipment back to Nairobi for repair."

"And I suppose the broken microscope is not one of them?" Ruth flicked a finger toward the floor.

The man looked down at the mess. Ruth had hoped he would reveal something, but he showed no concern. His strange manner spoke now of disease and misogynistic intent. Despite this, he remained... interesting. Ruth was seldom interested in men who were obviously interested in her.

"It was like that when I got here, ma'am."

Ruth laughed and crossed her arms. "Ma'am? Do I look like a 'ma'am' to you?"

"You'd like to know what you look like to me?"

Ruth laughed to hide her disgust and waved disparagingly to the man. "No."

The man looked at her again, but with interest-free intensity this time. "Well then, I have to get going. When you find Herriot, tell him that I'll get this stuff back to him as quickly as I can... and I'll bring the other stuff he asked for too."

"And when I tell him these things, shall I refer to you as 'that guy' or something else?"

"Jamal. Tell him Jamal will get these things back to him," he said. He had obviously moved on from the naked flirtation back to his current task, checking his cargo once again before trying to roll it out of the back door. He pulled the wagon backwards, but still had a view of Ruth as he backed out. "Are you Herriot's new assistant?" he said.

"No. I'm just visiting. And you? I'm surprised to find another American here who is not a tourist."

"I'm just here for work," Jamal said.

Ruth was confused by the statement. It indicated something within the man that had gone unseen until now. Yes, he was both more and less than he appeared. She hoped to see him again before she left. "Indeed. By the way, you didn't ask me my name." She grinned.

Jamal had the wagon out of the room and was just about to close the door. He stood in the open doorway for a moment and Ruth thought he was giving her another appraisal. It was an expected response.

"No, I didn't," he said, and calmly shut the door.

Ruth stood in stunned silence for a moment before making her way back to the front of the house.

Son of a bitch!

* * *

Jamal had not felt this much joy while sober in many, many years. The hot sun beat down and his pulse beat back. Victorious, he pulled the inert mass of Herriot along the streets of St. Edmund, all the while blowing kisses to random women and waving to men working on the rooftops or cobbling the road.

He decided to leave the box of guns in the house, fearing that if he got too cocky and lingered, he might run into another package hunter and thus ruin his perfect day.

His thoughts ran to the woman from whom he'd just walked away. Her beauty was one thing, but her other qualities had him electrified and eager for a sexual outlet. He could see that her primary strength exuded from her person, not merely her appearance. She had been tempered with something, her soul an alloy of everything he desired. All other women of beauty seemed like the raw and useless ore they were: weak shells devoid of purpose or trust. This woman was ironworks and cotton panties.

Jamal was not new to the seduction of females. He had never been alone when he chose not to be, a simple bout of bar-hopping always yielding a consort for the night. But, when he had tried the usual flirtation and attitude-laden words that always proved effective on this woman, it was like an arrow trying to pierce the armor of a tank. He had learned long ago that while he might entice many women to get naked with him, few would accept or understand his preferences for sexual conduct. She must have seen him for what he was. Not good.

So he took the high road of mock disinterest. It was a reliable code that Jamal lived by when it came to women.

He had almost made it to his truck when something brought his senses back to St. Edmund. In the last cottage on the main road to his left, Jamal saw something magical. Through the open door, a view of a small woman painting on a large canvas drilled into Jamal's mind. He left the wagon in the middle of the street and walked inside.

* * *

Ruth searched the town, but could not find Herriot. She even walked out to the field where wisps of uncollected cotton still fluttered about the plowed red dirt. Each person she encountered shook their head when she pleadingly said, "Herriot?" She decided to go back to the lab and wait for him, hoping he had just gone somewhere she'd not thought to look. She assumed that his skin could not handle the intense sun of Kenya, so perhaps she had missed him during her hunt.

Once back in the lab, Ruth sat on a stool and tried to re-kindle her anger. Regardless of what was happening, she liked the guy and did not feel inclined to unload her frustration on him... not fully. Genetically different or not, he was a man. She wanted to find the other Thrones who had set her upon this quest, however, and unload fully. Herriot must know where they were. She hoped.

As her internal fury cooled, she scanned the lab once more for something to entertain her. The smashed microscope sat where she had first noticed it. Ruth picked it up and placed it back on the table. While handling it, bits of glass and other damaged parts could be heard clattering about inside the device. *Not good*, she thought. Continuing the cleaning process, she picked up several volumes that had also fallen on the floor. She assumed they had been on the same table as the microscope, so she put them there. It made her think.

After surveying the table and its orientation, Ruth knew it had not been overturned then righted. It was bolted to the floor.

Perhaps the microscope and books had been pushed off the table. The fact that some of the books had landed several feet away piqued her curiosity, so she looked around the room for more signs. She also realized that the stuff from the table had been pushed *toward* the entrance of the room. Ruth began to shake as she walked back to the table and looked again at the broken microscope and zoological textbooks.

The soft inhale and exhale of the lioness's breath was now portentous. She wondered how long Herriot was going to keep the animal here before terminating the sedation and beginning rehabilitation. Ruth felt more relaxed now around the sleeping carnivore, but it was eerie to be in the lab without Herriot. She forced herself to walk over to the Queen.

The lioness slept soundly. Ruth reached out to touch the molten-gold fur once more, but remembered Herriot's insistence on sanitation and withdrew her hand. As she did, she noticed a small piece of paper under the lioness's jaw. It looked torn and protruded queerly as if it had been stuffed in haste under the animal. Ruth stepped back to look over the rest of the scene, but found no other pieces of paper or anything else suspicious. There was, however, a fine-tipped marker lying on the floor.

Ruth stood in terror as she looked at it, as though she were looking at a murder weapon instead of a simple writing tool. The cap of the marker was red, so when Ruth pulled the torn piece of paper from under the lioness, the red script struck her with such force she almost fainted. It took her mind a moment to right itself before she could read the single word that was scribbled on paper. It looked more like a splatter of blood than a word, but Ruth had no problem reading the script.

Taken...

She snapped her gaze around to look behind, hurting her neck. Nothing. No one was here. Ruth remembered all that Herriot had told her, his story and what it might imply. Then thoughts of the man named Jamal flooded her. His strange nature and how it had affected her. He was attractive, yet sinister, and Ruth had sensed some danger that immediately fled once he started flirting with her.

What was in the wagon?

Ruth thought for a moment before falling to the floor. She wept. She didn't want to be here. She wanted to go back to Wyoming, back to Campolo, back to grading papers, back to gawking students and old men. The man had abducted Herriot while she stood and watched.

* * *

The woman was under the influence of the Muse and painting steadily. Jamal saw that she was working with some sort of acrylic paint. He surveyed the work-in-progress and was overwhelmed by the image's genius and beauty. Shapes with distinct borders and contrasting colors created a dance of light and dark. The scene on the canvas combined both urban and wild environments, the skyline of Nairobi evident on the right of the piece. The city was dark, with shades of ash and charcoal built in geometric perfection.

The woman had used layers of paint to give the buildings depth, some shallow and some coming out at the viewer. At the base of the structures were black swirling masses that might have represented anything. Jamal thought they were people, but he couldn't say why. Within many of the nebulous shapes was a hint of bright orange and yellow that seemed to shine. *Souls?*

He turned his attention to the left of the painting, the portion that the artist was currently working on. It was almost complete. The jagged peaks of Mount Nairobi towered near the top of the scene, and above it, shafts of white light arrowed down to strike the wheat-colored fields below. The woman was using metallic colors for this part of the piece and the green leaves of the trees and the wheat buds glinted with life. Within the field was a collection of huts and houses that might have represented St. Edmund. Dark forms of people, heads high and bathed in radiance coming from the sky, surrounded the structures.

For a moment Jamal could feel tears well, though he did not comprehend their source. The painting was standard yet innovative, as if this woman had not merely copied other artists, but instead was communing with them, fusing their essences with her own creativity.

He was struck with a sudden and painful clarity of mind. He thought of the last time he had tried to create something. Had he truly died, as Tennyson had said? Was he a different Jamal Battle now, a wraith serving the whims of others and devoid of a real life? His previous life had not been much different, Jamal reasoned, so he had no desire to contemplate what he had left behind. He was free now... so to speak. He was falling to earth at a thousand miles per hour. He would make the most of it before the inevitable impact. Painting was not a necessity.

If the painter had noticed Jamal's entry and observation, she did not acknowledge it. She continued her brushwork, forming concentric circles of lighter paint around the tiny heads of the townsfolk.

He turned to leave, his triumph suddenly dampened by the sight of the beautiful painting. He wanted to know why he felt what he did, wanted to think about it. But the weakness in him died and he walked mechanically, pulling the wagon with him as he left the way he came.

CHAPTER 10

It did not matter that Ruth was an American citizen. It didn't matter that she had just spent half a day on an airplane. It didn't matter that she had witnessed Herriot's abduction. Nor that she was exhausted. She had to file through the purgatory of U.S. Customs like everyone else.

It had been two hours already, and she sat on the hard, tiled floor. The line had stopped moving about an hour ago—something about an emergency and how no customs agents were available, or so rumors indicated as they filtered back through the vast line of people. Ruth placed her luggage on the floor to form an uncomfortable nest. She tried to sit back against the suitcase, but her body rebelled. Nothing short of a presidential suite, complete with a fluffy bed and hot tub, could possibly cure her condition.

Her travels had also been plagued by male attention. For almost five hours she had deflected the advances of a man who sat next to her on the plane. He was a writer and claimed to be "the next Hemingway." Ruth knew that any artist wanting to be "the next" anything was a hack. Besides, his voice was annoying and he had absolutely no attractive features. Ruth had feigned sleep for most of the flight as a defense.

And while she sat there, eyes closed and trying to tune out the trite conversations around her, she had thought of

Herriot, Kenya, Jata, and *The Book of Beasts and Green Things*. She had *met* the man-who-is-not-a-man, doing exactly what the text claimed. Visiting an environment that had inspired a faith-based text was intoxicating, and despite feelings of sorrow that came with the situation, Ruth was motivated to dig deeper.

Tears came when she thought of Herriot. He had not been what many would consider charismatic, but something about the Throne beckoned to the love and purity in Ruth's heart. It was not difficult to see that this quality had called out to the people of St. Edmund as well.

They had answered. Herriot's origin narrative was horrific, and the emotional scars she sensed in him served as adequate testimony. Now his fate had caught up with him and she had been useless in that moment. Her years of learning and social avoidance had made her impotent—a foul champion for Herriot in his time of need.

"Hey, are you okay? We'll get through here eventually, ma'am. I promise you," a voice said from above. Ruth realized she had been crying and quickly wiped her eyes and nose with a naked hand. She dared not look up, but feared not giving a reply, so she composed herself and looked up innocently. The speaker was an older gentleman in a gray suit and narrow-brimmed hat. "I'm fine, thank you. Just have stuff on my mind. The waiting doesn't help."

"I understand, Miss. That I do," he said, giving her one last glance before turning around.

She scrubbed her face once more and stood up. The chatter of the people in line increased at that moment, followed by several weak cheers. Ruth stepped to one side to gain a view of the Customs counter. There were four clerks now, each taking people from the line. Ruth gathered her luggage and joined the line's movement, at a snail's pace, but a pace nonetheless.

Her thoughts now focused on getting home and resting. One last fight was needed to get there, but at least she was back in America. No more language barriers or random acts of violence. Finally, it was her turn at the counter. She stepped up.

Everything was routine. The agents checked her luggage and documentation. Once complete, they politely bade her to walk on. So Ruth was shocked when two men calmly walked up behind her, held her elbows, and directed her toward an open door in the side of the walkway that led to the main concourse.

"Please come with us, Miss Long," one of the men said, but Ruth knew she was coming with them regardless of her thoughts on the matter. The door was held open by a fourth agent, a woman, and the whole affair was calm and serene.

"What's the matter?" Ruth hissed once they were inside the corridor.

"Please, ma'am, no questions. The U.S. Customs Office has been instructed to detain you temporarily for an FBI investigation. We are bringing you to an interview room. You will not be harmed, so just try to relax," the woman said.

Ruth was not relaxed. She wanted to press the woman further, but knew it was pointless. The men escorting her kept hold of her arms, but were gentle and did not force her in any way.

They walked through a maze of passageways and offices. At last they reached their destination: a small room with a table and several chairs. Ruth swooned. The men helped her into a chair at the end of the table. They departed while the woman stayed. "Can I get you a glass of water?" she asked.

Ruth shook her head. A minute later a man entered the room and sat down across from her. He was broad and had sharp features. He wore a black shirt that had the letters "FBI" embroidered above the left breast.

"Miss Long, my name is Harold Gruber. You are being detained because we have reason to believe you are linked to a terrorist organization that has recently threatened national security. Do you understand what I am telling you?"

"No, I don't understand." She had no energy to stop the tears.

Gruber's face grew stern and he leaned forward. "You are familiar with the organization called the 'Thrones'?"

"Organization?"

"Yes."

Ruth wanted to climb under the table and sob. "I'm a Professor of Religion at Campolo University, sir. I don't know anything about terrorists."

"Why were you in Kenya?"

"Vacation."

Gruber tapped the table with a finger. "This is the wrong way to start, Miss Long. Because you are a licensed Professor, or at least aspiring to be, you know that what the FESB knows, the FBI knows. We are aware that you spoke privately with someone impersonating Walter Hendricks, Assistant Director of the FESB."

Ruth had already assumed this had started with the events at the Garner House, but something else must have happened. If she had been suspected of anything before, she would never have been allowed out of the country. "Is this about that meeting?"

"Not entirely, but let's start with just that. We know that you've never talked to Hendricks before, so the reason for the impostor is still a mystery. What did he give you in the security case?"

They know everything. "Just a copy of my thesis... my old thesis, that is."

Gruber's expression became almost murderous. Ruth was afraid. He spoke into the air. "Bob, bring it in."

Ruth wondered what *it* was. A man entered and handed Gruber a familiar document. He placed it on the table and spun it around so Ruth could read the heading: *The Book of Beasts and Green Things.*

"Don't lie to us, Ruth," Gruber said.

A slow burn of anger grew in her. "I didn't do anything. This guy pretending to be Hendricks gave me that document. It's just a story about religious experience in a town in Kenya. I'm a religion professor, so you figure it out. I was curious about the situation surrounding its genesis, so I went to St. Edmund in Kenya to check it out. That's it!" Ruth screamed, the slow burn becoming fury.

"That's it?"

Senses returned, shaken loose by her outburst. It felt good. The clarity also focused the memory of Jamal. Perhaps this was related? "You guys took Herriot, didn't you?" Ruth gripped the edge of the table tightly.

"Who's Herriot?"

Ruth felt dread at the thought of giving Herriot away, but was soothed instantly by another thought. Gruber had not read the document. "You figure it out. Now, I want a lawyer before you continue to harass me with your ignorance." She snapped her fingers.

Gruber sat back suddenly, apparently trying to stifle his anger. Ruth was not consoled. She didn't care what the FBI thought: no one jumped on her like this without good reason. As Gruber collected himself, Ruth did the same, channeling her personality into something both submissive and dangerous.

"I'm sorry, Mr. Gruber." She leaned forward. "It's just that one moment I am awaiting the end of a very long and arduous journey, and the next I am being picked apart and my integrity is being questioned. Excuse my lack of focus.

Perhaps we can start again? I will tell you everything I know to the best of my knowledge, if you let me."

Gruber's face softened, but Ruth saw more shock than forgiveness. Taking a breath, he made a face she assumed was a smile. "Yes, Miss Long, I agree. My advice is that you tell us the truth in its entirety, please, because we know much more about this than you might believe. Now, I'd like to know why the impostor Hendricks gave you a copy of this... uh, *The Book of Beasts and Green Things.*"

Ruth smiled back at Gruber as warmly as she could. She pushed herself back from the table to kick her right leg up over her left, doing it more slowly and demonstratively than necessary. She continued by stretching her back with a churning motion that started at her hips and moved up to her shoulders. She had no interest in seducing Gruber, so she made the movements subtle and smooth to show resignation as opposed to sexual intent. The desired effect was simply that of gaining rapport. Besides, the woman who had escorted her to the room was still there, standing against the wall. Ruth shot her a smile as well. "Mr. Gruber, let me lay out my position on this matter as clearly as possible. I have been working on my thesis for many months now. Several weeks ago, I was informed that my previously approved thesis topic was now unapproved, that something in the subject matter had piqued the ire of the FESB. At the request of my advisor and the Dean at Harvard Divinity School, I went back to Boston to meet with them and clear this up."

Gruber interrupted. "And you instead went to the Garner House in Providence to meet with Hendricks."

"No. I went there to meet with Dr. Faulkner, my advisor and mentor. He'd sent a driver for me. Once there, however, I was introduced to someone I thought was Hendricks. He gave me the Book because he thought I'd enjoy it for fun, or so he said."

"But you did more than read it." Gruber sat forward and raised a hand to interrupt. "You went to Kenya."

"Yes."

"And you met a member of the Throne organization?"

"I met a man named Herriot."

"Herriot?"

"If you had read the document sitting in front of me, you would not find the name so bewildering." Gruber growled.

"Sorry." Ruth smiled and waved a hand. "I'm running on fumes here. Anyway, Herriot was... different."

How much do they really know?

"Different?" Gruber cupped a hand and drew it towards himself, as if to magically extract Ruth's thoughts.

"He was not from Kenya."

"That's it?" Gruber sniffed and his nostrils flared. "I know they're from the U.S., Ruth. That is not the question."

Ruth pushed, but felt confident that Gruber was blind in many things. "Herriot was a vet, too. That's different, right?" Ruth gave her best idiot's grin.

Gruber sighed. "So, was he healing animals and whatnot in this, St. Edmund?" He looked at the wall while rubbing the side of his face.

"I guess." Ruth shrugged.

Gruber's expression grew sharp once again, but without anger. His consternation persisted for a moment and he said nothing. Finally, he cocked his head to the side as if he'd concluded some inner problem and spoke. "What do you *know* about the Thrones?"

Since meeting Herriot, conflict had raged within Ruth's mind. One side was given to the facts, facts which indicated that the Thrones were nefarious: they twisted and manipulated people, systems, and public sentiment. This interrogation added strength to that assumption.

On the other side, however, was Ruth's instinct and intuition. She had been manipulated, yes, but St. Edmund
was more than a charlatan's trick or merely a figment of
imagination. Herriot was also very real. She trusted that
his outward attitude was genuine. Besides, he had told her
his story. She was a total stranger, so why tell her that he
was essentially on the run? There was something in the
mystery of Herriot's origin and intention that added
strength to that side of the argument too. "Initially, I
thought they were just a legend."

"Legend?"

Ruth realized she was leading Gruber to Herriot's true
nature. She changed direction. "Just some religious or political nuts, you know? But Herriot was just working in St.
Edmund, like a normal guy."

"Did you talk to him?"

Ruth's change in tone had not gone unnoticed, apparently. Gruber was suspicious. "Yes. He told me that he had
fled America and made a home in St. Edmund. He was
one of twelve, he said."

Gruber looked interested, his body showing hunger for
what Ruth was spouting. He also looked surprised. He
didn't know about Herriot's abnormal biology. She was
failing to keep Gruber away from that fact.

"Twelve? We've only identified five. That's good information, even if it's only hearsay. We have an interest in
them based on several recent events. Before that, they were
merely a NSA-monitored name-group, the term 'Thrones'
being under surveillance. We monitor hundreds of thousands of word-groups a day for such a thing."

"Really?"

Gruber merely grunted.

"So you're looking for the guy who impersonated Hendricks?" Ruth said, seeing that she was losing his trust.
"That was the 'event' that kicked this all off?"

Gruber scowled at the question. He was hesitating, which answered Ruth's question. "No," he said. "To be more precise, I should say 'partially.' We think we know who pretended to be Hendricks, but we hope to apprehend all of the members of this organization. Something else has happened that makes the Thrones a greater threat than we initially calculated."

"May I ask what?"

"Under normal circumstances, I would not tell you this. But the truth is that you need to know who these people are and what they are about. The FBI is convinced that you have only been used as a hapless propaganda device—or are being groomed to be one.

"We think that the Thrones manipulated you into going to Kenya so you would meet one of them, who would, of course, seem innocent. This would inspire you to write about them, publish *The Book of Beasts and Green Things* or any of a host of scenarios that would legitimize the Thrones in the mind of the public. In the meantime, they would be free to carry out their attacks and operations, and when we intervene, they hope to galvanize the primarily Christian populace into defending them and demonizing the government."

Ruth vibrated with each word, Gruber's assessment nearly identical to her worst fears. But everything was halted by his last statement. "Attacks?"

Gruber looked at her with intensity, as if he thought she already knew. "Let me get to the real 'event' in question. Two days ago, a military facility in Idaho Springs, Idaho, was infiltrated."

Ruth's internal conflict bubbled up as one side, the side of reason and fact, surged forward with this new information. "How many people got killed?"

"Killed?" Gruber shook his head. "No one was killed, Miss Long. A death toll was not the target. We are still unsure, but we think that it was a botched theft. The facility is a training ground for Army and Air Force LarcSuit troopers—mechanized infantry and combat control specialists. They also test out new prototypes there. Under normal circumstances, it would be suicide to attack such a base."

"The Thrones attacked?" Ruth could not imagine Herriot attacking anything, though he had said many of his "brothers" had different inclinations, different skills.

"Someone broke into the base. Apparently, they waited for a response involving LarcSuited troopers. *Waited.*"

"The Thrones attacked *suited* soldiers?"

"No, *he* attacked suited soldiers. There was only one invader… without a suit of his own."

"They killed him, right?" Ruth laughed in disbelief. "Mr. Gruber, I'm not much into military tech, but even I know how dangerous those things are."

"No, they did not kill him. Instead, he single-handedly incapacitated three troopers before escaping."

Ruth said nothing. LarcSuits were one-person armies.

Gruber mirrored her thoughts. "Our LarcSuit supremacy, combined with our automated military units, comprises the major tactical advantage of the U.S. military over other nations in conventional combat. LarcSuit security is a matter of national security. Remember the Henley bank jobs fifteen years ago?"

"I do." Ruth had been in high school.

"We can't lose any of this technology, not even parts."

"But this assailant, he didn't take anything, right?"

"That's correct. He was, however, able to subdue a LarcSuit using physical means. He had no devices, weapons or equipment of any kind."

Ruth was at a loss. She understood the implications of what Gruber told her, but it was unexpected. She was waiting to hear a story of bloodshed and terrorism, not this. "What does this have to do with the Thrones?"

"We received a missive the next day. It was an *apology* for the incident. The message was signed by a person named Musashi. Based on the intelligence, we have linked this man to the Thrones organization."

"Is he a Throne?"

"I'm not sure I understand. 'Thrones' is an organization, not an identifier. They might call themselves that, but they are a U.S.-based terrorist organization with unknown motivations. The five we know of have chosen aliases: this Musashi, for instance, is actually named Valentine Carter. He's 25 years old and was born in Indiana. They're people, Miss Long. Ordinary people. Because the ones we know about are all the same age, we think they have connections going back to childhood. Also, they are all runaways. None of the families knows of their whereabouts."

Ruth sat in a fog of disbelief and confusion. Gruber's testimony was compelling, but there was more going on than the activities of a simple terrorist or criminal group. She needed time to think, time to digest the myriad facts, implications, and simple assumptions that were assailing her from all angles. The interrogation had become an interview, both for her and for Gruber. She hoped the change in attitude would lead to her preferred outcome: that they let her go.

I'm just the hapless propagandist who didn't know any better. Ruth stared at the wall. It must have troubled Gruber, because Ruth's mind snapped back to the room at the sharp sound of Gruber's palm striking the table.

"Thinking of something we should know about, Ruth?"

She scolded herself for being so careless. The man was a nipple, but Ruth's continued freedom lay in giving him the satisfaction of being in control and *thinking* he possessed all of the information available. "Please excuse me, Mr. Gruber," she said, flashing him a warm grin. "I was just thinking of how stupid I've been and how these guys have taken complete advantage of me. I'm a teacher, Mr. Gruber, and my place is in the classroom. The Thrones tricked me. I can't thank you enough for taking the time to inform me of what they are up to... and how they've been setting me up."

Gruber sat back and looked stunned. "Ah, of course, Miss Long. This situation was well beyond your understanding. I had to make sure you weren't involved in a criminal way, but after what we've talked about and the various pieces of evidence collected, I don't think you knew what was going on."

Ruth's body tightened. "Evidence collected?"

"Yes," he said, becoming flustered. "Your house in Cheyenne was searched. Nothing was damaged, but the team was thorough when searching for documents, weapons and recording devices. The good news for you is that we found nothing incriminating."

Ruth should have expected this. She had not. Her house was sacrosanct. She seldom invited anyone over, and if she did, they stayed for only an hour or two. Now her sanctum had been invaded and desecrated.

"We found a copy of the Book, of course, and confiscated it. No record of the document could be found on the Internet, so we think we are safe for now. Anyway, all of the items in your house were returned to their original location and nothing was broken. I have one more thing to ask you, Miss Long."

"Yes?" Ruth said, knowing what was coming.

"Do you have any other copies of the Book? We want to preclude its circulation."

"Why?"

"Are you serious? These guys can try to dupe others with the same trick if need be. Given, they can write anything they want, but we'd like to stem the effects of this attempt."

"You think the Thrones wrote the book?"

"Who else would write it?"

"Somebody in St. Edmund." Ruth was again betraying her vow to tell Gruber little.

"I doubt it. Ruth, they want you to think there is some 'New Order' in the making. We've stopped dozens of such groups. Now, answer the question: do you have any more copies of the Book?"

Screw you, jerk. "No."

"I hope that is true, Miss Long, for the sake of innocent people both in the U.S. and abroad. If you are lying, we'll find out. I don't believe you have bad intent, Ruth, but you're a professor, and by nature an idealist. Excuse my prejudice."

"And excuse me for saying that you're an idiot. I don't have any other copies of the document since you've raped my homestead. I've excused you enough. May I go?"

Gruber huffed as his hands became fists. Ruth uncrossed her legs, straightened her back and folded her hands on the table. She looked at Gruber, forcing a look of finality into her expression.

He glanced at the other woman along the wall and nodded. She walked to the door and knocked. It opened. "You're free to go, Miss Long. Thank you for your cooperation." Gruber was speaking through nearly closed teeth. "Don't bother looking over your shoulder. We'll be watching you from every angle imaginable."

Ruth got up and walked to the door without looking at him. She and her escorts emerged through the hidden doorway. Her luggage was waiting for her. "Have a nice day," the woman said, and the agents went back through the door. Ruth heard a loud *click* as the door closed and she was alone in the concourse junction. Looking at her watch, she sighed. The interview had eaten up all of her layover time and the flight to Denver left in only 45 minutes. By the time she walked to the gate, they would be boarding.

Thank God for small miracles.

CHAPTER 11

As the doors slid open, Jamal entered the lobby while pulling the wagon borrowed from St. Edmund. Without adequate knowledge of anesthesia, he had opted for tight restraints, a gag and violent reassurances to keep Herriot quiet. No one seemed to care as he traveled the New York streets.

Jamal put his nose in the air as he strode across the black marble floor, conforming to his idea of what New York businessmen did on an average day. As expected, he was intercepted halfway by security. A mob of gray-and-brown uniformed guards enveloped Jamal without exuding alarm or tension—an obvious requirement of their brief not to spook the business-people and tourists.

"Stop." A rotund man stepped in front of Jamal, a hand raised.

Jamal stopped. He towered above most of the men. The impulse to fight them for sport surged through him, but he realized that a conflict would certainly land him in jail. There would be no point. He grinned at the guards, trying to look innocent.

"What's in the… cart, or whatever the hell it is?" The fat man pointed at the wagon.

Jamal had not rehearsed his delivery of Herriot. He knew the likelihood of walking straight into the Andros

Tower and making a "drop-off" was ridiculous. Strangely, however, this was the course of action he had decided upon when he rolled Herriot's prone body down the gangplank of the cargo hydrofoil they had taken from Crete.

Once in New York, he had hailed a taxi and told the driver to take him straight to the heart of Tennyson Holdings. Now, standing in the lobby and surrounded by security, Jamal took a moment to survey the luxurious court for the first time.

The rocks lining the labyrinthine waterways feeding the falls and swirling garden pools appeared to be volcanic pumice and glimmering obsidian. The whole effect was that of a dark Eden, one that might have existed deep underground, undisturbed by the hopes and machinations of common men.

The garden had been transported, captured by the minds of men and taken to satisfy the tastes of one. Jamal's mind jumped to an image of the macabre chamber in the penthouse. The lobby garden was similar. Careful observation revealed serpent and vaguely reptilian sculptures hidden within the garden foliage, items that the casual observer would not notice.

"Sir, I am going to ask you one last time. Why are you here and what's in the cart?"

Jamal looked down at the guard and saw his hand was resting on a holstered pain-ray. Another guard had stepped back and was speaking into the air, obviously communicating with the centralized security in the tower.

"Oh, sorry. This place is something, isn't it?" Jamal looked up and swept a hand around. "Can't really think straight in here, can ya?"

"Well, you'd better think straight before the police get here. If you have reason to be here, we'll call 'em off. If not, you picked the wrong building to step into, asshole." The fat man tilted his head towards the ground, transforming his double-chin into a triple-chin.

Jamal laughed in spasms. It did not have a positive effect. The guards began to close in. "You guys are sharp and I admire that." Jamal put his arms up. "I have a package for some executives upstairs, if you know what I mean."

The fat guard shook his head. "Deliveries come in at the receiving entrance in the back, pal. I think you better sit tight over here for a minute. Guys?" He gestured to the others to move in. They converged and two grabbed Jamal by the arms. Upon making contact, they immediately let go and the entire group of guards jumped back and away from Jamal, several screaming in pain. The shock was fleeting, as Jamal had planned, and he knew that if he toyed with the men any longer the situation would go beyond his control. Most had taken out their side-arms.

The fat guard had stumbled while trying to move quickly, falling to one knee and now panting. "He's got a pain-suit!" he said through gasps. "Take him out!"

Jamal mustered his voice of command. "All of you holster your weapons and step back. You, reach into my shirt pocket. It contains my clearance. I said, put your weapons away or you'll be looking for another job... or worse."

The men remained in a stunned circle around Jamal. People within the lobby were leaving quickly, the scuffle now an incident. Several of the men brandished pistols and others, pain-rays.

The pain-suit Jamal wore was a microfiber skin worn under normal clothing and it contained millions of nano-emitters that flooded the surrounding space when activated, either willfully by Jamal, or through external triggers. It emitted focused electromagnetic pulses that penetrated the skin just far enough to stimulate nerve endings, inducing an optimal amount of pain.

Pain-suits were illegal. But, Jamal had found, that did not stop them from being sold. And Jamal had money.

The guard leader stepped forward, but did not holster his weapon. He plunged his meaty hand into the narrow pocket of Jamal's black button-down shirt, pulling the surrounding fabric to the point of tearing.

"Careful, Bub. Don't set the suit off again." Jamal widened his eyes.

The man's face contorted in rage and fear, but he took a breath and searched through the pocket gingerly. He pulled out a thin billfold and ID-carrier. The guard glanced at the ID and quickly waved it in front of a black plate hanging from his belt. Jamal assumed that each of the men had com-implants in their ears. As they waited, Jamal watched the fat guard's eyes widen as he, no doubt, was listening to the information now being vocalized in his implant, the information fed from Jamal's scanned ID.

The man looked as if he wanted to run. He put his gun back on the magnetic holster that protruded grotesquely from the side of his ample belly. His gaze darted from guard to guard, most of them still holding their weapons at the ready.

"Put away your weapons. Put 'em down! Everyone go back to your stations. Now," he said in a harsh whisper. "Please excuse our response, Sec-Commander Battle. We didn't know who you were."

"It's no problem, Captain...?" Jamal had not been sure if his latest fake ID would show his "promotion," but it must have.

"Peterson, sir. Captain Peterson."

"I'm going to proceed to the elevator and continue having a good day. Is that all right with you?" Jamal looked ahead, ignoring the man.

"Yes... Yes, of course, sir. Have a good day. Do you need any help with your, ah, package?"

"No, thank you. Just tell security I'm going to the top with something important, so I won't be accosted again, all right?"

"Yes, sir." The fat man scrambled off to reinstate order in the lobby. Several heavily armed security troopers had emerged from a hidden location and lay in wait behind a canopy created by hanging foliage and falling water. They wore a shade of charcoal that blended well with the blasted volcanic rocks. Jamal marveled at the integration of beauty and security, but was also confused as to why a location such as this must be ready for a fire-fight.

He walked behind the reception station in the center of the lobby and proceeded to the elevator bank in the back. The center car stood open and invited Jamal, as if waiting specifically for him. It was the only car that accessed the penthouse, as well. He wheeled Herriot inside.

If Herriot was trying to move or make noise, Jamal could not detect it. He had trussed the mutant in a way that precluded any tapping or shaking short of full-body motion. Jamal had also constructed a canopy over Herriot's body, using some cardboard. The tarp lay over this, so that if Herriot moved inside, it could not be seen through a suspicious shift of the tarp.

Jamal got the wagon inside the elevator car and took out his security cube. Before he could insert it into the receptacle and begin the upward journey, a starched businessman clad in Wall Street's finest livery tried to monkey past the wagon Jamal had intentionally placed to impede entry. Jamal grabbed the handle of the wagon and swung it to intercept the man, slamming it into his hip and forcing him to step back.

"What the fuck are you doing? Do you know who I am?" the well-manicured, petite man said.

"Try to get in here again, and you'll find out who the fuck I am, piss-ant."

The man stood in shock, his face painted with years of hatred and triviality. He said nothing as the doors shut slowly. Jamal made a fist and slammed it into the side of the wagon. "I hope there are more freaks like you to round up, buddy. I should have made this career move a long time ago."

The wagon's contents made no response.

Jamal had not prepared for his arrival at the penthouse. As the doors opened, the nerves of his face exploded into an inferno of pain. The animal within drew Jamal's body into a ball, his large form collapsing to the floor behind the cart. If his rational mind were still working, he might have made out the chattering of the form within the wagon, the convulsions of the bound occupant making the wagon vibrate.

The pain ceased for Jamal momentarily as he hid behind the cart, but quickly the agony resumed, now over his entire body. His bowels emptied and his nails rent deep gouges in his shaved scalp, primal fury replaced by self-destructive impulse. Jamal convulsed violently as he screamed, kicking the walls of the elevator and the wheels of the cart.

Then the pain stopped.

Jamal was half-creature, half human, and he felt the idea of psyche trying to invade his being, but he resisted. Slowly, he remembered his name, his life, and that he was in a small space called an elevator car. Blood ran from the ripped flesh on his head and face, his spasms having been so pronounced that the nearby wall and floor beneath were splattered with red.

He tried to get up, but his legs would not listen to his plea. He pulled himself up using the wagon, its burden now inert. As he climbed to his feet, he looked over the wagon and out through the open elevator door. A single man stood there. He held a small box in his hands and, as

Jamal's mind was resurrected, he knew that the item was
the source of what had made the elevator car a part of Hell
for several seconds. But before any more thoughts could
form, Jamal passed out. He awoke to find himself sitting
on the floor beside the elevator, his back propped against
the wall. Instinct told him that not much time had passed,
but he was not certain. His senses flooded back in gentle
waves. First, his vision became focused and coherent, followed by his motor functions, as he held his hands up and
surveyed the dried blood on his hands and under his fin-
gernails. Faint voices and other sounds crept into his
ears—trickling water and the hum of the tower.

Jamal felt a stinging pain around his head. Reaching to
his scalp, he gently felt around to survey the ruined flesh,
the self-inflicted wounds of flayed skin.

Anger surged into his limbs, forcing him to his feet. He
looked around for the wagon, but it was gone. He stepped
away from the wall in the direction of Tennyson's office.

"Now, now, Jamal. All in good time," a voice said from
behind.

Jamal wheeled around and saw Arthur Reston stepping
around the corner. He wore black: a suit, shirt and tie. His
movements appeared languorous, but Jamal knew better.
Reston stopped several feet away from Jamal. The distance
implied guilt and Jamal vibrated with fury.

"You attacked me," Jamal growled and stepped toward
the man.

"Easy." Reston stepped back. "My apologies, Battle, but
you could have picked a more clandestine method of delivering your cargo. When security told me someone was
coming up named 'Battle,' I couldn't just assume it was
you. Perhaps you and your mission were compromised.
Perhaps certain things had transpired that allowed for a
security breach into the penthouse by unauthorized personnel. You are, Battle, unauthorized. Understand?"

"Fuck you," Jamal spat.

"In any case, your identity has been verified and your presence here temporarily tolerated. You can thank Mr. Tennyson for that grace. Is he not gracious?"

Jamal gazed into the man's eyes. Whatever Jamal had thought, whatever Jamal had done, he was not like Reston. He was not given to this strange sycophancy or the pervading murk of something dark and sinister, a force that Jamal could not shake while inside this tower.

"The package. Am I not great?" Jamal said in mockery, as he extended his arms out and up.

"You have delivered a package, yes." Reston smiled queerly, his plastic features flexing.

Jamal grew fearful for an instant. "It is what you wanted, right?"

"What I wanted? I want nothing."

"Goddamnit, you know what I mean, Reston."

"Yes, it is what Mr. Keenan Tennyson hoped for. I must say, Battle, I did not expect you to succeed."

"You could have told me that the package was a person—it would've helped."

"Ah, but the package is not a person, is it? *It* is property, now recovered and safe within the Tennyson Empire and causing no further trouble."

"I was told there are twelve packages. Are they all like this one?"

"Patience, Jamal. We will send you on your way before you know it. Mr. Tennyson would like to congratulate you. Others returned without such a marvelous payload, and they regrettably will not be working for the company."

"How many?" He didn't care.

"Just think, you could have been one of them—but you're not. Are you not comforted?"

Jamal said nothing. Reston was unsettling in general, but the more he spoke, the more his strangeness penetrated Jamal's resolve. Jamal was serving Tennyson, and in turn, Reston. He was, indeed, working for the company.

"What do I do now?" Jamal said, ignoring the question. Reston stepped to the side and pointed. Jamal turned and beheld the ancient and alien chamber again. The black statue stood ominously, holding less interest for Jamal this time. The twisted figures on the frescos, inhuman slayers of nameless origin, continued their endless war against the marauding serpents. On this visit, the effect was menacing and held dangerous portents for Jamal, far from the wonder and creativity the images had inspired before.

But Reston was not pointing to the chamber itself. Instead, he gestured to the hallway on Jamal's right. The rough-hewn cobbles ended several feet down the passage and gave way to thin carpet, the kind found in offices. "Several meters down on the left you will find a washroom. Clean yourself up as best you can. Mr. Tennyson abhors individuals who don't care about their appearance." Reston smirked.

"So I see." Jamal smirked back, fluttering his fingers at Reston. If the gesture angered the man, as he had hoped, he could not see it. Reston simply grinned.

Jamal walked through the center chamber, carefully stepping over the black stone canals inlaid on the floor and went into the bathroom. His wounds were not serious, though they remained symbolic of his submission to Reston's assault.

After washing his hands and gently blotting the crusted blood surrounding the rents on his scalp, he surveyed the rest of his clothes. Some blood had gotten on his shirt and pants, but because they were black and dark gray respectively, he almost didn't notice.

He looked in the mirror once more before leaving. His eyes glittered like gems in the overhead light. The gouges lent him a ghoulish appearance.

Outside, he found Reston waiting. They walked back through the center chamber and on to Tennyson's office. Reston looked over Jamal and then down at his own clothing, smoothing the fabric over his arms and chest. "I do not have to reiterate protocol terms, do I, Battle?" Reston made eye contact.

"No," Jamal said, startled by the gravity in his own voice.

"Good." Reston said and opened the door.

Jamal entered behind him and stood in the same spot that he had during his initial meeting with the most important man in the world. The lack of adornment and security once again struck him. The wall of perfect glass held a different view than before, the sky above azure, and adorned with soft white clouds. A sprawling mass of earthen brown and gray stretched below, the colors a collective of thousands of buildings, vehicles and people stirring in the structured chaos that was New York City. From this altitude, Jamal thought he could see the curvature of the planet. A god among insects, or an insect among gods—either thought was easy to embrace while looking through the transparent wall.

Finally, he focused on the quiet man seated at the desk. He now recognized the material used to construct Tennyson's colossal desk because he had seen some special lumber awaiting transport at the dock in Africa. It was zebrawood. The grains alternated light and dark.

But today Keenan Tennyson did not match his desk. A suit of light cream made him glow within the dark room. Jamal thought it did not match the man's personality, but what did he know about this man, really? Again, Tennyson was typing away on the large com-pad and ignoring the presence of visitors. Jamal considered walking out just to make a statement. Thinking of Reston's pain-ray and his willingness to use it, he found patience.

Tennyson looked up. His face was unreadable, but there was something... warm around the edges of his eyes. Aside from that, the man continued to exude perfection—a living blade with an eternally sharp edge.

"Mr. Battle."

"Yes, sir," Jamal said, the presence and attention of the man automatically drawing his respect and discipline.

"You are alive and well, it seems, though your methods have left you... tattered in places, have they not?"

Reston chuckled.

"Have I delivered the appropriate property to you?" Jamal said.

"You are standing before me." Tennyson's gaze pierced Jamal. "Does that answer your question, Mr. Battle?"

"Yes." Jamal did not appreciate the man's theatricality, no matter how minimalist.

"Then I am sure you are overflowing with trite and worthless questions that you know not to trifle me with. But, as you have done your service, I am inclined to reward you with several important pieces of information."

True, Jamal hoped for more information regarding future packages, given that "Herriot in Kenya" had been barely enough to go on. His luck had provided success. He could not rely on luck in the future.

"You will be more sparing in your use of Tennyson Holdings' resources. I've been informed of gross losses of funds and stolen equipment that is costly, both to replace and to pay for in regard to government fines."

Jamal was not affected. Money was no object to this man.

"Future packages will arrive like the first—alive and well," Tennyson continued. "That is paramount. A dead package will be repaid with... recompense equal to the lifeless package itself. Understood?"

"Yes, sir," Jamal said, without sarcasm.

"Additionally, you will use all of your resources to recover the property quickly. You operated within a window of time for the first package that no longer exists. You may have competition in the future that is not aligned to our interests; therefore, time is of the essence."

Jamal almost asked "*what?*" but refrained.

"With that in mind, you will exercise any means necessary to impede, misdirect, or terminate these conflicting organizations. Understood?"

"What about internal competition?" Jamal thought fondly of the accountant who had tried to stab him.

"There is no internal competition. Your success has allowed me to discontinue the use of other vendors, so to speak.

"Now, since we are in concordance, you may leave."

Jamal realized he was smiling, and that Tennyson had realized he was smiling too.

Though fearful of the consequences of even mild insurrection, he risked it anyway in light of his new position as the only vendor. "Sir, I cannot. I need more information."

Reston tensed. Tennyson held the same cosmic serenity, a patience light-years in depth and immeasurable in energy. "They are my property, Jamal. That is all you need to know. Giving you any more details than that is both unnecessary and impractical. We will give you information needed to retrieve them, and nothing more. You may leave." Tennyson resumed his typing as if he were alone.

The last command held something more than Tennyson's usual speech. Malice and mathematics: these were the only words Jamal could conjure to explain what he felt in the man's tone. He did as he was told and walked out of the office.

Reston followed and shut the door. "A dangerous gamble, Jamal."

"I don't have anything to lose."

"You have plenty to lose. This new life of yours, for example. If you succeed, then you will be free to retire into that pit of decadence that you value. We know your heart. Insects and parasites fight to live for as long as possible. You are not complicated."

Jamal began walking towards the elevator. His fantasies regarding Reston had become muted. The man had punched him, pain-rayed him and, in general, been very rude. Despite all of this, Jamal wanted to leave without any attempt at revenge. "Where am I going next?"

Reston was a step behind. They stopped outside the elevator and Jamal turned around, expecting an answer.

"Don't come here again. If you do, I will be waiting with something more lethal than a pain-ray."

"I'll do what I have to." Jamal snapped his fingers in Reston's face. The man did not flinch.

"And you *have* to never come up here again. In the lobby is a box. It contains information on several new targets for you to secure at random. It also outlines how you should 'drop off' your deliveries from now on. Your success has earned you some convenience. Don't abuse it. Oh, and the information is on temporary film. It will disintegrate within one minute of being exposed to air. Make sure you record or memorize the information."

"Don't want this getting back to Tennyson Holdings, do we?"

"You don't exist, Jamal. The fact that I call you 'Jamal' is a farce in itself. Your name has been stricken from every record, including forged ones. No one will link you with us because there will be no 'you.'"

"Anything else?"

"Go easy on the cash. We can still find other vendors if you prove too costly. Oh, and some of the other packages might be more formidable quarry, resisting you with skillsets of greater tactical value than veterinary science."

The doors of the elevator opened. Jamal glanced inside briefly and stepped in, still facing Reston. "Where in the lobby is my box?

"Did I say lobby? I don't know where it is," Reston finished as the doors closed.

Jamal exhaled, angry now with the intrigue. Looking down he saw a small brown box on the floor in the corner. He reached down and picked it up.

"I need to get a new job."

CHAPTER 12

The remainder of the trip was the antithesis of its beginning. Ruth slept on the flight home. No one spoke to her and she awoke as the other passengers began to disembark. She shook off the grogginess as best she could and made her way through the concourse to the baggage claim. She got her bags and walked out to the street, hoping to find a free taxi cab.

It was around 7 p.m. and the sun was perched majestically above the Rockies to the west. The descending orange orb cast purple shadows that swallowed the mountains and plains below. Ruth took a moment to watch, thinking of distant Mount Kenya. The image brought sadness but also hope. Ruth scanned the vacant ochre fields that stretched to the west, looking for lions. There were no lions.

There were no taxi cabs either, so Ruth turned to go back into the small lobby and call for one.

"Looking for a taxi, ma'am?" The voice was rich and familiar in a way.

Ruth turned around. Before her stood a man wearing a long black coat and wide-brimmed hat. He was smiling. He was also very tall.

This close to him, Ruth could see his skin looked dark and too perfect. His features looked familiar, and if she had had any doubt as to *what* stood before her, the close examination dispelled those doubts.

She had slept on the flight, but she still felt wasted and delusional. She also felt numb to any adversity that might come her way. "I don't see a car?"

The man seemed startled for a moment as he wheeled around.

"Oh." He pointed behind Ruth. "My car is right over there. The black one."

Ruth looked and saw a black sedan. "It doesn't look like a taxi." She reached into her purse, hoping to find her compad in time.

"No, I guess it doesn't. Nevertheless, I will drive you home in it if you would like."

Ruth stepped back. She resisted the urge to run. Too many things were happening too quickly. She had no time to think about what to do, and she was not even to be allowed to get home and sleep in her own bed. "I think I'll just go inside and get a real cab, thank you," she said and turned to leave. She was ready to ignore the strange visitor, pretend he never existed, and pretend she did not know he was a Throne.

"Ruth! Wait. I—"

Ruth spun around and stalked up to him, forcing the Throne back. "You! You are ruining my life and I don't know why! I'm not going to write anything for you, I'm not doing anything for you. In fact, I'm going inside to call the cops and get my new FBI buddies involved so they can catch you!" But she continued to stand there, breathing in gasps, holding back tears.

He held his hands out in a gesture of peace.

Ruth was ready for war. "Why are you doing this to me?"

"Herriot is in trouble," the Throne said, quivering.

His tone stopped Ruth dead. She was not sure who was more distressed: herself or the Throne. His face was very much like Herriot's, but different in subtle ways. The nose was larger and the cheeks wider. But the man's eyes struck Ruth the most. Within, she saw fear wrapped in leadership. It was not a human look.

"From whom? The FBI doesn't know who he is. I don't know who he is! I don't know who you are!"

"My name is Massoud and the FBI is not who we are afraid of."

Ruth tried to calm down. Herriot had mentioned Massoud during their first, and only, conversation. "Then who are you afraid of?" She put a hand out in resignation.

"You, Ruth. We fear you, we fear innocent people and we fear those who know of us. Trust me, if we cared only for survival, we would not be talking to you."

"Then why did one of you give me *The Book of Beasts and Green Things?*"

"We can talk of that later. I am here because I needed to talk to you before our adversaries had you convinced of both innocently fallacious and intentionally deceitful information."

"And I should trust a group of mutants who want to make a statement by messing with the government and fooling with society?" Ruth instantly wished she could take the comment back. Massoud's body language and expression showed that it had cut him deeply.

"I am sorry that you think that, Ruth. I'd just like the chance to give you our side of the story before you make any more decisions. Things have become convoluted, as I knew they would. Now things are moving forward and we have no more time for subtlety."

"And what decisions do I need to make?"

"I can't define such things for you, Ruth, nor pretend to, given the circumstances. Allow me the pleasure of escorting you home. By the time we get there, I promise you will understand the times much better and know what decisions lie ahead."

The setting sun was descending to a blinding angle and Ruth tried to stay in Massoud's shadow so she could see his face. She was exhausted and this exchange had taken the last portion of coherent thought. Rolling her suitcase forward, she waited for Massoud to get the hint and take it from her.

He did. Together they walked to the car, packed Ruth's things, and drove off into the shadow of the indigo mountains.

"First, Ruth, I'd like to apologize for all of the trouble you've been through. I can't tell you that the future will be any easier either, so if it's any consolation, I admire the attitude you've held throughout this ordeal." Massoud drove slowly and deliberately, concentrating on the road.

"You just met me." She looked over at the Throne. "You don't know what I think and what I'm going to do."

Massoud's eyebrows rose and he sighed. "True. I don't know what you're thinking, but I have kept abreast of your progress. Most would not be in the position you are in now."

"And just what is my position? My life is being destroyed one day at a time."

"You may feel that way, Ruth, but it is not so. Through all of the intrigue and misinterpretation, both by you, and by the government and our enemies, you remain free. You can go back to your old life or continue forward. It's a blessing you must understand before you make any more choices."

"Blessing? From whom?"

"God, of course."

"Which God?"

"The God of Abraham, the God of Isaac, and His son, Jesus Christ."

Ruth put her hands over her face and laughed. The government would be right in terminating the Thrones before they came to grips with their inhumanity. Insurrection was inevitable. "There's no God for you. If you're not human, and a defect with Pure-Life created you and your kind, then Humanity is your God. How the hell can you claim to be Christian?"

Massoud kept his eyes on the road. Ruth was in the passenger's seat, her legs drawn up and clasped in her arms. She felt caught in the clash of science, religion, and politics. Though she was concerned for people in general, ethical quandaries did not interest her. If computers could convince people that they were human, just as the first Turing Test passed by a computer had the previous year, then how the hell could there really be a God?

"There was a time when Africans were informed of their inequality due to Old Testament justification," Massoud said.

Ruth did not flinch. "The descendants of Ham. What's your point?"

Massoud blinked and glanced at Ruth, his eyes returning to the road before they really left. "Even after the coming of Christ, after His work and words were chronicled, parts of mankind chose to justify evil by an irrelevant and fallacious connection with previous text."

New versus Old Testament? "So religious text is nothing—it only serves the whims and rhetorical aims of people in power. I've felt that for a long time."

"Yet you went to Africa, searched out a town that may not have existed, to find a man-who-is-not-a-man because of a simple text, a chronicle. Why?"

Ruth's point was countered and beaten. "You've derailed this conversation," she said, without anger.

"I have not." Massoud chuckled.

That *did* anger Ruth. "I asked you why you're a Christian."

"And in response I posit this: Why is anyone Christian?"

Ruth let her legs drop and leaned forward. "For the same reason that anyone is of any religion. You're born into that tradition and you follow it to varying degrees, depending on how it affects your desires and psyche. Zealots buy in for the security and solidarity, using their 'faith' to justify atrocities and injustice, as with the megachurches several decades ago. Hey, the Catholic Church just won't go away, as another example. Mystical Christians don't want to rule out or ostracize the growing Eastern fashions in their communities, so they just fuse them together. It worked for Judaism and Greek philosophy in Christianity, so it will work with any religion or ideology."

Massoud grinned and shook his head almost imperceptibly. "And then we come to the impasse that all people of faith and un-faith come to when they disagree," he said. "Anything I tell you can be reasoned into absurdity."

Ruth slapped the dashboard. "That's the coward's way out!" She realized she was out of line when the car swerved, but she did not apologize. Current events had startled her; let Massoud be a little startled too. The Throne breathed harder and sniffed before speaking again. "And that's the atheist's need for blood, the belief that God doesn't exist because His followers can't win an argument against the intellectually superior, just as those who are weak cannot win a fight with those who are physically superior."

Ruth had hoped the ride and subsequent conversation would clear some things up, not muddle them. Now she was having a freshman-style religious conversation with Massoud.

"Ruth, I've drawn this out and I don't need to," he continued. "Simply put, we believe that our existence is not a mistake. We believe we are meant to be here."

They were nearing Ruth's house. She didn't bother to ask how Massoud knew the way. "What do you want from me? You've been staging all of this, guiding me and betting on the results."

Massoud turned abruptly towards Ruth. He held her gaze for a second. "Not at all, Ruth. You and I are talking because of your choices and yours alone. Given, my brother Twain thought it prudent to give you a piece of someone's writing. My apologies for his ruse. Much of what he does is inappropriate, I admit, but everything we do is for a purpose, even if we act autonomously at times." He sighed. "Actually, most times. Anyway, Twain was motivated by our changing situation. No one could have predicted that you would go to Africa to investigate. In truth, Twain told me that he hoped you would just write about us and get the public interested. We were all pleased that you did much more than that."

Ruth had no more energy or patience. "We're almost to my house, Massoud, so answer my questions. What do you want from me?"

"We do not want anything of you. The only reason I felt the need to visit you personally is this: our time will come to an end soon. We don't know how and we don't know when, but we do know that the world-that-is will not suffer our presence much longer. In the short time we have, we've done our best to resurrect the truth in the minds and hearts of human beings. We know we are not human, but we are not forsaken either. Remember that when we are gone. That is all that we ask of you, Ruth. Do not forget. Do not forget what you saw in St. Edmund."

"And what did I see in St. Edmund?"

"The world as it can be."

Massoud pulled over in front of Ruth's house, not using the driveway. She looked out at her once-safe abode and felt an ominous tension surrounding the place. From here, the house looked the way it had always looked. But Ruth knew that it had been violated. She had been violated. Part of her wanted to go somewhere else, to tell Massoud to keep driving.

"It was very nice to meet you, Ruth," Massoud said. "I would help you with your bags, but it is safer if I don't. And safer for you."

Ruth felt sick in her stomach when he spoke. It reinforced the feeling of degradation created by the FBI's presence in her house and the probability that spying devices were watching her arrival. Ruth remained still. "What's happened to Herriot? Who took him?"

Massoud looked at her and out toward the house. He then scanned his mirrors. "I don't know."

"I met a man in Herriot's lab who I am certain kidnapped Herriot."

The Throne's eyes narrowed. "It seems that you know more than I, Ruth. What else?"

"His name is Jamal. He struck me as confused, yet ruthless. I was scared of him... so scared that I didn't realize he probably had Herriot sedated and in a cart, ready to smuggle him out of the town. I can't be sure, but..." Ruth started to cry. She covered her face with her hands. Massoud's hand came to rest on her shoulder. The gesture was warm and comforting in a way that was beyond Ruth's understanding. His touch was like that of a parent to a child, but also a lover to a lover, or maybe a friend to a friend. She felt imbued with strength from that touch and quickly composed herself.

He withdrew his hand once her tears began to dry. Several deep breaths helped to restore her calm. "You can't take responsibility for Herriot's abduction, Ruth. You can't stop them from coming for us."

"Why don't you hide? You can fit in just like you are now."

"Ruth, it would be a lie. We know why we are here and the lines are drawn. Our voices will sing until they are silenced. We can't stop that, and neither can you."

"I just don't understand." She got out of the car.

"I think you do, Ruth." Massoud's voice drifted through the still air and Ruth turned back, bending over to see his face. "With all that you've studied, you know what transpires in a community in regard to power, faith, and belief. You know better than most what these situations embody and how they end." Massoud glanced nervously around. "Ruth, our time together is over. You have to go into your house and find the truth for yourself. I have my own course to run. Though I am sure that the authorities have taken the Book from you, I also do not doubt your ability to safeguard that chronicle of Herriot's work. Am I mistaken?"

Ruth looked down and grinned, a bit embarrassed at being predictable, but also proud of herself. "You are not."

"I'm glad to hear it. Now go, Ruth. And Godspeed on whatever path you follow."

She was not sure if the Throne had actually answered her questions. She felt safe in Massoud's company, but knew it to be a weak and childish indulgence if she tried to prolong the encounter. She retrieved her bags from the trunk and shut it. Once she was clear, Massoud drove off, red lights fading into the west until the car climbed a low rise and disappeared over the hillcrest.

Glad to find the front door locked, Ruth found her keys and opened the door. She had feared that once the authorities had opened her life for inspection, it would never be sealed again. Her privacy and integrity would be irrevocably ruptured and her life would ooze out into the night, never to be collected.

She inspected each room in succession. Everything was in order, but she felt no comfort. She had to reclaim the house for herself. With that in mind, she began to wash all of her clothes, starting with those in the drawers the agents had unquestionably rifled through. Her underwear went into the washer first, something about her need for sanctity being embodied by those hidden garments that lay closest to her body.

While she scrubbed dishes, wiped down table tops with cleaner and folded loads of clothing while washing others, the pain and fatigue of the journey took hold. It struck when she walked from her washroom to the living room, her arms laden with clean laundry. The bundle slipped from her failing embrace and she sat down in the red chair of her ancestors. She leaned back and instantly slept.

She dreamed of twilight over black rivers and airplane seats.

CHAPTER 13

The dream melded with morning light, a haze of imagination fading slowly with yellow rays of reality. While the dreamscape might have been lit by the radiance seeping through shut eyelids, Ruth remained firmly wrapped in the surreal environment of her sleeping mind.

Human-like forms lay everywhere, some that looked like the Thrones and others that looked like golems of metal, clay and rock.

Ruth was besieged by howling and chatting things, their voices horrid and pain-filled. Some were deformed; some were injured. A man-who-is-not-a-man writhed at her feet, grotesque flipper appendages in place of proper arms and legs. He looked up and Ruth looked down. Though he was ruined flesh, though he was something that should not be, she looked into his face and beheld eyes of blue flame. Eyes that belonged neither to an animal nor to a mistake.

She cried out for them to leave her, but they pressed on. The sky above began to change from a noxious brown color to an inferno of flame and swirling shadows. She could make out marauding shapes, large things moving quickly towards her and the hideous crowd.

Ruth spun around frantically, searching for a place to hide. She was atop a small hill of dirt and the land that stretched beyond was barren and flat. But suddenly a silver tree appeared — a glimmering growth that stood at the bottom of the hill in front of her. It had not been before, but she began to make her way to the tree in hopes of finding a place to hide before the descending horrors could find her.

They were closer now and she could make out wings and hulking masses the color of gunmetal, surrounded by clouds of smaller forms like specks. She had expected monsters, but what approached were massive machines made of sleek angles and queerly angled fins. The specks were floating men, men in black uniforms who carried guns, swords, and boxes.

Ruth was filled with terror beyond anything she had felt before and, with primal force, made for the silver tree. The twisted forms writhed with renewed fury, pleading with her not to leave, asking for her forgiveness, asking for life. They limped or pulled themselves after her. Ruth was impeded by the throng of fingerless hands and crawling bodies. They prevented her from getting off the hill and she cried out to them. She begged them to let her go. They begged her to stay.

She was within a prison of sweating, deformed bodies and carcasses. From the sky above, the dark armada began their assault, blinding streaks of flame and booming gunfire raining down all around her. They killed the mutant beggars one by one. The dying creatures screamed for mercy, screamed for forgiveness.

But there was none. Ruth dropped to her knees and threw her arms around herself, hoping to avoid the flailing hell of exploding bodies and burning flesh.

In a moment, the concussions ceased and Ruth was enveloped in silence. She uncovered her face and peered out. The disfigured mob was gone and only a putrid, murky substance remained. It ran down the hill like oil and Ruth was afraid to walk through it. She looked again to find her silver salvation, the one place she could escape to.

But the tree was burning.

Ruth screamed, yelling out for the tree to stop burning. Already the leaves were beginning to melt off buckling limbs and form molten pools on the dark soil beneath. The flames seemed to be only *around* the tree, not actually on it, as if the inferno was slowly crushing inward on the holy foliage and squeezing out life. Lines of char and oxidation ran throughout the majestic trunk, and Ruth wept as the giant died slowly, more for the loss of its beauty than the loss of her shelter.

"Are you all right, ma'am?" The aerial marauders had landed and Ruth was now surrounded by black-suited men. One of them was speaking. "Wake up, ma'am. Wake up! Bob, I think we may need the medic. She's unresponsive."

Ruth tried to find the source of the voice. The trooper closest to her turned and gave her a view of his face within the helmet. Ruth screamed and fell backward. Instead of skin, the soldier had scales of dark ruby. His eyes glowed softly, yellow orbs split by vertical pupils.

The world changed.

The light intensified and suddenly Ruth was on the floor in a familiar room. Her living room. Sleep fled and she regained a sense of time. A man knelt beside her.

Ruth thrashed in an attempt to get away.

Hands shot from every direction to find purchase on her hands, arms, and legs. One of the hands brushed her left breast on the way to her waist. It maddened Ruth beyond reason and she lashed out with all her strength, trying to punch, kick, or bite anything she could.

"Ma'am. Ma'am! Calm down. You're safe. We're not going to hurt you," the same voice from her dream said.

She continued to fight. Something was wrong and she should fight it. Eventually the assailants immobilized her arms and legs. She hissed at them, spitting at faces and continuing to squirm. "Get out of my house!" she shrieked. The dream voice said, "Ruth Long, we are with the FBI. We thought you were in danger so we came by to make sure you were safe."

"Maybe she's high on something?" another voice, this one female, said.

Ruth stopped resisting and looked up, taking a moment to find the woman who had spoken. "Maybe you should get out of my house, you fucking bitch!" Ruth felt spittle escape her lips and roll down her chin.

The woman's eyes widened before her entire visage transformed to a hatred matching Ruth's. The woman opened her mouth as if to say something, but remained silent when the first speaker raised a hand.

"Miss Long, just calm down." The man turned back to Ruth. He was young—younger than Ruth. "On the count of three, we're going to let you go. After that, I will explain everything as long as you are calm. Don't try to run and don't try to attack us—either physically or verbally. Okay?" Young or not, the man's voice betrayed a feeling that he and his company were completely innocent and Ruth was a criminal.

She was calming by the second, at least from her earlier animal terror. But, stoked by the lead agent's hubris, the simmering anger at more FBI intrusion was ramping up. Ruth tried to holster it, hoping for the right time to use it. Somehow. "Okay." She let her body go limp. "You guys scared me. I was having bad dreams. You can let me go now. I'm all right."

The man looked at her, revealing that his primary concern was whether he was appropriately using the power granted to him by the FBI, not whether Ruth was happy or calm. Finally, he smiled at her angelically and said, "Okay. One, two, three…" All of the hands let her go.

Ruth sat up slowly and looked around. Nothing in the room had been disturbed. She took a breath and tried to soften her features to avoid any further bodily contact with the agents, consciously raising her eyebrows and faking a smile. "Why are you here? What happened?" Ruth said, as amicably as she could.

The first speaker, the man she had heard in her dreams, motioned for the others to back off. Some went out the front door, leaving only three agents in the room with her. One of them helped her up. She sat quickly in her antique throne.

The agents assumed they could take the same liberty and sat down on Ruth's couch. Stifling the impulse to tell them they had not been invited to sit, she sighed and took a moment to assess the situation. She must have either fallen or crawled out of the chair the night before, finding the carpeted floor soft enough for hours of sleep. This assumption was verified when Ruth saw a small dark spot on the carpet, right where her drooling mouth must have been.

She calmed herself, quelling another urge to send the agents out the front door by force. She knew that would not happen.

"Ruth, as you probably know, we have surveillance in the house. When we saw you on the ground for that long, we feared you were either dead or under the influence of some drug, poison, or psychotic condition. We had to make sure you were all right."

Ruth responded before getting her weapons in check. "So, what was it then? You decided to get some action from an unresponsive, unconscious woman? And you brought friends too. How nice," she fired, the boiling fury engulfing the agents.

They froze. The lead agent leaned back apprehensively, and looked down at the ground. Ruth didn't give a damn if she made these people feel uncomfortable.

"Miss Long, I think you should calm down. We would not have come if we didn't fear the worst," he said.

"The worst? The worst is taking a long trip from Africa and getting jerked around by people like you at Customs, then having you show up in my house. That's the worst!"

"Ma'am..."

"No! The *worst* is knowing everything in my house has been finger-fucked by the FBI!"

Ruth reached over to a side table and struck a pile of books, sending the tomes skidding across the floor.

"Miss Long." The agent sat forward, eyebrows furrowed. "We are still Federal Agents. You need to calm down. We can arrest you for being uncooperative and combative."

"Uncooperative! Oh, I'm cooperative. I was gonna say that having cameras in my house watching my every move was the *worst*, but if I can get this kind of service just by lying down, well that's gotta be the *best*, right?" Ruth sat back in the chair seductively and ran a hand down her thigh.

She kept this up for another few seconds, watching the men. They looked startled, and she made eye contact with them, each in succession. She saw the inklings of disappointment rise to be quickly replaced with forced professional bearing.

The lead agent stood up. "Ma'am, we are concerned for your safety: that's our job. Try to be proper, please?" He raised a palm toward Ruth. She locked eyes with him and saw resignation.

He looked down at the other agents, snapping his fingers. They stood up and waited.

"Can't a girl get a little sleep after a long trip? Even if she's a little dirty and likes to sleep on the floor?" Ruth asked seriously, but didn't wait for a response. "If you gentlemen don't mind, I'd like to take a shower and begin my day." She stretched out her arms and flexed her back in a feline manner, her chest forced out and her head nodding to one side.

The lead agent had steeled himself against her attacks, so when she began to stretch, he looked away and ushered the other two towards the front door. "Sorry for the inconvenience, Miss Long. Do take care," he said in a strained voice.

As the door opened and they began to file out, Ruth yelled after them. "If you hurry back to your command station or whatever it is, you might catch some of my shower on camera!"

The lead agent slammed the door.

Ruth sat back and exhaled, closing her eyes as she whispered, "Using sex to drive men *out* of a house. That's a first."

The water temperature was just below scalding. Ruth let the rushing water surround and cascade over her body, hoping it would take the tension of the last few days, especially the last hour, from her weary muscles and down the drain.

But the dark dream echoed in her mind, bringing with it apprehension stronger than the effects of the shower. Ruth could not remember when she had last had such a vivid dream. The images were unsettling, but the agents were infuriating. Both together had driven her to hysteria.

She bent her head down and let the water work to relax the muscles of her aching neck.

The world had become an amalgam of over-the-counter destinies and blameless holocausts. Every passing day granted the human race more abilities. Banished diseases, faster transportation, cheaper stuff, all of it running and running until the whole planet seemed a putrid blur, full of decadence and madness seething below a chrome exterior routinely polished by the affluent and the ignorant.

Her thoughts drifted to the Thrones. Their existence had not affected Ruth in any significant way. It was just another "Oh, they've finally figured out how to..." event. Japan was the first nation to become "android-driven," their robotic servants numbering one to every three Japanese citizens. In America, immortality was within reach for the super-rich. Worldwide, house-pets and even children were "engineered" for optimal traits. The existence of the Thrones was pedestrian in contrast, right?

No. Ruth could not convince herself otherwise.

She wanted to forget about the dream, but the implications were obvious even as the images faded from memory. So Ruth forced her conscious to focus on the second of the morning's shocks: the marauding FBI agents. There was little to ponder regarding the legal home invasion. She was under guard, under surveillance, and under suspicion. The mood of the FBI agent this morning was proof.

They had been polite enough, but Ruth was no longer open to negotiation. Her sexuality was a violent tool when the mood struck her to use it. That was seldom, and usually followed by weeks of shame. Currently, she felt no shame.

Some men use fists, some women use breasts. In a world of violence, what power did she have?

The wrong kind of power. The situation reminded her starkly of a volume of biblical literature. In Judges, a seductive heroine named Yael drew an enemy king into her tent, fed him, waited for him to sleep, then drove a tent pole through his head. Why couldn't Ruth think like Yael and fight on? She tried to believe she could.

But she could not. There was no reason to incite the FBI with her lewd behavior, no reason to push against a force that might decide her fate.

If she waited, the whole mess would go away and she could get back to the classroom. She could go back now, if she wanted. Her month of leave was only half over and Dean Rupert would be tickled if she cut it off now and went back.

No.

The FBI expected her to *cooperate*. Massoud expected her to—do something. Rupert expected her to come back and do her job or quit, whatever it took to restore order to the Ivory Tower.

But what do I expect?

Her mind raced to Jata, an instant friend, whom Ruth could trust with her life. Of greater importance was the idea that St. Edmund was filled with such people, every one of them ready to live, love, and forgive.

Herriot was in St. Edmund, helping those people live better lives with his skills and talents. He wasn't a talker; he wasn't some charismatic charlatan driving those people into a vile cult. He just *was*, and it was beautiful. He was gone now, perhaps dead.

Suddenly, the flames of consequence and passion spun round her soul, giving it no recourse and no alternative to what now drove her forward. Ruth turned off the water. Her flesh was red and pulsing with heat.

She toweled off the last vestiges of pain and uncertainty and went to her room to pack the suitcase she had unpacked the night before.

CHAPTER 14

It was cold.

Jamal hated the cold. When he was ten, the temperature in January never got above ten degrees Fahrenheit. He had worried that the fields would freeze and nothing would ever grow again.

Jamal's father had responded with a discussion on permafrost, but in an effort to allay Jamal's fears rather than incite them. Permafrost was in Siberia and Scandinavia and Canada, not Minnesota, he had explained. Jamal thought that there must be frozen places in the Boundary Waters that never thawed. He thought his father was lying.

This place was different. Winter had welcomed the Alps into its loving embrace. Jamal struggled to find passage along the mountain ridge, hoping to get to the next hamlet before nightfall. As the late sun set, Jamal made out sparse settlements scattered like embers across the snow, their windows glowing orange.

Of course, Jamal should not have been out hiking on the mountains in winter. Many a mountaineer had died while trying to traverse the icy rocks and shifting drifts, avalanche and hypothermia claiming the boldest of adventurers, or so a tourist pamphlet he had found in Zermatt had said.

But he was not here for adventure. He was not here to ski, or for *hefeweizen*. He was not here to try out the local wines made in Martigny. He was on a business trip.

Jamal had a very important meeting with someone staying in the village of Geranach, not far from where he now was. The other party was not aware of this meeting, but Jamal would be kind enough to let him know when he saw him. If and when Jamal found him, the meeting would be concluded as soon as possible.

From the information Jamal had, the Throne named Henry had been in the area since Wednesday. Today was Friday. This was unprecedented, given that Henry seemed to wander with no direction or destination, staying in any one location for only a day or two. Jamal had been following him for two weeks now, never catching up enough to initiate that important business meeting.

And because of this delay, he now regretted going after this particular package first — given that he had his choice of targets from an extensive list. Henry was proving to be a challenge.

Jamal had initially considered this erratic movement to be flight. After several interviews with those who had seen or spoken with Henry, however, Jamal reconsidered. The mutant, or "Throne," as Jamal had learned they were called, was a simple wanderer who moved quickly once on the road. The vast network of trains and buses made tracking him in this part of Europe arduous, but Jamal's odds of finding Henry improved as they moved farther into the less connected French and Swiss Alps. The whole affair had begun in Morocco.

Geranach was 20 kilometers directly to the east of Martigny, high in the Alps and accessible by only one road. That road meandered to the south before twisting around a mountain to reach the town. The total distance by road was 30 kilometers. Jamal decided on a more direct route.

It had been a simple matter to "commandeer" a snow-mobile. That had taken him up and over a pass to the east, but the terrain grew rocky, and eventually impassable by any vehicle. He ditched the ride and hoped to clear the last mile quickly on foot. He had clung to the side of the mountain as he crept along a narrow embankment, the distance to the forest below not certain, but certainly fatal for a falling hiker.

Darkness fell quickly, and the trail widened. In the valley beyond, he could see the lights of Geranach.

The village reminded Jamal of a smoldering campfire that a careless camper had left burning. The hidden chalets and their lamps would light up the forest floor and engulf the world in flame and ash. As he approached, the unattended embers became an alpine town, sitting peacefully in the grip of full winter. Most buildings had snowmobiles parked outside, and Jamal watched a truck motor through the center of the town and down into the deeper part of the valley.

A festively lit building stood out. The house was a traditional chalet of four stories that towered over the rest, with two ornate lamp posts flanking the front entrance. Every town, village, and collection of tents had a bar, Jamal mused. Geranach was no different.

He trotted the rest of the way down a perilous slope and emerged from the veil of pines wreathing the village. He could see the large building and, as he watched, a host of loud and stumbling patrons emerged. Jamal had little doubt that the building was what he hoped for, but as he read the heavy sign that swung on pivots in front of the large porch, even that little doubt dissolved. The sign read "Geranach Taverne."

Jamal looked around for anything tactically useful. The streets were clear and the whole town felt as if it were dead or dying.

He hated winter, hated snow. Jamal longed for heat and conflict and whenever he found himself encased in the vapid, useless peace that came from low temperatures, it made him cagey. He was hungry as well.

He decided against stealth in favor of appetite-induced hedonism when he entered the tavern. He was a hungry and thirsty traveler. That was true enough. The air within was hot and rich with meaty aromas. The interior was a great hall with long tables stretching back to the rear. Those tables were full. Jamal's joints ached from the journey, but more from the chill of the mountains than physical exertion.

A cacophony of voices rained down on Jamal, as they did in any place filled with the drunk and drinking. French and German were the primary languages he could make out, but the dark walnut bar and decorated paneling that clad the walls echoed a chaotic din of lust, anger, and sorrow: a language that Jamal understood.

He drew many glances when he entered. Most of the patrons looked at him as though they had never seen a black man before and they probably hadn't. On previous nights while in the mountains, Jamal had allowed rudeness to grow into all-out brawls, inciting the old and young with taunts while they gawked. He decided against that indulgence this evening, given that he was officially working.

He sat down at the bar and ordered soup and a drink, in English. The Friday-night festivities resumed and if anyone was speaking ill of him, he couldn't understand it. The food came and Jamal consumed it ravenously, draining the dark beer quickly. He needed sustenance, but he wanted to get out of the place as quickly as he could. For all he knew, Henry had already moved on, so he looked around without appearing to look around. It was a foolish hope to think the Throne might be sitting in the hall, just going about his business. It was foolish to think that he could just walk in and find the Throne.

Jamal was a fool.

His first indication that Henry was there was a group of quiet men who sat at the far end of one vast table, almost smothering a central speaker whom Jamal could not hear at this distance. He saw the man was black as well, which struck Jamal cold. He picked up his beer and casually made his way over to the gathering. The black man, whom Jamal now saw had strange features, was telling a tale of some sort, in French, Jamal guessed.

The man spoke in flowing tones, gesticulating for dramatic emphasis during the more intense parts of his tale. Jamal sat as close as he could, planting himself behind several drunk indigenes. The audience laughed at regular intervals, several junctures in the story warranting a sharp "Non!" from a random crowd member, followed by the storyteller's strong response of "Oui! Oui!"

Jamal recognized familiar features in the storyteller's face. A large brow and deep-set eyes captured the attention of the audience, though his skin was a rich shade of brown. Reston's list had included several facts that might aid Jamal. Many he had worked out by himself, such as the fact that Thrones could easily blend into the masses by way of heavy clothing and makeup. But if you knew what to look for, they might as well have a blinding arrow above their heads pointing down.

Jamal could see that arrow and there was little doubt that his quarry had been found. In the towns he had passed through, the people told him Henry was a kind of minstrel, traveling from place to place and telling tales for the simple joy of it.

It made no sense, but nothing in this whole situation did. The only coherent thought in Jamal's mind was the promise of freedom and revenge, once he had successfully rounded up this gang of freaks. He reasoned that the Thrones were either a mistake or an enhancement made possible by Tennyson, but the thought stopped there. Jamal did not know and didn't want to know.

The tale ended and the patrons erupted in sounds of victory and elation. Satisfaction rolled over the congregation. It seeped into Jamal as well, though he had no idea why he should feel satisfied.

But he did. It was as if the men at the table were celebrating for him, for the end of this journey and to his future success. The laughing and ruddy-faced crowd was handing Henry over like a burnt offering and Jamal sat in silence as the men jabbered.

Jamal eventually moved away. Several patrons remained at the table, but they had broken into private groups and conversed among themselves. Henry sat back and sipped from a glass. He looked up for a moment at Jamal and tipped his glass in acknowledgment. Jamal nearly laughed at the perfection of the moment. He raised his own glass in response and got up to move closer.

"Great story, pal, but I'm afraid it was lost on me," Jamal said in English as he sat down.

"That's sad to hear," Henry said in a hearty tone.

"You can tell it to me on the trip back." Jamal was still sore about Herriot's ruse with the blue liquid and had no intention of getting sidetracked this time.

Henry smiled warmly and tipped his glass once more. "Ah, the ending to every tale is often a story in itself. It will be so for me, but will it be so for you?"

This was not the response he sought. Jamal tensed and reached into his jacket. He carried a pistol, an immobilizer and a pain-ray. He held off on making a selection. Henry must have been waiting for him. Jamal might be in a trap, the jaws of which were closing as he thought. He glanced around, expecting to find an attacker or surprise that Henry had staged. But the raucous atmosphere of the tavern rolled on; Jamal saw nothing except drunks and flowing beer.

"No, nothing for you to worry about." Henry raised his hands, palms up, before returning them to his glass.

"You know who I am?" said Jamal.

"Of course not, but I'm sure of your purpose for being here," Henry said. "You probably know who I am, but in any case, my name is Henry. Nice to meet you."

The Throne stretched out his hand to shake, but Jamal leaned back instead. Henry seemed serious. Jamal scanned his face for tension, but found only a relaxed and nonchalant freak. He wore a long, dark brown jacket. Apparently, no one had wondered why Henry still wore it, though the tavern was sweltering. He also wore a knit cap, pulled down low to cover his ears.

They looked different, but only as much as people with Down Syndrome look different. Jamal was sure he'd be able to spot a Throne anywhere. Also, Henry had an aura much like Herriot's. He seemed jovial and expressive at rest, despite an apparent lack of expressive ability in his mutant face.

"I'm Jamal." Jamal's resolve was tested by this simple yet disarming display of fortitude from Henry. "You know why I'm here?"

"I probably know why you're here better than you do." Henry chuckled.

Jamal believed that. He didn't want to know why he was here beyond the simple plan. Get the Thrones; get his life back... or *a* life. Go for revenge and then go deep. It was the finest plot he could hope for. Henry was clever, though, and Jamal actually feared what the Throne might have for a defense.

"Do you have a room here?"

"Yes." Henry was calm.

"Let's go there and talk privately, eh?" Jamal put his hands on the table as if to push down and get up.

"Oh, it's too late to try and force me into your net, my vile spider. The truth is that I would not hurt you even if I was allowed, but you are as bold as you are arrogant. If you want me, then get me."

Jamal cursed. The bar was too full for his usual destruction, but he had no other choice. He pulled the pain-ray from his belt and held it under the table.

Henry took the cue and looked down at the weapon. "And what do you think that is going to do?" he said, with eyebrows raised.

"What it's made to do." Jamal almost fired the weapon on impulse.

"And that is?"

"To motivate people."

"And what would I be motivated to do?"

"Move," Jamal growled.

Henry sat back and laughed, his body convulsing in fits as great gasps of air fueled his booming voice. "Move?" He leaned forward suddenly, looking Jamal in the eye. "But I am moved, oh dark assassin who sits at my table, wishing for shadow, vying for silence, seeking my soul without paying a dime."

Henry was yelling, almost singing with fury. Jamal looked around and saw several patrons direct their attention to the table. "Shut up," he hissed.

"That is one of the many gifts that I do not possess, my dear Jamal. But I do have several others that are called for right now." He started to clap. His hands beat harder with each strike, increasing in strength and quickening in rhythm. The other patrons began to whoop and call out, hoping for a song or other such entertainment. They began to clap along.

"What are you doing?" Jamal slapped his empty hand on the table, matching the grand beat of the tavern. He had no choice.

"You come to my table and offer pain. I, instead, offer eons of wisdom." Henry stood and looked around the room, which now offered commitment from every face and every joyous voice. He began to sing:

> The voice of Time, that loathsome wretch,
> Carves cold with wind and stream
> But forever slays the fall of Man,
> And Adam finds the seam.
> He fights and toils to get them out,
> With ax, and flame, and might
> And suffers this turn, his lives are spent,
> 'til Time kindly ends his fight
> So bright, young man of pain and death,
> His trysts are deep but dead
> And Eve stands by to find a cause,
> But Adam's blood shan't be fed.

Whether the crowd understood Henry's words was irrelevant, for they cheered and beat varied drinking vessels on tables with abandon. Jamal sat back and watched, Henry now towering above him while working the tavern into frenzy. The Throne indeed had a defensive device. Jamal dare not interfere with such entertainment.

With that understood, Jamal sat and watched. Henry's song was beautiful. His voice bellowed with dark and deep notes, finding a vocal floor that not many men were gifted with. It spoke to Jamal, despite the circumstances. To join point to point with a line—a verbal shade here and pause of silence there—the poem was crafted with the same care that one might employ while building a clock or a monument. *Or a painting.* The thought penetrated before

Jamal was able to lock away that part of his mind. He counted to ten and felt his eyes dry and his body slow to a dead calm. Slowly, reflexively, a familiar defensive energy rose from the depths and his body began to hum with an opposing vibration. Henry's beautiful song had awakened it from dormancy. It surged upward and out into Jamal's being, filling him with hate.

He calmly holstered his weapon, got up from the table and made his way through the surging crowd of patrons, now on their feet and pressing in to get closer to Henry's table. Once through the wall of seething bodies, Jamal continued through the front door and out into the street.

It was beginning to snow. The flakes were caught by mountain winds and blew steadily through the town. He walked out into the middle of the street, illuminated by the tavern's high street lights. He looked around and found a suitable host for his plan. A small truck was parked on the street next to the tavern. Jamal jogged up to the back of the vehicle and reached into his coat. He had several hidden pockets filled with useful items, things he thought he might need. Geranach required the contents of several pockets. From one of them, he pulled a small black cube — about two inches on each side — and dropped it into the bed of the truck.

The night was crisp and Jamal felt the beginnings of enjoyment. What exactly he was beginning to enjoy was a mystery. He thought that perhaps the snow-covered town, with layers of pines beyond and a glowing slate canopy above, was the source of this growing warmth. No, he was just excited about what he was going to do.

Henry liked to sing. Jamal could make music too.

Snatching two more black cubes from his secret pockets, he ran to either side of the Geranach Taverne and tossed the cubes back a short distance, each of them landing where he estimated the middle of the tavern hall to be.

He glanced around. The street was empty and most of the houses were dark now, so he was sure that no one saw him run across the street and crouch against the corner of a house. Jamal now had a clear view of the tavern on the other side of the street. "Boom."

He pressed a button on the fourth black cube that he held in his hand.

The truck erupted in a flash of white heat, followed by billowing black smoke. Countless windows broke, shattered by reverberating concussions bouncing off the mountainside and down into the valley. Pieces of blasted asphalt and twisted metal fell in every direction, damaging nearby houses.

Jamal leaned back against the side of the house as a truck door flew by and landed several feet away. Once most of the debris had landed, he moved back to his original position to get a view. It would take most people a few seconds to get up and investigate, so he paused for a moment and then pressed a second button on the cube.

Pillars of flame and chunks of snowy earth blasted up vertically on either side of the tavern, the entire structure vibrating visibly from the twin explosions that held it in a concussive resonance. Glass and bits of wood rained down from each story. Jamal wasn't sure if those blasts would take the building down or not. He hoped they wouldn't, but he had abandoned caution in the wake of anger when he planted them. As he watched, the tavern began to settle.

The front doors opened and the Geranach Taverne vomited a mass of screaming drunkards and tavern staff, many of them holding their ears in pain and stomping over fallen fellows. Jamal enjoyed the turmoil. He wanted to enjoy it.

No — he enjoyed it. These people were in the way. Henry's pride was the harmful force here. He had tried to use these people as a defense. Their pain was his fault. Jamal

clung to these thoughts. Casting emotion aside, he watched the havoc unfold and waited.

After nearly a minute, most of those who could walk
had come out of the tavern and were running in all directions, putting distance between themselves and the anon-
ymous assault. Finally, a heavily garbed tall man emerged
from the open door and staggered out onto the street. He
held a hand to one ear, but instead of running, he frantically scanned the town, seemingly assessing the hurt
townsfolk while searching for something else.

Jamal was the something else and he knew it. He calmly
got up from his hiding place and walked out to the street.

Henry saw him immediately. His body was tense and
his legs bent some, as if he would run or attack. But he did
neither. As Jamal approached, his frame relaxed, but a look
of pure horror remained fixed on his non-human face.
"What are you?" Henry's mouth quivered as he spoke,
blood dripping along his cheek from several wounds.

Jamal was stunned by the question. "Me? What the hell
are you?"

Henry's face slipped from horror to sorrow. He looked
around and with each second, his view of the carnage
brought more tears. "I don't understand why you did
this."

A part of Jamal's mind was blocked off so he could not
think clearly. Henry had brought this about; Jamal was just
doing what Jamal does. "You thought you were clever.
Brutal beats clever every time."

He watched as Henry looked down. At his feet lay a
man, possibly unconscious, possibly dead. "Help me help
these people," Henry said through tears, bending down to
tend to the fallen body. Jamal stepped forward as he bent
over, slapping a small patch onto the back of the Throne's
exposed neck. Henry snapped his head back in an effort to

stop him, but the patch had already found purchase on his flesh and the adhesive stuck.

"Don't you get it yet?" Jamal said.

Henry jumped back and looked at Jamal, anger mixed with the tears. "I'm not going to hurt you! I was just trying to get you... trying to get you to... uh," Henry fell to a knee as his eyes began to close. He grabbed at the patch on his neck, but his strength was gone, his body now incapacitated by the sedative. Henry's body slumped across the man he had wanted to help.

Jamal suppressed an impulse to vomit. The illness was sudden and intense but passed quickly.

He collected himself and knelt. He rolled Henry over and, with a quick inspection, ensured that the Throne was not injured besides being knocked out. There might be numerous bruises under Henry's thick clothing, but he seemed fine. Jamal had bagged his second package—alive. "This couldn't get any better."

The headlights of a vehicle lit up the street as it turned the corner. The car stopped in front of the tavern and a woman hurried out of the driver's side, rushing over to a man who sat on the curb nearby. The woman was spouting French.

Jamal felt no emotion as she passed. He looked at the running car. The lights were on and the driver's door still open. He accepted the situation as providence without pondering the reason or source.

He pulled Henry's large frame over to the car and loaded him into the back seat. The woman was nowhere to be seen, so he calmly got behind the wheel and shut the door. The inside was toasty, hot air blasting from the dashboard ducts.

Jamal climbed in but did not drive away. People ran across streets, others writhed on the ground. Others just stood waiting. It was Jamal's song, a piece crafted with...

Malice, pain, regret, fear fear fear... A fist slammed into the steering wheel and Jamal awoke from the trance. The fist was his, though the voice in his head was not. Jamal cut out all analysis, relying on simple facts to guide him.

I'm in a car. Jamal put the car in gear and drove away from the people, the scattered debris, and the bright flames. Once through the chaos, the veil of pines enveloped the road once more as Geranach ended and the rest of Switzerland resumed. Jamal drove on, and it was several minutes before he remembered that he had someone sedated and captive in the back seat, that he did this for a living, and that the song that continued to flutter through his mind from the tavern was not his.

CHAPTER 15

Ruth awoke in panic. The essence of images conjured by slumber remained: falling, loss, and... something nameless. It churned within like regret and resonated hollowly as she struggled to wake up.

The room was dark and served as a black canvas for the dream memory. Pictures began to emerge from exile as they were called back by weariness and lack of sensory input. She rolled from the bed and staggered over to the thick drapes. As the opaque fabric parted, the light of morning pierced her pupils. She squinted and covered her face. The images fled, going into deep stasis as the web of nerves, needs, and growing cognizance reclaimed her mind.

She was barely dressed, and so stepped away from the window on the 25th floor of the Hotel Fisher. New York held many unguarded windows to peep into—with scenery much more scandalous than Ruth in her underwear—but she felt no inclination to offer strangers anything personal. She turned to look out the window, taking in the towers of stone and glass.

The growing cold arrested her introspection and she crossed her arms over her chest in an effort to staunch the escape of heat. Ruth drew the curtains to a crack.

An important day required important preparation.

The last two weeks had been long and full of discovery, doubt and travel. Ruth had lied, stolen, and impersonated several people in an effort to collect data. This was so she could make up her *own* mind about what was going on and what level of involvement she was willing to commit to. From Wyoming to Minnesota to Houston, Ruth had visited several important places and people that gave more insight into what Herriot had told her. A Pro-Life clinic in Texas; a retired physician in Eden Prairie; a police station in upstate New York—all of these encounters had provided Ruth with the information she demanded as a scholar. But the details were no longer relevant; the decision she had made as a result of those details was. The last two weeks had led Ruth to New York City.

She quickly showered and dressed, building confidence in her mind, although her crusade was most likely hopeless, a course of action that might ruin her forever. But Ruth controlled what she could and it was important that her appearance be just right: subtle, yet dangerous. She had spent more on her outfit than she had on the entire trip.

The purpose was not to look overwhelmingly enticing, but to suggest open promises. Her destination was in the heart of formal business, where professional women were free to express themselves in the same manner as teenage girls. The stakes might change, but the methods often did not. Ruth could work with that.

She put on a new set of lace underwear. No one would ever see it, of course, but it did much for her resolve to know she looked good in her skivvies. She seldom went beyond comfortable and unflattering unmentionables. The luxury of lingerie was enough to banish the tomboy in Ruth and get her in tune with her mission.

Next she put on her armor.

The suit was intended for the winter, and though Ruth had considered submitting to the New York dogma, was not black. Deep gunmetal gray, the pants and jacket held a faint luster when viewed at a certain angle. The pants possessed light gray pinstripes that were nearly invisible unless one looked closely. She wanted people to look closely.

Once she had put on a white blouse, Ruth pulled the tight pants up onto her hips, the fabric hugging her lower frame. She assessed the effect before a full-length mirror in the small, but amenity-rich hotel room. She turned to make sure the view from the rear was as she remembered it in the dressing room. *Definitely can't wear this in class.* She smoothed the fabric over her buttocks and swiveled her hips. Satisfied, her attention climbed to her top. The blouse was loose, but suggestive. Donning the short jacket, Ruth marveled at how the slightest hint of cleavage beckoned the eyes down. She found it intoxicating and hoped others would as well. The outfit was professional and inappropriate. It was perfect.

To complete her attire, Ruth reached into her suitcase and found a recently purchased pair of leather heels. She was already six feet tall, so when she slid her feet into the shoes and stood up, her towering height was commanding. Ruth knew that she would walk by a thousand women between the hotel and the Andros Tower who looked better than she did, but what could armor protect if not the ego?

She looked good and that was enough. Besides, when the battle began, her enemy would have more to worry about than Ruth's cleavage. Smiling, she put on a long black coat and left the hotel.

As she walked to the subway station and boarded a train, Ruth felt as if she fit in. Of course, anything and everything fit in New York City. She sat in silence while the subway car whisked her through the length of Manhattan. She felt good.

She got off at her desired stop and emerged from the concrete and graffiti to stand in front of the Andros Tower. At first she looked up with her mouth open, but snapped her head down and walked on, pretending that she had been here a million times before. The brief view of the tower's endless vertical plane of steel and glass remained in her mind.

Ruth focused on the tower's entryway. An air-curtained tunnel served as the main entrance. She walked through several layers of heated air. Inside, the air was overly warm, but dry.

She stepped to the side to avoid being trampled, the rest of the working world filing relentlessly around her. Taking off her jacket, she looked down into her own shirt and adjusted her cleavage to that perfect balance she was so proud of. Ruth looked up and met the venomous gaze of an old woman. Ruth grinned innocently, but the woman sniffed hard and walked off.

Ruth looked around. There were lush gardens with exotic plants. There were numerous waterfalls and bubbling channels of water flowing though sculpted rocks. True, it was a marvel of human imagination and art. It also resembled her idea of the Gates of Hell.

She walked into the center of the vast space, expecting a troll to descend upon her and demand a payment of gold or her soul.

She giggled in an attempt to abate a growing uneasiness. The volcanic rocks that surrounded the lobby appeared natural, but they also seemed to be worked in a menacing and strange way. Many of the large stones were flat on top—too flat. They reminded Ruth of sacrificial altars. Perhaps it was all just imagination, but she sensed the mind of a madman.

She focused on her task and forgot about the vile gardens. A large reception center lay near the rear of the lobby. Ruth tried to move sexily as she strode across the lobby.

The reception center had four individual booths. Only one was occupied. Ruth walked up to the fat man sitting there and pressed her hips into the countertop while bending forward. The gesture was lost on the receptionist, who looked up blankly with sad eyes. "Can I help you, ma'am?"

All this time, the thought of doing something *unexpected* had driven Ruth forward. She was battling against the collective expectations of everyone. Now she stood in front of that action and had no idea what to say to the disaffected, unhappy man who didn't even seem to notice that she was a hot chick. It was a bad start. "I have an information-delivery for Mr. Keenan Tennyson," Ruth managed.

Alarm flashed across the man's face, but quickly gave way to mild sorrow. "Ma'am, uh, I don't think you've ever been here before, eh?" He looked like a stray dog in the pound.

"No, I haven't." Honesty might work.

The man paused as if Ruth had said something meaningful. He gave her an expectant look that she knew lazy clerks gave when they did not want to bother explaining themselves. He sighed heavily and looked down, then up to Ruth. "The corporate Tennyson Holdings receptionist is up on Floor 20."

"Thanks. I'll just go up there then." She started around the desk toward the elevators.

"Uh, ma'am." He turned his head, but not his body. "You can't just go up there unannounced. You need a pass."

Ruth returned to where she had been standing. "Well, can you give me one?"

The clerk sighed again. "That's my job, but I don't know who you are. Are they expecting you?"

"No, I am not expected." Ruth put a story together quickly. "My name is Ruth Long. I am a professor of Religion and Theology at Campolo University. In my possession is a report of concern to Mr. Tennyson and his associates. I know that people do not simply 'drop in' on Mr. Tennyson. I expect only to pass on the information to one of his assistants. The details are not only beyond what you need to know, they are confidential. "

The man looked unaffected. "And you have no contacts?"

"No. But please, sir. I need to get this information to Tennyson's organization as quickly as possible."

"Ma'am, can you give me more than 'it's confidential?' If that was all it took to get up to the twentieth floor, we'd have idiots in new suits coming in daily. Yeah, they'd be selling and talking and lying their way into whatever... lotta people want Tennyson's attention—and money," the clerk said, obviously amused with himself.

"Fine. Write this down: Tell the receptionist on the twentieth floor that I have the current global locations of every Throne. Also tell them that after I leave here, I'm having lunch with several friends of mine who are in the FBI."

The fat clerk, whose nametag said "Ralph," seemed locked in some internal battle. His brow was furrowed and tight. He stared down at the desk in consternation. Ruth waited. Finally, his facial muscles relaxed as he tapped at something on the desk that was out of Ruth's view. "One moment, ma'am," he said and turned away.

She could hear him speaking softly into the air, hopefully contacting the office on the twentieth floor and not security. Painful eons crept by as Ruth saw him nod, shake, and tilt his head at each juncture in the conversation.

Ralph turned back to her and smiled. "Someone will be down to escort you up. Just wait over there for a moment." He gave her a sad smile.

"Thank you very much." Ruth went to the side of the counter to wait.

She felt that a little lie wrapped around heaps of truth was the most powerful, and most sinful, lie anyone could tell. She also felt that carrying a battering ram around was more efficient than finding a key. So she had used a battering ram. Now *someone* was coming down to escort her.

This might be bad.

Ruth doubted that she could get out of the building now even if she wanted to. The place must be layered with nano-trans cameras and other surveillance gear. Given the power of Tennyson, they probably were doing a background check on her while she waited. But she had little time to ponder her situation, as her escort had arrived.

She watched a lone figure walk from the center elevator toward her. He was an extremely handsome man. His suit was similar in color to Ruth's own, a steel hue that gave him a mechanical appearance. Dark hair, recently cut, matched his angular but attractive face.

Besides his physical attributes, Ruth was struck immediately by something dark and hidden that the man exuded. Perhaps it was that way his body moved, as if each step and gesture had too much force behind it, or perhaps it was the weak smile held in place by habit, an expression that did not reach his hypnotic brown eyes. He extended a hand and said, "Miss Long, I'm Arthur Reston, Keenan Tennyson's corporate advisor."

Ruth reached out in response. He accepted her hand and the touch was both seductive and dominating. Despite her intuition, she was drowning in Arthur Reston's attractive countenance. "Thank you for seeing me without notice. I hope to conclude this meeting as soon as possible," Ruth said, as steadily as she could.

"And why is that, Miss Long?" Reston crooned, his eyes showing an expression of power and — promise.

Ruth had never met a man like this before. A tendril of focus sprouted in her struggling mind. "After I conclude our meeting, Mr. Reston, you will understand everything. I assume we are going somewhere more... private?" In truth, she wanted to remain in the lobby, close to security guards, cameras and most importantly, the exit. But business was business.

"You assume correctly," Reston said. Ruth thought he could sense her fear. "You may call me Arthur."

"You can call me Ruth, Arthur. Now that we are on a first-name basis, can we continue the date?"

The response came from some incisive part of Ruth, one that had a mind of its own. But the comment shook Reston some. His face tinged with surprise before the gladiator mask fell back into place. He leaned forward and offered her his arm. "Right this way, Ruth," he purred. She took his arm without responding, and they walked to the rear of the lobby to board the center elevator.

Reston smelled of soap and motor oil. It matched his well-manicured hands and full head of hair. Ruth guessed he was in his forties, but he seemed the type to age very, *very* well. Even so, she was uncomfortable with their isolation. It allowed her to focus nakedly on his attractiveness. He looked forward as the elevator traveled, exuding a clear signal of disinterest in Ruth.

"So, where are we going?" she asked.

"To Keenan Tennyson's office in the penthouse." Reston continued to look forward.

"This must be an important issue."

"It is *very* important to Mr. Tennyson, Ruth. He would enjoy interviewing you personally, so that no miscommunications exist. I sincerely hope that you have the information you claim. A most unsavory situation might result if you and Mr. Tennyson are not communicating smoothly."

Ruth's infatuation died instantly. She scolded herself for allowing the luxury of seduction, given the gravity of what she was doing. Reston reminded her of the man she had met in Kenya, the man who had stolen Herriot right in front of her, the man who was the real reason she had decided to come to New York. Jamal.

Reston and Jamal looked nothing alike, but they both possessed something primal and enticing that Ruth wanted, though not from evil men. Reston was already pushing her and acting as though he wasn't.

She took out her battering ram. "That is my hope as well, given that I've decided to come to Mr. Tennyson first before contacting any Federal Agencies." Ruth failed to suppress a note of triumph.

"I don't think that will be necessary... or possible."

"Oh?" Ruth was unnerved by the man's placidity. "So you've hacked my time-delayed messages to the FBI?"

"All eight of them." He looked up at the floor indicator impatiently.

Ruth tensed. Reston must have sensed it. "Truthfully, Ruth, did you think that would work?"

So Tennyson had been watching her all this time.

"The FBI's interests are often our interests," Reston said.

Ruth was beginning to lose heart. "In that case, I will give you information that the FBI doesn't have."

"That would be most beneficial, Ruth. You have a good head on your shoulders. I'd like to see you free to use it in the future."

Ruth said nothing. Reston was dangerous—she had no doubt. The elevator chime toned and the doors opened. A short hallway brought them into a round room. The floor of rough stones appeared to have been cut from the Great

Pyramid at Giza and transported here. Ruth stepped carefully to avoid the trickling water that bubbled and flowed between the stones.

They walked without pause, but Ruth had enough time to look at the central statue, a nude and voluptuous woman holding a black orb and broadsword. Ruth's gaze rolled over the statue, and she tried to block the chamber's ambiance.

Ruth was not enthralled at the prospect of meeting Keenan Tennyson, especially not here. Nevertheless, they continued to the other side of the strange chamber and stopped at a closed door.

"Enter," a voice said. Reston opened the door and beckoned for Ruth to go in first.

Inside the office, a man sat at a large desk in the center. If Reston's starched appearance was impressive, this man's presence was overwhelming.

A sharp face framed by white-winged hair looked up at her. Ruth was captivated. He looked immortal. He reminded her of some ancient Near-Eastern king such as Sargon, Sennacherib or Nebuchadnezzar. He wore a suit of black, his vest a contrasting light gray.

The man peered at her with an expression that might have been malice, hatred, or even simple annoyance. Tennyson's face could speak to whatever paranoia Ruth fancied.

"What information do you have, Miss Long?" he said in a voice that crept along the walls and flowed through Ruth's body.

She did not care how much money or power the man had. "I want Herriot."

"You are here to give me information, information you offered. It is extremely rude of you to demand anything."

"And it is rude of you to bring me up here without at least offering me coffee. Can't you afford it?" Ruth knew the comment was stupid, but she needed to blunt the edge of Tennyson, Reston and the whole damn Andros Tower. She needed a little mirth.

Reston materialized by her side and Ruth jerked away reflexively. Tennyson shook his head. Reston only grinned, smoothing and re-buttoning his jacket as if he had been reaching into it for something.

"Miss Long, you have been the victim of much misinformation. I don't know who this 'Herriot' is, and none of Tennyson Holdings or its wholly owned subsidiaries is involved in this FBI investigation," Tennyson said.

"What about Jamal Battle?"

Tennyson spoke quickly—too quickly. "Jamal Battle is dead. He was a former employee—a sub-par employee at that—who died while on assignment."

"Then why did I meet him in St. Edmund, Kenya?"

"You didn't."

"If you give me Herriot, or tell me where he is so I can find him, I'll call it off." Ruth had feared this encounter from the beginning. But the fear was hardening into defiance.

Keenan Tennyson continued to resemble the powerful yet inert statue that quietly guarded the penthouse chamber. He breathed deeply, seeming to draw every molecule of air and ray of light to his body. He was more than a man in a black suit, Ruth saw.

"And you think it is my turn to say 'call what off?', but you are mistaken. You have invaded my business, my home, with nothing but childish intent and baffling stupidity.

"Under the law, I have taken every action to correct a defective product that manufactured… unexpected results, results well known to the government. Miss Long, you are the perfect example of what happens when the wrong people get involved with a changing world and changing technologies. There are and always will be unexpected results. I've built an empire by defeating religious degenerates, by out-thinking politicians, and by being very, very frugal with my resources. You have been fortunate enough to glimpse human progress on such a scale. You should feel privileged."

Throughout this diatribe, Ruth's rage grew. This man, the richest and most successful person in the history of the world, had the intellect and work ethic of a corrupt bank manager.

"Now, Miss Long, do you have anything real to offer or may I proceed?" Tennyson tapped a pen on his com-pad and ignored Ruth. "We've ensured that you are no longer welcome at Campolo University or any other teaching institution. Your past transgressions are now public knowledge."

The information struck Ruth like a crushing wave. She had not expected this. But instead of flooding her consciousness with doubt and fear, the wave washed around her internal fortress, the force spent, leaving only weak aftershocks to lap at her towering walls.

"Your dean, Rupert, was called just after you arrived here. We explained that your hiatus is not a vacation, but a trip to engage in criminal activity. You misled him and he has suspended you until your candidacy is officially cancelled."

Tennyson was notorious for engineering the success and failure of hundreds of famous people, both in business and in entertainment. Watching him snap her life apart nonchalantly was a strange view into his everyday life. Ruth detached herself from any thought directed at her future life and focused on her reason for being here. Besides, she did not trust anything this man said.

She continued with her original plan. "I offer the rest of the Thrones—all of them—in return for Herriot."

Tennyson waved his hand dismissively. "Miss Long, this farce is over. You have nothing to offer."

Ruth looked down at her watch. It was time. She looked past Tennyson. From this angle, she could see only an overcast sky through the picture window beyond. "You have surveillance in your lobby, I assume. Right now, all eleven of the remaining Thrones are waiting outside for my safe return. Once I come down, with Herriot in hand or his whereabouts known, they will surrender to you. If I do not return to the lobby in ten minutes, or they see the arrival of police or your own forces, they will scatter. Trust me, Mr. Tennyson. They are very good at blending in when needed. You'll never find them again. This is your only chance to get what you want."

Tennyson looked sharply at Reston, who opened the door of the office and left. Tennyson resumed his furious tapping on the com-pad.

Reston returned, his genteel veneer replaced with soldier-like bearing. "Three of the subjects have been identified. Because of the many tours and general traffic, we can't identify any more."

Tennyson looked rabid. His mask had fallen and Ruth was horrified at the scowling visage that lay beneath. "You said *all* of them, Ruth." His voice was murderous.

"They're there." Ruth shook, but held her voice steady. "It's your risk, Mr. Tennyson. Please accept it like the strong man you are."

Tennyson smashed a fist into the desk. "I don't think you understand the situation," he said, his body vibrating with anger.

"And you don't understand me. You've wasted two minutes. Give me Herriot and you get the rest." Ruth had to keep him calm until it was time to leave.

The CEO looked again at Reston and some unspoken communication occurred. The servant left.

An eternity passed and Ruth drew all of her fear into an internal compartment of her mind, stemming the flow of desperate impulses that might ruin her plan.

Reston rolled a wheelchair into the office. In it was a mass of wrappings and wound dressings. Even in his pain and misery, Ruth felt Herriot's steel gaze as he peered out with his one unbandaged eye. Ruth rushed over to the chair and kneeled. As she leaned over the Throne, tears fell on the thin robe that covered his body. "What have you done to him?" Ruth said, without taking her eyes from Herriot.

"Biopsies. Tests," Tennyson said. "He's our only specimen, so we needed to keep him alive. Frankly, I will be surprised if he lives past today. Normally, it is unwise to revive someone in his state from a chemically induced coma. But he isn't exactly like you and me. Is he?"

Ruth continued to sob over Herriot's broken form. The guilt of not preventing his abduction had never left her. His condition stabbed at her anew, and she felt herself unraveling.

"You have what you want and are no longer welcome in my building." Tennyson snapped his fingers. "Mr. Reston will escort you to the lobby where you will deliver what you promised."

Ruth rounded on Tennyson and took a step, but Reston held a pistol aimed at her. "Ruth? This way please." He gestured with the gun.

She looked back at Tennyson; his mask was firmly back in place. She took control of the powered wheelchair and left without looking back.

Reston held the gun up and stood close to Ruth as she wheeled Herriot by. "There's probably more of him on microscope slides and in test tubes than there is in that chair," he said, as he nodded down at Herriot.

Ruth ignored him. She noticed Herriot trying to look around as she rolled the chair over the rough stones, the bumps no doubt causing him added pain. Occasionally a weak moan escaped from the cloth wrappings over his mouth.

Reston accompanied Ruth and her charge. He said nothing and stared at the doors as he had during their ascent.

The elevator arrived in the lobby and the doors opened. Ruth started to roll Herriot out.

"Stop," Reston said.

Ruth wheeled around. Reston had the gun down low, pointed at her. "I have to go out to the street. They won't think I'm safe with Herriot until I get *out*," she said.

Reston scowled. "They must come here. Fair trade. They walk in and you walk out."

Ruth started to push Herriot into the lobby. "No."

"You don't get to say *no*." Reston stepped in front of the chair.

Ruth stopped. She looked at her watch. There was only a minute left. "Fine. Let me talk to them." Ruth made to leave again.

"I'll have security escort them to the elevator." Reston did not move.

"You don't know where they are." *We have to go, now!*

"I don't need to. I'll take what we can get. If any escape, we'll find them. Just as we did with this one."

He reached into his jacket and pulled out a phone. He was going to call security. Ruth had failed. Her plan relied on keeping the guards from acting until she was ready. She wasn't ready. Now she had delivered more of the Thrones to Tennyson and was still in custody herself. It was falling apart.

"Security," Reston began. "I need you to—what?" He turned, looking out into the lobby. "They need Federal authority to do that." His attention was no longer on Ruth, but on something happening at the reception desk. "Well, I don't give a fuck what he wants! Tell this Agent Gruber that CEO Tennyson will talk to him when he can. Just—Goddammit, just wait. I'll be there in a minute."

Ruth plowed ahead with Herriot's wheelchair and struck Reston in the hip. She ran.

Reston screamed behind her, but they were rounding the receptionist desk by then, going out of view of the elevators. Once into the sparse crowd, Ruth slowed to a fast walk.

People walked by and in front of her, tangling their paths with hers. She continued toward the main doors, traveling as close to the far wall as she could. She looked back and saw that her beloved receptionist Ralph was deep in conversation with several people wearing jackets bearing the letters, "FBI." Five armed SWAT troopers lay in wait next to the desk as well, suited in full body armor and carrying enough firepower to fight an army.

"They're early," Ruth said to Herriot, who had stopped moaning and now held his head up, looking out to the sunny street beyond.

Just before entering the tunnel, Ruth looked back. Reston stood by the desk now, surrounded by the FBI agents and SWAT troopers. He was speaking forcefully and waving his hands in agitation. She and Herriot were safe from him for the moment.

Once on the street, she turned left and started down the sidewalk. They walked five blocks. Ruth was struck by the lack of attention they drew, given that she was dressed in a suit and pushing a bundle of rags down the sidewalks of Manhattan.

They had walked almost another block before two men stepped out of a coffee shop and moved to intercept them. She smiled and waved a hand over Herriot.

The men were both tall and dark-skinned, their features obscured by heavy layers of clothing and long cloaks. At first they walked calmly up to Ruth and Herriot, but one lost his composure and ran to the chair, falling to his knees. "Herriot! Lord in Heaven, what did they do?"

"Twain." The other man looked around nervously. "Get up. Perhaps it would be wise to remember that our enemy is just around the corner?"

Ruth saw the pain and love in Twain's eyes as he assessed Herriot's pathetic state. She empathized. "What happened, Massoud?" Ruth said to the other Throne, though she already knew.

"We saw the police, FBI or whatever, arrive. It was a red flag, so we fled just as I promised we would. Now, I'm the one who should be asking *what happened?*"

Ruth was in shock from her success. For several days now she had maintained contact with Massoud, and he had cooperated in her request to meet at the Andros Tower. The Thrones had mustered in the lobby as she asked them to. They had no idea they were bait.

"How many of the others were with you?" Ruth said, ignoring his question.

"Only myself, Twain, Musashi, and Tesla. Musashi and Tesla will meet up with us later. We seldom group up in one place unless we know it is safe."

Four! Ruth had promised Tennyson all of the Thrones. Of course, the plan involved *not* giving Tennyson anything, but it was still a shock that Tennyson and Reston had not done more to protect themselves from deception. They were eager. Too eager.

"How did you get him out?" Massoud nodded at Herriot. "What did they want in return?"

"You'd think better of me if you didn't know that," Ruth said and winked. She looked back to ensure no one had followed. Though they stood out in the open on the sidewalk, pedestrian traffic was low and she could see clearly down the block.

Massoud looked at Herriot and warmth filled his face. When he turned back to Ruth, his expression became serious. "The ends don't justify the means, Ruth."

She nodded. "No, but sometimes we must be as clever as foxes."

Massoud seemed satisfied, and smiled as he put a hand on Ruth's shoulder. She had simply told him that she would leave either with Herriot in hand or with accurate information as to his whereabouts. In case of the former, she wanted them to be ready for a getaway. She assumed that one of the Thrones had hit the curbside cab-call button, because a taxi van pulled up just as Massoud withdrew his hand from her shoulder and looked around.

She had used the Thrones as bait, knowing full well that her call to Gruber, who happened to have an office in New York, would end in a visit from the FBI to Tennyson Holdings. She had told Gruber that the Thrones were there and part of Tennyson's operations: a writhing mass of naked lies and dangerous information. Massoud and his company might have been caught by Gruber as well. Yes, better if the Thrones knew nothing of her methods.

Ruth had turned to open the door of the cab when her body responded to an impulse caused by something she had just seen. Shock turned to disbelief. Several people had just walked by their meeting place beside the road, and someone in the crowd had triggered an alarm in her subconscious.

The large cab was wheelchair-ready and a small ramp extended. When Ruth failed to get in, the driver yelled something unintelligible.

"Ruth? What?" Massoud and Twain had successfully loaded Herriot and were now seated inside, peering out in distress.

She scanned the people who had just passed her. One of them might have been... she made a quick decision. "Go! I'll meet up with you at Columbia Circle with the rest. Wait for me." She reached over to shut the door.

"You can't risk it!" Massoud offered his hand through the open door.

"You have to trust me, all right?" Ruth shut the door without further discussion. The cab sped off.

It was not simply the stab of recognition of the passing man that had piqued Ruth's suspicion. It was the fact that he was pulling a dolly with a large, man-sized box on it. Ruth could see that its contents were not light, as the man struggled to keep it balanced while moving at a steady pace. The scene reminded her of Herriot in a cart right in front of her. And that scene included the same man pulling the cart.

At a pace just short of running, Ruth hurried back toward the tower. Massoud had told her that not all of the Thrones were in contact with each other, that many had interests both separate and remote. Even though Massoud could call a few when needed, there were others out there.

Jamal was out there, too.

She was only a hundred feet away from the lobby entrance when she saw him. He wore a pea-coat with the collar turned up. The collar did nothing to hide his shaved head and tight features, as Ruth could see every time Jamal turned his head slightly. Finally, he looked back and Ruth had no doubt. It was Jamal Battle, laden with a coffin-sized wooden box that a man—a tall man—could fit into. She ran.

Slowing to a sedate walk, she followed him back into the building she had just escaped from.

* * *

As he wound his way through newsstands, food hawkers, and bums, Jamal realized that he needed a better way of getting the Thrones from their hiding places to New York. Perhaps he could rig some kind of medical stretcher, put a cover on it, and be ready for each extraction? Henry was only his second catch and Jamal knew he would become more efficient with practice.

These thoughts dissolved as he approached the entrance to the Andros Tower. Reston's instructions were for Jamal to drop off each package in the rear of the building, at the utility access station. Jamal felt good today, so he thought he'd defy Reston for no good reason and enter through the front door once again with his illegal payload.

The street was full of gaunt business people, addicted to themselves and their society. Jamal looked at the insects crossing his path, loose facsimiles of what people were meant to be. It sickened him, but his disgust could not dampen the victory of delivering Henry. He had thought often of Geranach. Never before had he acted so incisively while in a moral haze. True, Jamal knew the methods he had employed there were extreme and did not lend themselves to secrecy or efficiency, but beyond that something infected his mind. Regret. He fought bitterly with this demon called Regret, a long-vanquished foe now alive again in the pit of his conscience.

With anger, he thought of all the moments past where regret had held him fast and impotent. He could never pass through emotion and carry on, always locked down by feelings of what should have been or could have been — what he was and was not. The day had come when he had locked this weakness up forever and become ardent instead. He crushed fear and crushed people, no longer a slave to guilt.

But the truth was the thing called Henry had pierced his armor. Each step from Geranach bore drops of Jamal's spirit blood, as the battle raged and burned within him. He thought back to the joy of the tavern and Henry's great song. He remembered the tears and disbelief at Jamal's power and will. It should be a testament to Jamal's growing strength, but instead it was the source of his hesitancy.

He walked into the air-cushioned entrance and was aware of someone next to him. He glanced over to find another business insect, albeit a sexually enticing one. She seemed enraptured as she looked at him, though the spell was one of anger and torture rather than interest.

The face: Jamal examined it. "Ruth," he said flatly, not stopping.

She walked in step and looked forward. "Jamal Battle."

Was this woman one of Tennyson's other undead assassins? He slowed to grab at a gun in his belt.

Her hand touched the back of his arm. The contact was sensual, fingers running up several inches, then back, to take a firm yet gentle grip around his forearm. "I can't hurt you, Jamal. Just keep going," she said.

"Why are you here? I got nothing for you unless you get in my way. You don't want what I have to give."

They walked together now, Ruth to Jamal's left and the top of the dolly resting on Jamal's right shoulder, his grip tight on the upper handle.

"You don't know what I want," Ruth's hand pressed on his arm in a way that conjured images of both sex and violence.

Dazed, Jamal could not navigate the fog growing in his mind. This woman was the fantasy, the dark and great thing he'd walked away from in St. Edmund. Now she was here. Was she just an imagined thing, a byproduct of his growing instability?

"So tell me, Jamal, why are you doing this? How did a man like you come to work for Reston?"

Jamal's body charged for conflict. His vision blurred and then focused. He realized that, unwittingly or intentionally, the woman had tested him for a weakness. "Reston is dead and I am Death. I don't work for anyone."

Ruth's hand began to stroke his arm. They had entered the building and were halfway through the lobby. "That's not an answer."

"Your question was lacking detail."

"Let me ask another then. You have a Throne in the box. Walk out of here with me and let him go."

Jamal went for his gun again.

"You can't do anything in here. Walk out and stop this," she whispered next to his ear.

Jamal saw the crowd of law enforcement at the reception desk. He ignored Ruth for a moment to assess the danger: armed cops and agent-looking assholes. He stopped. Through the assembly, Jamal could make out Arthur Reston. He looked upset and was arguing with one of the suits. Not taking his eyes from the situation ahead, Jamal leaned back and allowed the dolly and box to stand upright, taking the weight off his shoulder. Ruth let go of his arm. "You assume too much about me, Ruth."

"So you'll leave with me? Now?"

"I've been with better-looking women than you—two at a time. Your charm is worthless."

She stepped back, a look of fright painted on her face. Jamal did not understand this woman. He was tired of her effect on him. He wanted to leave with her, but for the most base and animalistic reasons. That must be what she had in mind, so it was a trap.

Ruth leaned in seductively, the fear gone from her expression. "I bet that was expensive," she said, then pushed him hard.

Jamal stumbled backward, but kept his feet. Ruth was on him, her hands plunging into his coat and onto the butt of his gun. With a quick motion he slapped her across the face. She went down, and instinctively he pulled out the pistol and trained it on her.

She sat back on the ground and Jamal swore he saw a smile on her face right before she screamed. "Ahhhhhhh! He's got a gun! Somebody help me!"

Jamal looked around to run, but his mind locked between his need to escape, his need to carry Henry, and the fact that he held a gun and every eye in the lobby was now on him. He just stood there, not knowing what to do, as Ruth continued to scream.

People ran in all directions and he heard the thump of boots from across the lobby.

"Drop your weapon! Police! Drop your weapon now!"

Jamal threw his hands up, but held the gun firm. The armored troopers had closed the distance quickly and had him in the middle of a semicircle. His ego was completely gone and, though an impulse to fight came naturally, he was paralyzed in disbelief. His dark fantasy, this woman of fire and dripping sex, had conquered him.

A trooper stepped forward and snatched the gun from his hand. Once he was disarmed they descended, forcing him to his knees. He looked down at the marble floor, his own visage captured in the black polished stone. He saw voids where his eyes should be. Transfixed, he didn't respond to each command and question. He was struck in the back and he went down. His view of the floor was broken when he rolled to the right. It allowed him, however, a glimpse of someone leaving the lobby. He watched beautiful, three-inch leather heels walk into the distance, their steps irregular as their owner struggled to balance a heavy box on a dolly. Jamal saw the heels and the box go out onto the street and around the corner. It was only then that his senses returned.

A familiar voice stabbed downward. "Yes, he is part of security, I assure you. Please let him go," Arthur Reston said. "As you can see, he's not very good at what he does, is he?"

CHAPTER 16

Jamal emerged from the subway and ran on. He had no intention of staying at the Andros Tower to regroup, facing the wrath of Tennyson. Ruth could not have traveled far.

So he ran several blocks, using a transmitter link to his com-pad to track Henry. Jamal had tagged both Henry and the box he rode in immediately after capture. The nano-transmitters were Taurus Force Systems prototypes, virtually undetectable by physical or electronic means.

The transmitter he had implanted in the back of Henry's arm was active and sending information to Jamal's small com-pad. No doubt Ruth had taken to vehicle transport by now, a taxi or car, as the locator ping traveled north over the com-pad map for several blocks, starting and stopping periodically.

Jamal had opted to take the subway north in an effort to intercept. The gamble had paid off as he now sat in the middle of Columbia Circle, positioned in front of the moving transmitter. The com-pad display showed a small green dot moving steadily through a map of mid-town Manhattan. Jamal had no need to view the display, however, as a synthetic voice hummed from his earpiece, giving updated location status by cross-street reference every 30 seconds, or if the transmitter changed direction.

It was coming his way.

There was a chance that Ruth would take the Lincoln Tunnel, trying to escape across the river. Jamal was struck by how little he knew of this woman. Was she working for the Thrones or was she a contractor like himself?

He also knew little of the overall situation. The Thrones were part of something Tennyson Holdings was working on or had worked on—that was certain. And whatever *that* was, Tennyson did not want the authorities involved.

The SWAT officers and mysterious agents came to mind. Jamal doubted that Reston had planned that meeting; it was the first time he had seen Reston physically agitated, quivering and flushed with rage. The man was not unflappable after all.

These thoughts led back to Ruth. She had found him somehow. In Kenya, Jamal had assumed she was some worthless scientist, assistant, or idiot tourist who happened to visit Herriot's lab at the wrong time. Now, after feeling her wrath upon him, he thought otherwise.

She was beautiful, but not the most beautiful. What this woman possessed in spirit, though, transformed her above-average physical attractiveness into something more. She decided, she risked, and she acted with power while striking out. Jamal had no words for this entity, this creature of legend and fantasy. Ruth was his enemy, but that realization held comfort instead of resolution.

I need to stop her from stopping me.

The automatic voice chimed in Jamal's ear and pulled his mind back to re-snatching Henry. The com-pad informed him that the transmitter was only two blocks south and still coming his way. Then another voice erupted in his ear.

"Jamal. This is Arthur Reston."

Jamal gave a verbal cut-off command to the earpiece to hang up on Reston. Nothing happened.

"I have overrides on your equipment, you dullard. The only way to silence me is to remove the earpiece, which I am quite confident you are not in a position to do right now."

Jamal looked out toward the street, giving Reston a small percentage of his focus. "What do you want?"

"Return to the tower. You've corrupted this operation greatly, but not irrevocably. I'd like to talk to you personally about what your next course of action will be."

Jamal laughed, drawing the attention of a quiet family sitting on a bench beside him. They looked at him with wonder. He looked back and smiled. "You're talking to me now. I don't need to come back."

"Jamal. Just come back and I'll help you."

Jamal could detect the pleasure in Reston's voice, though he was trying to hide it. "Fuck you."

The man and woman collected their three children and scuffled off toward a street crossing. Jamal laughed again.

"Battle, I am coming to the conclusion that terminating your employment may be in our best interests."

"I dare you to give me the pink slip."

"Come back to the tower and I will."

Jamal ignored Reston's aggression. "I have the location of the Throne I captured. If you bug off, I can get back to work and make the best out of a bad day, asshole."

He waited for a response. The com-pad told him that the transmitter had now stopped at 8th and 57th. He looked down the avenue as if he'd recognize their vehicle. The only thing he saw was New York traffic. Somewhere in the morass were Henry, and perhaps Ruth.

Jamal jaywalked to the other side of 8th and 58th, stopping at the southeast corner, among several street vendors and people waiting to cross the street. He stood calmly behind a group of young high-school girls standing by the curb. They giggled and chattered.

His locator chimed again. Two cars approached from the 57th Street intersection. One was a silver car and the other a taxi van. The SWAT officers had taken his pistol and stripped him of his other armaments, but Jamal felt confident with only his fists.

As the taxi approached, numerous scenarios scrambled though his consciousness. A sudden realization struck and he froze.

Just as suddenly, he made a decision. Jamal relaxed and stepped away from the crowd of girls. The light on 8th Avenue turned red and the girls rushed out across the street. The cab pulled up. Through the back window, Jamal could make out his enemy, Ruth.

He turned to avoid detection. But Ruth's presence compelled him to foolishness. Jamal faced a vendor stand that sold news-feeds and other sundries. Among them were flowers. He snatched a bunch of daisies, the only flower he recognized.

The street hawker yelled after him. Jamal ignored him and walked briskly to the curb and out into the street. Jogging to the rear door of the cab, he saw Ruth turn and look out. A muffled scream leaked out of the vehicle and she shied away from the window. He stood holding the bundle of flowers. His intent was intimidation.

Jamal felt anything but intimidating as he extended the flowers toward the window. Ruth was now leaning away and gesticulating wildly, the driver's head shaking as though there was a disagreement. Other forms seethed within the cab and Jamal realized he had made a good decision. There were three others, probably Thrones.

The cab lurched forward and screeched off as the light turned green. Jamal withdrew the flowers and held them at his stomach. He peered down into the white petals and noticed how ragged and damaged they were. Some were wilted and others had been crushed or ripped.

The flowers were pathetic, but pathetically beautiful. He spun around and got out of the street as more traffic approached. Walking back to the vendor stand, Jamal slapped a large-amount bill on the countertop.

"Sorry," he said. The hawker continued to chatter, but Jamal wasn't listening. He turned and walked south on 8th Avenue, not sure where he was or what he was doing. Something damaged yet alive was breaking into the normal clockwork of Jamal's brain. He was using the daisies to scare Ruth and the Thrones. No, he was going to see if she would... Jamal did not know why he had walked to the car with daisies. He was, however, sure of why he did not capture the whole bunch of freaks and their handler right then and there. He focused on that.

The next decision was where to go. The Andros Tower might be the worst, but there were other resources Jamal needed that went beyond the means of the key cube. With luck, his decision to let Ruth get away with the now easily traceable Henry would be rewarded.

"Jamal, I've been watching you since you left Columbia Circle." Reston's voice sounded within the earpiece, his timing apropos.

"Yes?" Jamal said.

"You let them go."

Jamal felt dread rise within and forced it down. He had made the right decision. "Yup."

"I trust you have reason. If not, a pink slip is on its way. From several directions, I might add."

Jamal did not bother to look around. He had no doubt that whatever clandestine security forces Tennyson had, they would be able to find and capture him. "I think you owe me a Christmas bonus instead, Artie."

"Oh? I'd dispense with the humor before my security reaches you. They have been instructed to bring you back to the tower, but not necessarily with a beating heart."

Jamal grinned at a bum who was digging through a trashcan. He walked over to the man. The bum looked up with dilated pupils and a face caked in filth. Stench surrounded the man. Jamal took a wad of cash from his pocket and held it out. "You might be back in the trashcan tomorrow, but today just got better."

The man said nothing. He looked apathetically at the cash, then reached out and took it. He walked off without giving thanks or looking back.

"The Thrones are seeking safety in numbers," Jamal said to no one.

Reston was no one. "But as of now, you have failed to retrieve a single one."

"You have Herriot." Jamal became serious.

"I don't understand this name, 'Herriot.' I only know that a very rude woman illegally extracted a piece of Tennyson Holdings' property this morning."

Jamal was stunned. Ruth was much more cunning than he thought. "Tough bitch."

"Hardly. She's a loose end you left behind. Her interference is due to your stupidity."

That was hard to believe. Jamal had never met her before Kenya. But he banished the thought reflexively. He was a retriever—let Reston worry about the back-story. "Hey Artie, you know that if your guys get to me, I'm gonna press this button on my com-pad that will fry it out. All of the information on it will be lost." Jamal ignored Ruth's origins to get to the point.

"And why would I care about that, Mr. Battle?"

"Because you would have no link to the locator implanted on the *package* I tried to deliver. The one I was recently robbed of because you can't keep cops out of your building." Jamal continued to walk.

After a minute of silence, Reston's voice returned, calmer now. "Safety in numbers, you say."

As if on cue, a catering truck pulled up to the curb just ahead of Jamal. Several men got out and looked around. They didn't look like caterers. One of them gestured for Jamal to approach. He stepped past them and hopped into the open van door.

He sat down in an empty seat. The interior of the van had nothing but central seating and racks of equipment. The other men got back into the van and closed the door. They sat next to Jamal and the vehicle jumped twice and then took off.

"Indeed, Mr. Battle. Perhaps a bonus is warranted, after all," Reston said.

* * *

"It's not safe for us to be together like this," Massoud said after the encounter with Jamal.

"I don't suggest splitting up into groups." Ruth was shaking.

"Wouldn't it help?"

"No." Ruth pulled her hair back behind her ears, fearing any loss of peripheral vision. "They know where we are now, but even Tennyson has some obligation to follow the law, especially where millions of New Yorkers can see."

"So you think Jamal was called off at the last minute?"

Ruth looked out the window, expecting to see the assassin standing there again. "I don't know."

"He frightens me," Henry said.

Ruth looked at the Throne. His face was a mix of soot, makeup, and exposed paper-like skin. His expression betrayed complete exhaustion and dismay. Like the others, he had identifiable features. Despite his current state, Ruth sensed that he was usually a jovial creature, since his speech was both light-hearted and poetic.

"I'm sorry that he hurt you, Henry," Ruth said, as she took his hand in hers, gripping it tightly.

Henry attempted a wan smile but his face fell back to sorrow. "He frightens me in the most beautiful way, Ms. Ruth. While his masters may have embraced a ruthless path, I feel this Jamal is not what he thinks he is. I am bereft of hope for a man in such a situation."

Ruth continued to shiver occasionally as her body was released from adrenaline shock. Pursuit she had expected, but finding Jamal before her and only separated by a quarter-inch of glass was not the type of early warning she would have liked.

Further, the man had stood there with a bunch of daisies, as if Ruth was supposed to take them from him out of adoration. She knew Jamal was sick, but the action was beyond comprehension. Even so, she had to believe that he was indeed sick—not evil. The comparison of Reston and Jamal had returned to her. Reston was gone, but Jamal hung on to something—worthy of redemption. But he had not actually *done* anything good for her or the Thrones. She looked at Henry and was starkly reminded of that fact. "He's an assassin or something. If any of you encounters him in the future, you run. Got it? Shoot him if you have to." Ruth felt cold.

She looked around the cab to find three sets of eyes on her. Their expressions ranged from awe to satisfaction to confusion. Herriot was asleep, and his bandaged head lay back against the headrest.

"Yes, ma'am." Massoud patted Ruth on the knee. "But we don't kill people... ever."

"So you said." She had not believed that the Thrones were truly pacifists. But now that she had spent time in their midst, it was hard to ignore their sensitivity and compassion. How they had made it this far in life was a mystery.

Massoud continued, "Once we get to our new home, I don't think Tennyson or the FBI will have any way of reaching us. We expect the end despite this."

"What *end* is that?" Ruth had heard this before. The Thrones seemed to be fatalistic.

"Your guess is as good as any. As you've already witnessed, the world cannot tolerate our existence indefinitely."

Ruth looked out into the passing concrete and glass, pedestrians and cars, and lights. She thought of retrieving her belongings from the Fisher Hotel. That she was now a fugitive from the FBI also occurred to her.

"What did you think of *The Book of Beasts and Green Things?*" said Massoud.

The question surprised Ruth, but she allowed her brain to shift into a scholarly mode of thought.

"It's intriguing. More so because I was able to see St. Edmund for myself. Herriot might not know it, but his presence changed those people's lives… for the better. Someone, and I wish I knew who, was diligent and artful in the way they captured the situation with text. Personally, I wish more people could read the Book, if only for the exposure to something so…" — Ruth struggled for the word — "…blessed."

Massoud stared at her without speaking. He seemed to be expecting more and Ruth realized that she had more to say. "What are you guys doing out there in the world? I understand if you want attention and protection, but why was Herriot alone with no way of defending himself?"

"It's the risk we all take," Massoud said.

"Risk? For what?"

"Ruth, you must understand what motivates us. In the early days, we thought that it was just a common, human type of drive, something that scholars, athletes, and business leaders all had. But as time passed, we each identified a blinding power within. Herriot, Henry here, Twain—we all have special interests and passions that go beyond simple decisions and intent. Our lives guided us, through pain and possible death at times, to special duties wherever we went."

"Duties?"

"Henry will always tell stories. Herriot will always grow and heal and act as though he's done nothing. You understand yet?"

"No."

"That's because there is nothing to understand, but rather to recognize. If you think that the Book is worthy of passing on—that the influence on St. Edmund from Herriot's presence and gifts is good—perhaps you'd be interested in other situations, places where we've been and done what we could."

"You want me to go to other places like St. Edmund? I—"

"No, I want to know if we could interest you in short-term employment."

"What would be my title?

"Chronicler."

"Chronicler of what?"

"Of all the writings our human friends have given us over the years."

"Like the Book?"

"Yes."

"Wouldn't you want a linguist or cultural anthropologist to do that? I make a living by teaching disaffected students about what something 2,000 years or more old meant when it was written, not what we *hope* it means."

"I am not inviting someone of the aforementioned professions. I am inviting you," Massoud said.

"I don't have a choice, do I?"

"My dear, you *always* have a choice. Henry and Herriot are here with us because of your choices."

Ruth was torn. She could go to Gruber, tell him everything, take whatever punishment they had for her and get back to living. Get back to... sitting in a classroom, teaching instead of doing.

But Ruth had made her decision to burn bridges before she came to New York. She could not go back. "You gentlemen are in need of some friends."

Massoud sat across from her and held her gaze. His expression reminded Ruth that she had not answered the question.

"Fine. I accept the offer, but only because I'm on the run too. We need time to figure this out, tell the authorities what Tennyson Life-Sciences did. I want to make sure that all of you get somewhere safe. Once I am sure the world can't hurt you, I'm going back to whatever parts of my old life I can salvage. You want me to look at papers? That's fine too. But really, I'm just looking out for you. Agreed?"

"Our ship leaves San Diego as soon as we get there." Massoud did not seem surprised.

Ruth was. "Ship?"

"Yes. Airplanes often have — excessive security, no?" He smiled.

Ruth shuddered. Being a fugitive and thinking like a fugitive were very different. This would take time.

"There's something else." She looked out the window. "I'm convinced that all of you are, in fact, man-made."

"And why is that?" Twain said.

Ruth turned back. Each of the Thrones wore a perplexed expression, nearly identical in every way. She chuckled. "Because you're all men."

CHAPTER 17

The signal stopped moving after a week. By then, Jamal had acquired the necessary provisions from Tennyson's empire. All that remained was to meet with the transport pilot at the Taurus airfield in Silver Spring, Maryland.

Jamal stood in the middle of his hotel room. His pride lay in the uniform-like attire he had recently purchased. Pressed black trousers and polished boots could pass for both military battle dress and downtown fashion. A tight microfiber sweater wrapped him in mild pressure, the shirt touching every inch of skin and muscle as he moved. The final piece was a fitted, high-necked jacket, the straight collar accentuating the sinew in his neck.

He appraised his image before the room's mirror. He had shaved his head that morning and several nicks remained, marked by dried beads of blood. He had grown accustomed to the damage and never did anything to hide the cuts. Instead he waited for the blood to wash off in the shower or simply flake off. When he was young, it was a habit of his to pick at the wounds in the hope of taking the scabs off early. Now, he wore them with pride.

A soft beep toned within his ear. "Jamal Battle, answer now."

He waited. Another beep followed and Jamal paused before speaking. "Yes?"

"This is Reston."

Jamal was expecting the call.

"The locator tracking information you gave us has maintained its integrity. We have a positive location."

Reston repeated information Jamal already knew as if they were in a boardroom. Jamal had come to tolerate the man's formality, though he knew Reston's true nature once the executive veneer and pretensions were stripped away. "So they haven't moved. Is that what you're trying to say?"

"Do not waste my time. The locator has remained at the same GPS coordinates for over three days. Perhaps one who wished to retrieve the locator would find the situation prime for such an action."

"So you want me to leave."

"I have no such intention. I am merely informing you of various facts that might aid you in—whatever it is that you do. I am not advocating any activity that would be in opposition to U.S. and International Law."

"Of course you're not," Jamal said. His connection with Tennyson Holdings had grown over the past weeks, but they would cut him off if things got out of control. He was certain of that.

As he stood before the mirror, he forgot he was having a conversation with Reston.

"Mr. Battle?"

"Thank you for the information, Mr. Reston. I will put it to good use," Jamal mocked.

"Perhaps. As we've seen, our property has more protection than we thought possible."

Jamal scowled at his reflection. His uniform was nothing. Although the situation suited what Jamal hoped to accomplish—capture the Thrones, all of them—his memory stung with thoughts of Ruth's maneuver that had freed the Thrones and left him on the floor with guns held to his face.

Ruth was his target. The Thrones were secondary.

"By this time tomorrow, I doubt that you'll be able to find me in New York." Jamal reviewed a mental checklist of the things he had packed for the journey. The list was complete.

"And by this time next week, we will have our property or not. Either way, you will no longer be in our employ."

Jamal commanded the call to end and the connection was cut. He was alone again. The hotel room was adorned in a New Classic styling, with metal minimalist furniture and wooden objects—carvings on the tables and molding along the walls. Jamal hated it. There was no color, no beating heart to give the room life. The world was filled with such rooms and the small minds that envisioned them, and the even smaller minds that enjoyed them. Two abstract drawings were the only other adornments. He was in one of the finest hotels in the world and they could not even afford colors and heat for patrons who expected more than insect comfort.

Jamal looked again at his own colorless form. The black fabric drew in light and color and vanquished them, leaving only darkness and obscure promises. He wanted to suck in the light of the room and streets and worlds he traveled. His garb represented his disbelief in the world he inhabited.

He gathered his bags and walked out. Twenty minutes later, he was on the train that would ferry him to the equipment and utilities he needed.

He was ready to do his job.

* * *

When they arrived in San Diego and boarded the yacht moored at the Cays, Ruth was weary from the five-day drive from New York, and not looking forward to a sea voyage. That aside, she was ready to get underway. Their destination was the Galapagos Islands. The journey would take several days. Ruth realized she could use the rest.

She had learned that Herriot had lived on the Galapagos Islands before coming to Kenya. There, he had provided his expertise to restore several of the islands as biological preserves, tourism over the past decades having taken a large toll on the beauty and stability of the islands.

Massoud had tried to explain that not all of the Thrones were cloistered science nerds or mischievous impostors. For several years, a group of them had been working with the government of Ecuador. The goal was to help the small country reach a state of economic independence that it had never had. It was only recently that the country had gone back to using its own currency, the sucre, after using the American dollar for decades.

The revival was tied to the Thrones, Ruth was told, namely an individual called Chanakya. He was a master of economics and finance and had given President Hector Flores the counsel needed to grow Ecuador into more than a tourist spot and collection of exploitable resources for more developed countries.

It was this symbiosis between the Thrones and the government of Ecuador that now provided a haven for Massoud and his brothers. Ruth realized that the Thrones were far from helpless, if still non-violent.

The Thrones' gifts of charity had been returned many-fold, securing them vast financial resources, and in some cases, government protection. The Throne named Tesla had pioneered several seminal technologies within the power transmission and conversion fields. Again focusing efforts in Ecuador, the research labs and factories in this field were tied to the growing economy and President Flores's goal of building the nation into a "first-world" country.

The high poverty and subsequent migration of citizens out of Ecuador every year were changing. Instead of catering to outside interests, the nation was building sustained internal food production, as well as a healthy list of exports. The Thrones had helped conflicting cultures work together, leveraging the nation's microclimates effectively. Now Ecuador possessed a nationally owned oil pipeline, the largest shrimp export trade in South America, and large palm oil reserves harvested sustainably from plantations in the Amazon. They also exported the greatest amount of bananas per year, as they had for decades.

The Thrones were more active than Ruth had expected. She had tried to understand why they were interested in this small, yet eclectic South American nation. When she asked Massoud what made Ecuador different from other nations, he told her that it was a collection of physical and cultural factors that exemplified South America. If Ecuador could reinvent itself, any South American nation could.

Ecuador had no laws concerning cloning or biotechnology, only that they forbade external companies from moving in to do research away from the laws of their home nations. So when the Thrones made their presence known after building several beneficial businesses, no one in the government had cared that they might be "illegal" biological products from the U.S. Instead, they had welcomed the enthusiasm and intent the Thrones had for the nation and people of Ecuador. The country was still recovering from the Americas War, though they had avoided the worst of it, compared to their near neighbor, Venezuela.

Though Ruth had come to believe what the Thrones told her, the whole affair seemed naïve and campy. She hoped to see some of Ecuador's "revival" for herself. And she wanted to meet Chanakya. Ruth knew that business relied on growth and survival: nothing less, nothing more. There was no such thing as altruism in business, no matter how it was framed. She remembered St. Edmund, and suspended judgment.

The *Groovy Booby* dropped anchor in the inlet off the pier of Puerto Ayora. A 120-foot touring yacht based in the Galapagos, the ship was captained by a man named John Burns. The Thrones had chartered the ship indefinitely and the captain was a jovial, though occasionally lewd, man who seemed committed to them.

As crew members disembarked using the two landing *pangas*, Ruth watched them go. She stood on the bow, leaning against a rail, and looked down into aquamarine.

"You can go ashore on the next trip, Ruth, and relax for a few hours before we continue on." A shadow approached from her right and stopped.

"This isn't our final destination, Massoud?" Ruth surveyed the cluster of structures clinging to the side of the island, looking as though they could all slide into the sea at any moment. The town did not strike her as a place the Thrones would live in.

"No. Some of the crew members were only on for that trip, so we're getting the normal crew complement back. Some were on leave, some were convalescing."

"Convalescing?" She turned to face Massoud.

"Several of the mates were out on a fishing run in a *panga*. They hooked a big mako shark. Instead of cutting it loose, they brought it on—thought they could bring it back without incident."

Ruth was not versed in fishing of any kind, least of all deep-sea endeavors. But she knew a mako was both large and dangerous. Her mind conjured an image of a ten-foot shark in an eight-foot boat.

"John was bitten and Raoul broke a rib when the beast thrashed around," Captain Burns said, as he walked up behind them. "Grumpy got smart and dumped the thing back into the deep." He took a position on Ruth's left and leaned back onto the railing.

He was a short, stout man. Ruth trusted him. Burns was cautious, honorable, and very shrewd. Despite his incessant sexual comments and coarse language, he was a good man. He stood now in a white uniform, a silly captain's hat on his head. Ruth was surprised to see him this clean.

"I was pretty mad at them at first, but hell, some shark meat ain't bad," he said to Ruth's breasts. She snapped her fingers and the man looked up to meet her gaze. It was a recurring problem, partially due to the man's lack of height and Ruth's overabundance of it.

He smiled in apology. "A tuna or wahoo would've been fine, though. When you live on and off the sea, sometimes you put her to the test just to see what will happen. Sometimes you get put in your place. It happens to us all... even me, from time to time." Burns looked across the inlet.

Ruth felt safe enough to take her eyes off him for a moment and turned to take in the view again. Their ship lay off the southern coast of Santa Cruz Island. A large volcanic peak loomed in the distance and, as the terrain sloped downward towards the sea, Puerto Ayora sprawled just before the rocky shore. From her vantage point, Ruth could make out quaint and colorful buildings, each flanked with lush palm trees. Smaller buildings and boardwalks seemed to ooze down to the water, while derelict pier posts had been recycled for new walkways and smaller piers that extended over the broken surf.

The inlet was protected and the flotilla of boats, ships, and yachts that had collected around the port rose and fell gently in the morning tide. A mist was fading from the verdant forest beyond, the mountain revealed through gaps in the morphing fog.

The sounds of seabirds and other creatures tore through the quiet, adding to the richness of the area. Ruth caught something in her peripheral vision and looked down to see two sea lions rocketing under the bow, their sleek bodies leaving shimmering bubble trails in the blue water that reminded her of airplane contrails.

"The islands aren't famous for habitation, of course, but you may find Puerto Ayora satisfying. We have to pick up Musashi, too. That's one of the reasons we stopped," Massoud said.

"What are the other reasons?"

"Our ultimate destination on Floreana Island is — inaccessible during the day."

Now in the Galapagos, Ruth was encountering the extensive support network employed by the Thrones. From Captain Burns to the supposed endorsement of the Ecuadorian government, this place might harbor them indefinitely. She had not believed Massoud when he first told her of their connections. She felt less needed with each passing minute.

I need them more. Ruth had no doubt of it as she looked off over the open sea.

"After twilight, we leave. Make sure you're back by then." Massoud squinted as he looked out, and then pointed. "If I am not mistaken, I think I see both of our *pangas* returning as we speak."

Ruth decided to make the most of the landfall by finding a café. She basked and sipped espresso as the sun massaged her body and the caffeine quickened her mind. The café deck extended out into the inlet almost 30 feet. With her legs extended and resting on another chair, she found the lapping of surf and honking of birds explained the inner workings of the Galapagos Islands more adequately than a travel brochure ever could.

As her thoughts ran together, revealing paradoxical ideas and increasingly unreal landscapes, Ruth was startled by a scraping sound under her chair. She leaned to the side and looked under it.

"Oh!" She laughed as she recognized the creature. A lone marine iguana lumbered with little grace under her legs and on to the edge of the deck. The animal was armored in fine obsidian scales, now looking the color of slate as they had dried in the hot air. Its head was covered by a crown of lumpy and uneven spikes, blunt and the color of tapioca. The scraping sound that had awoken Ruth was produced by the iguana's large hooked claws dragging along the wooden surface, claws designed to find purchase on rocks in a turbulent undersea environment.

She had seen several iguanas since arriving. Most were basking in the sun and moving very little. Suddenly, a shadow crept across her field of view.

"May I sit?" the shadow said.

Ruth shifted in her seat to look up. Before her was a tall man. After a short examination, she realized he was a Throne. No makeup hid his sickly-thin skin with vessels that looked as though they would hemorrhage with any movement. He wore a light button-down linen shirt with billowing blue linen pants to match. He had the same physical characteristics as the rest of the Thrones, but with several notable differences.

This Throne had a shaved head, his standard light-brown hair gone in place of wax-paper skin and veins and arteries pulsing beneath. He was also extremely muscular; his awkward frame filled in with tight sinew and defined muscle. That alone served to make him even more grotesque. Ruth felt guilty that the Thrones' appearance still evoked discomfort, but she hoped that would fade with more time in their presence.

"Please excuse me, ma'am." His voice was higher than that of the others, yet melodic. "My name is Musashi. Massoud told me where you may be found and I was excited to finally meet you. I thank you for what you have done for my brothers."

Ruth sat up and brought her legs down. She stood up, extending her hand. "Nice to meet you. Just call me Ruth, though."

He took her hand warmly. Musashi radiated the same benevolence as the other Thrones, but also something both powerful and alien. Ruth liked it.

"Of course, ma—of course, Ruth." He smiled, but she could see he felt awkward.

"Please, sit," she offered. She guessed that he was not accustomed to being informal. She also remembered that this was the Throne that had "attacked" a U.S. Army base. His physical prowess was apparent, yet he also seemed childlike.

Ruth looked over to where the iguana had been, but it was gone.

"Are you enjoying your visit to the Galapagos, ma—Ruth?" Musashi said.

"Very much, thank you. And you?"

"I've spent much time here over the last year, yet it is never mundane. It is a spiritual place that gives much to those who hunger. I am ever full while I train at our new home."

"Train?"

"Yes. Massoud knew he could never talk me into joining our brothers permanently if I could not train, so we built a dojo. In fact, some of my more understanding human friends have visited our estate on Floreana to train with me. It was most generous of them to share their wisdom and guidance." Musashi glowed. Ruth was utterly at a loss.

"Masters, really," he continued. "Some traveled from Japan and some from the United States. My masters have been both mentors and friends. They have never treated me with dishonor, though they were aware of my — differences."

The Throne was rambling on. Ruth did not understand. "You're a fighter? Karate and stuff like that?"

"Excuse me? Yes, yes. Please forgive my rudeness, Ruth. They are masters of several different martial arts. I spend most of my time learning the wisdom of ages from such teachers. I also have, with their approval, of course, begun to develop new styles and arts."

"I thought the Thrones were peaceful? Aren't martial arts ultimately — violent?"

Musashi looked at her with sudden dread. Eyes wide, he attempted to speak, but only worked his mouth open and shut several times before sitting back.

"Oh God, I'm sorry. I didn't mean to offend you." Ruth cursed her lack of tact. "I'm sure you're 'peaceful,' I just meant that the study of such things surprised me."

Musashi was a placid lake now, grinning at her. "No apologies needed. It is a weakness of mine perhaps, but I've struggled to understand my gifts against what my brothers and I are committed to. I can assure you that I have never killed nor intentionally harmed a human being.

Many of the arts I practice use defensive and aggression-neutralization tactics to obtain victory. I do not inflict damage to the human body. Coercive *pressure* perhaps, but not damage."

Self-defense was a worthy discipline, at least. "I see. So you're the Thrones' bodyguard."

Musashi took up a defensive posture, as if he were blocking a punch. "Not at all!" He lowered his hands. "We have accepted our potential fates and will not endanger others for the sake of our survival. My life directed me into the martial arts. I found a way to serve others with these skills."

More "we are destined for slaughter" babble, this time from the tough one. Many questions bubbled up from Ruth's brain, but she held them back. Despite the muscles, Musashi was extremely sensitive. Especially concerning how he fit into the current Throne situation. She decided not to push him. "Well, I find those skills intriguing. Perhaps you can give me some basic self-defense training when we get to the, uh, homestead."

Musashi looked delighted. "I would be honored, Ruth. You already have much in physique and size, so I'm sure you could learn."

Not that much in size, thank you. She took the compliment anyway.

Musashi rose and waited. Ruth looked at him and suddenly realized she was breaking some unknown protocol. As she jumped to her feet, he smiled and bowed slightly. "A pleasure to meet you, Ruth Long. I look forward to speaking with you soon. And training, perhaps?"

Ruth wanted to shake his hand, but his hands remained by his sides. She gave an inexpert bow of her own. "Yes. Nice to meet you, too."

Musashi walked through the labyrinth of small café tables to the road. Ruth sighed and slumped back down into her chair. The encounter, though pleasant, had broken the afternoon's spell. She decided to go back to the ship and wait for their departure, which occurred as soon as she was on board.

After an hour of travel, darkness enveloped the sky and a canopy of stars, marred by fast moving clouds, replaced the sun. Ruth chose to retire for the several hours it would take to reach their final destination. The sounds of humming engines and water running along the hull put her to sleep shortly after.

The barking of male voices awoke Ruth. She wasn't sure how long she'd slept, but she was not ready to get up. As she fought to stay conscious, she realized that they had arrived. With renewed vigor, she sat up and rubbed sleep from her face. The voices outside were punctuated by bursts of engine noise, the pulses of thrust Ruth had come to expect whenever the ship docked or maneuvered. She dressed, glancing out the porthole of the stateroom.

Initially, Ruth saw only darkness, but as her eyes adjusted, she recognized that what she had taken for the darkness of night was rather a black rock wall only feet from the side of the ship. No one was yelling topside, but Ruth was concerned about her obstructed porthole view. She was not a mariner, but she knew that rocks and hulls had a very bad history of not getting along. She decided to go topside and investigate.

At the top of the ladder, Ruth saw light from above. She saw that the *Groovy Booby* had docked inside some kind of cave. A walkway with mooring gear and cleats clung to the port side of the ship. To the starboard side was only black rock and barely three feet of space between. Large rubber bumpers had been installed at intervals on the wall to keep the boat safe from the jagged edges.

She looked aft and found the opening to the cave almost 50 feet behind the *Groovy Booby*. The cave was large and, as she examined the wall and its proportions, Ruth could see that the rock had been worked. The enclosure was manmade. Further inspection revealed ceiling joists and support struts along the walls, made of a dark metal.

The crew was occupied with securing mooring lines and connecting auxiliaries. Ruth saw some men working on the pier who had not been on the ship. She assumed they were some sort of support staff for the facility. The whole environment spoke of a hidden lair and clandestine operations. She felt she should be disembarking from the *Nautilus* instead of the *Groovy Booby*. Captain Burns chose that moment to leave the pilot shack and climb down to her. "It's a pleasure to meet you, Captain Nemo." Burns gave her a blank look before he smiled. He had obviously missed the allusion.

She touched his arm and smiled. "Where are we?"

"We are on Corona del Diablo," he said.

"What?"

"The Devil's Crown."

Ruth remembered reading about the island in her brief Galapagos research. That was before her com-pad had shut down a few days into the journey. It belonged to Campolo University, so she was convinced that Tennyson had spoken the truth about her demolished career. She lamented her loss until they arrived in the islands, where she forgot much of the misfortune in her life.

She remembered that the Devil's Crown was neither large nor habitable, the island being more of an undersea volcanic structure that broke the surface to form a circular "crown." It had been a favorite among divers and snorkelers for its rich sea life and reefs, before the area was closed to tourism by the Ecuadorian government three years ago. "The Thrones live on the Devil's Crown?" Ruth found it ironic.

"We have come to call this place the Jewel," Burns offered.

Ruth frowned. "The jewel in the Devil's Crown?"

"Funny, huh?"

She looked over to the pier. At the far end, away from the water's entrance, Ruth saw that a passageway led into the rock. "So, they carved this out?"

"Massoud can explain it to you." Captain Burns raised a hand to end the conversation. Sometimes the man was actually respectable. "Go ahead and get your stuff. I'm only staying for about an hour before we shove off and get back to Ayora."

Burns winked at her as he passed, barking orders in Spanish to one of his hands. She did as she was told and returned to her stateroom, gathering her half-packed luggage before returning to the deck.

Massoud stood at the foot of the gang-plank and waved. She walked over, laden with too much luggage. Massoud stepped quickly in front of her and grabbed the suitcase and day bag. She tried to pull away, but he tore them from her before she could get her balance for any real resistance.

"Ruth, allow me." Massoud smiled.

"Sure, whatever."

"Let's get off and get you settled."

They walked across the gang-plank and on to the doorway at the end of the pier. Beyond it ran a narrow passageway of black volcanic rock. They continued on for about 40 feet before coming to a round chamber. The passageway resumed in the far wall of the room, but on either side, large windows of segmented glass looked out to the left and right. The glass was thick and embedded with metal connectors that linked to a metal support frame stretching from floor to ceiling.

Ruth walked over to the left window. Peering out, she saw little except for the reflection of the ceiling light above. Cupping her hands around her eyes, she leaned forward. A clear sky and shining stars materialized above. Dark monoliths hulked in the distance. Looking down, she saw jagged rocks protruding from the lapping, luminescent waves. They were inside a large rock structure. It was wondrous. "What is this place?"

"Home," Massoud said, walking to the other window. Ruth was about to prompt him to say more when he sighed heavily and rubbed his nose, turning his attention back to Ruth. "I heard the captain tell you that this place is nicknamed the Jewel."

"Yes."

"The Devil's Crown is a rock formation located less than a mile north of Floreana Island. Floreana is uninhabited, but provides some of the most unique vistas and wildlife in all of the Galapagos."

"Massoud? Please excuse my rudeness, but I've read all of that in tourism articles."

"Yes, of course. What you didn't read about is the Ecuadorian government's new initiative to restore the islands to a better time, with increased wildlife populations free of invasive species. They also commissioned the construction of human habitation that blended into the environment, while being separate from it."

Ruth was dumbfounded. She walked past Massoud without her bags and followed the tunnel further in. The rock had been carved out in some places, but the bulk of the area looked like a natural formation.

"It was once a space formed by cooling masses of volcanic rock. Like lava tubes, but more of a fluke event than anything else."

Ruth gave herself over to exploration. The complex was a labyrinth of interconnecting chambers and tunnels. Quite simply, it had everything one would need to live. Generators, food storage and steady supplies supported the unique habitat. A large balcony allowed for all the clean and open air a person could need, if the black walls and subterranean gloom became too much. The balcony looked inward towards the main island of Floreana.

It was a paradise hideout.

A tunnel connected the main complex to the sleeping quarters, which were built from two large pressure vessels anchored into the seabed, 60 feet below the water and nestled on the inner circle of the "crown." Massoud left Ruth to relax in the small room allocated to her. A small porthole looked out to the sea from her room. She was overwhelmed by the view of undulating sea creatures and stretching indigo.

There was a knock on the doorjamb.

"Come in." Ruth glanced at the door as Massoud entered and then back to the porthole. She was captured by the beauty around her.

"They're going to come for us." Ruth felt as though she were speaking to the ocean outside, instead of to the Throne. She was sitting on her bunk, and she felt it sink with added weight as Massoud sat down beside her.

"Who?"

Ruth turned to look at him. He was staring at the floor.

"Whoever."

Massoud nodded without looking up. "What should we do, Ruth?"

"Stay behind me," she said, with forced confidence.

"We didn't bring you here to put you in harm's way." Massoud looked up, his face suddenly intense. "We are safe. The Ecuadorian Navy, though small, has several patrol boats that make extra rounds through this area. If you look out the porthole again, you'll see some of the ballast hatcheries near the habitat. We are developing better fish farms for the country. That is their 'story' if any foreign country inquires as to why they have security around a natural wonder that is now forbidden for visitation. And they are not lying. The fish farms are highly experimental and proprietary. This place has been given to us as a last stronghold, but it also represents a large investment by the Ecuadorian government and the nation's businesses to promote open-ocean farming."

Ruth listened and reveled in the harmony of human excellence and the natural world. She then thought of Reston and Jamal, of the dark bereft places in their hearts that were both hidden and yet screaming out at the same time. She did not understand what made men become such creatures. She had no doubt, however, of what such men could do. Proud as she was of finding Herriot and rescuing Henry, she knew it was only a matter of time before the Thrones were all found and attacked, regardless of their provisions and assurances from others. She had come to understand the Thrones' attitude towards eventual capture. "There is a greater investment at stake. They will come," she said.

"Then you must go." Massoud sighed and Ruth knew he agreed with her.

She almost told Massoud that she had used him and the others as bait for her scheme, but thought better of it. *No reason for them to know.* "No. I've made my choice and you have my services until I decide to leave or I am forced to leave. So please, be a gentleman and show me around. I am particularly interested in the dojo Musashi told me about."

"Yes, of course. Let me show you your 'office' first. We have much work for you to do."

Ruth could not prevent a smile. "Work is good."

CHAPTER 18

Despite the AC-48 Griffon's reputation as the most stealthy and gentle transport ever built, Jamal's ride was rough.

"Sorry for the chop, Sec-Commander," said the pilot, "I don't know what the fuck is going on in the air out there. This gotta be the roughest goddamned shit I've ever flown in. Especially if the Griffon can feel it, you know?"

As the only passenger, Jamal had passed much of the time by wandering through the narrow passage connecting the cargo bay to the cockpit, prepping his gear several times too many. But for the last two hours, he had sat next to the pilot, because the man's glibness, while annoying, was better than silence. Jamal had little to think about anyway, having run through the possibilities of what he might find and what he would do. Rumination had never served Jamal in any useful way: not in his life as a soldier, not in his life as Tennyson's retriever. So he sat next to the pilot and emptied his mind of thought and emotion, leaving only spinning gears and timed mechanisms set to act with precision and incisiveness.

Within the timing, within the rotating steel, rays of thought formed and streamed outward, threatening his perfect nothingness. He thought of several things: first, the woman painting in St. Edmund; second, Henry's fervent song in Geranach. Each had a quality that called to him, a soft voice that did not judge or condemn, but merely spoke to... the heart?

Suddenly, he wished he had a blank pad of paper and charcoal. Just to pass the time, of course.

Focus! Jamal examined the view before him. Narrow cockpit windows framed only darkness. No stars were visible, nor clouds, nor lights below. The environment was perfect for their arrival: no outlines visible in the sky and the wind would mask the little noise the Griffon produced. A tactical insertion vehicle, it was small for a transport and made to carry a specific payload: LarcSuits. That was a thought he did not fight. Mechanized death and power— Jamal finally had it and Jamal would finally use it.

The loquacious pilot invaded his solitude. "How long you been a Larc jockey?"

The man's mouth never stopped. "Almost five years," Jamal lied. He wanted to flip some random switches to give the pilot something else to do than talk.

"Then this drop will be nothing for you." He reached over and lightly punched Jamal's arm. "That's good to know. Sometimes I get knuckle-fucks who, despite being trained, can't seem to get out of the drop bay without damaging the Griffon—and the suit too. Everyone thinks they want to get into those suits, ya know, but I think it takes a special type to pilot them. You gotta be born with it."

Jamal had trained for about a half-hour in the tactical assault suit that now stood like a statue in the Griffon's drop insertion bay. It was easy to fly and easy to use. He had fired well on the range, flew without crashing and landed just as well. So given the pilot's testimony, Jamal felt he was 'born with it.' Besides, he figured that he'd get a little training while flying from the Griffon to the Throne-freaks' hideout. When he found his quarry, they would bow before him and ask to be spared. Perhaps a few random deaths and a grand use of ordinance would drive them to their knees, begging.

The fantasy grew and Jamal harnessed it, preparing for the coming violence. This was the last thing he had to do — he was sure of it. After capturing *all* of the Thrones, he would be free. Perhaps he could take the suit, too. *I was born with it.*

"See." The man whirled his fingers in the air. He was feeding off Jamal's silence. "You know what I'm talking about. Fucking amateurs running around in those things all the time."

"Drop time in seven minutes!" the pilot screamed. Jamal's earpiece did nothing to amplify the sound, but the pilot's voice was distorted and nearly unintelligible.

The Griffon continued to buck against the oscillating wind streams and thermal chaos outside. A serious drop in altitude had occurred as Jamal was entering the LarcSuit. He fell to the side and struck his face on a crate. Now secured into the suit, he felt the growing sting of the contusion rising on his cheek. The situation was fighting him, but he could not be stopped.

While he waited, the Virtual Intelligence of the suit made system and body checks, measuring Jamal's heart rate, circulation, and relative brain activity. Though the suit did not run on thought, he knew it was sensitive to changes in hormone levels and overall electrical activity in his brain. An internal injector pumped Jamal with stimulants that focused his senses, speeding up his decision center. As he tried to analyze his own state, he felt like writing poetry while destroying a city. The drugs made him into a Zen Berserker. *Born with it, born with it, born with it...*

"One minute. I hope you know how to fly in this shit!" The pilot's voice entered Jamal's elevated cognitive process and was immediately seized. *Why is he speaking so slowly?* "Drop point is the south-east portion of Floreana Island. Current satellite intelligence indicates no positive presence for humans on the main island. The Corona del Diablo to the north has several signs of life, however, so steer clear of that on your training run. I'll be here at 2200 hours tomorrow for egress. Over?" the pilot said, not savvy to Jamal's real mission.

Jamal started to smile, but his face was now covered with a sensor skin that helped to control the suit. A smile might have undesirable effects. "Roger that." Jamal was certain that only he, Reston and, of course, Tennyson, knew why he was here. It was not for training. The seconds counted down in the display on his visor. At zero, Jamal could feel the slight vibration of the bay doors opening, then a tearing jolt as the LarcSuit clamp released.

He fell.

The lighted view of the cargo space was replaced by the yawning blackness of the earth below. Several warnings toned in his helmet to inform him of an overly quick descent. He moved easily as the suit reacted to his needs, aiming him at an angle, his helmet down. But he kept rotating and was soon plummeting straight down. He threw his arms out in reflex, but the encasement of steel, plastic, and microcircuits did little to catch the rushing air.

"Shit!" He was going in as a human bomb. He tried to remember what to do. He had flown the suit before, but not performed a drop in it. The training manual made it sound easy enough, so Jamal thought he would figure it out when it came time. It was time.

Wings! The wings! "Deploy slow descent," Jamal said, suddenly recalling the right command. A faint vibration danced along his back as the controlled descent equipment engaged. To the top right of his display, he read the words *descent wings deployed*. Jamal looked to either side, examining the flight surfaces that had extended from equipment pods on his back. He could feel the suit reacting now to airflow instead of just gravity.

"Activate automatic insertion protocol." The suit responded with a *beep* and gradually Jamal leveled out into a much, much slower descent at a shallower angle. He was in the pipe.

The suit knew where to go and Jamal needed only to follow its Virtual Intelligence, unless he decided to deviate and go manual. There was little to see in the gloom, so the optics detected the island and outlined it in faint green for him.

Several seconds later, he leveled out further and flew straight over the island. He felt the thrust of his hover jets as they easily found stability, the choppy air that had tossed the Griffon so violently now gone, restricted to the higher atmosphere.

Soon Jamal could see the shore below unaided, as lighter shadows moved in and out to reveal the ocean surf. The suit banked to the left and the view shifted. Sharp volcanic rocks and sparse vegetation were visible in the island's interior.

He decided to take command of the suit as he retracted the descent wings and fully engaged the hover jets to prevent an inadvertent loss of altitude. He wobbled in the air for a few seconds before finding competence with the controls.

The display told him that he hovered 200 feet above the surface of Floreana Island over a flat plateau near the southern coast. A cinder cone towered to the northeast and Jamal was hidden in its shadow.

He brought himself down in the forest near the middle of the island. Once on the ground, he took refuge among the spindly trees of the interior. His display told him that no threats existed and he was alone.

He looked down at the suit. The surface was flat and did not reflect any visible light. The chronometer displayed a local time of 2 a.m. He assumed that the facility to the north was heavily guarded. He *hoped* it was. But Jamal was sure that nothing lay between his location and the Devil's Crown save ten miles of volcanic rock, lizards, birds, and a narrow strip of water. He targeted the compound in the distance and resisted the impulse to fire several concussion grenades at the rock, disappointed that stealth was needed more than brute force. Jamal was still under Tennyson's mandate to bring the Thrones in alive, but he doubted that he would be able to hold back once in the compound.

He had no idea how many of the mutants would be there. They might have found the locator and set a trap. Jamal had decided that the Thrones had been underestimated because of their "peaceful" demeanor. The LarcSuit would level the field — level it with fire.

He took a breath and surveyed the display. His body was normal, with no side-effects from the chemicals surging through his system. The net effect of the drug was a battle haze without the haze: Jamal was sharp and calm.

Intoxicated with focus, he put one leg in front of the other, gaining speed as he ran north. The distance was crossed in several minutes. Though Jamal could have easily flown over the jagged landscape, there was a possibility the noise of his jets would alert the Throne compound. Sound traveled well here.

So he ran. Instead of going directly to the beach across from the Devil's Crown, he crossed to the west and traveled up the large cone that formed the northern-extending peninsula named Punta Cormorant. The power and force grew, each step reinforcing his belief that he was invincible.

He climbed to the top of the mountain and looked out. Circular rock spires jutted from the sea and in the deep gloom they towered as jet monuments. Jamal magnified his visor to find out more. Proper intelligence gathering required that he scan as many sides of the compound as possible before making a move, but Jamal had seldom followed the proper way to do anything and he was still alive. As he looked the Crown over, he found nothing. The rising of the sea against the rocks was detectable and the rocks extended a bit to the north and east...

Suddenly, he saw light coming from somewhere within the formation. It was faint, but as he magnified his optics, there was no mistake. On the side of a larger spire was a lit opening. Jamal couldn't believe it. The opening was large and a flat floor ran into the rock.

Jamal made out several chairs. *A patio?* They faced out into the night but held no occupants. He had expected to find a hidden guard or some sign of protection in or around that area, but he detected none. For nearly half an hour, he sat and waited. Nothing stirred.

He decided that whatever the situation, they would not expect attack by a tactical assault LarcSuit. Their bullets would do nothing. They couldn't harm him with force. The only way he could be beaten was if the whole area was rigged with explosives and he was inside. That *might* kill him, but...

Jamal shook himself mentally and focused. Reston had finally told him what the Thrones were: mistakes. They were genetic aberrations that would be an embarrassment to the company if the public or government found out — not to mention the lawsuits. Jamal could not understand why the parents of the Thrones had never come forward.

He reminded himself that he was up against pacifist mutants. They wouldn't hurt him, even if they could. All that was left to do was to rain down fire and pain on their secret lair, take the freaks off to the boss — with an acceptable casualty or two — and collect his pension. Jamal engaged his flight jets and rocketed off towards the Devil's Crown.

He went in straight, looking through the open balcony and into the compound itself as he got closer. A passageway wound off and to the right. The beginning of a large chamber could be seen to the left. The walls were rough-hewn and black, as if cut from the surrounding formation in haste — or simply because of a lack of skill. As Jamal approached, he saw that the floor of the balcony was set with mosaics in bright greens and blues.

But he had no time to examine the artwork: he was coming in too fast and gave a command for the suit to boost backwards. The shock threw his metal-clad feet out and up, and Jamal nearly plummeted into the sea before righting himself to a hover.

Slowly rising, he matched the height of the balcony once more and watched. The floor was covered in small polished stones, creating images of green foliage and a host of Galapagos creatures, such as turtles, lizards, and sea-lions. Quite abruptly, Jamal had the impression that he was invading a tourist resort.

This is the place? He looked up into the large balcony entryway. The hallway stretching to the right was dimly lit, but was discernibly empty. Extending out from the left opening, however, oozed a dancing shadow. Jamal's energy pulsed, knowing that he finally had found an outlet for his growing aggression and unease.

He came in slow, the faint hiss of the LarcSuit doing little to mark his approach. Jamal cleared the low balcony wall and landed. Enhanced by the suit, his hearing detected light thuds and an occasional grunt, the sounds reminiscent of what issued from a man who was exercising.

Jamal lunged forward into the balcony opening and on toward the left. His vision filled with a brightly lit, high-ceilinged room. The floor was sanded wood, with shelves and racks lining a circular wall. A man in white stood near the far end of the room, his back turned.

Jamal surged into the space and stomped toward the man, his armored feet breaking the floor timbers with each footfall, unloading several rounds from his arm-mounted small-caliber barrel up into the lights as he moved. Glass shattered, the raining debris skittering harmlessly off Jamal's visor. With his left munitions launcher, he fired a flare at the wall ahead. The orange fire-bolt bounced several times from wall to wall, finally coming to rest near the center of the room and igniting patches of broken flooring.

Jamal screamed, raising mechanized arms, basking in the chaos, destruction and fire that engulfed the once serene dojo.

Triumphantly, he leveled the arm-gun at the still figure and waited for the inevitable surrender. The flare continued to burn, but the man made no move to put it out, no move to run. He did absolutely nothing to acknowledge that Hell-on-Earth had come to visit, bringing explosive force and alloy steel.

Jamal quickly examined the man to ensure that he was not wounded, that he was not damaged in a way that could put him into shock. No one could remain calm during such a barrage—not even Jamal. But this man appeared to be that no one.

The figure began a series of choreographed maneuvers with a sword. Jamal was now the one in shock, mesmerized by the dance, the perfection of movement as the man made graceful arcs with the sword and accomplished natural transitions in stance. The trance prevented Jamal from immediately recognizing what the man was. But the harsh crimson and orange light of the flare and the long shadows could not mask the truth.

The swordsman was tall, with oddly shaped shoulders and a thin torso. His legs were too long, though the body in motion seemed to move more fluidly and gracefully than any human body. He was also shirtless, though his skin was a near shade to the light cream-colored pants he wore. The exposed skin was a map of veins and arteries, lacing his wax-like back and chest.

This is the right place. But this Throne was like none that Jamal had ever seen. He was big, much larger than Jamal, and he moved like a hunting predator.

This Throne also had skill with a blade. Herriot was some kind of scientist. Henry was a rotund storyteller. This Throne was a warrior.

Jamal had prayed for this from the beginning, and the desire lingered to fight this Throne with his bare hands, without the LarcSuit. He longed for a fight he could savor. But the idea of breaking this Throne, of stripping him of training and honor by mechanized force, was just as tempting.

Despite the anger, despite the fire and destruction Jamal could feel running through his own veins, the serene beauty of the Throne going through exercises was more unsettling than any counterattack. The lines and shadows created by the whirling figure invaded his resolve.

Suddenly, he was more interested in the image before him and how it could be captured in a painting. Calamity churning around a single point of light: flames and decay seemed powerless in the face of such precision and discipline. The scene reminded him of the woman's painting in St. Edmund.

Instantly, Jamal's internal defenses cast the ideas away and reinforced a sense of power, conquest, and hatred.

These fucking mutants are a mistake. I'm ending this now and forever.

The Throne brought the sword up and Jamal thought he was going to attack. But the Throne placed the katana into the scabbard at his side with a flick of the blade, a quick downward motion and a final bow. He stood erect once more and was still.

Jamal fired off several more rounds just above the Throne's head, not caring if he accidentally blew the mutant's head off. The rounds hit the wall behind, some lodging and some ricocheting around the room. The Throne before him grinned, *grinned*, the way a father might at watching a child. Fury erupted within and Jamal slammed his fist into a nearby wall, shattering the wooden frame of a shelf and smashing into the rock beneath. Wood bounced off his armor and onto the floor.

The Throne continued to grin and then turned and walked across the chamber to a wall of mounted weapons.

"Stop." Jamal heard his amplified voice boom in the chamber.

The Throne did not stop. Instead, he untied the katana from around his waist and placed the weapon on two horizontal hooks where it must have usually hung. "You need me alive, no?" His voice was as calm and powerful as his deadly dance.

The question was nonsense. Jamal believed that it was meant to confuse, just as the mocking expression served to distract him. The Throne started to rummage through a tall cabinet.

Jamal stepped forward and clubbed him on the back of the head with a gauntleted fist. "No."

The warrior-Throne went down. Jamal's mind stung with the realization that he might have killed the thing, though he had never actually decided on how many of the Thrones he would spare. He would kill a few, probably.

But the swordsman writhed for several seconds before getting to his knees, a slick trail of blood now painting the back of his head and neck as it flowed freely from where Jamal had struck. He got up and stumbled back to the same cabinet.

Jamal did not stop him, doubting that anything lay within the cabinet that could harm the LarcSuit. He hoped that the Throne would do something stupid, like attack or try to run. He stood watching, mildly amused, but ready to move on. He turned his attention to the cargo pod at his hip, the one that held sedatives and binding gear.

"I assume you are the one named Jamal," the Throne said, through obvious pain. "I've heard much about you. My name is Musashi."

Jamal stopped. For a moment he suspected that the Thrones were somehow ready for his assault. He spun around, expecting ambush or worse. But the hallway was still vacant. Turning back to Musashi, he could see that the small flare-created flame had grown into a sustained fire. Smoke was beginning to fill the room.

Jamal pulled a tranquilizer gun from the cargo pod and ensured it was set to the proper dosage. He looked up and saw that Musashi had found what he was looking for. He drew out something that appeared to be made of thick leather and metal and resembled leather gauntlets or boxing gloves. While the majority of the device wrapped around the forearm, there was a metal piece that extended down the arm and past the hand, the end forming a flat hook. They looked homemade, with absolutely nothing in their appearance that hinted at mechanical or electronic devices.

Musashi looked up and his face held a serene expression that was not a grin. The expression was dangerous because, disciplined or not, Jamal could feel confidence emanating from the Throne in crushing waves.

Jamal shot out his arm to grab the Throne by the skull. He resisted the idea of squashing Musashi's head and instead threw him, lightly this time, down to the ground.

"Stay down!" he said. He checked the tranquilizer gun again and stepped forward to put Musashi down permanently.

But as he bent over and reached out, Musashi erupted from the floor, dodging the gun and launching himself *at* Jamal. The suit's display malfunctioned and sent hazy images as Musashi struck at Jamal's helmet, hitting it right between segmented seams. Jamal reached over to crush the Throne's head with an armored fist, but missed. As he spun, he knew the Throne was on his back, striking at weaknesses in his armor.

This was unexpected, but the assault was useless. The LarcSuit had no weaknesses from personnel — any that existed had been engineered out of the current designs. But as he tried to grab the fleet Throne, as he wheeled and wheeled in an effort to snatch or throw the mutant off, Jamal could not keep up, and was failing. Cargo pods and other external pieces fell to the ground at his feet. He aimed the arm-mounted gun over his head at a location he thought Musashi to be, but Jamal watched as a flat hook lashed out and damaged the weapon in the ammunition feed, rendering it useless.

Jamal screamed. *This is impossible!*

He could not feel Musashi's mass as he scrambled up and down the suit, but the Throne was there. Jamal could only flail in panic as the Throne drove his hooks into seams and joints, doing damage with each strike. Then something important broke and Jamal's visor display went bright white, rendering him blind.

In desperation, Jamal ran straight ahead in an attempt to crush Musashi against whatever wall he could find. Nothing formed in Jamal's mind except primal impulse and reflex. No thoughts of conquest and no thoughts of pleasure. His fantasies were replaced with dread and distress.

As he gained speed, a sharp crack behind his head reverberated through the helmet and into his spine. Jamal's natural vision returned as the helmet was ripped up and off. Quickly, he realized that he had run out onto the balcony, missing the walls completely. Part of his brain saw the starry sky and smelled the salty-sweetness of ocean mist and island vegetation. Another part saw only death, death in the surf below, death the answer for a life of confusion and pseudo-victories. He was beaten, beaten by a genetic freak with no weapon except his hands. Jamal's violent façade of fire and steel had failed him.

But the best answer to this was only a few feet away. Jamal charged on toward the end of the balcony, hoping to end this torment and take the warrior-Throne with him. Suddenly, the suit went dead and Jamal's limbs froze. He went down under the ton of weight that was now released from powered control.

"Get off me!" As he looked down into the mosaic floor, into the green eyes of a giant tortoise, Jamal felt overwhelming fright at being paralyzed and nothing else.

Something touched his exposed neck and his fear became muted. The invasion of chemical force took hold and he enjoyed this realization briefly before losing focus. The eyes of the tortoise looked inviting, peaceful, friendly... Jamal remained lucid for some immeasurable minutiae of time before falling into emerald eyes and not the emerald sea.

CHAPTER 19

It was just him?
Voices filtered into Jamal's brain.
Yes.
As consciousness grew, Jamal struggled to listen, to digest what was being said. He feebly latched onto the sound of each voice. Both were familiar.

"We need to bind him for now. Do you have any handcuffs?" the woman said.

"No. I'm afraid we did not anticipate a need for prisoner accommodations. I also would prefer not to use any more of Herriot's anesthesia inventory," the second voice said.

"He's not a prisoner, but I don't know what he'll do when he comes to. It's better if we detain him for now."

"And with that, Ruth, I agree. His mind is only clouded. The man is far from emptiness."

Jamal understood enough for anger to rouse in his guts. He attempted to move his body, but none of his limbs obeyed—not even his eyelids. Faintly, he heard himself moaning.

"Ruth, might I make a suggestion?"

"Of course."

The words faded. Jamal's nerves burned as they tried in vain to move his body. He wanted to revive himself fully,

instead of enduring another second of this paralytic purgatory. But his eyes remained shut, mysterious images and
emotions running through his senses, calling him to sleep.
He submitted to unconsciousness once more.

* * *

The man was still. He looked dead. As the assassin's
chest slowly rose and fell, Ruth reminded herself that Jamal was not dead.

He slept on a large cot, his legs bound with mooring
rope. A glass of water and some bread waited on a table. A
bucket also lay next to the cot in anticipation of any sickness from the anesthesia. His hands remained unbound so
he could make use of these amenities, although Ruth had
advised against it. She had wanted to expedite his removal
from the compound. This had resulted in a heated discussion with the Thrones. Their opinions concerning Jamal
and his situation had angered Ruth initially. Despite the
pain he had caused, the Thrones felt sympathy for the man
and wanted to keep him in the Jewel.

As she sat by Jamal's bedside, Ruth felt more confused
about her decision to stay by the Thrones' side. She was
ashamed because she wanted to leave. The only thing that
prevented her from doing so was the work.

Work.

Before coming to the Galapagos, her greatest fear had
been to be out of work. Not out of money, but to be without purpose. With the oceans of Throne-centered stories,
articles, and random missives scattered in the "office" be-

low the main compound, Ruth had more purpose than ever.

I have to get back to work. She got up and turned to the door. As she did, the man's hand reached up and hooked onto her forearm.

Ruth jumped back and Jamal's hand slipped, falling to the floor. His arm was extended awkwardly. She saw that his eyes were open to slits. His body tensed feebly several times as he attempted to retract his fallen appendage, but there was no strength and he was still. He breathed slowly, as though unconscious once again.

She did not know what his intent had been, but she risked a courtesy by lifting the limp arm off the floor and positioning it across his chest. He did not move.

Ruth examined him again. Jamal was handsome, his features intense and powerful even as he slept. Massoud had told her that the man was afflicted, his illness being of the heart and not the body. But Ruth felt no inclination to suffer the illnesses of others. She had learned long ago that diseased people spread disease. Better to stay away from them. She started toward the door once again.

"My father was a U.N. delegate from the U.S.," Jamal whispered.

Ruth turned around but did not walk back. Jamal raised his head an inch before letting it fall back to the pillow. His eyes remained half-closed.

"What?" She doubted his lucidity.

He laughed. The act was more of a weak smile and a few convulsions than true laughter. "Mom? I don't want to..." Jamal's face contorted.

Ruth stepped back into the room and sat down facing Jamal, on the bed opposite. He continued to speak.

"Back in 2022, there was a boat full of Nigerian refugees. They had been gassed with some biological agent that reduced them to animals—harmless animals, but animals all the same."

"The Venter Syndrome." Ruth remembered the incident: it was the worst loss-of-life incident on American soil. Approximately 13,000 people had died.

"I was only a kid, but I knew about it from the news and what my mom told me. Dad lost his job and was eventually murdered for his part in what happened. Most of the people involved wanted to sink the ship at sea. The automatic captain had brought them near the coast of South Carolina, within U.S. waters. That made it a U.S. problem—all eyes on us. My father pressed to have biodefense teams take the ship in and get the people to a facility where they could be treated."

There's no treatment for Venter's. She knew the story well, but let Jamal speak.

"Told everybody there's no treatment... Bullshit. It just costs a lot and no one wanted to flip the bill for a bunch of poor Nigerians. That's fucking history for you."

Ruth gasped. "Your father was Julian Battle?"

"My father knew that they could be cured." Jamal ignored the question. "But the artificial bacteria got out anyway and... I'm sure you know how many people in Charleston were lost." Jamal spoke quite clearly, though his voice was a rasp and he kept his eyes on the ceiling as he spoke.

Ruth was bewildered. Julian Battle was famous, or infamous, for his involvement in the Charleston Venter Syndrome Outbreak. Some blamed him for the catastrophe. Others considered him a saint.

"He lost his job, because of course it was his fault for having a fucking heart. Several men who had lost loved ones plotted his death. They succeeded."

Ruth was not ready for this. She only knew that Julian Battle had died in a car accident shortly after the Venter outbreak. But no—the man had been murdered.

"My father thought he was doing the right thing, but he should've blasted those diseased little bastards into fragments and scattered them across the seafloor."

Ruth wanted to say something. The man was giving personal information and probably did not know it.

But before anything resolved in her mind, Jamal sighed and was silent. Ruth saw that his eyes were closed. She left him to his peace.

CHAPTER 20

Jamal regained consciousness while standing. A strong arm held him up. In the only dream he could recall—and there had been many—he was being called to and dragged out of a bed. Now, as fresh air invaded his lungs and bright light leached through to his squinting eyes, Jamal knew it wasn't a dream. His head throbbed with pain and the last thing he wanted to be was awake.

"One leg, then the other." The voice was friendly.

Jamal thought for a moment that he was in a hospital. He opened his eyes fully and made out the shape of a low-walled area that gave way to a two-toned blue blur beyond. Swirling mosaics of flora and fauna thrived beneath his feet. *I'm still here.*

As he focused, the blues materialized into sea and sky. A chorus of animals honking, bellowing, and shrieking filled the area in a haze of natural sounds. The smell of brine opened his nose and provided the final shock needed to restore his senses.

He stood up under his own power and looked over at the man who half-dragged, half-carried him. It was the Throne who had flayed his LarcSuit.

Musashi locked eyes with Jamal, his expression the same landscape of serenity as before. Jamal tensed and tried to get away, suddenly realizing that his wrists were tied together and tethered to his waist.

"You have nothing to fear," Musashi said. "Just rest now before you decide that our quarrel must continue."

"Fuck you," Jamal said but felt little in the comment. The only feelings with any will behind them now were hunger and resignation. He was still alive.

"Sit down here. The sedative was better suited for large felines, but it works adequately on humans as well. It will take a day for the after-effects to pass." Musashi helped Jamal into a chair before taking another beside him.

They sat in silence for a moment, and Jamal breathed in the pungent and fresh smell of the Galapagos. Their view looked onto Floreana Island to the south, the cinder cone Jamal had once rested on over a mile away. He wanted to fly back there. He imagined the Griffon coming back, circling the island before abandoning the search. "What will you do with me?"

Musashi sighed but remained silent. Jamal sensed that the Throne was slow to speak and perhaps was collecting himself first. He hated people like that, thought it was weak, was a power-play on others instead of "discipline." But he waited all the same.

"Do you believe in a world without war, without violence?" Musashi broke the silence.

"I don't care." Jamal feared the Throne was starting an interrogation, one that would eventually include pain.

"Jamal, you are not a prisoner," Musashi said, as if reading his mind.

"Really." Jamal jerked at the bonds in response.

"I'll take care of that once we have talked. As I said, you are not a prisoner. Rather… a guest. You may leave at any time. The only stipulation is that you are not to carry anything resembling a weapon. If and when you choose to leave, we will provide passage for you as far as we can."

"What if I don't take that offer?" Jamal braced, waiting for Musashi to strike in some way.

"It's a free gift. If you choose to tie your wrists back together once they've been untied, you can."

Jamal looked into the Throne's deep-set eyes. They looked sincere. "And if I pick up a weapon?" Jamal fought to distrust the Throne, but his will to defy was oozing away.

"I'll talk you out of it." Musashi remained calm and was smiling.

"You're confident you can do that?" Jamal wanted to test this free gift. If these mutants were that naïve, he might be able to get free and capture them after all. As he thought this, he remembered the previous night's rout.

"Yes. I feel your rhythm and understand it," Musashi said. "Can you say the same of me?"

Jamal did not understand the statement. He moved on to something he did understand. "Where is my suit?"

"We cast it over the wall of the balcony into the sea." Musashi pointed.

"What?" Any hope of using the suit to escape was gone. He knew he was a prisoner, regardless of the mutant's promises.

"It was much too heavy to transport through the compound. The sea bottom where it fell is only 24 feet deep. Earlier this morning, a work-boat with a heavy-lift winch lifted the suit out of the water. It is now on its way to Puerto Ayora."

"Tennyson will want that back." Jamal wanted it back too.

"Yes. We've already contacted—indirectly, of course—Taurus Force Systems. With any luck, they will find the suit waiting for them in London."

Jamal had underestimated this organization. They could smuggle, evade capture, and protect themselves. But they could not be potent or sophisticated enough to elude the man who ultimately hunted them. "Tennyson knows where you are."

Musashi sank back into silence for a moment. "Yes. Herriot found the locator in Henry's arm after your arrival. It was the only logical way you could have found us."

Now Jamal sat in silence. He felt smug in knowing that his plan had almost worked. It was also difficult not to enjoy the ocean view before him. "Are all of you here?"

"Yes. You did well, my friend."

"I came to capture, or kill, all of you."

"And now you sit and enjoy our hospitality. Can your malefactor, Keenan Tennyson, provide better choices than you can provide for yourself?"

The ambiguity was tiring Jamal, his mind not fully aware or able to grasp anything complex or convoluted. Musashi was intriguing. His warmth was genuine and hard to dislike, even more so because Jamal knew the freak was a formidable fighter. He was not weak. Jamal was also in awe of one who had trained himself to defeat mechanized armor suits. But the awe drove him back to hatred, and thoughts of revenge.

Musashi got up and stepped over to Jamal. He had a long knife in one hand.

Jamal kicked hard, nearly knocking himself and his chair over. Before that could happen, Musashi grabbed the arm of the chair and pushed it, and Jamal, back to stability. "I'm cutting your bonds. Please trust me." The Throne did not wait for an answer before bringing the knife to Jamal's bound wrists. With several quick movements he cleaved the knots and coils.

Jamal watched the Throne's face as he cut. There was no obvious deception in the act and he felt the tatters of cut bonds fall away.

As Musashi stood straight again, Jamal followed the movement by leaping from the chair and snatching the knife cleanly from Musashi's hand. Bringing it to the mutant's neck, Jamal felt a surge of spite and triumph.

Musashi did not move. His face bore the same serene expression that Jamal remembered from their first meeting.

"Would you like my 'free gift'?" Jamal was quivering with energy, his actions spurred forward by a mix of both vengeance and fear. His mission had failed. He could not retire as he wanted. He had lost his glorious suit of armor. And most heinous of all was that his enemies forgave him. The world inside Jamal's mind was burning to ash.

"Tennyson will kill you whether you return with us or not." Musashi spoke softly. "You must know that."

Jamal was stunned, both by the Throne's composure and the statement itself. The knife blade rested across the Throne's jugular and Jamal was poised to cut and end the mutant's mistake of a life. But he was confused.

"They sent you to test our defenses. If you happened to succeed, all the better. Tennyson is a master pragmatist."

Jamal's mind spun and, as an observer, he watched his arm start to lower the knife from Musashi's neck. "A Tactical Assault Suit?" He heard the fear in his own voice and fought to stay angry.

"Jamal, I know you are still recovering from our... contest last evening, but surely you understand what is happening?"

"You beat me!" He returned the blade to Musashi's neck. "Now I beat you."

"No, you were beaten from the start. They sent you in a suit because now a suit is missing. You stole it. *We* stole it."

"But..." Jamal did not want to admit the logic.

"They will come bearing the justification they need. We have already been made into a 'terrorist group' by Tennyson's propaganda. This event is the final justification. The flood is coming."

Jamal lowered the knife. A lost suit: a piece of protected technology extremely important to the U.S. government. "But you sent it back," he whispered.

"Tennyson never expected you to succeed on any level. Your purpose was always to provide intelligence, nothing more. Dozens of other would-be assassins like you have been killed, most by each other, some by Tennyson's lieutenant, Reston."

Jamal sat. His new life, his new beginning, had been a death-march all along. "How do you know that?

Musashi took his seat. Nothing about his bearing showed that he had just been held at knife-point. "We may have taken a stance of non-violence — even ignorance in the face of certain doom at times — but we've never been oblivious. There are others out there, other Tennyson assassins, I assure you."

When Tennyson had told Jamal he was the chosen one, he had never questioned it. Now, he felt the weight of his own stupidity. "I need to leave."

Musashi turned to look at Jamal. "Before you do, we would like to talk to you — all of us."

Jamal sat in numbness. His mind slowed and gave no insight, no introspection, and no apprehension either. He was instead aware of his lungs slowly filling and emptying, the air coursing in and out, in and out. The beat of his heart was regular, if slightly elevated. It pulsed with steady resolve, with steady rhythm.

Rhythm.

Without looking away from the rolling surf below, Jamal extended the knife back to Musashi. He felt the weight leave his hand as Musashi took it. Jamal let the rhythm of the sea and air and birds and his own heart fuse and mingle. He let it fill his mind and for a moment, he was still. Soon, very soon, there would be decisions to make.

But for now, he said nothing, thought of nothing, and felt nothing save his own rhythmic breathing. Lost were thoughts of murder and malice, though they had only fled temporarily in light of this turn of events. Jamal felt a small comfort, sitting amid the sounds of wild birds and the feel of warm air. It compelled him to say one thing: "I need a new job."

Musashi put a hand on his shoulder. Not accustomed to accepting physical contact, Jamal was encouraged by the humanity of the gesture. He did not shy away from it, though it was alien.

"And we can help you find one," Musashi said.

Jamal continued to sit and enjoy a moment of peace. His thoughts were weak, but they were his own.

Epilogue

Ruth stood at the threshold, looking at Jamal's back as he sat on the balcony. Musashi sat with him. They spoke often, but in hushed tones and without any obvious emotion. She had come to learn that such signs were good regarding men in discussion. It also indicated that Jamal had accepted defeat. Whether he would maintain such acceptance was another matter.

Ruth slipped away without making a sound. Although she wanted to speak with Jamal now that he seemed calm, she was content to delay that potential meeting for as long as possible. She made her way to the deepest part of the compound, a chamber that had begun as an empty space within the volcanic formations. The void had been expanded and built into a round chamber with walls that curved gently upwards to form a domed ceiling. At its center sat a hollow stone container with a flat top.

It was here that she read much of the literature concerning the Thrones, collected from around the world. She had brought in a small table and chair to support her research, the stone container serving as a desk for her com-pad and reading. One day the container would serve as a document vault for the work at which Ruth currently slaved.

The media were varied; most of the writings had started as little more than Internet posts. Others were handwritten manuscripts sent by mail or collected personally. The chamber held a morass of printouts and books. Ruth could navigate the area easily, but she dissuaded others from coming into the chamber while she was working.

Massoud had told her what the room was for. The Thrones wanted to leave a record of their existence, something that could not be defiled by media spin or cover-up. Therefore, the chamber was in essence a tomb, not for their bodies, but rather for their memories.

The stone container would house their stories—what they thought and what others thought about them. The chamber was a secret, however, and not even the Ecuadorian government knew about it. They knew about a research station at the Corona del Diablo, but only as living quarters for the Thrones and the studies they engaged in. Ruth had come to find that Ecuadorian biologists and their students often visited the Jewel. They ran small hatcheries for protected fish species and other creatures, one of their many hopes being to restore the reefs and surrounding waters to the flourishing dive sites they had been several decades before.

So the Thrones' paradise was both open and secret, both a public space and a protecting fortress.

Ruth had urged Massoud to take additional security measures. The first was to ask the Ecuadorian Navy to patrol the area more often. That had been accommodated. The other had been the installation of cameras and early warning devices on nearby islands. That had also been accomplished.

Those measures had been in vain. Though Jamal had been defeated, it was by coincidence that Musashi had been awake in the middle of the night—and training. What would happen next time?

These thoughts faded as Ruth concentrated on her work. She categorized each missive or story by which

Throne it pertained to. Each of the twelve had equal representation. Her aim was to take the best pieces and put them into a bound text—or perhaps several volumes of bound text—and place the edited work in the stone container. Once that was complete, the container and chamber would be sealed indefinitely.

Ruth sat down and began to read a testimonial received the day before, this one from a town in Minnesota called Blue Earth. She began to read:

"It was good for us to find our son was not dead. Our shame knows no bounds for abandoning him, but we are sure his education was looked after. That was the very least we could do. With the laws surrounding what we feared, however, the least appeared to be the most at the time. Only in hindsight do we now understand how cowardly we were in his time of need.

I cannot say that Robert and I were not relieved when we got word from our son, however brief and without emotion that word might have been. I also cannot explain the pain that it caused us. To be honest, we had hoped never to hear from him again.

He was always clever, though, and Robert assured me that while our son may not be socially adept, he was able to act and survive when need be. A fuel station sits on the site of the old clinic. It is a reminder to us every time we pass it. I try not to look.

Our son, James Walters, is certainly dead. But his ghost is with us, and at the request of that apparition, I send this simple missive to both validate our hope and shame, to confess our undying love for James. He loved the earth, the black and rich Minnesota dirt that held the keys to life, or so he told us every time we compelled him to leave his backyard garden and come inside. James had few friends, but those close to him were in awe of his un-

*derstanding and drive to study, to learn as much as he
could of the botanical and biological mysteries of God.
We did not understand. We still do not. But the only
consolation we can hope for is that his ghost has found a
place in the world that needs his skills, that has called him
to be fulfilled. We saw the blessings that he espoused in
his short time in Blue Earth. What a world it would be if
James could share his gifts with everyone."*

Loose tears splashed down on the page in dots and
Ruth could not read on. She dabbed at the pages with a
tissue from the table. Portions of words were now satu-
rated and smeared by her efforts. It was only a printout
and Ruth had no reason to worry, but she fretted over the
page as though it were the only surviving manuscript of
an ancient text.

Since she had begun collecting Throne-related material,
the Thrones themselves had assisted her by requesting
documents from their friends and contacts around the
world. Ruth received these documents via mail or email.
Some were mysterious and she was left to piece together
exactly which Throne a given document was about and its
context. The printout before her was one such document.

The Thrones spoke little of their lives before exile, many
having suffered much pain and confusion at the hands of
others. The relative tone of the message in Ruth's hands
denoted intelligence and education, perhaps affluence. It
was from Minnesota. After a brief moment of recollection,
Ruth had no doubt as to which Throne the missive pertained to.

Herriot.

He must have written to his parents and given Ruth's
email as a return address. She had no inkling what he
might have written. She would never ask. Ruth also knew

not to offer the missive to Herriot. He had suffered enough.

She smiled as she thought of Herriot and the rest of the Thrones. They were all here. They were all safe. Regardless of the future, Ruth sat in the basement of their secret hideout—a secret hideout everyone seemed to know the location of—and protected them, loved them, and watched over them.

Ruth forgot about the future and continued to discover the past. She read on...

* * *

Jamal waved the truck on, deciding instead to walk the few miles from the fields to the town. The men in the truck began to talk and laugh, gesticulating in response to concepts and feelings that Jamal had come to know could not be articulated by an English-speaking, or more precisely, an English-thinking person. A small grin reached his mouth as he watched the truck accelerate and move on, sending nutmeg-colored dust up into the darkening sky. The day of labor in the fields had been long, yet it was satisfying to Jamal's soul.

The days went by more slowly now, Jamal having the time and sobriety (broken at least once a week, but better than in years past) to enjoy his work. His freshness did not merely come from a lack of alcohol, but also a lack of rage, of primal emotions and confused regrets. They flared occasionally, pushing him to anger and tension once again. But the presence of St. Edmund and its people served to soothe the pain. His friends could feel when he was sliding back and knew exactly what to say—or not say—to help him along. They did not validate his behavior, but Jamal knew that, no matter the challenge, no matter the hatred, he was not abandoned.

That was new. Jamal walked away from the setting sun toward St. Edmund, in the direction that the sun would soon enough return to as it rose. He thought of it and the colors that would stretch over the landscape in the early, middle, and then late morning. Images coalesced and he breathed into them, calling them from dust and directing their nascent spirits to go forth and multiply. He kept them in his mind and decided on the colors and textures needed to make them real as he walked the final half-mile into town.

He had a closet-sized room in the main building that he called home. With only space for a mattress and a small table, Jamal could do little there except sleep and dress. Being far from retiring for the evening, he walked past the white house and his room.

He thought briefly of his first visit to St. Edmund. Finding the strength to forgive oneself was the first lesson that he had learned from Massoud. It was hard to realize. Jamal felt the shame and self-loathing surge when he thought of the man he tried to be, of the demon he had tried to forge himself into. The scars remained and reconciliation would not easily be forthcoming. Jamal focused on forgiveness instead and allowed the shame to fade.

He walked on and rounded the corner, continuing to his destination. The door to the house was open, as always, and Jamal entered without a word.

Maria was finishing a simple portrait. The man was dark-skinned. She had used dark purples, blues, and brown paints to fashion a bold and enlivened image. Orange eyes peered out impossibly from the dark recesses of the face. They were not evil eyes, the muted colors instead giving them the appearance of flames within a night scene, or inner light firmly in control of a once-forlorn fortress.

Jamal looked at it and tried not to think. He busied himself at his own workstation: a large easel with a canvas, standing next to Maria's. The painting-in-progress was simpler than the one beside it, but "simple is often the beginning," as Musashi said. He had also said that "simple" was *always* the end. Jamal was not clear on much of Musashi's philosophy, but this maxim seemed to make sense. He focused on the simplicity of what he wanted to accomplish, on the minimum of voices needed to say the most.

The painting was a blurred image of Mount Kenya. Only the land and mighty spires of the mountain were complete. The sky was white canvas. Jamal allowed his evening walk and the colors, thoughts, and memories that came with it to mingle in his mind. He mixed several base oil paint colors together on his palette, closed his eyes and saw the sky again: twists of burning autumn and cool twilight. Sentinels of dust and sand carried their messages up into the heavens, their masters invisible and their purpose hidden. The scattered greenery of the basin floor melted into shapes and colors identical to the rocks that surrounded them. The animals were there too, but Jamal knew he had to capture their presence without showing them to the world, that he needed to keep their secrets in confidence and their whereabouts protected. He opened his eyes.

Feeling the pressure of being stared at, Jamal turned to his left and met Maria's eyes. Her warmth washed over him. She had stopped working on her portrait of Jamal and was looking at him expectantly. She gestured to the clean, bone-white portion of canvas that rose above Jamal's Mount Kenya.

"Eh?" she said. He looked back to the painting and felt the new images loading into his body from the recesses of his mind. His fingers vibrated with the colors, the textures and possibilities. He could feel the sky as much as see it. Looking back to Maria, he replied "Yes."

She smiled and calmly turned back to her own painting. Jamal dabbed a brush into the first color he would use, the first voice of the conversation that would speak eternally to all who looked on this painting and wondered at the mystery of being.

Jamal drew the brush across the canvas, forever changing the blank white to something more, and finished the first of many, many strokes.

Jeff Stover was born in Mechanicsburg, Pennsylvania. Jeff strives to write thoughtful tales that are both psychologically and theologically stimulating. He is also an avid ice hockey fan and a U.S. Navy veteran. Jeff currently lives near Denver, Colorado, with his wife, Sara, and daughter, Gabrielle. Learn more about Jeff and other Blue Throne writers at www.bluethrone.com.

www.bluethrone.com

Visit our website for more titles, information, and services from the Blue Throne fellowship.